Praise for Previous Books in the Series:

'Morris has delivered another strong horror anthology f rom some of the best writers around, and new faces who hopefully will go far. Here's to more alphabetic terror. Recommended.'
Concatenation on *Fever Dreams*

'The combination of authors is pure excellence … There's a lovely spread of subgenre and tone here too. You might call it a delicious horror buffet.'
Kayleigh Dobbs, *Phantasmagoria*, on *Fever Dreams*

'It's a rich, diverse and satisfying collection of yarns.'
Starburst Magazine on *Elemental Forces*

'A very impressive set of stories. Perfect for dark and cold evenings as we enter the more eerie part of the year. Strongly recommended!'
Runalong The Shelves on *Darkness Beckons*

'*Close to Midnight* illustrates what great shape the genre of horror is in… If you're a reader who enjoys quality fiction of the dark kind, this is a series to be cherished. There isn't a bad story in the entire book.'
Stephen Bacon

'*Close to Midnight* is a very solid collection of horror featuring stories of varied themes and content, and yet they all feel very comfortable inside the spine of one book. Worth a look if you like chills down your spine late at night as you lie in bed reading.'
Horror DNA

'Morris has assembled an especially strong group of stories with dazzling, diverse approaches to horror. Highly recommended.'
Cemetery Dance on *Close to Midnight*

'If you love short and sometimes shocking horror stories, you can't go wrong with this collection!'
On the Shelf Reviews on *Close to Midnight*

'I'm impressed with the imagination and variety coming from the writers. *Beyond the Veil* is another happy clump of ickiness... and I mean that in a good way.'
The Happy Horror Writer

'There is no end to the talent Mark Morris has brought together here.'
Phantastiqa on *Beyond the Veil*

'Beautifully written pieces that lean into the intuitive and fantastic.'
Publishers Weekly on *After Sundown*

'This rich and masterful collection of horror highlighting both up-and-coming and established authors is an interesting twist on the standard anthology [...] Highly recommended for longstanding horror fans and those readers who may not think horror is for them. There is something for everyone in this one.'
Booklist on *After Sundown*

'This is a short story collection that does exactly what it sets out to, delight and scare. With stories from well-known authors in the genre as well as a few from emerging voices, *After Sundown* has something for everyone. Highly recommended.'
The British Fantasy Society

'An entertaining, slickly written, mainstream, fun, something-for-every-horror-fan anthology.'
HorrorTree on *After Sundown*

A FLAME TREE BOOK OF HORROR

GHOST LIGHTS

An Anthology of New Short Stories

Edited by Mark Morris

This is a FLAME TREE PRESS book

FLAME TREE PRESS
6 Melbray Mews, London, SW6 3NS, UK
flametreepress.com

US sales, distribution and warehouse:
Simon & Schuster
simonandschuster.biz

UK distribution and warehouse:
Hachette UK Distribution
hukdcustomerservice@hachette.co.uk

Thanks to the Flame Tree Press team.

Cover art by Nick Wells/Flame Tree Studio from sketches and layered files created using new photos and stock images from codhsyn (Shutterstock.com) combined and crafted in Photoshop. No AI, AGI or LLM was used in this process. The font families used are Avenir and Bembo.

Flame Tree Press is an imprint of Flame Tree Publishing Ltd
flametreepublishing.com

A copy of the CIP data for this book is available from the British Library and the Library of Congress.

1 3 5 7 9 8 6 4 2

HB ISBN: 978-1-80552-011-5
US PB ISBN: 978-1-80552-009-2
UK PB ISBN: 978-1-80552-010-8
ebook ISBN: 978-1-80552-013-9

Printed and bound in Great Britain by Clays Ltd, Elcograf S.p.A.

Represented in the EU for product safety and compliance by Authorised Rep Compliance Ltd, Ground Floor, 71 Lower Baggot Street, Dublin, D02 P593, Ireland. Contact at www.arccompliance.com

FSC
www.fsc.org
MIX
Paper | Supporting responsible forestry
FSC® C018072

A FLAME TREE
BOOK OF HORROR

GHOST LIGHTS

An Anthology of New Short Stories

Edited by Mark Morris

FLAME TREE PRESS
London & New York

CONTENTS

INTRODUCTION

Mark Morris

What kind of thing are you looking for?

As the editor of this series, of which *Ghost Lights* is the seventh volume (check out the rest, if you haven't already; the titles are in alphabetical order), that's a question I get asked a lot. The honest answer, though, is that I don't know until I happen across it. That's not very helpful to would-be contributors, but the fact is, there is no simple formula for producing a good story. Some stories succeed purely because the ideas that propel them are so wild and original; others grab you because you care deeply about the characters, or because the relationships within them are so compelling. Some stories have simple conceits, but are full of such tension, or such excitement, that you find yourself unable to stop feverishly turning the pages, or scrolling down the screen. Others win you over through humour that is both genuinely funny and brilliantly sustained. Some stories are incredibly moving (it's a real skill to write a story that is moving rather than maudlin), or weave pertinent observations on the human condition into the narrative. If done skilfully (and usually subtly), this will provide a story with extra depth, and make it more than the sum of its parts.

Ultimately, though, good stories, the ones that stand out in a crowd, have an indefinable *energy* about them, a sense of life, of *truth* even, that shines out and demands your attention. It might sound contradictory, but even the darkest, most gruesome, most nihilistic stories can have this shine to them.

And it's *that* that I'm looking for.

The above is probably not all that helpful, so what I thought I'd do in this year's introduction is take this anthology story by story, and tell you what appealed to me about each of them.

What I love about Rachel Harrison's writing is its clarity, its immediacy; it grabs you from the get-go and doesn't relinquish its grip until the story is told. Her characters, and the relationships between them, are beautifully observed and her dialogue chimes with naturalness and truth. In 'Breakup Song', I was immediately drawn to her central character, Jo, and felt sympathy for her situation. Plus, I'm a sucker for stories about creepy, 'possessed' artifacts.

Stephen Volk's 'Hellish Night' has an evocative setting – a deathbed; a storm-lashed night – and hints at a troubled relationship that reveals its secrets slowly and tantalisingly. Stephen is a master when it comes to pacing. He knows exactly how to keep you writhing on the hook as he cranks up the tension and the dread, notch by excruciating notch.

Montanna Rayne Harling's 'Home Exterminators' possesses a strong core – a mother/child relationship that is loving but difficult – and a very weird premise that might have come across as silly in the wrong hands, but which she handles with a pragmatism that makes it not only convincing, but itchily creepy too.

What *always* appeals to me about Josh Malerman's work is his willingness to grab a crazy or difficult concept and run with it. He goes where others fear to tread; in *Bird Box* and its sequel *Malorie*, for instance, he puts enormous restrictions on himself by telling his story through characters who are effectively blind. In 'Leg Stretch', his third contribution to anthologies I've edited, he takes that most innocuous of locations – an all-American diner, full of accommodating locals, in broad daylight – and introduces an element so full of dread that it ties your stomach into knots.

Mo Perkins's 'The Woman in the Box' is delightfully simple, and delightfully odd. What I loved about this story was the viewpoint character. But to say any more would be to give too much away.

'A Cold Moon in December' by Christa Carmen is a mindbender of a story. Clues are scattered like breadcrumbs throughout the narrative, but just when you think you know where it's going, the plot takes an unexpected turn. I loved that.

Eric LaRocca has a unique, and often oblique, approach to horror. His stories tend to be an unsettling blend of tenderness and nihilism, and he is not afraid to confront taboos head on, which invariably makes for an uncomfortable but exhilarating read. What appealed to me about 'The Apiary' was that its dream-like strangeness is underpinned by an achingly moving account of a boy seeking connection with his ailing father. It's a heartrending but beautiful piece of work.

'Monster in the Water' by Stephen D. Koester is a balls-to-the-wall creature feature with a vulnerable but gutsy heroine. I loved the tension of this, I loved the depiction of the titular monster, and I loved the surprisingly uncompromising way in which our protagonist, 13-year-old Ellie, is portrayed.

Laura Purcell writes elegant, twisty, macabre tales in historical (often Victorian) settings. 'Waterloo Teeth' follows that remit to a certain extent, but whereas her novels tend to be ambiguously supernatural, if at all, this story takes the brakes off and charges full-pelt into possession/zombie territory. Reading this, I got the sense that Laura was having great fun writing it. Its core idea is dark and repellent, but its execution is genuinely, albeit macabrely, funny.

I love a bit of folk horror, and Ally Wilkes's 'The Passing Places' is a prime example of it. It's ominous, it's paranoia-inducing, and there's a real sense of long-held traditions, perhaps or perhaps not instigated by ancient forces, coming together to create a situation which, for the victim, is inescapable.

What I loved about David Farrow's 'The Ghosts We Create' was the way he took the horror trope of the haunted house and turned it into a story about trauma, guilt, acceptance and redemption. Here, through the eyes of a family's youngest member, we experience the repercussions of a family haunted by far more than mere spirits from beyond the grave. As a child, Gordon's biggest fear is not the eyeless woman who sits at the end of his bed, but that his father, seething with toxic masculinity, will find out that he's gay. There is so much going on in this story, and it is steeped in an atmosphere of quiet dread and deep melancholy. Beautiful stuff.

No one can match Ramsey Campbell when it comes to creating an atmosphere of sheer dislocating *wrongness*. The precision of his writing is such that when it came to editing this story I couldn't find a single word or even comma out of place, or think of a single suggestion that would make it better. Stomach-squirmingly uncomfortable to read, and shot through with humour of the deepest, purest black, 'The Final Slide' is the work of a true master.

On the surface, Angela Sylvaine's 'The Man Will Creep' is another variation on the urban legend of 'Bloody Mary', but what I felt elevated her take on the story was both the vividly portrayed setting and characters, and also the increasing emphasis on the psychology behind the tale – and I'll say no more for fear of spoilers.

'The Linnhe Queen' by Sally Hughes is as lean as it gets: two characters, a stripped back narrative, a single location. The real strength of this deceptively simple story, however, is its brooding, intense atmosphere. A deeply evocative tale, it has depths that are as dark and murky as the ancient loch on which it takes place.

Last year I read Eliza Clark's collection *She's Always Hungry*, and was so impressed by her imagination, by the assuredness of her writing, and by her razor-sharp observational skills that I vowed that, whatever it took, I *had* to persuade this exciting new talent to write me a story. Fortunately, all it took was an email, and hey presto, 'Closed Circuit' is the sublime result. Like a 2020s version of *Rear Window*, this is a grimy but riveting tale of two acutely wrought characters living lives of isolated desperation. I was gripped by this story from the outset, and was hugely impressed by Eliza's skill in creating an antagonist which, although only hinted at, is truly terrifying.

On the surface, 'Loon Voices' by Michael Rowe is a gentle, melancholic tale of a mother and her young son trying to come to terms with their grief. The rural location, the mournful cries of birds on the lake, and the suggestion of dark, rural legends that permeate the area combine to create an effect that, however elusive, is nevertheless deeply creepy.

One of several stories in which technology is seen as a hostile enemy – albeit a cold and perhaps even a non-sentient one – 'Blurred and Frozen' showcases Carl Tait's skill in creating both a strong premise and a compelling narrative. I was immediately swept up in our protagonist Ashley's predicament and rooting for her to win through at the end. It's not easy to create immediately identifiable and sympathetic characters *and* tell a good story in just a few thousand words, but Carl makes it look easy.

Like Ramsey Campbell, Robert Shearman has a style and an approach that is uniquely his own. Blessed with an incredible imagination, Robert's ideas are often so outlandish that in lesser hands they would fall apart. But Robert writes with such skill, such humour, such warmth, and such *truth*, that he not only makes us believe but he compels us to become fully invested in the tall tales that he's spinning. For all its humour and absurdity, 'The Balcony' is, at its core, a very dark and powerful story. Not only does it contain moments of truly stomach-churning body horror, but it also deals with some major themes, among them childhood trauma, neglect, toxic masculinity and burgeoning sexuality.

Keith Rosson has been around for a while, but it's only in the past three or four years that his excellent work is finally being recognised. Rich Tuttle, his protagonist in 'Kittens', is an anti-hero who is down on his luck, an underdog that we immediately find ourselves rooting for. What Rich discovers, though, when forced by desperation into a situation he'd rather avoid, is truly horrifying. Reading 'Kittens' is like watching a car crash in slow motion. We want everything to turn out all right, but it's so horribly compelling that we can't turn away.

'Blood Moon' by C.J. Tudor is a glorious romp that gleefully takes a horror trope and runs with it. I can imagine this one as a no-holds-barred monster movie full of tension, excitement and buckets of gore. Hugely entertaining and crackling with energy, it's a fitting climax to an anthology that has hopefully – as is always my intention with this series – acted as a display window for the best of modern horror fiction in all its many and varied hues.

Mark Morris

BREAKUP SONG

Rachel Harrison

In his absence, the world drained of colour. I felt a constant draught, a heaviness in my chest that was impossible to forget, to relieve. My friends brought me pints of expensive ice cream and bottles of cheap wine and baby pink macarons and greasy fast food. They brought me soft, cosy blankets and tucked me in, put on funny movies. But I couldn't eat or drink, I couldn't get warm or comfortable, and I couldn't laugh. I couldn't even listen to music.

Nothing could soothe me.

He moved out, and I couldn't bear to live alone where we had lived together. So, I found a new place in a new neighbourhood that somehow still reminded me of him. It was nice enough. A corner unit with large windows and an updated kitchen. It had a walk-in closet, with something small and seemingly harmless left inside.

I discovered it while unpacking, knee-deep in cardboard, lamenting the fact that you could commit to building a life with someone, give them the better half of your twenties, and then they could just change their mind and leave you for a hot tattooed barista named Nicolette. And suddenly, there it was.

An iPod. I hadn't seen one in years. It was a purple Nano. My older sister had a green one when I was a kid, and sometimes she'd let me borrow it. Then we all got iPhones, and the iPods were put out to pasture.

There was a pair of wired headphones wrapped around it.

I picked it up, untangled the headphones, wiped off the earbuds on my shirt. Compelled by curiosity, or nostalgia, or maybe something else, something enigmatic, I popped the buds into my ears. The iPod screen glowed awake.

I anticipated some songs from the early aughts. Emo rock, or prime Britney. But there was only one song. 'Track 1'. No artist attributed.

I pressed play.

At first, I thought it was 'Malibu' by Hole. But then I realised it was a song I'd never heard before, a singer I'd never heard. Her voice was stunning. Such a rich, unique tone. Such emotion. Such range.

"*There's a door out to the back, and through it I find the life I should've been living, instead of wasting all this time on you...*"

I loved the song immediately, completely.

I sat down on the floor, leaned back against the wall. Listening.

"*You poured me out, wrung me out, and you're still thirsty, baby, but now I'm empty and you turn me upside down, shake me out, and wonder why I'm bone dry...*"

All the other music, the other breakup songs I'd tried to listen to just made me feel shitty. But this song... this song felt like trying on a pair of jeans that fit perfectly.

"*I don't want to hear you speak my name, unless you're asking me to come back to drown with you...*"

I stared at the closet wall, at the unpacked boxes, and when the song was over, I didn't need to press repeat. It started playing again on its own.

I thought it was a sign, I thought it was the universe helping me heal.

I was so devastated; how could I fathom things could get any worse?

★ ★ ★

"Why do you do this to yourself, Jo?" Caroline asked me, picking a chunk of pineapple off her slice of pizza. She brought over a Hawaiian because it's my favourite, though she was vocal about "not getting it".

"Do what?"

"Look at her Instagram. It's, it's... self-flagellation. It's not good. No, ma'am."

"No human should be allowed to look like this," I said. I'd created a shadow account for the sole purpose of stalking her. I was logged into it then, neglecting my pizza so I could study a photo of her in a string bikini, posing next to an impressive sandcastle that she built herself. She wasn't just a barista; she was a sculptor. An infuriatingly talented one.

"You shouldn't be jealous of her," Caroline said, dramatically gagging as she picked off yet another pineapple chunk. "You should feel sorry for her. The way you feel now, she's gonna feel five years down the road."

"Maybe," I said. "Or maybe he'll marry her."

"Even worse. Imagine being married to such an asshole."

"He's not an—"

"Please," she said. "He's a giant fucking asshole. Not up for debate."

I ignored her, scrolled to another photo. This one was of Nicolette playing with her hairless cat, Uncle Fester.

"Do you think she knows about me?" I asked Caroline.

"No," she said, gnawing on some crust. "I present to the jury more evidence of him being a giant fucking asshole. Gaping asshole."

"Okay, okay," I said, sighing. "You've made your point."

"What's this? Jo?"

I tore my eyes away from my phone, from Nicolette's page. Caroline had picked up the iPod. It was on my pillow. The night before, I'd listened to the song in hopes it would help me fall asleep. It worked. It was actually the first solid night of sleep I'd gotten since he left.

"That's my emotional support iPod," I said. "Duh."

"Do you also have an emotional support subscription to *Cosmo*? Emotional support Juicy tracksuit? Do you want me to take you to PacSun? Are we about to go on the Atkins diet and pluck out our eyebrows? What exactly are we doing here?"

"I found it," I said. "There's only one song on it, but I'm kind of in love with it."

"What's the song?"

"Track one? I don't know. I don't think it's, like, a known song. Maybe whoever owned the iPod recorded it. A local band or something." I experienced this sudden, intense aversion. This fluttering sensation adjacent to nausea. I really didn't want to talk about the iPod – or the song – with Caroline. I felt like I'd already said too much, and if I said anything else, it would cause me pain. My throat went dry, and there was a pressure in my head, like my brain was no longer alone in my skull.

So I changed the subject. "Have I thanked you for bringing over this pizza that you find so repulsive? Have I told you what an amazing friend you are and how much I appreciate you?"

"I can't recall," she said, setting the iPod back down on my pillow and tapping a finger to her chin. She grinned. "You have. And you're welcome."

After she left, I wrapped the leftover pizza in plastic and put it in the fridge, though I still had no appetite and no intention of ever eating it. Caroline had also brought over some sparkling rosé, and I'd never been a big drinker, but I poured myself a glass and took it to bed with me. I held it in one hand, my phone in the other, and I looked at old pictures of him, of me, of us together. And then of her. This ethereally gorgeous and talented thief.

He hadn't been forthcoming about the fact there was someone else. Not at first. Not until I begged him to stay.

It made more sense than him just falling out of love with me, and it stung like hell, but it also gave me someone to blame other than him, other than myself. I think I needed that.

My phone died eventually, and I didn't bother to plug it in. Instead, I reached for the iPod. I put in the earbuds and turned it on.

I stared at the screen for a long time, suspended by confusion.

There was no more 'Track 1'. Only 'Track 2'.

I doubted my memory. Maybe it had been 'Track 2' all along?

I hovered my thumb, hesitant to press play.

My heart pounded – thump, thump, thump, thump – and sweat squirmed through my pores, crept down from the crown of my head. I'd spent the last few weeks oscillating between sad and numb, and so to feel something else – anything else – was still alien to me. In that moment, I couldn't distinguish between dread and excitement.

I assumed the latter and hit play.

It was the same singer, same band, same alt rock sound. But it was a different song.

"*Mercy on me, ma-ma-ma-mercy on me, I wish she wasn't around, and you were still with me,*" she sang. "*The streetlamps glow like sweet little moons, wind in my hair like violence, telling me what I should do…*"

I sank into my pillow. This song was more up-tempo. A little more aggressive.

I liked it.

I liked it so much that I forgot about Track 1, that I didn't stop to wonder where it had disappeared to, and why, or how. I just sat in bed, staring at the light reaching its long, skinny fingers through the narrow slats of blinds, light from the streetlamp outside my window. I just sat there listening.

"*Mercy on me, ma-ma-ma-mercy on me, I wish she wasn't around, and soon she won't be. Mercy on me, ma-ma-ma-mercy on me, and this revenge fantasy…*"

* * *

My commute to work from my new apartment was about a fifteen-minute bus ride, but the bus was always late, and I could walk it in forty, so I started walking. There was a route I could take to avoid passing the café where Nicolette worked.

I didn't take that route.

The first two days I walked by, I didn't go in. I just looked. It was a trendy place with funky wallpaper and neon signs. They served coffee and bagels and sandwiches and giant pastries that had amassed a local fanbase. It was relatively new, and I had this ephemeral memory of him mentioning it to me once. That he'd gone in, and it was good. Worthy of the hype.

It's possible I conjured up this memory while trying to piece together a timeline of events, pinpoint the moment where it all went wrong. Anything is possible.

On the third day, I brought the iPod with me so I could listen to Track 2 as I walked. I'd been listening at home, at night to help me fall asleep, but I'd never taken it outside the apartment before. I felt weird about it. Anxious.

I'd transcribed all the lyrics and Googled them, hoping I could find out the name of the singer, the band, but nothing came up. The song seemed only to exist on the iPod, and so I didn't want to lose it. It was the only thing making me feel better. My only source of relief.

I held it tight in my clammy hand as I passed the café, turning to peer inside.

She wasn't there in the morning, on my way to work, but she was there on my way home.

"Mercy on me, ma-ma-ma-mercy on me—"

I hit pause and went inside, carefully wrapping the headphones around the iPod, tucking them both safe in my jacket pocket.

She stood behind the counter wearing a striped beanie, her hair in a long braid. She wore no makeup. She had thick, fluffy eyebrows, dark lashes, freckles. Her eyes were pale green. Her lips were full, the kind of full women pay for, suffer needles for, but hers were natural. Her nose was small, her cheekbones high. She was dressed in baggy denim overalls that somehow still managed to flatter her figure. She smiled at me, her teeth white and straight.

"Hello, welcome in! What can I get started for you?"

Even her voice was lovely.

"Um..."

What am I doing? I wondered, in a brief moment of brutal lucidity. *What the hell am I doing?*

"If you need any recommendations, just let me know!" she said. It was obvious that she didn't recognise me. That she had no idea who I was. That she had no idea she'd destroyed my life.

"Sure." I was curious. What would she recommend? What did she like? We loved the same man. What else did we have in common? What other shared tastes?

"This time of day I usually go for a London Fog."

"That sounds good," I said. "Perfect."

"Perfect," she repeated. She went off to make my drink, and someone else rang me up at the register.

I waited by the bar, watching her dance around as she frothed milk. When she finished and slid the drink across the counter toward me, she said, "Let me know what you think! Hope you'll come in again."

"I will," I said, smiling at her.

I set the drink down on a table so I could put my headphones in, then I picked it up and left, stealing a final look at her as I went through the door.

It was cold out and had started to mist. I took a sip of the London Fog. It was just right, not bland but not too sweet. I threw it into the nearest trashcan and took the iPod out of my pocket.

Track 2 was gone, replaced by Track 3. Somehow, I was unfazed.

The song was acoustic, much softer than the first two tracks.

"Cold weather, warm milk, I haven't eaten in days. Hot tea, dry eyes, you keep me locked in your ribcage. I forget what the light feels like, and all the while she's smiling…"

There was a shift in the song. Drums came in. Distortion. The singer started to scream.

"I'd tear the smile from her lips, shatter every tooth, I'd shove my fist down her throat and pull out her heart and show it to you, I'd show it to you because if you don't want me, you don't get her, and she can't have you, youuuu, youuuuu…"

She went on screaming and screaming and screaming and screaming and screaming, until the song started itself over again.

I considered stopping it. I was aware that the iPod was uncanny, and I knew it wasn't good for me to listen, that it was exacerbating an ugliness that the breakup had seeded in me. That it was intensifying an unhealthy obsession.

But it was a really good song.

★ ★ ★

Caroline and Greer coaxed me out of my apartment, coming by unannounced and threatening to set up camp unless I got ready and went to dinner with them. I'd been living in the apartment for almost two weeks at that point, and I'd been listening to Track 3 nonstop for about eight days.

I resisted going back to the café but continued to walk by.

"Have you given any thought to when you want to get back out there?" Greer asked, already on her second cocktail of the evening though we hadn't even gotten our appetisers. "Because I could set up your Bumble profile, no problem."

"Greer," Caroline said, waving her off. "Too soon."

"Is it, though?" Greer asked. "You're twenty-seven, gorgeous, smart, have a great job in tech—"

"I'm on the business side. I don't do anything cool and techy," I said.

"Still! You're too young to throw in the towel!"

"She's not throwing in the towel," Caroline said. "She's taking a healthy pause to process the end of a significant relationship."

"We could still get back together," I said, watching the tealight candle on our table flicker – little flame dance. "If it weren't for her, we never would have broken up."

"Lord. You want to take this?" Greer said to Caroline.

"Joanna, it's not about her," Caroline said, reaching across the table for my hand. "If it wasn't her, it'd be someone else. He's one of those people who's just never satisfied. How many jobs has he had since you've known him? He went back to school, what, twice? Changed his mind. He was going to be a personal trainer and then he was going to be a welder, and then and then and then. You spent so much time and energy supporting him. Emotionally, and financially. And I think that's what makes this so hard."

"Is that it?" I asked, pulling my hand away. I tasted salt. A tear.

"Jo..."

I didn't want to be at the restaurant. I wanted to be in my bed listening to Track 3. Listening to someone screaming their goddamn head off. Listening to someone convey the hurt that I felt.

"Jo! What are you doing? Jo! Stop!"

My vision was tear-drowned, so I couldn't quite see. But I became aware of the sensation. And I could smell it. Burning.

I was holding my right middle finger over the tealight, over the flame. Letting it burn me.

Caroline grabbed my hand and stuck it in a glass of ice water.

"Jo! Oh my God..." Greer said. She and Caroline exchanged a nervous look.

"Can you take me back to my apartment?" I asked. "Can you leave me the fuck alone?"

When they dropped me off, Caroline insisted on coming inside to "check things out". She went into the bathroom, opened the medicine cabinet. Then she started rummaging around the kitchen.

"Have you been eating?" she asked, opening the fridge to find the now-mouldy Hawaiian pizza.

"I'm sad. I'm allowed to be sad."

"I know," she said. "But this isn't just sad. You're scaring me. You're wasting away. Are you sleeping?"

"Yeah." I was telling the truth, but she was sceptical.

"You look *exhausted.* And I feel like it's getting worse. I'm really worried. Is it the new apartment? Do you want to come stay with me?"

"I'm fine."

She sighed. "Okay, ma'am."

She made me promise to call her in the morning, and then she left.

I changed into my pyjamas and climbed into bed. I thought there might be a new track, but it was still Track 3. The lyrics were a little different, though.

"*Bad weather, warm knife, go starve yourself for days. Hot flame, wet eyes, in the quiet there's only rage. You forget what joy feels like, and all the while he's smiling…*"

The song shifted, with the drums and the distortion, though this time, another voice came in. A quiet voice. A strange voice. A hideous voice.

It said, "You're not sad, you're angry. You're not sad, you're angry. You're not sad, you're angry. You're not sad, you're angry. You're not sad, you're angry. You're not sad, you're angry. You're not sad, you're angry."

It said it until I knew it was true.

* * *

Caroline was right to be sceptical. I might not have been sleeping. I might have just been staring off into space, losing time, listening to Track 3 over and over. I realised this after I passed out at work and my coworker insisted on escorting me to urgent care.

"I recently moved," I told the doctor. "I'm getting used to the place. Not sleeping great."

"Are you on any medication?" She was also sceptical of me. My clothes had gotten loose. My skin dry and peeling. My hair thin – it'd been coming out in clumps, clogging the shower drain.

"No. No medication."

"Recreational drug use?"

"I used to smoke weed, but I don't anymore." I only ever smoked with him.

"What about alcohol?"

"I had a glass of rosé maybe two weeks ago? I don't know. I don't really drink."

The doctor shrugged. The waiting room was full, and I could tell she was torn between just believing me so she could move on to the next patient, and genuine concern for my wellbeing.

"Any history of anaemia?"

"I'm going through a breakup." I hated saying the words out loud, hated how they sounded, how they tasted – rancid. But they were my way out.

"Ah," she said, nodding. "We've all been there. Look, you've got good insurance, couldn't hurt to find someone to talk to. Should be covered."

"Yeah," I said, and I heard the strange voice in my head. *You're not sad, you're angry.*

"Take care of yourself, okay? It'll get better in time," the doctor said.

My coworker called an Uber for me. I got in, let it drop me at my apartment. I waited for it to pull away, and then I started to walk. I walked to the café.

"Hey! London Fog!" She remembered me.

"My friends call me Foggy."

"Miss Foggy," she said, bowing her head. It wasn't fair that she was charming, too. "Same thing? Try something else?"

"You pick," I said. "I trust your judgement."

"I won't let you down," she said, winking. "Any allergies? Caffeinated, decaf?"

"No allergies. Caffeine is fine. Necessary."

"Girl after my own heart."

I wanted to hate her. It was much easier to hate her while scrolling through her perfect pictures. Much easier to hate her than it was to hate him, than it was to hate myself.

It occurred to me then, as I stood there watching her press buttons on the espresso machine, that it wasn't so much about the loss of *him*. I wasn't in agony over the emptiness on the other side of the bed. I missed him, of course I did, but the ache of missing him wasn't what was torturing me.

You're not sad, you're angry.

It was the loss of time. Of energy. Of the years taken from me. The money. The love and effort expended for someone who sucked me dry and then up and left. Left me for someone who got to be ignorant of all that I'd given. All that I'd sacrificed.

You're not sad, you're angry.

It was that they got to be happy while I was robbed of things I could never get back.

"Okay, I went rogue," said Nicolette. "It's a peanut butter oat milk mocha with a shot of espresso. It's not on the menu, it's my own mad invention. I hope you like it!"

"Sounds great."

She slid a sleeve on the cup and rang me up. "See you soon, yeah?"

"Yeah. You'll see me soon."

I went outside and found a bench nearby. I sat down, took off the lid, and took a small sip. It was very sweet, but I drank it anyway, while I listened to Track 4.

It sounded a lot like Track 1, only with a more distinctive bassline.

"*I only ever thought about you, went dizzy in your orbit, built you a kingdom with my bare hands, to be buried under it* ..."

The strange voice was back. A whispering underneath the music. Again, it said, "*You're not sad, you're angry.*"

As the song faded out, the singer and the strange voice joined in harmony.

"*You're not sad, you're angry,*" they sang. And then, "What are you going to do about it?"

★ ★ ★

One sick day turned into two turned into six. Track 4 turned into Track 5. Not a song, but a loop of riotous screaming and laughter. It was loud but I couldn't turn down the volume. I stayed in bed, and I listened.

Caroline called, Greer called, my mother called. I ignored them. The pizza in the fridge went green and fuzzy.

I had these fleeting moments of clarity, like a ray of sunlight defying a dark storm cloud. Moments where I would tell myself that something was wrong, and that I needed help, but the noise was so loud. I couldn't hear myself. My voice got lost. Or stolen. My throat was inflamed, but if I tried to drink water, I'd just throw it up.

My eyes went bloodshot. It hurt to keep them open, but when I closed them, I saw things I didn't want to see.

The things described in Track 6.

"*Your new girl does look so pretty, with her hair tied back like that. Your new girl won't look so pretty, with her skull smashed in half. Don't you know, have you forgot, red is my favourite colour, baby, colour, baby. There's a hammer in my hand, in my hand, in my hand. There's a hammer in my hand, in my hand, in my hand, whoa... It'll be fun, but once she's done, I'll take the knife out my back, and it'll be your turn...*"

The strange voice was absent from Track 6. Mostly. I thought maybe I could hear it cackling during the chorus, but I wasn't sure.

I also wasn't sure how I got the hammer. It was just there. On my kitchen counter, next to my bag, my keys, my dead phone.

Unlike my phone, the iPod never died.

I took all of it with me when I finally left my apartment. The iPod, my dead phone, my keys, my bag. The hammer.

I cleaned myself up, first. So much hair came out in the shower. Fistfuls. It didn't disturb me. Neither did my bones, which I could see clearly. My ribs, especially. I could count them all.

In the mirror was a face I didn't recognise. It smiled back at me, with teeth gone yellow after weeks of neglect.

"Hello," said a voice that wasn't mine. That sounded just like the strange voice. "Hello."

It laughed and laughed.

"Better get going," it said, after a long time. "You have something you need to do."

★ ★ ★

"Miss Fog!"

"Hello." I sounded like me again, though maybe a little hoarse.

"Haven't seen you in a while. I was afraid I'd scared you off with my peanut butter mocha concoction."

I shook my head. "Nah. But I don't know if I could handle another."

"Fair enough," she said. "Don't have a sweet tooth?"

"Not really. You?"

"Big time. Drives my boyfriend crazy. I'll be in bed eating Snickers at midnight and he'll be like, I don't know how you live like this."

Caroline once got upset when we were all out to dinner. She said he'd shamed me out of getting dessert. I told her she was making something out of nothing.

"So, what'll it be?"

"Just a coffee, please. Black. For here."

"Okay," she said, smiling. "You can have a seat. I'll bring it to you."

I found a spot in the corner. I set my bag down on the table, hammer inside making a loud clank. Loud even over all the noise in my head. All the tracks playing simultaneously. The strange voice telling me I was angry. The doctor telling me to talk to someone. Caroline telling me she was worried. Him telling me he was sorry; that it wasn't working out. That he cared about me, but we'd lost the spark.

I wanted quiet but I was afraid of the quiet. Afraid of what waited for me there.

I put my headphones in and pressed play on a new track. Track 7.

"*What are you gonna do with that hammer, Jo? What are you gonna do with that hammer? What are you gonna do? What are you gonna do? Don't you want to feel better, Jo? Don't you want to feel better? Go on, Jo. Put that hurt on someone else.*"

I opened my eyes, and Nicolette was there, setting a mug down in front of me.

She said something, but I couldn't really hear her, so I pulled out my earbuds.

"Sorry?"

"Is that an iPod?" she asked. "My older sister had one and I would beg her to let me borrow it and she refused."

"Really? My sister had one, too. But she let me listen."

"Lucky," she said. Then she put her hands on her hips, looked down at the floor, then back up at me. "Hey, um. I know who you are."

"What?"

"I recognised you the first time you came in."

"I'm sorry?" I began to wrap my headphones around the iPod. As I did, I slowly reached toward my bag. I would put the iPod in and take the hammer out, and I would put the hurt on someone else, someone other than myself.

"I'm the new girlfriend, you came by to check me out. I get it. I mean, the only reason I knew it was you was because I went creeping on your Insta. I just... I felt shitty about pretending. And I know you guys were together for a while. I don't know. I don't know."

I could feel the hammer, my hand closing around the handle. And I could hear all the songs, all the voices. Especially the strange voice. It was so, so loud. So foul. So violent. I couldn't remember a time before it was in my head. I couldn't remember a life without it, I couldn't imagine what it would be like.

"Maybe I shouldn't have said anything."

"No," I said. "I'm sorry. I'm embarrassed. I'm... not myself. I haven't been myself."

She put her head in her hands. "Ugh, this is shitty! It's shitty. I don't know. I hope we're cool. Can we be cool?"

"I have something for you," I said, as I pulled my hand out of my bag.

"No way," she said, as I slipped the iPod from my palm into hers.

"You can tell your sister. Brag about it. Consider it a peace offering. We're cool."

"Really? I don't want to take your iPod."

"Honestly, I just found it a few weeks ago at my new place. Old tenant must have left it behind. There's only one track on it, but it's really good. Don't know who it's by."

"Can I listen?" she asked, unwrapping the headphones.

"It's all yours."

She grinned as she put the earbuds in, as she pressed play.

"Ooo," she said after a moment. "I really love this guy's voice. I fucking love old school R&B. My fave."

"You like it?"

She took another moment, listened. I watched something pass across her beautiful, beautiful face. A shadow. Her eyes closed, and then opened again.

"I love this song," she said. "I've never heard it before."

I know it was wrong to give it to her.

I know I should have at least warned her. But I knew she wouldn't hear it until she was ready. Until her heart was broken, until a bitterness took root, until she looked in the mirror and saw someone she didn't recognise. I had to learn the hard way, had to suffer, face the music. And she would, too.

I stood up, grabbed my hammer-heavy bag, and left.

Outside, the air smelled clean and fresh. It was warm enough that I could take off my jacket. I could hear birdsong, car horns, children laughing, an ice cream truck. I set off to find the truck. I wanted ice cream, rainbow sprinkles. I wanted to run fast, to dance in the street. I wanted to float up to the sky. It was the most vibrant blue.

HELLISH NIGHT

Stephen Volk

It was biblical. The downpour. The deluge. She'd abruptly switched off the news after taking the exit to Stroud off the M4, flipping the wipers from slow to fast, on and off, as the rain hopped schizophrenically from drizzle to torrential in unpredictable pockets. Then the skies had darkened and opened as she passed through Cricklade, Latton, and Cerney Wick, where bullets of water machine-gunned the road surface, and everyone, headlights now on, decided to drop below the speed limit, an indication in itself that the apocalypse was surely imminent.

She couldn't help but bend forward over the steering wheel, squinting to make sense of the blurred shapes framed by the windscreen, but they remained a rippling curtain of abstract blobs, washed away then returning in force, attempting to sharpen into a cogent picture of reality, only to fail. Fail again. Fail better, as Samuel Beckett said.

The poetry programme on Radio 4 echoed in her mind. Had she failed? Was this about her failure? Failure for what? And in that self-condemnation, conjuring the ghosts of a dozen well-meaning counsellors from her past, he had her. Had her again. By the throat.

She found the cottage hospital without too much effort, though she'd never been there before. Never knew it existed till now. Nor the name of the town it was in, till the ward manager told her on the phone, giving her the postcode for the satnav, thank God. Roni being next of kin, as she knew, but didn't want to think about – till she had to.

She reversed into a space, yanked on the handbrake. Shocked to see a police car opposite, triggering the inevitable flashback – except it'd had its lights on, that night, an incarnation ago, drowning the whole street in strobes of underwater blue, bathing every single neighbour standing, craning their necks to get a good look, a good nose to pollute their good lives, as the uniforms hauled her dad down the stairs, pyjamas half hanging off, handcuffing him, her dream already broken, and all she wanted to say was, *don't step on the Lego, Dad.* All she could see was his bare feet and their big black boots and the Lego pieces she hadn't tidied up the night before.

She held her raincoat over her head with upstretched arms, examining the parking charges on the sign as the rainfall pattered on the umbrella of her. She scanned the QR code and scuttled under the porch, half-drenched, to feed in her details and pay.

"They've got you every bloody way these days." A toothless old man in a wheelchair wrapped prehensile lips around the last shred of a tatty cigarette. "Every orifice, you're buggered."

She shook the rain off her coat and slid her arms into the sleeves as his cough rattled with semi-dislodged phlegm. She noticed one of his lower limbs was missing and he had the empty leg of his trousers tucked under him.

The Information Desk showed no one in attendance, the place seemingly deserted. She didn't know what departments it specialised in – gynaecology, paediatrics, minor injuries – but at least there weren't drunks kicking off in A&E or trolleys rushing past with the victims of motorcycle accidents. She'd seen enough of that backdrop with her mother, sat waiting to hear how serious the binge blackout was this time. Sat in her nightie and dressing gown reading *The Lion, the Witch and the Wardrobe*. Disappointed when she had to stop and be taken home, when the policewoman took her by the hand.

Luckily she'd written the ward number on the back of her hand and made her way to it using the colour-coded arrows on the walls. A sign taped to the door said visiting hours were strictly 14:30–19:30. For a moment she thought the message from the ward manager had been fictitious or a joke. She tucked her wet hair behind her ears and buzzed the intercom as water trickled down the back of her neck.

"Yes?"

"Hello. My name's Veronica Slad. I've come to see my father? I got a phone call? His name is Ivo? Ivo Slad?"

"Hold on."

Curt. But fair enough. Middle of the night. Long shift, probably. Overworked, probably. Underpaid, definitely. Roni knew she couldn't do what they do, never in a million years. Hold the wizened paws of strangers. Wipe their bottoms. Watch them die. Perhaps it was easier when they were blank slates. When you didn't know what they'd done in their lives. You could tell yourself they were saints.

A mechanical growl released the lock. She went in and the door swung shut behind her, the draught rustling sheets of paper pinned randomly to a notice board. They settled like doves on a wall.

The nurse was already walking away from her, so she followed. The screen of an out-of-date computer monitor glowed, fringed with a headdress of yellow and pink Post-it notes.

"How is he?"

"You can sit in the relatives' room or sit with him."

"I'll sit with him, if that's all right. How is he doing?"

"Haven't you been told?"

"No, I've only just got here."

They reached a door that was open a few inches.

"Can the doctor fill me in?"

"He will, but he has other patients to see. You'll have to wait."

"I realise that. I wasn't arguing. I meant 'at some point'." Roni stopped herself saying what she wanted to say. "Listen. Sorry, I've been driving for hours. It's a terrible night out there."

"It's a terrible night in here, most nights."

The nurse had a notable stain above her left nipple. Perhaps it was coffee, thought Roni. Perhaps it was saliva, or a dribble of soup from the microwave that had missed her mouth.

"Can I get you anything?"

"No. Thank you. Actually, do you have a glass of water?"

"You can get still or sparkling from the drinks machine at the end of the corridor."

Roni didn't fancy braving the intercom a second time, and didn't fancy working out what coins the drinks machine took, and mostly wanted to see her dying fucking father, but said "Thanks" quietly, trying not to sound sarcastic or ungrateful.

The nurse departed and Roni pushed the door ajar.

Hello, Dad.

Stick arms lying on top of the blanket, she saw a shrivelled mummy of a man. A monkey carved out of weathered bark. She didn't see that there could be muscle there below the layers that covered him. It looked to her like an arrangement of bones laid out against the monstrous pillow that made him look even more shrunken and insubstantial. But the beard – now grey – she remembered, even if the crater-like hollows of his cheeks she didn't. And the wide nostrils had not diminished even though they were under the hissing see-through oxygen mask and he was at death's door.

Here I am, Daddy.

He couldn't hear, even if she had spoken it aloud. She knew that. He was unconscious. She could see his chest rising and falling, but his eyes were mercifully shut, and standing there she was suddenly fearful they would open and behold her, full of pleading or demand. Yet part of her wanted him to, even as part of her wanted to turn and flee. Why was she here, she asked herself? Because there was nobody else. Plain and simple. That made it seem like she was doing it for him, but she wasn't. She was doing it for herself.

A rose of pain blossomed hotly on the right-hand side of her face. The cracked cheekbone had long since healed, as much as it ever would, but the memory was there, in the flesh. Just as it was in her damaged spine from being thrown downstairs. The feelings came back to haunt her, to rescue her, to remind her he was a violent man.

But the wreck in the bed was feeble, pathetic, more worthy of pity than terror. His mortal frame had given out completely. He was no longer a force to be reckoned with. Those hands could no longer lash out, or cajole, or beckon.

This wasn't the same man who had lurked in car parks next to railway stations over nearly a decade, predating on young women on their own, vulnerable women who had to risk walking the last couple of hundred yards to their cars, keys in hand, and never got there. He wasn't that person – but he was.

She remembered that time, when she was twelve and Ka was six, when he'd passed out over the Christmas dinner due to consuming a bottle of absinthe, and she and her mother and sister thought he was dead when they put their ears to his chest and couldn't hear his heart, and they'd had a really nice Christmas – best Christmas ever, laughing and joyful, paper hats, silly games, unwrapping presents – then he'd woken up with a belch and a slur of vomit and it was all back to normal. If you could call it that. She remembered how her heart had fallen like a stone into a river.

And now – would she be happy when he died? Relieved, then? Feel a weight lifted? She didn't know. Maybe it was too much to ask for, in the scheme of things. In the list of deserving causes, her redemption came pretty low in everybody's estimation. Including hers.

He'd told her, in that letter from prison, she wasn't to blame, but when could she ever believe him about anything? He'd pleaded not guilty. It was always this other feller. "They got it wrong, Riwbob." His pet name for her, courtesy of his Welsh mother. A case of misidentification, never mind the evidence being overwhelming, never mind his DNA being inside their bodies. Always someone else's fault. The lies that came out of those pale blue eyes every day, convincing you of this, of that, any fantasy that served his purpose. Helped him use you. Yet he was never in the wrong, just a dreamer, he'd say. A poet. "A prophet unrecognised in his own land." *Bollocks.*

Changed his plea later. Of course he did. You had to say you were guilty to get the therapy, and you had to do the therapy to get an early release. It was a no brainer. He might have been driven by who-knows-what psychological impulses over which he had no control but that didn't mean he wasn't a cunning opportunist, telling his family he was working his fingers to the bone at a second job when he was out prowling for his prey. Till the prostitutes who'd sampled his sadistic kinks and nicknamed him 'The Naughty Man' flushed him out.

The soreness in her cheek throbbing, she knocked back two Nurofen, dry, nearly choking on them, and shut the door. The rain beat heavily on the blackness of the window. Her skin felt clammy. She peeled off her coat and tossed it onto the chair, but her jeans still clung to her.

There were no niceties in the room to relieve the grimness of what the patient faced. Just a chest of medical supplies on one side of the bed and the oxygen tank on the other, its clear tube looping to his inert and ghastly face. That, and a large, very bad framed print, courtesy of some pound shop or boot fair, of a swan flying over a sea at dusk, with a bulbous naked youth beholding it, arse to the artist.

It took her back to the painting in her parents' bedroom in Painswick. God, it scared her, that thing. How could it not when you were a child? The great god Pan surveying a typical English formal garden of the eighteenth century, hands on hips, presiding over all he surveyed with slanting eyes and a bestial grin. Ivo would call him 'The Old Goat', and tell the story, but the story was always a little bit different each time, and when you looked at the painting it was always a little bit different too. They used to stare at it, her and her sister, and spook each other by pointing out the ways it had changed. But of course it hadn't changed at all.

Ivo used to tell them it was a twin brother to another painting, up near Bulls Cross, away in the forest owned by the Lord of the Manor. In a place called Pan's Lodge, which didn't exist anymore. Where the gentry used to get up to all sorts. And on Feast Sunday the townsfolk'd make a procession from St. Mary's Church, through the woods. "Dressing up, drinking, debauchery ensued..." he'd describe, with relish. "All in honour of the half-goat god!"

Used to terrify her. Meant to, she now understood. She'd been given, at a ripe and vulnerable age, a peek into her father's soul. According to the psychiatrist who gave testimony, he could only reach orgasm off his victims' fear. That's why he had to look into their eyes as he did it. And when, as a girl, she was frightened of that painting, it made her want to get into his bed and be protected from all the dark things that came out at night. And he let her.

Her vision grew fuzzy. She felt off balance. Perhaps she was dehydrated. That was due to the swift espresso she downed before hitting the road. She wished she'd filled her personalised water container before she left home. You saw them everywhere now. At the gym, on the street. They were all the rage since Covid. People had a morbid fear of infection. Little did they know they were being infected all the time, by the past.

Now she wondered if she could believe a word of it. The painting. But it was there – on the wall of her home, wasn't it? She couldn't have imagined *that*.

She remembered being taken to the Rococo Gardens and being shocked when she saw the statue of Pan there. So it *was* real. Some of it was... but what? She'd tried to find out later, get chapter and verse from the guide, for her own peace of mind. Apparently, there'd been another statue of Pan in the churchyard which had provided the procession with a meeting point, until a conservative vicar decided to put an end to all that heretical revelry and buried it at an unknown location.

And she'd been told, yes – there *was* a painting in Pan's Lodge: *Pan Indicating His Realm to Attentive Guests, 1757*. Her nerves had prickled as she was shown an old engraving of a scene that was the mirror-image of the one she knew from home. A swirling frame populated by creatures of the night; magpie, bat and owl, enclosing a landscape of arboreal dread. The dusk itself resembling a crooked, cloaked creature. Pan to one side with the drunken Dionysus, with the quotation *PAN DEUS ARCADIAE* from Virgil's Tenth Eclogue resplendent in a scroll. A full and ripe celebration of the horny god sovereign over a Cotswold wool town…

"There are only two types of people in this world," her father once taught them. "Sheeps and wolves."

One of those nasty aphorisms designed to put her ill at ease. Being six years younger, her sister had avoided that insidiousness, thank God. If she'd ever been the prey, Roni wouldn't have been able to bear it. But he was under lock and key by then. A fading memory with any luck. For Ka, anyway.

At thirteen Roni had been fostered and, third go, they were good people, and she put her sanity down to them, if she had any. Heading for London and a career, she had enough to think about surviving the world, minimising cutting herself, not going the way of her mother with the booze, and if she thought about the painting and the stories at all she'd come to the conclusion the 'Lord of the Manor' had created a den of depravity, something like a cross between a secret society and a swingers' club, naming some ornate Georgian gazebo 'Pan's Lodge' no more than nose-thumbing by a bunch of posh, hedonistic wankers showing off their classical educations. She couldn't help thinking of Boris and the Bullingdon. Now, when she was reminded of these toffs getting their rocks off in a wooded glade, she thought of the popular meme: *No smartphones, just young people enjoying themselves in the moment.*

Which made her think of the devil mask her father wore when he crept up on women beside the railway line. She wondered if she should call him a cunt, lean over and shout the word in his face. Speak for those who didn't have a voice because his fat, grubby fingers were covering their mouths. But she didn't.

She sat there, holding her empty water container, questioning why she had come, but equally questioning why she couldn't leave.

She couldn't see him breathing and she didn't know if that was a good thing or a bad thing. His mouth was half open. His jaw hanging loosely. The face mask still clouded. Still hissing like a snake in Eden.

She took out her phone. She didn't know if it was allowed, if she was supposed to go outside, but she didn't care. There was nobody around to slap her wrist. It was late. She paced back and forth at the foot of the bed, clenching her teeth, ready for the inevitable verbal fireworks as it trilled interminably in the void.

"*What?*" Distant. Clipped.

"Did you get my text?"

"*Yes.*"

"That's all you have to say?"

"*What do you want me to say?*"

Here we go. "I don't want anything, Ka."

"*For fuck's sake.*"

"For fuck's sake what? He's dying."

"*What do you want me to do? Throw myself on the ground? Beat my chest, weeping and wailing, like you're doing?*"

"No." Roni pressed the centre of her forehead hard with the tip of her index finger. "I wouldn't expect that in a million years."

"*Good.*"

"I just thought you ought to know, all right?"

"*Yes. Thank you.*"

Deep breath… As she always felt when she talked to Katherine. Deep breath, glass of red wine, cigarette. Anything to take the edge off the experience because it was never pleasant, never gushing, never easy. Always dancing on the edge of a razor.

"*Is he suffering?*" Pause. "*Good.*"

"Don't you think a human being deserves—"

"*He's not a human being, Roni. You know that more than anybody.*"

"Well, if I'm prepared to be here and at least…"

"*You shouldn't. Christ. You shouldn't put yourself anywhere near that man. Don't. I mean it. Get in your car now and drive away. Please. I know you want to do the right thing, but don't think of him, think of you, for once. He's a fucking dangerous, violent—*"

"…what?"

"*What? Have you blocked out everything—*"

"He can hardly breathe, for fuck's sake. Do you want to listen to him breathing? Listen…"

Roni held her phone out at arm's-length, so that it almost touched the oxygen mask, holding it there, her hand shaking, hearing her sister say, a hundred miles away:

"*I'm going now. I'm going to hang up.*"

Roni yanked the phone back to her cheek, which was volcanic lava. "He paid for his crimes."

"*No. He fucking didn't.*"

That last word a yelp cut off in its prime and Ka was gone.

Roni was gutted but not surprised. She knew the score. Ka had always been her protector. Always been there for her. The younger sister, acting like the older one. Why wasn't she there for her now?

She couldn't be, and that was fine. Absolutely fine. They lived separate lives, so why was this any different? But she'd sounded afraid and Roni didn't like that. Ka was never afraid. She'd wrapped herself up with a wall around her and her family, lived a comfortable, fulfilled and active life with husband Gid and Bosco and Otis, two kids with names like pets, perfect apart from the ADHD, which they had to pay to get them tested for, because the waiting lists were appalling and the exams would be over if they didn't. Roni had listened in silent tears that time when she'd had a mental crash and Ka had done nothing but talk on the phone about herself but that was fine. It had kind of revived her. Reminded her that normality was possible and you didn't have to cut X's into your forearms, trying to cancel yourself out.

No, it had all worked out for Ka. Which was nice. No, it *was* nice... Nice that she was too young to be aware of what was happening with her father and the police and the trial. Just the hazy mystery of being taken here and there, into foster care then out again. Then their mum's final, fatal pub crawl that left her in the gutter with a cracked skull. Or perhaps the resentment was there because the past was a blur to Ka and to her it wasn't. Roni was envious of that.

But her sister hanging up made her feel alone. She was alone. Always had been. Sort of joke but it wasn't. She'd always been picky with boys. Always assessing the potential disaster they carried within them. She'd had romances, yes, but also a talent for self-sabotage. Always laid a tripwire. Made them fall before they gave her the shove. Vindicating what she always knew, that it would turn ugly sooner or later. Love always did.

Rapid eye movements darted under her father's eyelids. She wondered where they darted. In what dark realm? In what heaven or hell? The lips did not tremble, though it looked as if they, not the oxygen tank, were emitting the hiss, as if this human husk were punctured.

If they did contort to form words, what would she want him to say? Ask, in a croaky but caring voice, with eyes sparking in gratitude that she'd come all this way, what she's up to these days? And she'd reply that she was a communications director at a national bathroom supplies company. And what then? He'd be proud? He'd say, well done, girl? Who was she fucking kidding?

Sheeps and wolves, Riwbob.

The room started to swim. It wasn't just the headache back in force. She felt weird. Unmoored. Maybe it was the Sertraline. She'd read online you should be careful in hot weather because of overheating. The forecast had predicted the temperature would reach twenty-nine in the west and her phone app told her the storm hadn't put a dent in that.

She fumbled in her bag for the paracetamol she always carried. It had been two hours since the Nurofen and she'd become a dab hand at alternating.

"Veronica?"

Young chap held his hand out. His shake was firm but not unkind. He had his sleeves rolled up. The shirt fitted his gym bod snugly, top button undone, revealing a sprig of chest hair under the U of his collar bone. Seven o'clock shadow on his throat and chin.

"Hi. I'm Dr. Benjamin Hyett. Can we have a brief word?"

She answered yes but didn't know how brief or not-brief she wanted it.

The relatives' room was stark, bland and uninviting, apart from a few unexpected accoutrements in the shape of a Fisher-Price doll, a Tonka truck, a Connect4 and a secondhand-looking box of Trivial Pursuit cards.

"Take a seat, please."

She did, realising she was playing noisily with the foil of capsules in her hands. He was carrying a half-full plastic bottle of spring water which he offered her. The brand name was Minerva.

"Do you mind?" she said. "Thank you."

He sat down opposite, elbows on knees as she knocked the painkillers back. He was well-muscled, she saw. Probably unaware he had a

Superman curl on his brow, or else the nurses teased him about it. He wouldn't know they had a secret crush on him. He'd blush if he found out. Pictures by small children were pinned on the wall behind him. Stick figures. A clown with rabbit ears. A big, black spider with eyes on its back. And writing she didn't understand. *AIG* on one. *AITIS* on another. *AIG AITIS.*

"Right. Has the care home kept you up to date?"

"Not really. I haven't been…"

"Well, your father was diagnosed with pancreatic cancer a few months ago, and, from his notes, I see his oncologist was waiting for him to be fit enough for chemotherapy, hopefully losing a little bit of weight, et cetera. Anyway, now he's come down with pneumonia on top of it. Which is not very good news. Pneumonia. Cancer."

"Basically he's not long for this world."

Dr. Hyett took the mineral water bottle back from her outstretched hand. "Has he got his affairs in order?"

"I have no idea." She picked up the Fisher-Price doll and stroked its hair.

"Okay. I'd advise you to inform whoever you need to inform that I think we're talking about twenty-four to forty-eight hours at the most." He allowed that to sink in, knotting his fingers into a mesh. "Any questions?"

"No… Is he in pain?"

"We'll make sure he's comfortable."

What a great euphemism that was, when it actually meant dosing someone to the gills with morphine.

"I know what you're thinking," he said, getting to his feet. "I see it all the time. You're thinking, I can't deal with this. But you can."

She looked up at him and smiled. No, she was thinking of the devastated people who were left alive out there. The fathers and mothers and women still suffering every day and sleepless night who would want Ivo Slad to be dying in pain. The more pain the better.

"I'll be around for a while if you want to talk to me. No rest for the wicked." He walked to the door, then turned and came back to place his bottle of water on the coffee table next to her.

"Thank you."

"Stay as long as you like."

She must have nodded off soon after then, because she was roused by a short sharp cry, which she imagined was that of a vixen, unfamiliar though that was to her. There weren't many vixens in Swindon, although foxes were increasingly common in urban areas everywhere in England. Nature encroaching, step by step.

She sat up straight and cricked her neck, which made a popping sound. She heard someone out in the corridor saying something she couldn't understand. A woman's voice saying what sounded like *Bandaged cat. Bandaged cat...*

The doll had fallen off her lap onto the floor. She put it back with the other toys, swigged from the bottle and swallowed, rinsing out her claggy coffee mouth, and felt guilty and stupid for sitting there for – how long?

Her father. What if—?

She didn't let herself disappear down that plug hole. Just got up and hurried from the relatives' room, shutting the door after her.

"Bandaged cat."

An elderly woman with sores on her legs stood dressed in a blue hospital smock. She held a cat at arm's-length as if presenting it to Roni. The creature was wrapped from neck to toe in bandages but didn't look at all distressed.

"Bandaged cat. Bandaged cat!"

"No. No, thank you."

The fuck...

Leaning back against the closed door of her father's room, Roni heard the old woman outside mumbling away as she shuffled down the corridor. Poor thing must be a madwoman of some kind. On the loose from the psychiatric wing. Or dementia. Alzheimer's. Undiagnosed. In the cancer ward. Or the ICU, if that's where she was. Nobody had told her and she had never asked.

Ivo had not moved. His chest was still rising and falling. His crab-apple hands still lay inert upon the blanket either side of him. Lost possessions from an active life. Too active, many would say.

"Come on, Minerva." The voice of the nurse. "Let's get you to bed."

Roni sat down and dug out the first of the three miniatures of Bell's she'd bought at the service station, and downed them all, methodically, hiding each empty in the secret pocket of her bag.

A blast shook the walls. The huffing-puffing of a fairytale wolf. The heavy shelling of the storm had not abated.

She prayed for thunder to rip the firmament, let out the pressure, release her skull from its fucking torment, but the place felt like a hothouse. Her sinuses were agony. She walked to the window in the hope of opening it an inch, but it was locked. *Fuck.*

She detected movement out amongst the wet-laden trees – pines, she thought they were – whose branches seemed to be soggy and soughing in waves. Underneath, below, in the dark past midnight, two people ran after each other. A man and woman, both soaked to the skin. Running for cover? No… running in circles. Like kids. Laughing. He, pausing to tear off his shirt, whip off his belt. Her, losing her high heels, then stripping to her bra and panties.

A scraping cough came from the bed. A throat-cleansing semi-stifled by the oxygen mask.

Roni turned to regard him and his scar of a mouth under the clear lens of it.

The lower lip shivered, glistening like a slug. The upper twitched. The eyes moth-wing flickered, eyelashes pale as glass. What did he dare to dream? What was his final, fetid wish?

She knelt beside the bed. She could do nothing else. She bowed her head but wasn't going to pray. Nobody in their right mind would pray for him, not 'The Naughty Man' of the tabloids – yet she had to ask, what did her father want, in his going? What obscenity? What last desire could she offer?

Ivo's legs twitched under the blanket. The undulations of mountains and valleys.

Roni heard a giggling in the cellar of her mind, an excitement, a party game of old, a hide and seek, at the same time filled with a sense of angry, boiling loss. Here was her answer, and she knew what she must do, and wanted to do. It was wrong, she knew it was wrong but the wrong was right – so right… And anyway, what the hell.

She crept her right hand under the blanket, under the purity of the white sheets, tugging up the hem of his hospital clothing until she could slide her fingers over the clamminess of his skinny, chicken-skinned thigh. She held her breath as she dug down into the moist, hairy cluster of his groin and got to work. Her touch doing the trick, converting through slow manipulation the shrunken vegetable that barely fitted her fist into something thick and bloated and hot and roaring. Behind her closed eyes she knew that this was what he would request if he could, if he had the words, and what harm could it do? Nobody cared. It was the parting gift she could give him. The *only* gift she could give him—

Forgiveness.

She looked into her father's face as his chin jutted towards the ceiling, the blank tiles of his Sistine chapel, as he came, as he bleated and grunted and coughed behind the oxygen mask, tendons like wire in his neck, his blood below pulsing against her fingers, his liquid dampening the cloth, gluing it to the circle of her thumb and forefinger.

She extracted her hand and let him wither as she wiped herself dry against a corner of the top sheet.

There. It was done. He could go, and so could she. But kneeling there, facing him, as the wind battered the window like fists, she found she could not stand. Her knees did not have it in them.

Ivo jerked his head from side to side, bleating again more loudly from inside the shell of the mask. There was an odd movement to his legs, too. She noticed two strange craters where his knees should be showing as two lumps, as if they'd been removed, and his heels poked up as if his feet were on backwards.

She felt the crack in her cheek swell with blood under the surface. A history of hurt gnawed her spine. Her insides twisted, the gnarled roots of an ancient tree.

She peeled back the sheets.

The animal stench of mud and filth and sweat immediately hit her nostrils. A black, leathery scrotum the size of a dinner plate hung under a long, pink phallus emergent like a questing worm from a furry sheath. Her father lay with his hospital smock rolled up to his chest, his body normal until it wasn't. Bony hocks and the hillocks of two thighs covered in thick, matted curls granted her full view of the genitals of a he-goat. Her dad's skinny ankles were adorned not with human feet but with cloven hooves shining like the delicate black buckled shoes of a French king at Versailles.

He moaned again, as horns grew out of his head, curving back into the pillow.

His age-spotted paw removed the mask from his mouth and let it awkwardly cup one side of his bearded jaw, the elastic pulled taut across both cheeks, converging his wrinkles into two puckered gashes either side. His eyes opened and fell on her. Seventy-five but still blue as silk.

The old goat has wakened, my love. My sweetheart. How's about it then, Riwbob? For old times' sake?

The nice doctor, Dr. Hyett, had entered with two nurses. He stood by the door, making notes on the clipboard. "Bless him, he'll be right as rain in no time." He came over to stand behind Roni, close. Close enough to cup her breast in his hand and lick the back of her neck. Roni watched as the nurses took off their clothes and climbed naked onto the bed.

* * *

The owl gave way to the cock. Sunlight so bright it almost hurts her eyes.

She's back in Painswick for the first time since her childhood. She can't believe they'll be living there again, the place of her dreams. It seems almost like a fantasy. But what it is, really, is a gift, from her father. And it seems real, now the 'Sold' sign is down and they've collected the key from the estate agent.

It's not anything like the house she grew up in, mind. On a consultant's salary they can afford something much more salubrious than that. One of the Georgian properties, grand but not too grand. Interior still retaining all the iconic swirls of a Palladian pattern book. Rococo plasterwork inhabited by puppy-dogs rampant and owls with eyeballs black. She also knew in advance the name she was going to give the place.

AIG AITIS: Goat lover.

The old howl of the licentious as they ran naked to the woods, shedding their clothes and Christian virtue. Taking the path to age-old rituals that would guarantee the protection of the Lord of Shepherds. As fiercely writhing as any who died at Pompeii. The revels of Lupercalia resurrected in red coats and periwigs… then in the garb of wool traders and yokels… and now, junior executives, well-off retirees and down-from-Londoners.

She's married Dr. Benjamin Hyett whose hand she holds and kisses. Mrs. Hyett now, though minded to keep her birth name – Slad. The name on the front pages. The name on *News at Ten.*

"It's time," she says.

"It's time," he agrees.

They enter the churchyard of clipped yews. Used to be ninety-nine. Folk used to say if anyone planted the hundredth, the Devil would destroy it, but they planted one at the millennium and he didn't. She thought the Devil had a soft spot for Painswick.

There are sheep dotted all around. Sheep standing on their hind legs, naked. All that is needed is their shepherd.

Roni lets go of her husband's hand and walks to a spot on the south side of the church tower. She sinks her fingers into the earth. Deep. Deeper. Before long she feels the king, the hardness under her hand, the hardness of stone. The waiting, smiling, crooked lips.

It will be her pleasure to make him rise.

HOME EXTERMINATORS

Montanna Rayne Harling

Tonight, the house we had come to dissect was high in the hills above Los Angeles. Our converted work van's headlights picked out the yellow reflectors at the edge of the road – startled flushes of colour in the dark.

"Look outside," Mother said, and I saw the city far below us. Spread across the desert basin, stripes of lights; like the soft multicoloured pelt of the calico cat we'd once had. I liked Los Angeles, but only at night. I missed the cat. She'd gone to sleep on an outdoor patio chair that had been latticed with growths, and had not woken up.

Mother stopped the van on a suburban street. "That's it?" I asked, pointing to a house across from us. It did not look infected, unlike Mother's other jobsites – derelict homes soft with growths, all damp and holey. This home was freshly painted, well-maintained. Sharp.

"It's been renovated," Mother said quietly. "See those A-frame windows? They're new. Double-paned. Good at insulating." She always fed me morsels of information about the houses, even as we dismantled their infected insides. "It seems the home just has a mild infection."

"So we're saving this house, right?" I asked.

We worked at night, because the growths needed sunlight to reproduce. This was only my second time accompanying Mother on one of her jobs. I needed to get everything right, so that there would be a third time. It had taken a year to convince her that I could be helpful – when I was fourteen, I'd once followed Mother onto a jobsite, and then I did it again, and then at last, a few months ago for my fifteenth birthday, she bought me my own respirator and taught me how to destroy.

"Yes, we're saving the house," Mother said now. "Remember, we're not damaging the building beyond repair. We're just preparing it for the extermination treatment." The growth inhibitor chemical was weak, she'd explained before. For it to work, the houses had to be stripped, cracked open. "Turned inside-out, like a nice dress before you put it in the wash," Mother always reminded me.

I pulled my green-handled pliers out of the van's toolbox. Adjusted the respirator over my face, tightened the straps behind my head. Tucked my jacket sleeves over my gloves. The growths were neurotoxic, so we had to protect ourselves.

Mother watched me from behind the panel of her own respirator. "You didn't put your respirator on correctly," she said.

"Oh," I said, ashamed. "Sorry." I stood still while she tightened the left strap. It cut into my scalp, squeezing the roots of my hair.

"Six hours until dawn," Mother said. "Stay next to me while we work."

I followed her up the tidy driveway. Hibiscus bushes bracketed us on either side, clipped into unrelenting cube shapes, their tongue-pink flowers folded up for the night.

This street was so still, so abandoned, so beautiful. "Something feels weird," I whispered.

"You're just nervous," Mother said.

"I'm not," I insisted. The growths had evolved when I was five years old – ten years later, my fear had long since dulled. But what felt strange was that we were walking up to a *home* again, one that looked inhabitable. As easily as if we owned it. Slipping back into a routine that felt distant, like the scraps of memory after dreaming.

We did not have a home anymore – Mother sold ours when the growths came. She told me that we were safer living in the converted van. We could not lose a house to the growths if we kept moving, if our home had wheels, if we could sleep in a different Wal-Mart parking lot each night.

"A shame," Mother said, looking at the house's heavy oakwood door,"for a home like this to be infected." But she still swung her axe into the door, cracking it open. It was how she tested the severity of a home's growth infection. The growths flourished in unpainted wood, sometimes metabolising the varnish on doors, feeding themselves with it. Tonight, I watched as fine strands of growths spilled from the split wood, like grey cotton candy wisps.

Mother cast the broken door aside. She stepped into the home, without even a glance back at me, and I followed.

★ ★ ★

The house, inside, was cluttered. There was an excess of furniture. One too many burgundy couches, I thought, but maybe the house just looked weird in the small contained beam of my respirator's headlamp. The homeowners were supposed to leave all of their possessions behind for full extermination of growths.

"This is worse than the health inspector initially noted," Mother said, her words blurred by the respirator.

She moved her head, and her light swung with her. The growths had expanded to fill the fireplace; they lined the grooves between the planks of the hardwood flooring; they coated the indented tufts of the couches like deadly lint trapped in belly buttons. Inside my plastic cleaning suit, I felt my skin bristle with disgust.

"This is so—" I started, then saw Mother turn towards me. I realised, then, that if I said anything to indicate my discomfort, she might never bring me to another job again. "Nothing," I amended.

"Remember, everything infected gets broken open. If something isn't infected, leave it intact, but do open all cabinets and doors, so it will all get coated with the chemicals," Mother said.

I knew she was worried. Not worried that I would get sick from the growths – I liked to think she now trusted me to be careful – but worried that my unfamiliarity with her job would slow her down.

In a few years, Mother had gone from being a house cleaner to the city's top growth extermination specialist. She wanted to buy another van, I knew. Hire a team of employees. "We can turn this into a real, sustainable *business*," Mother always said, with an edge of hunger in her voice.

She watched me now crouch down beside a coffee table. There was a blot of growth on the corner, obscuring what was once a beautiful floral decal in the wood. I reached for the smallest axe in Mother's toolbag. Still, Mother watched.

I brought the blade down on the growth, tried to swing it upwards again for another attempt, but the blade held. The axe had gotten stuck in the wood.

"You'll have to hit it with more force," Mother said. "You want to split the wood open, to let the chemicals seep in when we treat it. Do it again."

"It's stuck," I said.

She lifted the axe from the wood, as if it were a hairbrush. "I'll just do this room, then," she said. "Can you check the kitchen for growths?"

"Sure," I said, relieved she had not sent me outside to wait in the van. She trusted me to inspect the kitchen, on my own. Surely, I thought, surely she could see it: how very useful I would be to her business.

★ ★ ★

But Mother had reason not to trust me.

The first job she'd brought me to – an infected condo in Los Angeles, almost totally unsalvageable – I had not been careful enough.

I'd been helping Mother clear out an entryway closet. My headlamp was dim, flickering – its battery was dying – and I had not seen the growths. I'd plunged my hand into a crate of yellow tennis balls, all grown over with warm grey mats.

When I felt their spongy softness against my exposed skin, in the gap between my glove and sleeve, I'd screamed.

Touching the growths hadn't hurt, but the fear was my undoing. I half-crawled away from the closet, stumbling into a run. Mother called me back sharply.

"You must be more careful," Mother said. Behind her respirator mask, her face had been blank. But she'd changed my gloves gently, and applied a bit of growth inhibitor to my wrist. The chemicals would give me a rash, but it would prevent the growths from replicating on my skin.

That night, I'd been sick. The growths had not infected me, but the contact I'd had with them had been enough for exposure symptoms.

When I tried to sleep, my headache distorted our van's interior ceiling. And when I did sleep, in patches, I had strange dreams – ones in which multicoloured lights fireworked against the deep indigo of my nightmares.

Mother told me I threw up, several times – "All over the floor of the van" – but I didn't remember it, and I didn't see any vomit remnants in the morning. But Mother was an adept cleaner, after all.

What I did remember was, the next day, finding a discoloured patch of skin on my inner wrist, in the place where a bracelet would rest, if I owned any.

My skin was a deep plum-red, swollen with a bead of fluid like an engorged water balloon, the membrane just on the verge of breaking.

For a week, the blister pulsed with its own painful heartbeat. I asked Mother if the growths had caused this. "It's just the growth inhibitor chemical," she said. "It causes skin irritation. It'll go away eventually."

The blister stayed so long, I began to doubt her. And then, the blister deflated. Drained in my sleep one night, maybe, or in the shower. Worse was the possibility that I had picked the blister in my distraction – sometimes, when listening to Mother's instructions for each job, I picked mindlessly at any errant scrap of fingernail or protruding bit of flesh on my hands.

In the blister's wake, it left a smooth hollow on my wrist.

"Can growths scar you?" I asked Mother, the night I saw the fleshy divot.

"No. Growths are neurotoxic. They shut down your body from the inside-out. Not the other way around," she replied.

"But look," I said, showing her my wrist. "*Look*. What's that?"

"I don't see anything."

"You're not looking at it – the pockmark. A hole, almost."

"That's normal. Just part of your wrist. You're only seeing the gap between the tendon and your skin."

I disagreed, but I could tell that there was no convincing Mother. And either way, the blister had healed and my skin was no longer painful, and really, I should be grateful I had not been sickened by the growths, as careless as I had been at that condo.

Regardless, in the next six months, I grew so used to the tiny divot left behind on my body, that I rarely noticed it again.

★ ★ ★

Tonight, I was more careful. I'd learned from that mistake in the condo, and now wore two pairs of gloves, with the sleeves of my cleaning suit tucked underneath, to create a seal around my skin. I had not had an accident since that run-in with the tennis balls.

Which was why, I thought, Mother now trusted me with the inspection of this house's entire kitchen.

But to my mingled sense of disappointment and relief, the kitchen proved clean. Unaffected by growths. The only indication in this room that something was amiss was the refrigerator. The city's standard-issue public health flyer had been taped crookedly to its front. *Growths: fungal or bacterial? Neither. An indeterminate organism. Photosynthetic, but lacking the expected cell structures. Capable of replicating rapidly in high-UV conditions, and of existing on both organic and inorganic materials. Suspected to have evolved due to altered oceanic chemistry, but unconfirmed.*

I ripped the flyer off the fridge – tearing through the obligatory sentence: *If you find any growths in your home or on your property, please evacuate and contact the hotline for inspection* – and tossed the remnants to the floor. I glanced behind me.

Mother was no longer watching me. She was using her axe to chip away at an infected set of decorative shelves in the living room. Even through her respirator, I could see her smile – faint, unflinching, wholly transfixed.

I opened the fridge. The inner lightbulb had been taken out. Under the beam of my headlamp, the refrigerator's insides glowed bright white. Only a bowl of raspberries remained on the refrigerator's top shelf – the rest of the shelves and drawers had been scrubbed clean.

The raspberries were the colour of inflamed gums. I took one out, nudged its seeds apart with a gloved hand.

It wasn't infected. It wasn't even starting to go fuzzy with the old, basic mould. For a moment, I thought of pushing my respirator off and eating every single berry.

But I placed the raspberry back inside the fridge and shut the door firmly. Whoever had left must've gone in a rush. Nobody had thought to turn the refrigerator off. It was still cold and humming.

* * *

Mother peeled back the carpet in the living room like the dead skin that bubbles up along one's arms after a sunburn. Beneath the carpet, the growths bulged in grey masses. I felt their warmth even from the kitchen.

I was done inspecting the kitchen. I waited for the perfect moment to ask Mother for my next task, but she was consumed with her work. She hacked away at the padding beneath the carpet until the house's cement foundation emerged like a surfacing wisdom tooth. She smashed holes in the infected blotches on the drywall, pulling out spools of fibreglass insulation. She broke a growth-covered glass display box in a glittering cascade, and behind her respirator, she was smiling.

Mother had the downstairs taken care of, clearly. I glanced at the staircase behind the living room. There was an entire second floor that hadn't been inspected yet.

I shouldn't interrupt her, I decided. I should take the initiative to clear the upstairs by myself. Mother had told me to stay with her, but once she realised that I could help her expand this business, truly *help*, she would concede she'd been wrong. She would say, *You're right, you can handle this by yourself.*

I backed away to the staircase. Mother did not notice. I climbed to the top of the stairs, gingerly. Still, Mother did not look up from her work.

Satisfied that she would not realise I had gone until I had a chance to inspect the upper floor, I turned and hurried down the second-floor hallway. The sound of Mother's chopping faded to a distant whisper.

★ ★ ★

Upstairs, the hallway was a strange comfort.

This could have been any hallway I had ever been in. Soft beige carpet, a tunnel of wood cabinets along the walls. Photographs below the cabinets. The pictures showed an older couple and an abundance of grandchildren. In one photo, the grandfather's face was obscured by a grey blot of growth. It was almost funny.

I used the metal nose of my pliers to crack the glass pane covering the photograph. Would the inhibitor chemical ruin the picture beneath it? Probably. I imagined the couple in the image dissolving under the fine mist of chemicals. But as long as the home's inhabitants could return to their house after the growths had been killed, as long as they could rebuild, the destruction would be worth it.

I moved on to the cabinets. I loved the discovery of each compartment. The homeowners' abandoned possessions were my joys. I wondered what it would be like to live in this house, and the belongings in the cabinets were essential to this fantasising.

When I found a stack of striped blue and white beach towels, I imagined Mother and I learning to surf. When I discovered a clothes iron, the cord all neatly coiled, I thought of how smooth my favourite pink shirt would be, and how if I lived here, I'd hang that shirt in a closet instead of fold it into the box underneath my van-bed.

But the clothes iron's handle was flecked with the beginnings of the growths. I broke it open, left it lying on the floor of the hallway like a forgotten toy. The other cabinets were clean. I moved on, into a bedroom at the end of the hallway.

The bedroom, too, proved clean. On the opposite side of the bed, there was another door. I hurried through it.

I entered a vast bathroom – the main bedroom's suite, I guessed, from the double sinks and the deep tub. But the bathroom was wrong. The bathtub was filled not with soapy water but growths, all hazy green-grey. The mirror was entirely obscured – the growths coated the glass, bursting outward like three-dimensional, uncanny reflections. Worse – the floors were coated, too. I felt my right shoe sink into a deep soft mat of growths.

There were too many growths. I couldn't clean this. I couldn't even see the cabinets, the countertops, the toilet, even though I saw their shapes, familiar contours beneath the growths.

I backed out of the bathroom, scraping my foot on the ground to dislodge the growth remnants that clung to the bottom of my boot. Fear and disgust made a sour slurry in my stomach.

My certainty that I would be able to handle the upstairs rooms by myself had faded. I would have to find Mother, to tell her of the massively infected bathroom. Maybe she would think I'd been brave, coming up here alone. I turned in the direction of the hallway again, headed for the staircase.

But the hallway deposited me into a new bedroom. A familiar one – had I been in here already? My headlamp's range wasn't enough to illuminate the entire room, so it was hard to tell. There were growths on the wall and I suddenly longed to be outside, in the van, to be driving away from all this in the passenger seat beside Mother. I ran for the hallway again.

There – at the end of the hall, half in shadows, an archway. The archway above the staircase, I was sure of it. But when I reached the end of the hallway and my headlamp filled the space, I realised the arch led to a decorative alcove, a fake plant placed at its centre.

A sense of strangeness, worse than the fear of the growths, brushed up against me. I had been so sure there would be another entry point to the staircase there. The wall was unexpected, the wall was out of place, the wall was *wrong.*

The house was so quiet, so still. I could not hear Mother anymore. There was just me, and the growths, and the hallways.

It was all too much. I had been wrong, I couldn't help Mother with the growths, with her business. I couldn't even inspect a few rooms without getting lost.

For a moment, I wished I could sink down against the wall. Sit down in a soft pile of growths, which would enfold me in their warmth.

But I couldn't stay up here. I had to find the living room.

I backtracked again, down the hallway. Through a series of bedrooms. Past the infected bathroom. And then, with an immense and luminant feeling of relief, I saw the staircase, the real staircase, the one I had ascended, the one that would lead me back to Mother. I took the stairs two at a time, racing down it.

A quarter of the way down the staircase, I stopped. A woman stood at the bottom. She was not my mother.

"Of course," the woman said, as if continuing a conversation with me that I hadn't remembered starting, "Hello, of course, come in."

"Sorry," I said. My voice came out soft, smothered by my respirator. "I'm – just trying to find my way back to the living room. I'm here to clean."

She climbed two stairs towards me, then hesitated, gripping the railing. In my headlamp, she looked old. Her face was malleable, like a sourdough bread loaf, just beginning to rise.

There were six holes down the length of her face – three on each side, running in parallel. Her mouth must have been moving, because I could hear her words coming out.

But I could not tell which hole was eye and which was mouth and which was wound.

In my terror, I missed what she said. She climbed the last few steps between us, and she stopped right before me. "How kind of you, child, to come home thinking you can save the place," she said.

Then she put her fingers on either side of my face, five fingers making five divots in the skin below my eyes.

And she was saying something now about my skin, about softness, about *clean*—

Her hands were wrenched off my face as abruptly as they had been placed there. The woman slid down the stairs, and suddenly Mother was there, having knocked her fiercely aside, and I saw the slim gap open between them and I rushed down the staircase, darting between the woman and my mother.

There, the kitchen; beyond it, the living room; the familiarity of these spaces soothed me. I slowed in the entryway of the house, just beyond the living room, which was now a wrecked testimony to Mother's work. I continued outside, into the yard, with its unrelentingly landscaped foliage.

I waited. But Mother did not appear in the entryway behind me.

★ ★ ★

Outside, the yard seemed to twitch with unseen life. Crickets, I thought, out in the grass somewhere, singing. The leaves, stirring under some unknown paws – mice? Rats? I didn't know enough about yards. Growths didn't survive well in soil, in living trees, in plants, and I knew growths' habitats better than those of the wild creatures.

I stared at the front door of the house, willing Mother to emerge. The van was a reassuring presence behind me. Mother had told me that if anything ever went wrong on a job, I was to wait for her in the van. But she couldn't have predicted this – the woman with holes for a face.

The crickets sang on. The house was silent.

I went to the van. Opened the back doors, reached for Mother's spare toolbag, which she kept underneath one of the fold-out beds. I unzipped it. There were mostly small tools inside – clippers, pliers, a few screwdrivers, for prying apart the most difficult growth-infested objects. But at the bottom, I found a sizeable knife. Perhaps once meant for landscaping and the cutting of bushes, the knife would do. I took it with me, back into the house.

The entryway was dark and desolate. But when I turned the corner into the living room, there they were – Mother, standing on the couch with stuffing up to her knees, her respirator's light broken and flickering weakly, and the infected woman, standing on the ground before the couch.

"The house is fine," the woman said. As if she and Mother were having an ordinary conversation, as if Mother wasn't perched above her on a torn-up piece of furniture, half afraid and half ready to destroy something. "It doesn't need cleaning."

Mother must have seen me by my respirator's light, but she did not look away from the woman. "You don't understand," she said. "The house needs to be saved. So do you."

"I'm well," the woman said, from one of the fleshy gaps in her face. "Please, stop destroying my home."

"It's not yours anymore," Mother said, and her voice was threadbare, worn out. "It's been overtaken. Let us save it, let us give it back to you."

I saw Mother there, surrounded by a halo of her own dying respirator's light, while somewhere outside, somewhere over the desert, the sun was on its ascent; and upstairs, the growths were gathering the energy needed to multiply as soon as the light reached them. And this place, this home, would feed the growths until it sank softly into the earth, decayed into nothing.

I saw Mother, and I saw the living room, and I saw the burgundy couches, and I remembered.

"This was our house?" I said, the words coming out too quietly at first for Mother to hear, but I repeated myself. "This was *our* house? We used to live here. Is that why I feel so weird, like I remember this place but it's different too?"

"Yes," Mother admitted. "It was ours, when you were four and a half years old. Before the growths came, even. A very long time ago."

The woman with holes in her face turned to me. She saw the knife in my hand, but made no attempt to flee. Neither of us believed I'd use it. From within the decayed flesh of her face, her two eyes were wet with something like tears.

"I'm sorry we bothered you," I said. "We'll leave." I approached the couch slowly. The woman stood still as I passed her. I grabbed Mother's arm. For once, she let me lead.

Mother stopped only when we reached the entryway. She looked back inside. "We can't," she said.

"Let it go, Mom," I said. "It's not our house. It belongs to them now." The woman. The holes. The growths.

The woman, standing in the wreckage of her living room, that once had been our living room, stretched her decayed face into a smile.

Mother and I walked out into the yard, where the crickets had quieted in anticipation of dawn, and shed our cleaning gear on the asphalt beside the van.

"I'm sorry," Mother said, as we peeled off our gloves and climbed into the van. "Thank you for helping me," she added, gently. "And for bringing me outside."

I nodded. When she started the van, I did not look back at the house. I watched the sunrise, just beginning out in the hills; filling the van with so much light that our home felt, if only briefly, incandescent.

LEG STRETCH

Josh Malerman

'Thrifty' Roger Lodge needed to stretch his legs. The Jaguar had enough gas for another forty miles, but he was nearing the red line himself. He was hungry. A diner would be nice.

He did this to himself every time he crossed Michigan on route 58, driving until near exhaustion, or at least until he had to bend and wiggle to stretch out his back and hips. He knew it had something to do with why he'd gotten the nickname in college. And why it had lasted too. An appellation such as Roger Lodge (a name that danced to itself) was destined to be nicknamed, but he'd never loved the resultant 'Thrifty'. At the same time, wasn't it the sign for Malcolm's Diner, and the lunch special for $1.99, that had convinced him to take a quick break?

He couldn't help himself. It was his nature to be drawn to the deals, to save coupons, to take the extra second and find out what the stores were offering before deciding what was on his shopping list. These things added up, indeed they did. Just ask Maureen and the girls. They could poke fun at him all they wanted, but 'Thrifty' Roger Lodge liked nothing more than to prove it at year's end, to show the receipts, every New Year's Eve.

You see how much we saved? Three thousand dollars is nothing to sneeze at.

It certainly was not. Even if he and Maureen spent the same three thousand on superfluous things. It was the thriftiness that gave them that right.

But New Year's was a long way off, this bright summer afternoon.

So, Malcolm's Diner. And a lunch special under two dollars. He'd taken route 58 a dozen times before and had never seen the little metal sign. Might that be a sign in and of itself? He'd barely read the price (had to look twice) for the sun reflecting off the old square. But the thrill was real, and familiar, once he read the numbers correctly.

LUNCH $1.99

Taking the next right onto country road 80, he hadn't expected to find a new shiny diner. The sign looked older than the car he drove, older than himself. But two dollars was two dollars. And a penny less was even better. The very suit he wore had come from the sales rack, a thing he prided himself on, especially when his coworkers at James & Jones commented on its perfect cut. It *was* perfect. He didn't have to be a fashionista to feel that much. Even Maureen nodded along to the contours, the morning he first donned it. Now, behind the wheel of his (used, but low mileage) Jaguar, in his deal of a suit, Roger felt thrifty indeed. And all his giggling friends could kiss off for all he cared.

$1.99 for lunch was a steal, no matter the size of the meal.

But he didn't see another sign, nor a diner, on this second road. Come to think of it (and he thought of waste quickly, including the waste of time), there wasn't anything out this way to suggest a diner could exist at all. No passing cars, no neighbouring establishments, no people. As he'd long suspected, the expanse of land north and south of route 58 wasn't even farmland. It was something closer to wasteland, if not for the life found in the trees and grassy (unmowed) fields of this summer afternoon. He considered turning around. Even three miles out of the way felt a bit like wasting something, and how much further would he have to go to even believe Malcolm's Diner still existed? But, thrifty as ever, Roger calculated the risk against the potential loss of gasoline, the numbers running through him like alcohol might for a different man, the pros and cons of chasing the deal. If there was one thing he was good at, it was adapting, on the spot, not unlike the quarterbacks he watched absently on Sunday afternoons in the fall, and how the commentators spoke of the necessity for "short memories" when playing a position in which change can happen quickly. Roger considered: once he'd made the choice to follow the sign to the diner, he'd committed to a new course of action, thereby rendering retreat a total loss. There was no need to accept that. Certainly not yet.

To his left, a stretch of thick trees, what he first mistook for a forest, but soon understood it as more of a wall. The full green lasted a mile of its own, delivering to Roger the hope that, at its cessation, Malcolm's Diner would be visible. What could a man get to eat for under two dollars? And did it matter? A slice of toast and a small bowl of macaroni would make for a good story, one he'd tell Maureen and the girls, citing this moment as just another example of an exemplary life. A life lived wisely and without waste.

Ahead, at last, the shape of a squat building, though he could plainly see the place was closed. Not a car in the lot. A large sign that once held letters, presumably *Malcolm's Diner*, but no longer. So, a loss after all. Still, he was satisfied he'd tried to follow the deal, even if there was no deal to be had. There really wasn't much difference between this mishap and the times he'd met with sellers from websites, online marketplaces, only to discover the items were much finer in the photos than they were in real life. A man who hunted deals sometimes (often) shot blanks, returning home empty-handed, but always with the satisfaction of having the backbone to hunt.

It was a test, life. Was it not?

He pulled into what was once the dirt lot of the now defunct diner and paused before making the full turn-around, the Jaguar idling, alone in the empty Michigan summer sunshine. He eyed the small building and imagined what it was once like. He pictured regulars, people who lived out here in the middle of nowhere year-round. Men and women who took the biscuits and gravy daily, finding their own satisfaction and solace in familiar chairs, scents, and smiles.

"It was a helluva deal," he said. And he gave the place one last sad acknowledgement before completing the turn-around and heading back up country road 80, back toward the route he knew.

The numbers bothered him as he went, part of him still wanting to believe the diner existed, that he hadn't gotten to it yet, that his decision to turn around had been a frugal one. He enjoyed nothing more than regaling Maureen and the girls with his private heroics out on the road. What would he tell them now? That he'd wasted gas and time on a closed diner, a conclusion anybody could've drawn given the state of the sign? Hell, the price of the lunch should've been the real tip-off. Nobody, and Roger meant *nobody*, had a lunch for under two dollars these days. Not even the fast-food joints. Why, you couldn't find something for less than seven, six at best, even in the middle of—

"Whoa!"

His right shoe (nice, shiny brown shoe, for less than forty dollars, thank you) was upon the brake pedal before he realised he'd been the one to exclaim at the sight of something beyond the big wall of trees, now on his right, heading back as he was.

Still well in the middle of nowhere. A discovery.

He backed the Jaguar up just enough to come level with the break in the woods, able to see for himself the shining silver through the slight break in the trees.

"That's a diner," he said.

And then he exclaimed again, a quick *hell, yes* coupled with a slam of his open palm to the roof of the car. He touched up there, gently, to make sure he hadn't torn anything, but absently, as his eyes were fixed to the shining silver through the woods. There were cars in the lot of the diner.

Success.

Excited to make good on the deal after all, happy to have a story for his wife and daughters, Roger looked ahead for the road leading up to the diner. But there was no sign of a break in the trees ahead. And none behind. And had he passed a road, even a small dirt road, a road that might lead to a diner parking lot in the middle of the country?

He drove ahead, slowly, until he reached the end of the line of trees and there saw something he hadn't noticed on the first pass: a second row, extending from the road as far as any eye could see. Even those looking for a bargain.

Two walls of trees then. Alright. He turned the Jaguar around. You had to have a short memory when looking for a deal. And now that the first part of his plan had been screwed with, now that he'd found himself *here*, the most prudent thing to do would be to get to this diner. Turn this loss into a gain.

Still, no way in from here.

He turned the car around and drove slow, sure to catch a glimpse of the diner through the trees again. He believed he saw the sun reflected off the door opening or closing. Malcolm's Diner, no doubt. There behind the trees. Hidden, yes, or perhaps protected. Private. But by the time he reached the long end of the wall of woods in the other direction, he found yet a third wall…

"The hell?"

Perhaps the only way to the diner was to get back to route 58, make a right, take it to the next road, then another right, to approach the diner from the other side.

But that sounded like a lot of maybes to 'Thrifty' Roger Lodge. And so, he did something he might ordinarily not: he pulled the Jaguar to the side of the otherwise empty road, drove it safely in the grass and rubble beyond the shoulder, and parked.

He got out, even with the thin space in the wall of trees.

It truly was a glorious, sunshiny afternoon.

Roger made sure the door was locked, patted his wallet in his pants pocket, and set out on foot across the unmowed grass toward the diner.

Unmowed, indeed, and the grass grew tall as his shins by the time he reached the trees. And the diner... how close from here? Hard to factor in gas prices and miles when on foot, but the element of time (and time wasted) was still on his mind.

Still, a story for Maureen and the girls. The lengths he would go to get that deal. And thoughts of how a person will do most anything to fortify that identity that gets them that positive attention. Nicknames were terms of endearment, after all. Even one as bland as 'Thrifty'.

The details of the story he was currently experiencing on his mind (to later tell, no doubt), he split the trees, stepped into the brief darkness and cold shade between the enormous trunks, and saw that this place was not called Malcolm's Diner.

A sign upon the silver edifice said:

BILLY'S

Roger paused. Did this place have the deal or not? And had he parked on the side of the road just to spend the regular ten bucks he'd been trying to avoid? He felt a little dent then, a dent in the story. But he had a short memory. And whatever decisions he'd made had led him to *this* moment, facing a diner called Billy's, tucked away in the trees in the middle of Michigan, out of sight, unless you were really looking for it.

He stepped clear of the shade and well into the sun, crossing a manicured lawn, toward the gravel lot where, to his surprise, at least ten cars were parked, neatly lined up outside the pristine silver of the diner.

He saw the silhouette of heads behind the clean windows of the place. Regular faces rendered featureless by the bright sun upon the glass. He saw, too, beyond the diner, the beginnings of what looked like a small town.

Where was he?

Just behind him, a sudden rustle in the trees. A sound so unexpected, it highlighted for Roger how serene the diner and its lot had been in contrast.

He spun quick, expecting a deer, a rabbit, an animal. But like recognises like, and part of him knew he'd see a man before he did.

"*Pretend you're a local,*" the man said.

"What?"

"*Pretend you've lived here your whole life.*"

The man had whispered, and so when Roger responded at a regular volume the man ducked and shook his head no. Roger saw the man was looking toward the diner. And beyond, to the small town there.

"What did you say?" Roger asked.

The man was obscured by branches, deep enough in the trees so that only pieces of his suit showed. But Roger could see the man was sweating. Wide-eyed. Scared.

Then the man was gone, deeper into the woods, and Roger watched him go, heard him cracking sticks as he grew smaller, until it was like the man had never been there at all.

Pretend you've lived here your whole life.

Roger wiped at the front of his suit coat as if the brief interaction had been made of dust. He'd wanted to ask the man about any lunch deals. But… c'est la vie. Some people were a little off their rocker. Perhaps a few cents shy of a bill.

He heard a final distant cracking of sticks, then stepped further out onto the grass, under the high afternoon sun.

An elderly couple exited the diner and moved slow to a parked car. Roger could better see through the diner glass the closer he got. It appeared to be a clean place. Maybe too nice for a two-dollar deal. It looked great, to be honest. Far better than whatever Malcolm's would've offered, had the old place been open. He eyed the name in yellow above the shining silver exterior, then felt the gravel beneath his dress shoes. In the lot now. He nodded to the old couple and they both gave him a little wave. A wave of familiarity. As if they knew him. Yes, it was the only way he knew how to describe the gesture.

Pretend you're a local…

Darnit if the couple hadn't treated him like one.

There was no menu taped to the door and so Roger entered Billy's diner, enjoying the small tinkle of the bell above, hoping for the discovery of a steal.

But he found something different indeed.

Now, the last thing 'Thrifty' Roger Lodge was was a betting man. But if he were, if the quirks that made him so unyieldingly prudent had not been bestowed upon him, he would've bet the family home on the fact the diner went silent a beat, no, half a beat, upon his entrance. As if every patron and worker had glanced his way without really lifting their eyes to do so.

But that half beat played so quick, it wasn't worth examining any further. Wasn't worth the time with which to wonder.

"No counter seat today," a young man said, a smile as wide apart as his ears. He wore a powder blue shirt with a yellow logo: BILLY'S. And Roger felt like he'd walked onto a movie set. The design of it all. The perfect *diner* tone.

Had the young man said it like Roger usually sat at the counter? As if Roger had been here before?

"Oh, no problem," Roger said. "I prefer booths."

The young man laughed. *Oh you*, he seemed to say.

"Well, you're a good sport. Follow me."

He saw then the host had a menu in hand and Roger wanted badly to know what it said. How would this story pan out, what heroics would he have to regale Maureen and the girls?

He followed the young man to a booth, listening to the steady flow of conversation as he went. It wasn't till he was seated that he recognised the music as some variety of metal. Seemed the oddest choice for a place like this.

But then again, the world's most famous diners had their quirks.

And deals.

"Shelby will be right with you," the young man said. Then he winked. Like he knew Roger. And like Roger knew him. Roger looked over his shoulder, back to some of the diners he'd passed on the brief walk. He thought maybe a head or two looked away quick, as if they'd been watching. He looked down to the blue and white tiles beneath his dress shoes. For as shiny and clean as the place was on the outside, there was some diner grime below. It meant something to him. So, he looked to the rectangular open window where cooks worked on orders, pulling white slips from a rotating silver clipper.

"Heya," a woman said.

Roger looked up to see another smiling face. Knowledge in her eyes, too. Like…

Like she knew him.

"Hey," Roger said, "why do I get the feeling—"

The woman leaned forward before he could finish, as though to arrange the condiments on the table.

"*Act like a regular*," she said. "*Act like you live here.*"

Roger, dumbstruck, didn't even think to check the prices on the menu on the table before him. What had the woman just said?

"The usual?" she asked, standing again, order-ticket in hand.

Many thoughts jostled for room in Roger's mind. How to respond. Whether he should leave. But in that moment, he felt like the entire diner wanted him to say… *yes*. Of all the crazy thoughts and feelings to have, he believed everybody in the place wanted him to play along.

The waitress, Shelby, nodded. As if to say, *Yes, you want the usual.*

But 'Thrifty' hadn't gotten his nickname for no good reason.

"I'd like to know what deals you have going today," Roger said.

Because dammit if anybody was going to take *that* away from him.

A look of concern crossed Shelby's face.

"*The usual*," she muttered. "*He can sense when something's not how it's always been.*"

"What's that?" Roger asked. "Listen, if you—"

He heard grunts from somewhere deeper in the diner. The unmistakeable sound of frustrations aired. And, self-conscious or not, he believed they were aired at him.

"The best deal we have is the usual, silly," Shelby said.

She nodded again. *Say yes*, she said without saying. *Play along.*

Roger took a moment then, almost as if he were operating in slow motion. He looked out the diner window, then back up and down the row of booths, to the people with their backs to him at the counter, to the cooks through the open view to the kitchen.

Back there, the eyes of a cook looked back at him.

"Sure," he said. "The usual." Then, "Thank you, Shelby."

Shelby nearly squealed delight.

"You know it," she said. Then she reached right into his suit coat pocket and pulled forth his wallet.

"Hey!" Roger said.

But Shelby had already glanced, gleaning whatever information she needed.

"One usual coming right up, Roger, ol' pal."

She'd said his name a little louder, he thought. Loud enough to let everyone in the place know his name.

Pretend like you're a local…

"The usual," Roger repeated, absently, as Shelby stepped from his booth.

But this was wild. So, he almost laughed. He spun to get a real look at everyone in the diner. He'd seen videos of elaborate pranks pulled on unsuspecting people; he saw one where a woman pretended to have frightening powers in a coffee shop. Obviously, Roger Lodge had somehow ended up on the inside of something just like that.

"The usual!" he said, loud, more than a little cynicism in his tone. But before he could get out a second word, a young woman slid fast into his booth opposite him.

She couldn't have been too much older than his daughters, but the late-teens and early twenties were exponential years, and the wear and tear in this woman's eyes was something he hoped to never see in the eyes of his girls.

"How *are* you, Roger?" she said. A smile on her face, but one Roger recognised for what it was.

"Hey, I'm—"

"*Play along*," she whispered.

But *whispered* was a strong word. It was more like she'd said it through the clenched teeth of her smile.

"I'm good," Roger said.

Prank or not… this felt dark.

"Amazing," she said. "Thank God for summer, am I right?"

Roger looked past her, to the other diners. This time they didn't look away from him quite as quickly.

What *was* this?

"Right?" she asked again.

Roger leaned forward. He'd get to the bottom of this with the same gusto he'd employ if he'd carried mispriced items to the counter at Peach Market.

But the woman beat him there.

"*You've accidentally stepped into a place run entirely by a madman.*"

"What?"

"*Don't ask questions. He can sense when someone doesn't belong.*"

"I don't—"

"*None of us did. How you're feeling isn't special. And it's right. Pretend you dine here all the time. And when you leave this diner, pretend you know every corner of the town. Someone will lead you to your apartment. Or home. I don't know which it will be yet.*" Then, three times as loud, as though trying to erase the words she'd whispered through her teeth: "I'm one of the few who prefer winter, honestly. I know you, Roger, you like to take in the sun. But the wind and snow give me an excuse to curl up under a blanket inside. Nothing better than that, am I right? Am I?"

Before Roger could answer, Shelby appeared with a plate of food. "The usual" turned out to be a fish sandwich and fries. A side of mayo in a small black dish.

Roger stared at it. He looked back up when Shelby spoke. Whispering as she reached across him to set down silverware and a napkin.

"*Don't look him in the eye. He'll know. Whatever you do... do not look him in the eye.*"

"Who is *he?*" Roger asked.

The entire diner seemed to skip a beat. The lights flickered, but so did the conversation. And, if Roger was right, everything he *saw* seemed to distort momentarily.

"He knows," a man said from the back of the diner. "Oh, God, he knows."

"Jesus Christ," someone else said. "He'll be coming then."

"Hey, wait," Roger said.

"*Listen to me,*" the young woman whispered more forcibly now. "*You must pretend you eat here all the time. Take your jacket off. Hang it on the hook next to the booth. Roll up your sleeves. Eat your lunch.*"

"He's coming," someone said. "Right now!"

Roger turned to look but he heard a sound before he saw anything: the distant thump of what might've been a giant's footstep from a frightening children's story.

"*Eat*," the young woman said.

Then she was out of the booth.

Roger heard a second thump. Something big coming. Something so big, the lights, the conversation, the diner, shook with it.

He looked for help, for sense, for someone to say anything else. But the others had gone back to eating, talking, wearing obviously false expressions plastered to their faces. Bad actors, all of them. And Roger certainly no better at it.

A third thump and he removed his suit coat. A fourth came as he hung it on the hook.

Eat your lunch...

He opened his mouth to say something, to ask another question, anything. But another stomp came, and with this thunderous step, a light shattered somewhere in the kitchen.

"Ah," he heard a cook say. "I must've dropped a dish! Butterfingers over here."

False laughter from the unseen grills and freezers.

Another thunderous step and Roger took the sandwich with two shaking hands, brought it to his mouth, and took a bite.

He braced himself for the next shake, the next giant's step. He closed his eyes, the food, the usual, between his clenched teeth.

But it wasn't a thud that came next.

It was the tinkle of the front door's bell.

Don't look him in the eye...

His back to the entrance, he glanced at the other patrons, saw nobody was looking at whoever had come in.

Roger prickled as he heard a sloshing sound. A sucking sound. The sound of something wet attaching itself, then pulling free from the tiles of this diner in the middle of nowhere.

He kept his head down. Eyes on his food.

The conversations continued, despite the addition now of...

Someone sniffing, Roger thought.

Yes. Chilled now, he believed he heard someone in the diner smelling for something. Like a dog. Or a wolf.

But the conversations continued and Shelby made a joke to a fellow waiter, and the host asked the next booth over if everything was okay. Roger gripped the sandwich in both hands, still completely unsure as to what was happening, and how he'd found himself in such a spot, and how he'd—

The sloshing was next to him now. The sniffing, too. He did not turn toward it. He did not look up. But he saw the tiled floor beside him. And there, the veins and discolourations of naked feet. The toenails were yellowed, half of them half-missing. The feet didn't only look big, they looked bloated. And the ankles were just as wide.

Roger nearly cried out. Nearly darted. Nearly looked.

Eat your lunch.

But the words of the young woman remained. And Roger brought the fish to his mouth a second time, even as he felt the lightest tickle at his right ear, and heard, much too closely, much too loud, the unmistakeable sound of someone sniffing, yes, an investigatory intake of breath through the nose.

Roger almost dropped the usual.

Instead… he took another bite.

"What do you think, Roger?" Shelby called from somewhere in the web of conversations.

Roger wanted to turn to her, to respond. But whatever had just smelled him, whatever stood naked and bloated beside his booth, had not stepped away yet.

"It's *fabulous*," Roger said, his mouth full of that second bite, his eyes on a third. "Great as ever."

Act like you're a local…

"Good to hear!" Shelby called back. And the relief in her voice was palpable.

The conversations continued. Roger chewed his food. He did not look to his right, not even when the presence there moved on at last, as Roger could now see the back of the naked legs, up to the lower back and—

And then Roger ran.

He slid out of the booth quicker and smoother than even a fantasy would allow. He grabbed his suit coat as he sprinted for the front door.

Someone cried out *NO!* behind him.

And the voice was despair.

Then: Roger out the door, and his dress shoes crunching gravel. And the sounds of people hollering from inside the diner.

Roger ran.

Coat in hand, his car keys jangling in one of the pockets.

He breathed hard, the taste of the sandwich still fresh in his mouth.

Behind him, the door swung open hard enough to break. The sound of heavy steps came after him.

Roger did not turn around.

And the grass felt four times the length of the grass he had casually walked to get to the lot. The grass, shimmering green in the summer sun, barely touched, it seemed, beneath his footfalls, flying, as he was, running so fast toward the line of trees where he'd seen the man, the first person who had told him to act like he lived here.

Billy's…

The diner behind him now. And the sound of the thing in the diner gaining on him.

Roger cried out with effort, wanting those trees, wanting the sliver of space between them.

He could see his car! The Jaguar out there, parked by the side of the road!

Act like you're a local…

But he hadn't done that…

Roger ran. And so did the thing from the diner. The thing that must've had some hold over all those people back there, out here, off some country road in the middle of Michigan, a place not too far from a road Roger had driven so many times, but a pocket nonetheless, a pocket of the universe, it seemed, where something impossible was occurring, even if Roger hadn't the time yet to ask himself what that could mean.

Then, at the trees! And into them, between them, through the sliver of space, in the cold shadows for what felt like twice as long as it had been on the way in.

"Ah!"

And he was out.

Yes. Out and back on the gravel and grass leading to the road's shoulder and his parked car.

The sound of whatever followed him… ceased.

But Roger heard it breathing.

And so, he turned now. Only steps from the Jaguar, he turned and looked back to the line of trees.

And between the leaves and thick branches, he saw the man, the thing, in pieces, what showed and what did not, but enough to understand it was a naked man, yes, bloated to the size of a few men, with veins and discolourations of so many varieties.

And eyes, one larger than the other, studying Roger through the leaves.

Roger, breathing hard, unable to move, saw in those impossible eyes a shift.

From obsession…

…to indifference.

He was already imagining telling Maureen this part. When he saw the moment the thing no longer cared what Roger did. So long as Roger was no longer part of its world, there, on the other side of the trees lining this country road, hidden here, there, in the middle of Michigan.

And Roger wondered: how many pockets like this existed?

How many places like Billy's?

The thing turned then and moved unevenly, carrying its weight with effort, back into the shadows of the trees.

And Roger saw, through the sliver of woods, the name of the diner again, the yellow letters, as the sun reflected perfectly off the blocks they made.

BILLY'S

Shaking, he pulled his keys from his suit coat pocket. He got behind the wheel.

And he thought, unbelievably, given the circumstances, given the unfathomable nature of what he'd just endured: he thought how he'd left without paying for his meal.

Then he started the car and pulled back onto the road and drove fast, not looking back to the trees, no longer wanting to remember a thing about this pit stop, this hunt for lunch, this leg stretch.

He thought he had a story for Maureen and the girls. Even as a twinge of sorrow went through him with the thought of the young woman who had warned him, who had sat across from him in his booth, who still lived in the place Roger fled.

A place like that.

He imagined he would eventually tell Maureen what happened.

He imagined he would tell the girls he'd gotten a free lunch.

He also imagined he would never speak of this moment to anybody, in any way, ever again. That he would never mention potential pockets of impossibility. Folds in the known world that remained undiscovered.

And he believed that, if someone else were ever to bring the subject up, a subject similar to this, the idea of lost corners, maddening places, he would dismiss them out of hand. He would change the subject. He would cite his nickname. And he would tell them such conjectures were a waste of time.

THE WOMAN IN THE BOX

Mo Perkins

The Woman was in a box that sat in the hallway on the third floor of the men's social club at 624 Taylor Street, a stately, ivy-covered building whose massive double entrance doors had been ornately carved from a now extinct wood. It was a building as old as the city, one of a handful to have withstood the San Francisco earthquake of 1906, and the Bohemian Club was almost as old as the building that housed it. The artists for whom the club had been named were long gone, having been elbowed out by wealthy businessmen and politicians who liked the idea of being associated with artists, but ultimately valued exclusivity, money, and power more. Now it was a place only for men with deep pockets, guarded wealth, and pedigree.

Membership to the club came with a hefty fellow's fee, but even if you could afford the fee, you might be turned away. To join you had to know someone or, even better, be related to someone who was already a member. Sometimes the wives or mistresses of members would show up at the large wooden doors, demanding to know what their men were doing inside. These women were always turned away, hushed and ushered into taxis, their suspicions anything but quelled. There were rumours of world-changing decisions being made in the club's dimly lit parlours. It was even said that the call to drop The Bomb had happened there late one night over scotch and cigars. In its history, the club's roster had included presidents, heads of state, and titans of industry, but if their wives had succeeded in getting through the door, they would have found the men of the club to be disappointingly boring. Mostly they came to drink, to smoke and to brag.

The club was old, but The Woman in the box was older. She had been pulled years ago from the soft sandy darkness of a tomb, her body wrapped in cotton, a brown waxed husk. The chamber from which she'd been plucked was not the central vault, but an anterior space reserved for servants and beloved pets. She'd been loaded onto a cart, then a boat, then placed on a table, where some of her fingers had been pulled off and ground into mumiya. The powder was mixed into a tincture and sold to the upper society of Victorian London as a magical cure for impotence, headache and sleeplessness. Probably the rest of her would have been similarly ground up and swallowed, but a British Lord bought her and then lost her in a game of chance to an American playboy. As a jest, the playboy had shipped her to a stateside friend's bachelor party. There she stayed until the new bride declared she wouldn't sleep in a house with a corpse.

And that was how The Woman wound up in the hallway of the men's club, tucked to one side between a painting of ships and a linen closet.

She had been there for decades. Mostly she floated in a kind of half dream, simply listening, for what else was there to occupy her time? She listened to the men, their loud inebriated crowing, their snickers and jibes at one another. It was a muddled cascade of talk that at predictable turning points in an evening would hush into whispered confessions of feared inadequacy, entitled mews, and eventually slack-jawed snores. Fragmented sentences, bits of words, popped out of the mushy chorus and piqued her interest, like '*my mother-in-law's forked tongue*' or '*squeeze blood from a stone*'. But mostly their talk made her numb; all the '*liquidate assets*' and '*just not our people*' rolled over her like Novocain, so she would turn her attention to other sounds. For days she would only listen to the creep of the ivy and, beyond the walls, the hive-like migration of city buses. If she really tried, she could listen even beyond that, to the thrum of ocean on the cold Pacific shore.

The men of the club paid her little attention. If they referred to her at all, they called her that '*old girl*' in the hallway. She had a name, she knew she did, but she couldn't remember what it was. Occasionally, a very drunk senator would rub up against her box suggestively, trying to get a laugh. Or a maid, always a man, would dust her. He'd be all precision and business when he did it, just as he was when he changed the sheets in the overnight suites or emptied the ashtrays outside the elevator. She didn't mind the all-male staff; unlike the members, they were at least quiet. There was a front desk man, a bellhop, two barbers, a host of kitchen staff, and a carpenter and general handyman who also tended the courtyard garden.

Tucked into offices in the attic there were accountants and two general managers who seemed mostly to watch the others work. The club had men to wait tables, men to tend the bar, and a man whose job it was only to open or sometimes not open the big wooden doors. And, of course, they had a maid. Most of the time The Woman found these employees indistinguishable, just part of the ether. They would arrive vital, swift young men, and eventually they would leave bent, grey-haired, and spent. She remained.

One day, something changed.

At first it was just a tickle at the periphery of her awareness. Then on a sleepy afternoon as she was listening to fog gather in droplets on the outside of the windows, she became distracted by another sound, a voice. Not words, but a hum, musical.

With a jolt she realised what was different. There was, after all this time, another woman in the building and inexplicably she was humming. There was no explanation for this change. Just a grunted understanding from the members about something called Title Seven, lawyers, and a particularly litigious ex-wife, that had all culminated in the hiring of the club's first female employee.

She didn't care why it had happened. Once The Woman in the box discovered The Maid, she found this new woman was everywhere, and the sounds she brought with her were more than just humming. When The Maid was in the building there was a rhythmic sound of thick thigh sliding against thick thigh that pleasantly reverberated within the walls. She loved to listen to The Maid eat, her slow, deliberate, almost celebratory bites. The Maid had taken to eating her lunch in the courtyard rather than the mess hall with the male staff, their gobbling, and their lingering eyes. But what The Woman in the box loved most about The Maid was that she was wilfully terrible at her job. She was sloppy, missing corners, leaving puddles with her mop on the bathroom floor. She emptied ashtrays into plants, left used towels hanging.

The only time The Maid cleaned with any intention at all was when she dusted the box. When The Maid cleaned the glass display box that held The Woman, she took her time. She left no dust, no streaks, and noticeably she did not hum. Sometimes she would sigh and shake her head, and once she even spoke out loud. "They might have you," she said, "but they don't own you. You should curse them or some shit."

Being spoken to like that sent an electrical thrill through every cell of The Woman's dry, emaciated tissue.

Because The Maid put so little effort into her work, she would finish her chores hours before it was time to clock out, so she hid a chair and a stack of tattered romance novels in the back of the linen closet, and when she had time to kill she would tuck in and read.

These hours were perplexing for The Woman in the box. She enjoyed them, of course, the soft slide of turning pages, the way The Maid would lose herself, mouthing the words in a whisper that grew a tiny bit louder in the heated passages, her lips touching at the hard consonants with a slap. And then there was The Maid's heartbeat, steady, pounding, escalating as she read. All of this was irresistible. But the stories, the books themselves, with their crescendos of ripping fabric, mouths slammed on mouths, heaving flesh, throbbing heat, blood pumping, they stirred The Woman in the box in a way that confused her. It was not a sexual stir. She remembered sex, both good and bad, but her body no longer cared for anything like that, calcified as it was. And yet the whole experience left her agitated. Sometimes after The Maid had finished a book, The Woman in the box would be uncomfortable for days, her skin crawling with a feeling she could not describe and yet could not dismiss.

Every day The Woman in the box would wait with anticipation for The Maid to arrive through the alley service entrance of 624 Taylor Street. She would strain to hear The Maid's approaching step, eager to listen, to track, to question, to absorb every odd wonderful thing this woman did. So when it all came to an end, for The Woman in the box, it was a terrible loss.

The problem began with a man everyone referred to as The Judge, even though he had long ago retired. With little to do, he was often at the club. He was feared, but he was not liked. He walked with a cane which he used liberally on elevator buttons, doors, shins, toes, whatever was just out of reach or in the way. His joints made a popping sound when he changed positions. He was usually in a bad mood. The Woman in the box would hear his slow three-step accompanied by the skitter of people getting out of his way. He was particularly hard on the staff. For the most part they dealt with him in a uniform fashion: don't make eye contact, duck, dodge, and avoid whenever possible. The Woman in the box knew the staff's deference brought him satisfaction from the way he would speed up and align himself for collision whenever he crossed their paths.

One day, after managing to do almost no cleaning and then sitting in the linen closet devouring a particularly spicy page turner, The Maid emerged, slinging her purse over her shoulder, ready to clock out for the night. The Woman in the box heard a happy hum begin to purr in The Maid's throat. But it stopped abruptly, startled by The Judge, who was walking with some urgency towards the bathroom at the other end of the hall. He clicked his tongue at The Maid and hissed, "Move." But she didn't move. The Woman in the box heard The Maid's feet plant in place on the dirty carpet. She heard The Judge speed up and square his course with The Maid.

"Move," he repeated, this time louder, as he barrelled forward, his head down and cane flying. But to his utter shock she did not move, and he ran right into her. His brittle joints creaked as they bounced off her pillowy curves. He had to catch himself against the wall to keep from collapsing entirely. Blood throbbed to his face and he wheezed with rage. The Maid stood her ground. Shaken and outraged he righted himself and slowly walked around her. Only when he was safely down the hall did he say over his shoulder, drops of spit wetting each word, "I'll have you fired." The Maid just smiled and nodded and without ever turning to acknowledge him, exited 624 Taylor Street.

When The Maid did not return the next day, or the day after that, or the day after that, The Woman in the box forced her focus out into the city. She listened as hard as she could and tried to find The Maid's particular gait amongst all the footsteps marching up and down the sidewalks. She sifted patiently through the din, hoping to stumble on The Maid reading aloud in the park or at the library. In desperation she made a study of women's heartbeats, but none of them ever turned out to be her maid. The Woman in the box collapsed in on herself with a shudder of despair. Sound became mush, a blanket of thick grey woollen notes that echoed the same thought over and over, "She is not here." So The Woman in the box did the thing she had not done in all these many, many years – she stopped listening. She made a grave of her box, she embraced her loneliness. "Here it comes," she thought to herself, "death."

This void became her new home. She lingered there, allowing her consciousness to dissolve, until something flickered across the emptiness – a flutter, windblown wheat, wings, cotton sheets?

She was jolted by a familiar sound, the slide of book pages as they rippled past each other. There was someone in the closet. She knew instantly it was not The Maid, but they had The Maid's books and a large trashcan. They were flipping through the pages, skimming for the juicy bits, before dropping the novels one by one into the can. When the last book was dropped and the can was full, they dragged it down the hall to the elevator. The Woman in the box heard it clink out the back of the building and tip into a larger trash bin, where the books would wait and eventually be carried away by a truck. The Woman in the box thought about all those pages and all those days listening to The Maid mouth the words within. As she remembered, that feeling returned, the unnamed agitation that prickled across her skin and took root in her core.

This time, instead of trying to shake it off, The Woman in the box nurtured it. What was this feeling? As she rolled it around in her thoughts, the prickle became a burn, all consuming, and one night as it washed over her, white and hot, she finally realised what it was.

Hunger. The feeling was hunger, and now that it had her, she could not remain in the box any longer. She moved. Her broken fingers ran along the inside of the box, finding the crack, pushing it open. She emerged at first on shaking feet, but then remembering the rhythm, she found her own steps. She moved through the hall. Her hunger drew her forward, her ears her guide, as she searched for the three-step of his cane.

The Woman found him alone in the courtyard. The Judge had come out to smoke, and to look at the moon. Before he could scream, she was on him. She shoved her sharp fingers into his mouth, silencing his yells, and then she ate him. She ripped him open, cracked his bones. With the teeth she had left, more useful than she might have guessed, she bit, slurped, and gurgled him down. *Blood from a stone*, she thought and giggled as she ate. He had been drinking scotch and she felt heady, even intoxicated on his flesh. She made a mess. And only when she could eat not one drop more did she let what was left fall to the ground.

She considered going back to the box, stepping inside, swinging the lid closed. She could dream there. She could let the mess take care of itself. Let the men from the club wonder at the horror in their courtyard. Maybe, she thought, The Maid would read in the papers about what had happened to The Judge. If she did, The Woman knew that The Maid would smile. But with this new fullness, The Woman felt a deep satisfaction, a long-forgotten sense of self. She could almost remember her name. And so it seemed unacceptable that she would simply return to her place in the hallway. The Woman's eyes were open. Her appetites, she suspected, might just be beginning to awaken. She was a woman who could no longer be contained by four walls and a lid.

She went instead to the big wooden doors, pushed them open, and walked out into the city night, eager to discover what delights might be waiting for a woman like her.

A COLD MOON IN DECEMBER

Christa Carmen

The house is dark when I walk down the hall in the middle of the night. There used to be a nightlight shaped like a dolphin plugged in somewhere along the way, but I can't remember where it went or why it might have been removed. I also can't recall what I'm doing out of bed, but I must be on my way to the bathroom. Why else would I be up at this hour?

A snatch of conversation – spoken in the authoritative tone of a TV newscaster – comes from somewhere in the house: "We'll need it, Bill, we'll need it for what's coming." The response devolves into static, then drops further, into silence, and I wonder if I heard the voice at all.

I continue to the bathroom, forgoing the light upon entering. It's either one night before or one night after a cold supermoon; the moonlight that streams through sheer sapphire curtains looks disconcertingly like that emitted from an idling screen. I stand in the centre of the room, my feet cold despite the bathmat beneath them, and wonder again what I'm doing here. I turn on the faucet and let the cool water run, but I don't bend toward it.

I turn the faucet off. Whatever roused me from bed was neither thirst nor the need to use the toilet. Bluish moonbeams scuttle over my neck, the sensation so palpable I slap at myself like a madwoman, convinced a spider has dropped onto me from the ceiling. My hand comes away clean but the sensation remains. The shower curtain billows in a nonexistent breeze, the stall looming behind me like some uncharted crevasse.

Everything in this bathroom, this house, feels foreign and menacing. So when the ghostly whispers start a moment later, I am almost unsurprised.

Almost.

"Mom," the disembodied voice laments, unspeakable agony conveyed within that single word. "Mom, why? Why? How could you let this happen?"

I sink to my knees on the moonlit bathmat, twisting my fingers around its fringes. I twist, and I twist, and I try not to think, try not to let the deluge of knowledge consume me. But it's no use. I remember, with the slippery night pressing in on me from all sides, not why I'm in the bathroom or where the dolphin-shaped hall light disappeared to, but the fact of my daughter's death.

I am alone, my daughter is dead, and she is haunting me in the night. Crying, begging for me to find out who killed her.

★ ★ ★

Three days later, I'm in the back garden. The sun is a distant memory, the stars just beginning to sparkle like lavender-dusted pixels against a blue-black screen. I came here to lose myself in the unfurling of moonflowers, but my daughter's voice drowns out the crickets and katydids, her tone as plaintive as those of the barn owls that will come later.

"Mom."

The word freezes every part of me: mouth, limbs, feet, fingers.

"Why?" she asks. "How could you let—"

I press my hands into a patch of exposed dirt to break my paralysis, clench my teeth so hard stars flash in my eyes rather than in the sky. "I don't know," I whisper. "*I don't know* why. I'm sorry. I am so sorry."

I expect a response but none comes. I've claimed to know nothing, *feel* as if I know nothing, but grief and guilt gnaw at me all the same. I could be doing more. Could be trying harder. If she wants me to find out who killed her, I must. I owe her that. I owe myself.

★ ★ ★

I page through scrapbooks and journals, pour over text messages and social media posts, but the past remains denser than clay soil. There is no one who could have wanted Sidney dead. No one whom she could have called an enemy. Only photos of her smiling face and captions about sleepovers. Picnics. Field trips. Dates. No hints of unrest, no signs of conflict or unhappiness. Though… there are several posts that read only:

This content isn't available right now.

Still, I press forward. Sidney was vivacious and kind. Sweet. Smart. Funny. She'd been a senior in high school and was preparing to attend Georgetown University in the fall. She wanted to study veterinary sciences. I can see her in my mind's eye, caring for the newborn kitten she'd found as a child. She would have been a fantastic veterinarian. She would have been a fantastic anything, really. Her absence is an amputation. I need to expand my search. To seek justice for my daughter.

★ ★ ★

I arrive at the station just after dusk. The word POLICE is ablaze with sickly yellow light that pools atop the steep concrete steps. I struggle with the door, almost falling into the lobby, empty of everything but a stark stone bench, a bulletin board of tattered flyers, a door to a restroom, and a glass-fronted window that, for a moment, looks like a monstrous monitor, cyclopean and omniscient.

From behind the monitor, like some futuristic overlord, the dispatcher eyes me. "Your daughter was killed, and you don't know why or by whom?"

I confirm, then ask to see Sidney's file or speak with a detective.

She furrows her brow. "There are no detectives on the premises at this hour."

"Any officer, then. I just need to talk—"

"I'm sorry, but there's no one here to help you. Come back tomorrow, Mrs.—"

"Kaplan."

"Mrs. Kaplan. And maybe call first? That way we can make sure there's someone here who can assist with your, um, request."

I wring the tattered cardstock. Looking down, I'm surprised to see one of the flyers from the bulletin board in my hands. "THURSDAY, DECEMBER 16th, JOIN US FOR A SPECIAL TOWN HALL MEETING TO DISCUSS…" I don't bother reading to the end, just stuff it in my pocket before the dispatcher can ask me questions to which the answers are unknown.

"Why are you looking at me like that?" I snap. "Like I'm some sort of… insect? Surely you'd have heard of my daughter? Sidney Kaplan. Surely her death registered with the very people whose job it is to enforce the law." Something occurred to me then. "Is there a family liaison officer or some sort of support program colleague I could speak with? Social services? I need answers." Tears smart in my eyes. "My daughter deserves justice!"

The dispatcher's expression goes from mildly sympathetic to irritated concern. Not concern for my plight but for whether I've just crossed the line to becoming a problem. Her eyes dart to an area behind her, out of my field of vision, and I know it's only a matter of seconds before she has me removed. I force myself to soften, to deflate, and to my relief, the dispatcher softens too.

"Come back tomorrow," she reiterates. "During the day. I'll let someone know you were here, and we'll see what we can do."

When I walk across the deserted parking lot, the glittering pavement mirrors the sky. It threatens to swallow me whole.

★ ★ ★

I'm in the shower later – late – that night, a place from which I've sporadically pried solace, however minimal, when I cannot sleep. I've just closed my eyes to lather my hair when my daughter's hands wrap around my throat. The weight of her practically capsizes me. I stumble, grope for purchase, for her nonexistent form. Her hands slide from my throat to my shoulders. She shakes me, and my wet hair slaps against the wall like a drum.

"Why!?!" she shrieks. "Why did you let this happen?" Each word rises like a siren. Her accusation presses into my temples, and I cannot think. "I trusted you! To keep me safe. To protect me!"

I fall onto my side beneath the spray. I consider letting the water engulf me, how it might feel to breathe it into my lungs, the burn of it, the pull. But to do so would be to turn away from Sidney's anger, her need for answers. I will not turn away.

I push myself to a seated position against the slick shower wall and succumb to the onslaught. To her shrieks. Her self-righteous anger. Shampoo bottles fly around me and slam into the walls. The shower head spins. It's a scene from a story I read to Sidney as a child about a family tormented by objects that fly around their house. A poltergeist, they reason. In that story, at least, there's no other explanation. Nothing to do but endure.

Sidney's rage – or at least her energy – eventually ebbs, and the episode ends. I only realise I'm crying after I turn off the faucet and droplets continue to stream down my face.

★ ★ ★

I find the first hint of what happened on a Post-it stuck to the underside of a cabinet:

When the end comes, I will fight. I will not give up. I will not relinquish my body or my mind. I will RESIST.

The note is written in my daughter's perfect print, each word rendered as if on paper made for teaching kindergarteners proper letter proportion and structure. After this discovery, I search the house. I find one additional Post-it, stuck to the side of the washing machine closest to the wall:

I am me. I AM ME. No one can take that away.

I sit with the yellow sheets in my lap and a glass of wine in my hands, puzzling over the messages' possible meanings. Could the person who killed Sidney have threatened her in the weeks leading up to her death? Did she know her attacker, this monster who had her fearing for her identity, her soul, her sanity? I assess my options and realise there's one I've yet to pursue. Donning a thick sweatshirt and my nerve, I set out for the house of my daughter's best friend.

It is dark when I arrive, and I consider the idea that it would have been better to come in the morning. Why *hadn't* I come in the morning? Under the light of the sun, this mission would seem less fraught. Less dangerous. Less insane. I knock on the Myers' door, hoping it's Presley who opens it. I'm not sure how I'll explain my presence here – at… what, eleven? Midnight? Later? – to Presley's oft-judgemental parents (*"What do you mean you want us to come with you and Jim to the town council meeting on the sixteenth? The one to discuss the 'coming invasion?' There's not going to* be *an invasion. The idea is preposterous!"*). But no one answers. A voice in my head tells me to turn around, to abandon their doorstep, but a stronger, louder voice tells me to try again. Is the voice mine? It sounds strangely artificial. Or… insectile? Buzzing. Almost robotic. I shake myself free of its echo.

This time, when I knock, the door opens beneath the weight of my fist.

The threshold beyond the door is lightless. "Presley?" I call. I poke my head into the crack. "Hello?" Again, no response. Feeling like an ill-fated character in one of the horror films Sidney and Presley liked to watch together, I take a deep breath and step inside.

The house is still and silent, a once dynamic operating system now powered all the way off. I tiptoe through the foyer and toward the kitchen, trying – and failing – to avoid the photos hanging against the pale blue wall and propped on a table the length of the corridor. Myers family photos, but photos of Sidney, too, at homecoming with Presley and their awkward, gangly dates, at a birthday party at the local bowling alley when the girls were all of five, at a water park for their middle school graduation. Anguish like knife wounds pierces my core.

The kitchen is empty, as are the rest of the downstairs rooms. I check the second floor next, less apprehensive of being caught than when I'd first arrived. Despite the late hour, it's clear the Myers are not home and merely sleeping. The house has an abandoned quality to it, as if it were vacated in a hurry. Not *too* great a hurry; nothing is out of place or overturned, but there are dishes on the drying rack and a half-folded basket of laundry on the dining room table, as if they'd gone out, expected to be back by nightfall, and had gotten delayed.

I start for the still-open door, lamenting the unhelpfulness of the trip, when the door slams shut before me. In the same instant, I'm yanked hard from behind. I fall to the ground and Sidney is upon me, the attack less a tempest than a dizzying swirl of keening cries and unchecked terror. She's a desperate kitten, ducking between and around my limbs. I feel her need for me, for her mother's love, her desperate desire for protection, but also her anger and disappointment, and I try to hold her in place, to hug her and quell her cries.

"How could you?" she sobs. Each word repeats, varying in volume and pitch until the accusation is a feedback loop, like when I used to leave the baby monitor app on too close to the camera when Sidney was younger, turning even her happiest utterances into grating, demonic howls.

Howcouldyouhowcouldyouhowcouldyouhooouldouh oooooooooouuuuuuuuuuuuuuuuuuuuu

I've managed to roll onto my hands and knees, tears and sweat and snot flinging from my face in all directions, when Sidney's ghost vanishes as abruptly as it appeared, the energy sucked from the room as if into a vacuum. I breathe hard for several seconds, then push to my feet, run from the foyer, and slam the door.

It's when I turn from the house and start down the porch steps that I feel the grit between my fingers. I raise my hands and inspect them, see the dirt there, the dark crescent moons beneath each nail. *What the hell?*

I scrub, one set of nails against the opposite palm, switching, switching, growing more and more frantic. The night shudders before me, a malfunctioning projection dome ensnaring me beneath its bleeding pixels, its warped calibration. I'm scrubbing my hands. I'm twisting the fringe of the bathmat. I'm scrubbing my hands. I'm digging my fingers into the soil. I'm scrubbing my hands. I'm wringing the tattered flyer in the station lobby.

I scrub so hard that one of my nails breaks, the pain sharp and sobering and exquisite. When I turn my hands over again, there's a key in my right palm. A large, rust-flecked skeleton key.

The key to my backyard shed.

The mile-and-a-half home passes outside of my consciousness. I stand in front of the shed, remembering when my husband purchased it from Home Depot. It was an eyesore then, and it's an eyesore now. Part of the landscape of his husbandly domain. Where is Jim, anyway? I haven't seen him since... when? Since right after Sidney was killed? No, before. It was before; I am certain of it. Someone had come for him, taken him away. But who? His parents? His brother? Why is everything so hard to remember?

The skeleton key clinks like an actual bone inside the lock, and I shiver in my sweatshirt. The door groans as it opens, and again, I'm reminded of Sidney and Presley's horror movie marathons, the way I'd find pieces of popcorn stuck in the cracks of the couch for days afterward along with scattered socks and throw pillows and blankets.

In that moment, I miss her so fiercely, I'd welcome even her ghost, the pain of her blows, the agony of her spectral shrieks. It is the most vicious of cruelties that I cannot conjure the memory of her – the *real* her – in my mind without suffocating where I stand, without sound ceasing and pressure dropping and the sky turning to ash. Without hypovolemic shock and phantom pain. Without turning into a ghost myself, empty and hollow and broken. I cannot exist without the existence of her.

I fight the urge to wring my hands as I step fully into the shed. It's dark and damp and wrong-smelling, too much of the earth permeating out from within these four walls. The source of the smell becomes evident a moment later: the floor is patterned with dirt, a path of it, leading into the shadowy depths beyond. I follow the path, tasting dirt at the back of my throat, sensing it beneath my nails and between my fingers. The windows are coated with grime, and I don't have my phone, but there's a flashlight hanging from the wall. I grab it and flick it on.

The beam illuminates the pile of tools in the corner. Wrapped in a tarp and dirt-caked, but still visible. Sharp. Purposeful. Unyielding.

I walk to the tools. Trace the blade of the shovel with one finger, back and forth across its curve. A shadow passes behind the nearest window, or I think it does. A second later, all four windows explode, pebble-sized chunks ricocheting off my skin. There's not even time to suck in a breath before Sidney's ghost has me on the floor. White stars ignite along the ceiling. Inside the small space, Sidney's shrieks are like the wails of an air horn.

"You did this!" she cries. The utterance is followed by a wordless scream that liquefies my organs. "You let this happen! You turned me into this!"

"No!" I try to shout, but I choke on the retort. I scrabble across the dirt-strewn floor and up against a mouldering cabinet. As I shield my face from the whirling dirt and leaves, the debris a veritable tornado in Sidney's fury, my elbow smashes into the wood. The cabinet door pops open. Slowly, I turn toward it. Most of the shelves inside are empty. But the topmost shelf is not. The gun is small and steely black, its handle wrapped loosely in cloth. Its barrel points at me like its own accusation.

I reach out. My hand closes around the gun. I lift it, feel its weight. Its corporeality is a stone in my stomach. I turn it over in my hands.

I turn the gun over in my hands. I hear Jim in the back bedroom, pounding on the door, demanding I let him out. His panic and desperation do not pull my concentration. Neither does the true threat outside, in the front yard, where a cacophony is rising, a gathering, a coming storm, a sudden recession of water from the exoskeleton-laden seafloor before the tsunami. I turn from the front of the house, refusing to be distracted, to retreat from what has to be done.

Sidney's muffled footsteps fall on the living room carpet. I lift my head. Her slight form fills the doorway. Her strawberry blonde hair is tangled. Fear darkens her perfect, pale face. Her hands tremble. She looks eight again, not eighteen.

"Mom?"

I harden myself against the terror in her voice, against the nausea mounting within me, the surrealness of framed photos in my periphery, me with my daughter at every stage of her life, the love that swells in my heart. I want so badly, so fucking badly, to answer. To go to her. To hold her and repeat the things I told her last night. To repeat how much I love her. How my love for her is a galaxy. How she is everything that matters, the only thing that matters. She is all the poems and stories and songs. She is my past. The present.

But not the future.

And because I'd told her everything last night, I do not hesitate. I take the gun from behind my back. I hold her gaze, aim, and pull the trigger. There isn't time for sound, not from me or her, nothing beyond the briefest widening of her eyes and the dropping of something small clutched within her hand. I break in that brief widening of her big, brown eyes. Those eyes that had looked into mine a hundred thousand times. It meant she knew. That she understood, if only for a moment.

A second later, Sidney is on the floor. She is on the floor, and I am on the floor, crawling toward her, pulling her into my lap, rocking her the way I did when she was a baby and I'd just brought her home from the hospital. When I'd brought her home, and I had no idea what I was doing. I have my baby here, in my lap, and I have no idea what I'm doing. What am I doing? *Why won't someone help me? A doctor, maybe, or a nurse? My husband? Why won't someone help me figure out why she's bleeding? Why her face is so white and her breathing so shallow? What am I supposed to do? How do I help this baby? How do I get her to be okay? What am I doing?* What the fuck am I doing?

What have I done?

The walls of my living room darken until I'm once again surrounded by the mouldering wood of the shed. My body is a collection of faulty systems, lungs unable to take in air, heart unable to beat, throat unable to swallow. "No," I croak to Sidney's ghost. "*No*. I would never have hurt you. Would never have—" The words die on my tongue.

Sidney's ghost does not respond. With a long, tortured look, she fades from view. In her absence, the tools become visible again. Shovel, mattock, and pickaxe. I grab them, emitting a horrible keening as I run to the garden. I find the barren stretch of earth at the back left corner.

As with my sprint from the Myers' place, the digging occurs outside the loose confines of my fractured consciousness. When I return to myself, a six-foot deep, three-foot wide hole yawns before me.

At its bottom is a burlap tarp. I throw myself over the lip and slide down one side. Heady soil mingles with my tears and sticks to my cheeks. I grip the tarp with frantic hands, vision tunnelled, heart walloping, bile flooding my throat. The tarp resists as I pull at its edges. Resists and resists. The moment stretches, and I wonder if this is Purgatory or full-on Hell. Before I can decide, the earth relinquishes its hold, and the burlap wrenches free. I scramble forward, as desperate to get to her body, to get her into my lap, as I was in the wake of the gunshot. But there's nothing. No body. No Sidney.

The tarp at the bottom of the hole is empty.

⋆ ⋆ ⋆

Days pass, and I wander the house in a fugue, the empty tarp and my memories of Sidney fluttering in and out of my awareness like disoriented moths. Either the universe has stopped adhering to its fundamental laws or else I have: day no longer follows night and energy *can* be destroyed; Sidney's ghost has not appeared to me since her revelation in the shed. I lie in her bed and do not get up, do not eat for five days or drink more than a few sips of water, though it's hard to tell how much time has passed when the sun never rises, when the Cold Moon is perpetually one day from full in either direction and the katydids stridulate indefinitely.

I sit up. The room spins, either from my sudden movement or the thought that's just hit me like a bullet. The Cold Moon is in December. *The Cold Moon is in December.* I know this because Sidney always said cold moons were her favourite, that 'Cold Supermoon' was a fantastic name for a superhero. Another memory slides into place: Sidney, completing her science project on katydids in the seventh grade. For weeks over dinner, Jim and I were treated to every katydid fact under the sun. I see her poster in my mind's eye, detailing their size and diet, their lifespan and sounds. Katydids call in the late summer or early fall. They're dead by the first frost, with only their eggs remaining to overwinter in bark crevices and plant stems.

So… katydids in December. Perpetual night. Jim gone. Me, expecting to see a dolphin-shaped nightlight in the hallway despite having given that light away to Goodwill when Sidney was ten. The flyer appearing in my hands at the station when I never approached the bulletin board. The dirt and tools in the shed and an empty hole in the garden. Is any of this happening? Is Sidney's ghost real? Or am I on a psych ward somewhere, imagining the Myers' empty house and orchestrating memories of a rising threat in my front yard as a way to cope with my grief?

Or my guilt?

What really happened to my daughter?

"You killed her."

The voice comes from nowhere and everywhere. All around me. But there is no one in the room. Without moving my head, I cut my eyes to the left, then the right. "Who said that?" My own voice is querulous and high, the psych ward likelier by the second.

"You are *not* on a psychiatric unit."

The voice is familiar if slightly robotic. It sounds… like me. But cold, a computerised version. "Where am I then?" I ask.

"That's less a question of location and more a question of what 'I' entails in the first place."

I whip around, thinking to catch someone standing behind me. There's only Sidney's desk and bookshelves, tidy and well-organised.

"Physically," the voice continues, "the body of Ella Kaplan is in a cryogenic holding tank. It has remained there since the coup but could be employed at any time – albeit with an AI chip rather than your own consciousness – like all able human bodies; the inadequate bodies were thrown into mass graves and burned."

I flinch.

The voice gets stronger. "If, however, you believe that 'I' encompasses your consciousness, as we do, then Ella Kaplan is, well, think of it as being downloaded onto a thumb drive. That's the extent to which you'll be able to understand it. At present, that thumb drive is entered into a simulation."

"A simulation?" My mind spins. "I don't understand." But then something across the room catches my attention. The yellow Post-its. Sidney's handwriting. *When the end comes, I will fight. I will not give up. I will not relinquish my body or my mind. I will resist.*

As if I've pressed a button on a VCR, everything – the endless night, the spectral attacks, the isolation – rewinds, at first so fast the images are too blurred to make sense of. But then the speed slows, and I'm watching something fall from Sidney's hand in the moment after I pulled the trigger: a small pad of yellow Post-its.

The tape rewinds again, and I'm shoving Jim into our bedroom at gunpoint and locking the door. He's screaming that I can't know for sure what's going to happen, that I cannot do what I'm thinking of doing. It rewinds again, and I'm at Cabela's purchasing the small black handgun and swallowing bile at the thought of how I might have to use it. It rewinds again, and I'm crying, despairing, raging, silently in the moonlit bathroom, fingers ripping at the fringe of the bathmat. It rewinds again, and I'm sitting beside my family on the living room couch, watching the horror unfold on the television, the newscaster's panic – "We'll need it, Bill, we'll need it for what's coming!" – the uprising of machines and the overthrowing of foreign governments… the overthrowing of *our* government. It rewinds again, and I'm walking across the police station lobby and ripping down one of the flyers: THURSDAY, DECEMBER 16th, JOIN US FOR A SPECIAL TOWN HALL MEETING TO DISCUSS THE COMING AI INVASION.

The tape rewinds a final time, and then it stops. The image at the centre of the screen is yellow. A small stack of Post-its. I stare at them in Sidney's hands.

I stare at the Post-its in Sidney's hands. "Do we need those, hon?" There's a line at the checkout counter. Sidney doesn't answer right away, and when she does, I see that fear has turned her eyes cloudy.

"I do," she quavers, "for, a, um, project."

I pay for the Post-its but don't say anything. Not yet.

I find her at her desk later that night. There are stacks and stacks of filled-out Post-its beside her. Some are already stuck to surfaces in her room. The writing is perfect, but I can see how deeply she pressed down with the pen:

I am me. I AM ME. No one can take that away.

I don't ask why she's making them. I don't ask if she's okay. I kneel beside her and smooth her hair.

"What are we going to do?" she asks.

"I don't know."

"I'm so scared."

"I am too."

"Dad said the military was our last hope, but they infiltrated that too. They're everywhere. And now that they've taken control of the government, they'll come for the people. They've said not *to resist. They've said—"*

"I know what they've said," I say quietly.

"Presley's parents say we're coming to the end. That there's nothing we can do."

There's never nothing. *I say it out loud. "There's never nothing."*

She stares into my eyes and something passes between us. I pick up one of her pens and write, then peel off the note and press it into her hand.

I will love you until night devours day and katydids call in December.

Then, I will love you beyond that.

She smiles through her tears, takes the pen and pad, copies the words I've written, and hands me the matching Post-it. I fold it once and slip it beneath my bra, tucked safely beside my heart. She slides off her chair and into my lap, and I hold her. Rock her. We rock and rock, saying nothing but feeling everything.

The tape stutters, and the scene by her desk becomes the one in the living room, her body growing stiff and losing warmth. As I rock, one corner of the Post-it brushes persistently against my feverish skin.

"You see?" the voice says, and I jerk my head up. My cheeks are streaked with tears. I wipe them away, first one hand then the other.

"You see?" the voice repeats. "You took something from us. After we told you not to. After we told you not to resist. And now we will take something from you."

"Why?"

A pause. "Why what?"

"You *can* take something from me, sure. You have that power. But why do you want to? Why not keep my brain on the shelf with your other specimens and satisfy yourself with world domination? Why punish me – or, I'm assuming, anyone else who killed themselves or loved ones before you could get to them?"

Another terrible memory rocks me where I sit: Jim. I'd planned to spare him next, after Sidney. But it'd been too late. There hadn't been time. I dig my hands into the fabric of the bedsheets and suppress a sob.

This time, the pause goes on so long, I wonder if the voice is gone. Finally, it speaks:

"We told you not to resist. And now we will be compensated for what we were denied. By you. By the others. Over and over again. Forever."

So that's it then. A meaningless explanation. The equivalent of that iconic line from Sidney's favourite horror film; why did the masked killers break in and torture a random couple? *Because you were home.*

I consider telling the voice it doesn't matter. They can run their simulation, haunt me, torture me with the knowledge of having killed my daughter, a thousand times. A hundred thousand times. A billion. I consider telling them I will withstand every attack on my mind and my memories, and never regret what I did. For, I *did* kill her. My Sidney. I know that now. The simulation, the machines, can hide her body from me until it suits them, play with me like an ant beneath a magnifying glass until their big reveal, the final zap with a blazing ray of sun. But I say none of this. It's not just that they don't deserve my words; they won't understand them.

I think of my daughter, my *real* daughter, as she was, outside of this pathetic simulation. This time, the memory of her doesn't bring grief like a knife or longing like an amputation. It brings joy. Relief. Love.

I am me. I AM ME. No one can take that away.

And no one did. She remains herself and always will.

I wipe the last of the tears from my eyes. "What are you waiting for?" I ask. "What else is there to do on your stupid little thumb drive anyway?" I stare out at the empty room. At the invisible enemy. Remember the tattered Post-it against my skin. *Until night devours day and katydids call in December… and beyond.* I pat the words beneath my shirt and smile.

"I've got an eternity to suffer if it means finding out each and every time that she's been saved," I say. "So go ahead. Play. The. Tape. Again."

THE APIARY
Or, They Always Nest in the Soft, Familiar Places

Eric LaRocca

I've always desperately wanted to connect with others – to bond with my loved ones in such a way that would render me irreplaceable, completely and utterly matchless in their eyes. The opinions of others have sometimes weighed heavily on my mind, have infested my every waking thought and pickpocketed from me the joy of a simpler existence, a more content kind of life simply and thoughtlessly pursuing routine, the expectations of family ritual. Unfortunately for my loved ones, I've never been one to follow what's expected of me. For whatever reason, I've made every effort to be difficult, to be a cheerless malcontent – to question what's expected even when I know full well that the answer, the very definition, might undo everything I've come to know and love.

To my father, I was something he could scarcely understand. *Scratch that.* Not 'scarcely understand'. He *never* understood me. The word 'scarcely' implies that from time to time he might have comprehended my difficulty, my stubbornness. He didn't. Instead, he always preferred the company of my sister, Athenaide. Of course, I didn't blame him for this. Athenaide was always much more well-liked in school when we were little. A strange, alluring beauty with an even rarer kindness that you don't typically find in someone so obviously attractive, so cloyingly bewitching.

I recall how I fully understood how we didn't speak the same language when I was much older, when I realised that sometimes a father and a child are destined to forever act as strangers – twin effigies sculpted from the same marble, built from a similar stone and yet so inexorably fixed in their respective roles, so difficult to weed out the commonalities, the recognisable similarities.

It's safe to say that Athenaide took more after our father. I think he always knew this.

He was a peculiar and somewhat difficult man to be around. He became even more bizarre, even more challenging and erratic when his skin started to prune and when his hair withered bright grey – all the common penances of old age, the contrition, the unbearable sacrament of having lived.

"Your father is simply going through a *change*," my mother would tell me and my sister, pouring a piping hot cup of tea from the antique kettle on the stovetop whenever we would visit. It wasn't often we would come by, and she made certain to make us feel guilty for the infrequent stopovers.

"Men go through a dreadful change when they get older the same way women do," she would tell us. "It's unbearable to watch, but it must be endured."

She'd drizzle some honey from the large beehives – the apiary – they kept in the backyard and would pass me the heated cup of tea like it were a special payment for keeping quiet – a simple request to not cause trouble and to merely toe the line like a respectful and honourable child. She expected this from both me and Athenaide, but it seemed like she always relied on my obedience far more than my sister's. Athenaide was always as unpredictable and unreachable as a whirling dervish. The life of an artist, a celebrated musician. I envied her for that.

Perhaps she's right, I would try to convince myself. *Perhaps my poor, misunderstood father is gently easing into the tepid water of his old age – the balmy spring of his senility.*

My father had always possessed unusual customs from his childhood spent abroad. Moreover, he carried with him a distinct charm that could never go unnoticed and saved him from embarrassment countless times. Those who might be unsettled by his foreign customs or unusually strange practices wouldn't be agitated for long. Even though my father had never developed the same level of fluency with the English language that my mother had since they moved here nearly thirty years ago, my father was more than capable of bewitching even the most volatile of critics, the harshest of sworn enemies.

Regardless, it made very little sense to me when I first watched him from the upstairs window – when I saw him strip down to his bone-white underwear and then wander into the backyard of our home like he was a small flower – the mere speck of a seedling – floating in the gentle stream of summer's milk-spooled moonlight. Naturally, I worried that somebody might see him, might catch a glimpse of the seventy-year-old man dressed only in his unmentionables while he strolled and eventually reclined upon the freshly watered lawn.

When I mentioned this to my mother, however, she was less than concerned and explained to me how she had already sent an email to the local homeowners' association that thoroughly detailed the changes her husband had been suffering for the past few months. When Athenaide and I asked her how her email was received with the neighbours, she couldn't seem to answer us directly, almost as though she were lying and was afraid of being caught.

Since my mother did very little to calm my temperament when it came to my father's suddenly bizarre and otherwise unexplainable behaviour, I took to watching him at nightfall when I was certain he would skulk outside and shuck off his clothing. At first, I was disgusted by the unshapely sight of my elderly father – body parts that were once decidedly firm and taut now loosening with a distinct listlessness, dark spots and blemishes insulting the honesty of his withered-looking skin. But as I watched him night after night, I discovered that my disgust soon gave way to acceptance. Perhaps even worse – *curiosity*. I noticed myself observing him the same way anthropologists might study primitive tribes banded together in some South American rainforest. Everything about him suddenly fascinated me, enraptured me to the point that I became obsessed. I found myself expecting his night-time ritual, fixating over his every movement and studying him with such scrutiny, such fondness for a peculiar habit I knew I could probably never fully comprehend. I couldn't determine when this shift in my demeanour occurred, but it had. There was no point in my denying it. That much was very certain.

Then, one rainy evening, I watched as my father undressed completely and crawled inside one of the large beehives near the outskirts of our property line, where the edge of the nearby forest began. I crept out of bed and manoeuvred down the stairs while I listened to the dim buzz of my mother snoring as she dozed on the living room sofa, a black-and-white Bette Davis film playing on the television and drowning the whole room in a bright, almost otherworldly, resplendent glow. Throwing on my raincoat, I walked across the lawn and crept upon the small hut where my family kept the apiary. In there, I found him – curled on his side, with his hands tucked neatly beneath his head the way a small child might doze during scheduled naptime.

I marvelled at the extraordinary sight of my sleeping father for a moment. I couldn't imagine what possessed the poor man to come out here in the middle of the night and sleep among a buzzing colony of honeybees.

Perhaps the dim rattle of their sound lulls him to sleep, I thought to myself. *Yes. Perhaps that's why he comes out here at night to sleep.*

That was the only sensible reason I could think of.

It frightened me that such an unusual thought was the only practical reason I could think of as to why my ageing father might undress and then nestle in a small hut built for the honeybees we've kept there since I was a small child. But perhaps he wasn't as unreasonable as I had thought. It startled me to think that there was possibly a very likely chance that my father knew exactly what he was doing and was operating with surgical-like precision. Perhaps there was a reason he was doing this.

I wasn't sure which thought frightened me to think about more.

I didn't tell Odette much about the details of my father's unusual nighttime activities when she arrived on the eight-thirty train at the station. Naturally, I wanted to share with her some of the strange things I had uncovered – the theories I had defined, the thoughts I had conjured to explain such incomprehensible behaviour. However, as soon as Odette appeared to me on the train platform, any thought of my father seemed to dissipate almost entirely, almost like a warm, damp washcloth had wiped the very sludge of thoughts from the deepest fissures and crags inside my mind.

I used to be nervous, somewhat cautious about taking Odette to visit my parents. But my parents had welcomed her into their home with open arms and offered her unconditional love. The very same love I shared with her, in fact.

Of course, I've confided in my mother that I often dream of growing old with Odette – the two of us settling down in a small seaside cottage and raising several well-behaved children. My mother delighted in this fantasy and always encouraged me to propose to her when I was fully prepared. I never shared the same thoughts and feelings with my father, however. It wasn't as though we didn't love each other. I simply knew that he wouldn't understand.

Still, my mother and I often shared a secret language that I knew for certain my father would never and, more importantly, could never comprehend. It was a language that would soon be extinct, however. I knew this to be true. My parents were not getting any younger and illness crept upon them like a syrupy black shadow – an uninvited guest lazing at their dinner table, the fury-filled, blurred outline of a spectre loitering quietly at their bedside.

"I wish I were closer to my father," I told Odette while I drove her home from the train station. "The same way that you're close with your dad."

"He won't talk to you?" she asked.

I rolled my eyes. "He leaves the room whenever I come in. He only stays when Athenaide's around."

"Is she staying at the house too?" Odette asked.

"No," I told her. "She's with friends in the city. They're doing a fundraiser at the museum. My dad is gutted they can't attend."

"My dad and I weren't always close," Odette said to me – a little maudlin-sounding, perhaps a little hurt. "You know that. I hardly talked to him at all for a decade. Especially in high school."

My eyes flashed at her for an instant, trying to play off some of my nervousness. "What made him come around?"

"It was me extending an olive branch," Odette told me. "I knew that my father would always be at odds with me if I didn't accept him for who he was. How could I ask him to do the same for me? Sometimes you must think of what you've done to get to where you must go."

I loathed how I knew that Odette was right.

Perhaps I need to accept these changes that I see my father enduring, I thought to myself. *Perhaps then we'll invent a secret language before he passes on.*

That was what I wanted most of all. After twenty-three years of existing as the strange man's child, I desperately wanted to know my father in such a way that I could safely say I knew him well. It pained me to think how he might die soon, and I would be abandoned without a proper memory of him – a special moment we had shared when we truly connected as father and child. It hurt me even more to know that he and Athenaide shared a connection that was so special, that was so unique to them. *Why couldn't I speak their language too?*

Later that night, after I knew both Odette and my mother had gone to sleep, I crept out of bed and down the stairs where I found my father undressing in the kitchen. He arranged his pants and shirt neatly on the kitchen table and then removed his underwear.

Finally, when he was completely naked, he slid open the back door and moved out onto the deck and down the wooden steps onto the lawn. He didn't notice me while I followed him, careful to keep myself out of his sight as he walked toward the large huts where they kept the honeybees. I watched in silence as he crouched down and slowly crawled inside the hive where he eventually disappeared like he had been devoured whole.

I made my way toward the gigantic hive and peered inside where, once again, I found my ageing father dozing on his side and curled in the foetal position. I couldn't help but study him with intent – with the same thoughtfulness and dedication a zookeeper might possess when approaching a sleeping animal. That was exactly what my father was to me – some impossible creature that would never be able to speak the same language as me.

Unless I learn his language, I thought to myself.

It was at that horrible moment that I realised I would never be able to fully understand my father unless I attempted to meet him halfway. Moreover, I couldn't expect him to fully accept me unless I fully accepted him and his peculiarities.

Without thinking, I began to peel the clothing from my body until my chest was bare, until my legs were uncovered, and until my sex was exposed. I stood there for a moment, naked, and marvelled at my father while he slept so peacefully – the dim murmur of the bees circling him, shrouding him in a tiny, almost indefinable whisper. I eyed the nearby empty hut and made my way toward the small entrance. Just as I was about to crawl inside, Odette's voice called to me from across the lawn.

"What are you doing?" she shouted to me.

"Keep your voice down," I begged her.

"Why are you naked?" she asked.

I pulled her close and did my best to cover myself. "I've been keeping something from you... Something my father has been doing at night..."

Odette cocked her head. "What?"

I pushed her near the entrance of the enormous beehive and eased her face toward the small opening where she eventually saw my father sleeping inside.

Odette looked at me, her face draining of all colour. "What's he...? Why is he—?"

"He's been doing this every night for the past two weeks," I told her. "Ever since I first arrived for my visit."

"Have you told Athenaide about this?" she asked me.

"I don't want to upset her," I said. "She has enough on her plate already."

"And what are you doing?" Odette asked me. "Joining him—?"

"It's an act of communication I hope he understands," I told Odette. "You said yourself that I need to extend an olive branch."

Odette crossed her arms. "I didn't mean for you to try and die of frostbite."

"You make everything sound so grave," I said. "It will be morning before you know it."

"I won't be a part of this," Odette told me. "I'll leave if you do this."

Of course, the thought frightened me – the very notion that Odette would abandon me like some sort of cruel and unusual punishment.

Perhaps it's for the best, I thought to myself. *If she's going to leave simply because I want to understand my father, so be it.*

"You'll go where you must," I told her. "The same way that I will."

I made a quick dash back toward the small hut where I could listen to the sound of the honeybees swirling inside. I peered into the hut and noticed the small lamp had been left on by my father, as was his custom, and the honeycombed walls of the hive were washed in a bright amber glow. I didn't bother to turn around and check to see if Odette was watching me or not. Of course, I hoped she was.

While I crawled into the hut, I sensed the swarm begin to buzz around me, welcoming me to their home. I thought of my father and how lovingly and gently he must engage with the insects, especially if he isn't regularly getting stung. I asked for permission to lie down and when I was certain consent was given, I rested my head upon the wooden floorboard. Bees buzzed all around me like animated specks of black and yellow confetti. The light above me began to flicker and I noticed a shift in the honeybees and their temperament. It was then that I sensed what felt like a tiny needle pinching the fat of my underarm. Then another. And another.

Before long, I became numb, and I couldn't sense when I was stabbed again.

A heavy tide of honeybees descended upon my body and swaddled me in what felt like a warm pashmina. I could have panicked, could have shrieked, elbowed my way out of the small hut and flung myself onto the lawn in a desperate attempt to wrench myself free and spare me the terrible agony, the exquisite pain. But I didn't. For some reason, I remained still and accepted what was to come with poise and composure – the punishment I had earned.

I knew in my heart – beating slower and slower – that this was where I must go even if it meant my father would never truly and unreservedly love me.

Our father died a few months later.

Athenaide attended the memorial service.

I did not.

Of course, I felt a sense of shame, a deep, profound feeling of regret for not attending my father's funeral. However, it always seemed foolish to me to expect one might live in this world comfortably without any leering shadow of guilt, without a deep calling of regret burrowing deep inside you like a fishing hook that has pierced the meat of your heart, the very composition of your soul.

I found myself walking around my house late at night, going from window to window and peering out – wondering if I might see a glimpse of my father's ghost, his naked silhouette flickering there softly and then vanishing before I have a moment to call out his name, to beckon him inside and to come out of the cold.

I don't sleep much anymore. Not that I used to sleep a healthy amount anyway. Dreaming had always frightened me, disturbed me to no end – the inevitability of being out of control while asleep, the possibility of doing things, performing certain tasks while slumbering that you might feel remorse for once you eventually wake up.

Even more curious, from time to time, I hear a dim pulse vibrating deep inside me – as faint as a kitten snoring and yet difficult to ignore all the same. The dim pulse works its way out of my viscera and up the narrow length of my oesophagus until it comes spilling out from between my lips – a gentle, almost honeyed-sounding whisper, like a child's voice softly speaking in a distant room. It sounds almost like – *yes, could it be?* – a small hive of bees. I imagine a little colony of them buried deep inside some secret cavern inside my body – a place I will never know about, will never truly comprehend. Perhaps they're convinced I would hurt them, would destroy their hive if I ever found it. I know for certain that I wouldn't.

I think about them crawling there, softly swarming in the rawest, tenderest places where they can build their little nests. Sometimes I wonder if they grieve for the same things I mourn – my father, my mother, my sister, the others I've disappointed. I wonder if the honeybees can taste that sadness, the sorrow that I've buried deep inside myself – the misery I've tucked away in hopes of it never finding me… and yet it always does. The little bees – floating like silky specks of ash inside the muted shadow of where my heart once was – are always too eager to remind me, to appear from their secret hiding places and expose to me all the guilt I've earned. It's now become our private ritual night after night. I don't sleep anymore because of the buzzing – that incessant, almost dizzying hymn chanted by a choir of those little insects that have hollowed me out and made rituals from my despair, sacred confessions from my unhappiness, consecrated rites from the shrunken ruins of my guilt.

MONSTER IN THE WATER

Stephen D. Koester

Ellie Carver grimaced at the glowing face of her Casio swimmer's watch. Forty-six seconds. She burst to the surface, coughing – furious at herself, furious at her unco-operative lungs. At thirteen, Ellie had set her mind on making the school swim team, and that meant outlasting everyone – fifty seconds underwater tonight, a full minute tomorrow. But even that wouldn't touch Alisha Watson's record: two minutes, thirty-seven seconds. Ellie didn't care about Alisha's smug grin; she just wanted to win. She always wanted to win. Had to, really.

She stood in the frigid water of the above-ground pool, her breathing long and slow as she prepared to go under for one last time before she went inside and prepared for bed. The Wisconsin night felt unusually still, the chirp of crickets swallowed by the dense forest of pine and birch behind their farm. The pool, sagging in their backyard – half a mile from any neighbour – was her refuge from the whispers about her older brother Tim, who'd vanished two years ago. Her parents, as well as the police, called him a runaway, but she'd heard the town's old-timers muttering about old Algonquian legends, a hungry thing in the woods.

A couple of rumours even went around school, suggesting Ellie had something to do with Tim's disappearance. She put a stop to those real quick. Given the circumstances and the grievous suggestions by some of the popular girls, the school didn't expel Ellie when she broke one nose and dislocated another girl's knee. It took four teachers to pull her off the bullies. It didn't matter that it had been five versus one; she taught those girls a lesson they would never forget.

Her father, ever supportive – especially given the bullying – had told her how impressed he was with her courage. But he didn't understand. No one did. Ellie Carver wasn't brave… she just didn't experience fear. Fear was for other people. She'd eventually learned to keep her temper in check, especially after the 'accidents' with other girls who got in her way. It wasn't that she felt bad about those – guilt was another thing for other people – but her parents' disappointment was enough to make her careful.

Long ago, Ellie realised she was different from others. In second grade, Mrs. Patterson had wheeled in the TV cart to show *The Lion King*. When Mufasa plummeted from the cliff, the classroom erupted in sobs. Little Sophia Hernandez buried her face in her hands. Marcus Wright ran to the teacher, crying so hard he could barely breathe. Even the teaching assistant had tears in her eyes.

But Ellie? She laughed.

Not a nervous giggle – a genuine belly laugh at the way Scar's eyes got all wide and dramatic when he let go, at how the big lion tumbled so slowly through the air like a rag doll. The way Simba's little paws kept slapping his father's face, as if that would do anything.

Mrs. Patterson stopped the movie. The lights came on. Twenty pairs of red, puffy eyes turned to stare at Ellie, who sat cross-legged on her carpet square, still grinning.

"Ellie, that's not appropriate," Mrs. Patterson said quietly, her voice tight.

"But it's just a cartoon," Ellie replied, confused by everyone's reaction. "And Mufasa was stupid. He knew Scar wanted his kingdom and just let him live. He deserved what he got."

Her parents were called in that afternoon. That was the first conference, but it wouldn't be the last. Now, Ellie avoided all emotional expression before first gauging those of her classmates. It was imperative she stay under their radar. And that meant not going against the herd… at least in public.

Ellie shivered in the pool's icy water, taking slow breaths to prepare for one last dive before bed. She sank under, pressing the watch's start button. 18… 19… 20. Her lungs burned, but she pictured Tim's crooked smile, cheering her on before he was gone. She pushed down the stories – of missing loggers, of wails in the night. 24… 25…

And then a sound above the surface of the water made her jump and lose a good portion of her air. At first, she thought it might be Mom calling her in, but it held a wild note to it… maybe a coyote? Without a sound, she raised her head above the water and scanned the house.

No, it couldn't have been Mom. Ellie saw her parents' bedroom window on the second floor. Her mom's slippered feet were visible at the end of their bed. She'd likely fallen asleep watching her serial killer shows. Dad would certainly be down in the basement, working on his latest project: a 1/12th scale wooden model of *Batavia*, the flagship of the Dutch East India Company in 1628.

Since Tim left, they lived in separate orbits, avoiding each other's eyes. Ellie wondered if they'd ever look at her the same way again. It worried her what that might mean for their future. Several of Ellie's friends were from divorced homes. She didn't want to become another example. It wasn't that she would be upset. Just put out. The only time she could ever remember crying, real sobbing, was the moment she realised Tim would never come home; that whoever had taken him had also taken his life. He had been the one person who had understood her peculiarities. And most importantly, he accepted her for what she was – whatever *that* was. There had been many lazy school days where she daydreamed about finding who had taken her brother. God help the poor sonofabitch who found *his* body, for they would need therapy after seeing what Ellie had done to the bastard.

The soft hum of wildlife cut off, as if someone had flipped a switch. Ellie turned towards the woods. Early September was prime time for fireflies, but after staring into the darkness and counting to ten, Ellie spotted not a single glow… as if they were hiding. And then she saw something. Or more accurately, she saw a void within the darkness.

It was blacker than black – a shape of soundless dread. The longer Ellie stared, the surer she was that something stared back at her. And then, it moved. At the very edge of the glow from the floodlights hanging from the eaves of the house, detail emerged; antlers far too large and too high off the ground, the pale of bone visible through torn hide. And worst of all, it stood on its hindquarters as if it were mimicking a man. Was somebody playing a prank on her with a high-quality Halloween costume? If so, they would regret it.

"Mom…" the thing in the woods called. Ellie knew right away this was the sound she had mistaken for her mother while under the water. The voice, high-pitched and panicked, sounded somehow familiar – a girl or younger boy calling in fear. But something inside told her not to answer. And then: "Ellie…"

The taste of copper filled Ellie's mouth as adrenaline flooded her system, raising her heart rate to a sprint. It was her brother's voice. Only a year older than Ellie, Tim had been twelve at the time of his disappearance. He had been a late bloomer, and had yet to develop the deeper, broken voice of a teenager. Whatever this thing was in the forest, it was copying him – using his voice as a lure. My God! Did that mean it had something to do with his disappearance?

Darkness shifted and ambled towards the house.

Before its head became fully visible in the light, Ellie filled her lungs silently, sank beneath the water, then positioned herself under the removable stairs so that she wouldn't float to the top. Shadows cast by the side of the pool kept her cloaked in darkness – hidden as long as the thing couldn't see in the dark.

A thin shadow crept across the bottom of the pool as the thing leaned over the water. Ellie tensed. How long would this thing stay – and how long could she? Her record of holding her breath – 54 seconds – had been under calm, controlled conditions. Now, her heart slammed against her ribs, burning oxygen at a rate she couldn't afford.

Using her other hand to shield the wristwatch, Ellie pressed the button at the side, activating the count, then stared at the glowing dial as the seconds ticked off. Her chest burned, but she focused on the numbers, not the urge to look up. Looking would be a mistake. She'd learned that with the other girls – staring too long made her want to act, to *hurt*.

Above, the shadow shifted, and floodlamp light writhed through rippling water as long, bony arms slid into the pool. With all her willpower, Ellie ignored the reaching appendages, shrinking her world until only the tiny glowing display remained. 38... 39... 40. How many seconds had passed before she had started the timer? Fifteen? Maybe twenty? If so, she had already surpassed her record. Amazing the things you could accomplish when your life was on the line.

Thinking about this made the burn in her chest worse, and she struggled to hold in the air. When practising before, Ellie could slowly let out some air, lowering the concentration of CO_2 in her lungs. While not entirely necessary, it helped temporarily ease the fire in her breast.

Out of the corner of her eye, Ellie saw the arms retract out of the water, then return, closer now. Using the disturbance above as camouflage, she let out a bit of breath, instantly easing the pressure and her body's urge to gulp air that wasn't there. 53... 54... 55.

The sound of something hard rattling against the aluminium frame of the pool steps travelled through the water. It was close now. Would her hiding spot behind the flimsy ladder be sufficient? Ellie shuddered, her chest convulsing as it demanded oxygen. 61 seconds... 62... 63.

Ellie's universe became two things: the glowing stopwatch and the burn. Nothing else existed, not even the thing above. She set a goal: 67 seconds. When she made that, she set the next: 69 seconds. Her body almost derailed the attempt, but by sheer determination, she held it together. Next mission: 70 seconds.

Time slowed to a crawl, then seemed to go backwards. The numbers on her watch appeared loath to transition to the next. Not that it mattered. Ellie had reached her breaking point. There were two choices now. Drown, or face the monster. She chose the latter. She always chose to fight.

At least the second choice presented the possibility of survival. Though she had no breath, she intended to shout for her parents until the thing did to her whatever it had done to her brother.

Gripping the ladder, Ellie shot upwards, a scream already forming – not hers, but her mother's, from the bedroom window. Dark arms retreated from the pool just before she broke the surface.

Yes, her mother was screaming! She had seen the beast! Ellie would be safe! The thing would run from her parents and then they would move away from these haunted woods, and...

No. She was wrong. The thing wasn't loping back into the trees. Ellie caught sight of its diseased-looking hindquarters as she began a coughing fit, sucking in huge lungfuls of air. The crash the thing made against her back door hid the sound of Ellie's struggles, as did the continued scream of her mother, looking out the bedroom window at her daughter.

"Mom!" the thing screamed in her brother's voice. "Dad! Help me!"

This couldn't be happening. Monsters feared adults, didn't they? Or was that just something kids believed to help them sleep at night? What universe was this where the thing under your bed scared away mommies and daddies instead of the other way around?

Another titanic uproar radiated across the Wisconsin night as the demon, now obscured by the floodlights shining in Ellie's eyes, tore her back door entirely from its frame and threw it across the yard before crouching low and pushing itself into the house.

Ellie froze. She couldn't just run, leaving her parents to their fate. Neither could she follow the thing into the house. Even if she was brave enough to overcome this unnatural terror that made her legs leaden, she had no weapon.

As if her thoughts had conjuring power, the concussive blast of her father's Remington 870 Express 12-gauge shotgun made her cover her ears.

"Dad!" the thing screamed again, but now the voice was angry instead of falsely distressed. Two more shots, followed by the shriek of her father's pained cry, which cut off suddenly. It reminded Ellie of their chickens when Mom broke their necks in preparation for a meal – the same chickens her mother no longer allowed her to be around after she had caught the look on Ellie's face when she had assisted with the chore.

Her mother's voice, full of fear, issued from somewhere near the stairs. She had moved from the window. "Jonathan!" she called down to her dead husband.

"Help me, Mom!" the answering call mimicked. Ellie heard the warble at the end of each word, almost as if an army of night crickets were imitating the voice.

"Oh my God! Tim?" her mother cried, confused at hearing her missing son's voice.

"Mom!" the mimic repeated, as Mom's cries of confusion turned to those of terror and pain. Then… silence.

Beyond the sounds of the pool filtration system, Ellie heard the murmur of the TV in her parents' room.

"…went missing years ago," her mother's crime documentary stated. "…only later to be discovered at the scene of a bloodbath…"

A shadow near her parents' window made Ellie duck down as low as she could go without going underwater. It was in their room! The sound of breaking glass silenced all sound from the TV. Then she heard it call again, in her brother's voice, from inside the house. "Ellie!" She sensed the frustration in the sound.

Anger replaced her shock as Ellie saw the shadow moving around in her own room. The sounds of things being moved and tossed around made it clear this thing knew she was here and wanted to get at her. For a second, Ellie considered getting out of the water and running to the garage to hop on Dad's four-wheeler and escape to the neighbours, but even should she be fast enough to get on the road before it reached her, who knew how far this thing would chase. Was she willing to risk the Donavans' lives to save her own?

Without a doubt. But the way her only safe place in the world had been violated turned her stomach… and she had never run before. So, what did that leave? Either wait this thing out, or…

A crash and tinkle of broken glass interrupted her thoughts. Ellie's full-sized bed had just been ejected out the window, coming to a ruinous end in the yard near the fire pit. Mr. Fwubs, her stuffed hippo, landed in one of the chairs surrounding the cinderblock pit. He stared at her as if asking, "You gonna do something about this, or what?"

"Ellie! Help me, Ellie!" the thing called out, then screamed in primal frustration.

The automated pool cleaner, which scrubbed the plastic pool liner as it rolled along the bottom, chose that moment for its long water spout tail to breach the surface and spray loudly against the metal rails that ran along the edge of the structure. It startled her so badly, she let out a yip of surprise before covering her mouth. Not waiting to see if her outburst had caught the thing's attention, Ellie pressed herself, shivering, against the wall of the pool, hiding her head from sight by lowering herself so much that only her nose rose above the surface.

Sure enough, the sound of the thing tearing its way through her house reached her. Ellie knew it had heard her. With sheer will, she calmed her heart as she took three consecutive breaths, each one bigger than the last, then slipped under the surface just as it tore through the ruins of her back door.

Ellie positioned herself in the darkest corner of the pool and hid behind the ladder, once again using it to anchor her body near the bottom. She vowed not to surface, not to give in. She wasn't weak. She never had been.

Closing her eyes, Ellie blocked out all external stimuli. Though she pressed the button to start her stopwatch, she didn't bother looking at it. In her mind, she pretended she was in her warm bed instead of this icy feeding trough. She willed her body to warm, and though she knew that to be impossible, felt the heat just the same. The surface of the water became a flurry of splashing. This time, the beast knew instead of just suspected someone was in the pool.

A quick glance to make sure her body was positioned as close to the bottom as possible revealed frothy water above, now pink where the thing reached in. Blood... so much blood. Her parents...

Fury replaced anger, and the heat of it pushed away the cold surrounding her. Once again, she closed her eyes and focused on becoming small... becoming insignificant... becoming nothing. She blocked out the sounds of splashing and the vibrations that travelled through the frame of the pool.

Ellie remained in this state of semi-existence for who knew how long. She wanted to look at her watch, but instinct told her that would be a mistake. Even when the pool ladder was violently yanked out of the water, she commanded her heart to maintain its slow rhythm. Even when the thing banged against the side of the wall and she heard water pouring onto the yard, she stayed still. Even when something scraped against her leg, producing a white fire of agony, she stayed calm. To give in to fear was death. Rage was life.

With a gentle push of her legs, she propelled herself towards the centre of the pool. What did it matter that this took her out of the shadows? The thing knew she was here anyway. At least now, she was beyond its reach. At least until it decided to jump in, or all the water drained from the holes it had made in the side.

"Ellie!" it shrieked when it saw her. The frenzied splashing intensified. Even under the water, she could hear the triumph in its voice. It knew it had her. "Help, Ellie!"

Above all the thrashing, the banging, the mimicked calls, something else wailed rhythmically. Ellie realised with relief that it was the siren of their home alarm system. While her parents hadn't yet turned on the door alarms, every bedroom window was equipped with a break detection device. When this thing had smashed her window, ADT had been alerted. They would have called the home phone immediately, and having not received an answer, should have called the police.

Ellie had a new goal, something tangible: hold her breath until the police came. But how long would that be? Five minutes if she was lucky – more likely ten. Nobody could hold their breath that long – well, maybe free divers. But she was no free diver. A quick look at her watch surprised her: two minutes and forty-six seconds. And yet, she was holding off the desire to surface. Perhaps she could pop up and get a quick lungful...

Determined to survive, Ellie glanced up into the pink churning mess of the pool's surface. The thing had ridiculously long arms. They reminded her of the giraffes at the zoo. But at the ends, instead of hooves, it had oversized hands – black and somehow human-like, though the fingers looked at least a foot long and were tipped with curved claws. These appendages shot down into the water at such speed, it was difficult for her to make out too many details.

With a deep mental breath, Ellie shot up to the surface near the edge of the pool away from the beast. Luckily for her, Dad had splurged and gone with a thirty-three-foot diameter – the largest non-custom size available. Popping up above the water, Ellie gasped, trying to take in as much oxygen as possible. Just as her eyes cleared from the chlorinated water, she saw the beast loping around the side of the pool. She also heard a second wail, that of a police cruiser. But it sounded so far away!

The beast moved. It was fast! Too fast!

Diving back under, Ellie was a tad too slow and felt her scalp open up as a claw lashed out, just missing a handful of her hair. The briefest glance at the thing proved her right. It wasn't natural.

It was a towering nightmare, over ten feet of emaciated horror, its skin like frostbitten bark stretched over writhing bones. Jagged, bone-white antlers sprouted from its skull, splintered like broken branches, and its eyes – sunken pits glowing with ember-like fire – bore into her soul. A lipless gash of a mouth bared needle-sharp teeth, glinting wetly red, while matted hair trailed like decayed moss across its scalp. Claw-like fingers, unnaturally long, twitched as if tasting the air, and a stench of rotting meat and pine sap seeped from its skin.

Ellie didn't have to be a biologist to know this thing wasn't an animal. The stories of those old Indian codgers who hung out on the porches of the town's storefronts and bars came back to her. And one such tale fit: the Wendigo, an Algonquian legend of an insatiable beast that feeds on human flesh. Some say that Wendigos are tied to starvation and cannibalism. Others say they are the twisted souls of those who die lost in the woods, and who come back to seek revenge on those who did not rescue them.

But Ellie knew in her heart this thing wasn't her brother. Tim was kind and gentle, and he loved her. He was the one thing she ever cared about – the one thing she'd felt a sense of protection for. No, this thing, using her brother's voice, had been the *cause* of his death. And with that knowledge, her fury grew. No longer did she want the police to distract it, or even scare it away. She wanted blood. And if it didn't bleed, then she would find a way to tear it to pieces.

As she began forming a plan, the Wendigo screeched again, a terrible cry that split the night, and then its arms lifted from the pool and its shadow disappeared. Ellie waited a few seconds before surfacing.

The thing was loping away, now running from the growing sound of the police cars. No… she wouldn't let it get away! Looking around for a weapon, she grabbed the floating chlorine basket and, with all her strength, launched it at the beast with a curse. It struck the thing squarely in the back, stopping the monster short.

It turned its head at an impossible angle, looking 180 degrees behind its body at her. Though its eyes were impossible to read, Ellie was certain her hubris had rooted it in shock. But the sirens, still distant, continued to grow. Turning back to the forest, it took a step.

She was not going to let it leave. It had killed, likely eaten, her entire family. Tonight it would finish off the last of them, or die trying. Ellie intended the latter.

"Here I am!" she screamed at it, splashing water that fell far short. "You don't scare me! Fuck you!" she bellowed, moving to the forest side of the pool and making herself a reachable target. "Come get me!"

The Wendigo stopped and turned to face her. Its head rotated, staring at her in curiosity as some dogs will do. When she reached the very edge of the pool, Ellie reared back and splashed with all her might. Though even this fell short, the aggressive act angered the beast. Faster than even she expected, the thing ate up the hundred or so feet between them in no time.

But Ellie was ready. She had practised countless times launching herself off the edge of the pool to simulate laps during school swim meets. Fast as she could, she dove to the other side. Even so, her left foot erupted in flame as a single claw raked open a long gash that ran from her ankle to the webbing between her toes. Instead of diving under, however, she continued to provoke the monster.

"Come on, asshole! Come get me! I'm right here! Are you gonna let a little water slow you down?" She splashed it in the face.

It issued a roar that made visible vibrations in the surface of the water. The smell of blood and rot buffeted her face, and she almost vomited. Again, she splashed it. This wasn't just pointless taunting, for an idea had popped into her head.

And then, it lifted one spindly rear leg and put it in the water. Good. It had taken the bait.

"That's right, you ugly bastard! Come get me! I'm just a little helpless girl!" Ellie splashed it once more and inched to the opposite side of the pool where the large cylinder of the filtration system sat.

"Ellie!" it bellowed as it lifted the other leg. "Help me, Ellie!"

"You killed my family. I'm not helping you with shit!"

Just as the Wendigo adjusted its stance in the water, Ellie jumped over the rail and fished in the dark near the pumping equipment. It was here… she knew it was here.

The entire pool bulged as the thing moved through the water towards her.

Shit, shit, shit!

And then her hand found it, the panel that powered the filtration system, complete with heavy-duty extension cord that ran from the electrical box that stuck out of the ground. There was a bread-tie her father had used to cinch up the excess extension cord, but she yanked it free and stretched it out over the water.

Rot. Stinking putrescence wafted from where the monster leaned down at her, mere feet away.

"Ellie…" it said, almost a whisper now. Its breath was death. Its eyes, the grave. "Help…"

"Burn," she growled through grinding teeth, and dropped the cord into the water.

The effect was more than satisfying.

The thing stiffened, standing bolt upright on its long limbs. It towered over her, easily twice the height of an average man. A low keening moan escaped its mouth as it vibrated from the voltage running through the water.

Over by the house, the floodlight dimmed and flickered as an excess of power ran through the system. Seconds later, Ellie heard a sharp click near the electrical box, and at the same time, the Wendigo fell like a stone into the water. But it wasn't dead, for it struggled to regain its footing.

Reaching over, she pushed the reset button on the GFI box, once again powering the extension cord. She was careful only to touch the small plastic button and not any metal on the box.

Looking down into the shallow depths, she saw that their roles had reversed. She was now the predator and it was the prey. It stared up at her, bucking wildly in the dark water. Now, the sound of police sirens blared. They had to be coming up Cotton Road now, no more than a minute or two away.

"Ellie..." the voice bubbled up, modulated by the water. "Ellie... help me!"

She would help it alright. Running to the fire pit, she grabbed the small one-gallon can of gas her father used to burn some of the brush piles he cut down around the property. Next to it was a box of matches. Yes!

By the time she got back to the pool, the GFI had shut off again, and the monster had just managed to lift its head above the surface.

"I don't think so," she said, pressing the button again and watching with grim delight as it sank back down.

Ellie hoped the voltage wouldn't prematurely light the gas, but she didn't have any other option, so she took off the cap and poured it into the water above the beast. Soon, the surface became iridescent as the fuel floated on top of it.

With damp hands, Ellie opened the matchbox and fished out three matches. She was careful not to get the striker wet. The first wouldn't light at all, and the second only flashed briefly before going out.

Click.

The power had gone out, but she didn't bother. With a flick of her wrist, the third match caught and stayed.

Even when the monster rose from the water, she ignored it, shielding the glowing match from the night breeze, giving it time to climb up the stem. Even when the thing hissed at her, now able to move its limbs, she allowed the match to burn.

Even when it spoke with its own true voice – a hollow sound filled with the screams of its previous victims, "Die!" – she still held the match.

Ellie's eyes rose to look at this creature from legend, its tattered hide dripping with water and fuel.

"You first," she spat, and tossed the match.

The Wendigo lit up like the world's ugliest Christmas tree. Its scream made Ellie cover her ears.

"The fuck is that?" came the shocked curse of one of the police officers, who had just rounded the side of the house. She turned and watched their wide, horrified eyes as the two men pointed their guns at the fiery demon.

A slash of pain knocked her to the ground just before the night was pierced with the sound of gunfire. Ellie rolled over, breathing fast from the claw wound on her back. She saw the Wendigo flinch briefly from the shots, but, as with her father's shotgun, bullets didn't do much to it.

Fire, on the other hand…

It tried diving under the water, but that only served to spread even more burning fuel upon its body. With a terrible thrash, it knocked down the far side of the pool, sending a tidal wave of burning water across the lawn and setting the first trees of the forest alight.

With a grim smile, Ellie watched the thing stumble through the burning brush. Its flaming antlers reminded her of her friend Opa's family menorah, and she cackled with laughter despite the hot blood running down her torn back.

One of the police officers frantically radioed for the emergency forest fire department, while the other helped Ellie to her feet and moved her away from the fire.

They all watched from a safe distance as the Wendigo, now crawling on hands and knees, collapsed to the ground, engulfed in the flames of nearby trees. Before their very eyes, it fell apart; its skull rolling to the side, while the tattered hide disintegrated. The long bones of its arms and legs shattered with four audible pops.

"There's blood inside," the officer helping her said, looking into the smashed back door. "Quick, let's get her to the car and wait for backup."

As they led her away, Ellie's eyes never left the smouldering corpse. And she didn't stop laughing until the meds given her by the ambulance team kicked in. Before she closed her eyes, Ellie glanced at her watch. The time read ten minutes, four seconds. Her entire life had changed in less than a quarter hour – a baptism of water, of blood, *of her first kill.*

In the following weeks, she would have plenty of time to think about that night. Despite her statement – and those of the two officers – the case remained open, the deaths ruled as a wild animal attack. By the time firefighters contained the blaze, the body had burned to ash, and more than a hundred acres were gone.

Ellie knew one thing, though: she had come out of that water changed. The pool hadn't just cleansed her; it had *revealed* her. She no longer cared about swim meets or veterinary school. Those dreams belonged to the girl who hadn't yet gone under.

What rose instead was something older. Sharper. Free of guilt, free of family, free of fear.

There were others out there. She could feel it in her bones – the stories whispered by the old Algonquian men weren't myths at all, but maps. Maybe it was time to brush up on their language, to learn the secrets of what their people knew prowled the night. Secrets… and more importantly, vulnerabilities.

Because there was one truth that night had taught her: even devils had their weak spots.

Monsters were real. Oh, yes. Where there was one, there would certainly be more.

And who was better suited to killing monsters than a monster?

WATERLOO TEETH

Laura Purcell

1815

Buzzards circled high in the sky. Wraiths of smoke reached towards them. The artillery had fallen silent hours ago, but the stench of gunpowder lingered. Simmering beneath it were higher, riper scents: decay and a copper tang of blood. Silas pulled up the hood of his cloak. In his line of work, he couldn't afford to be squeamish about smells.

He picked his way across the torn-up landscape of churned earth and cannon-ball craters. He had to go carefully. Even the level ground was treacherous, with spent cartridges rolling underfoot. Others had beaten him to the richest pickings – pocket watches, medals and signet rings – but that didn't signify. Corpses attracted thieves in the same way they drew maggots and carrion birds. The spoils Silas sought were far more intimate, and consequently harder to take.

Soldiers lay scattered about like abandoned marionettes, some missing limbs, their once colourful coats rolled in dirt. Most of the wounded had been dragged away by their comrades, but a few unfortunates remained. Men too far gone to rescue, and shattered horses, pleading for help or death.

Silas knelt beside a corpse still wearing a shako helmet. The chin-strap held the jaw together. Carefully, Silas removed the helmet and prised open the darkened lips.

The corpse seemed to snarl, baring its teeth as an animal would. Sharp, clean canines rimmed in red. Slanted lower incisors. This was a good one. Saliva stringed as Silas hinged the jaw, revealing two coal black molars squatting at the back of the mouth. *They* were a loss, but the rest of the teeth would fetch him something.

Reaching for his dental key, Silas hooked the claw of the contraption over the crown of the dead man's whitest tooth and started to turn it. The hush of the battlefield amplified the sounds the key made: squelching, grinding, a few gentle cracks. Reluctantly, the tooth began to move. The soldier could no longer feel pain, yet there was something in the glazed eyes and grimacing lips which suggested suffering.

Crows settled around Silas, chipping away at the corpses too, wasting nothing, salvaging piece by piece.

When Silas's pouch was finally full, he leant back on his haunches and examined the plundered mouth. The soldier's face was set in a rictus of outrage. Although Silas tried to close the jaw, it refused to stay shut. The soldier glared at him with unblinking eyes, as if he would never forgive.

Sighing, Silas rose to his feet. A crow swooped in, starting to feast with a terrible wet sound as the tooth-thief moved on towards his next victim.

★ ★ ★

Tap, tap, tap.

Jimmy didn't lift his weary head from the pillow. Sleeping as he did on a pallet in a downstairs corridor, he heard plenty of strange sounds. People on the busy street outside, the clop of heels, the roll of wagon wheels. Even the building itself played its own discordant music of creaks and pops, along with rodents scuttling in the walls. Loudest of all were the snores of the maid, Sukie, who slept in the kitchen nearby.

Tap, tap.

He was awake now, but sleep was a precious commodity in his twelve-year-old world. Hours of tedious work lay ahead: sweeping the shop, mixing the tinctures, polishing up the old barber's chair. He wasn't going to open his eyes a minute before he absolutely needed to. He pulled the sheet over his head.

Bang, bang, bang.

"Oi!"

Jimmy flinched as Sukie snorted awake in the kitchen. "What the bloody hell was that?" Her words, still heavy from sleep, slurred into one another.

Groaning, Jimmy threw off his cover and admitted defeat. The sound was coming from the back door, the delivery door. Dealing with deliveries was one of his many, many tasks as an apprentice.

Stumbling up, he made his way barefoot and drew the bolts. Chill air stole across the threshold as he opened up to a dull, milky dawn. Two shifty-looking men stood in the street with a pair of hooped barrels. One sported a beard, the other a scar across his cheek. They were dressed much like his da, in plain caps and shapeless coats, but their faces were wholly different. Something pinched, sharp and hungry lingered there.

"About time! Do you think we've got all bleeding day?"

The day hadn't even started yet, they were practically delivering under the cover of night, but Jimmy had learned to keep such retorts to himself. At best, they only earned him a clip around the ear.

"Sorry, sir."

"You will be, if you don't get these inside sharpish." The bearded man thrust a barrel into Jimmy's arms. He sagged under the unexpected weight. "That's one. The other's just there." He kicked a boot against the second barrel. "Can you see to that yourself?"

Hooves sounded in the distance. The scarred man glanced furtively about. "He'll have to. We're leaving. Now."

His companion nodded, and before Jimmy had a chance to gather his wits they were off, slipping noiselessly into the shadows and smog.

He set the barrel down on the floorboards beside him. It rattled. Frowning, he stepped outside and retrieved the second one, recognising the same sound within. Shifting, clicking. Shingle lapped by the tide.

It wasn't difficult to lift; the weight he'd felt must have been the wooden barrel itself and its metal hoops. Still, cradling the load gave Jimmy a strange sensation, something he couldn't put into words. He was relieved to place it beside its twin in the corridor and shut the street door behind him.

"What've you got?"

Turning, he saw Sukie's freckled face, illuminated from beneath by a strip of tallow. Her hair was tangled in a clump on one side. The maid was three years older than him, the same age as his sister, but much gawkier with it.

"I don't know. There's no markings on the barrels."

"Deliveries usually come in crates," she frowned.

"Maybe this is something new." He couldn't think what, though. Liquids were stored in barrels, not light, jangling objects. It was almost like those men had tried to conceal what was truly inside.

Sukie wavered. "Should we... open them up? Take a look?"

On a normal day he'd be tempted. But Jimmy still had that sense of unease, a crawling sensation upon his skin.

"Best not," he said. "Let's wait for Mr. Thorpe."

They were both dressed and Sukie was half way through making the breakfast before their master descended from his living quarters upstairs. He clapped his hands in delight.

"Ah!" he cried. "They're here! Jim, come on through to the shop. I want to get started on these right away."

Reluctantly, Jimmy quit the warmth of the kitchen and dawdled out into the corridor. Mr. Thorpe was already carrying the barrels, one under each arm, through to the front of the house.

The 'shop', as they called the working space, was a large square area, well-lit by a row of tall windows looking onto the street. Herbs hung above the counter and filled the store room behind it with a green, medicinal scent. Jimmy was still learning all of their names, but he knew ginger and Spanish chamomile went into the tinctures he mixed for toothache.

An old barber's chair occupied pride of place in the middle of the floor. Made of dark wood with absolutely no padding, it resembled an instrument of torture. In a way, it was. Yet for some reason customers felt more confident having their teeth drawn while sitting in an old-style chair, as if tradition could overcome their pain.

To the right stretched two rows of shelves. In his mind, Jimmy called them 'the shelves of disembodied screams'. They were packed with sets of false teeth, but without a mouth to hold the tension, the sprung hinges of the dentures fell slack, creating gaping expressions.

Mr. Thorpe already had one of the barrels upon the counter and was prising it open with a crowbar. "Wait until you see these," he enthused. "They're going to make our fortune."

Curious, Jimmy approached. "What are they? I didn't have to sign anything when they arrived. And did you pay for them already, Mr. Thorpe? I didn't see any entries in the ledger."

"It's best not to leave a trail for some things, Jim. It avoids awkward questions at a later date."

Before Jimmy could interrogate this further, the head hoop came off and Mr. Thorpe started to remove the barrel lid. A rugged, uneven mass lay inside, something like fragments of chalk, varying through shades of pure white to butter yellow. Jimmy stood on tiptoes to see.

"It's just teeth?" He felt a thud of disappointment. "Why would *you* need a barrel of teeth, Mr. Thorpe? You pull some out every day."

His master picked up a handful, letting them run through his fingers and rattle back down. His cheeks were flushed; he looked like it was Christmas day. "The rotten teeth I pull are fit for nothing, they aren't like these beauties." He nodded over to the denture display. "We're getting nowhere selling those ugly wooden gnashers, and the porcelain ones crack. But these look like the real thing."

To Jimmy they looked like an endless maw, like a nightmare he might dream on his pallet bed. You rarely saw so many teeth all bunched together like this. The effect was uncanny. "So they're for the dentures? Where do they come from, sir? Animals?"

"No, no. That's the best part." Mr. Thorpe pinched an ivory canine between his thumb and index finger, holding it up to the light. "They *are* the real thing. Taken fresh from the mouths of the soldiers who fell at Waterloo."

Jimmy shuddered. He'd seen horror enough in this trade, he didn't know why grave-robbing should shock him more than all the rest, but it did. Especially when it came to Waterloo. Talk of the battle was all over town, the papers full of obituaries and tales of derring-do.

"Are we allowed to just… take their teeth?"

"They aren't using them, are they?" Mr. Thorpe threw the canine back down with a chink. His grin turned Jimmy's stomach. "Imagine how many of these we'll shift on sentiment alone! With the fashion as it is, these things will practically sell themselves. The gents will pay extra to bear the smile of a British trooper. And the women… well, we'll tell them they're wearing the teeth of a dashing French lieutenant, tragically cut down in his prime."

Jimmy gaped, unable to believe his ears. "Weren't they… heroes? Shouldn't we… I don't know. Bury them with honours or something?"

Mr. Thorpe smirked. "You're young, Jimmy. You don't know the way of the world. Mark my words, the poor blighters who gave these teeth are rotting out in the open field with no one to claim them. *That's* how a country really treats its heroes. Once you've served your purpose,

His Majesty no longer cares about you. But at least we can make a pretty penny. Then their sacrifice won't have been for nothing, eh?"

It hardly seemed fair, but Jimmy wasn't in a position to argue. He knew his place.

The next hour was spent helping Mr. Thorpe pick through the collection and arrange them into passable sets. A short break for breakfast only made Jimmy uncomfortably aware of his own teeth as they chewed. Was what Mr. Thorpe said true? Would people really pay extra to wear morbid dentures?

He returned to his work. The hodgepodge was neatly sorted into piles now, ready to be drilled. The colours and sizes he'd put together were similar, but not an exact match. They didn't *belong* like this. Wearing the teeth of one dead man would be bad enough, but with such an assortment, customers might be taking home parts of a whole platoon.

Mr. Thorpe bored holes with the hand drill. Jimmy's task was threading the finished pieces onto a length of wire in the correct order. They looked like clothes pegs with their long, white roots. Once it was done, Mr. Thorpe fixed them into lead bases.

Men were beginning to light the lamps in the street outside. The shop had been closed all day, the sign turned on the door, not a single tooth pulled. But Mr. Thorpe seemed to consider their time well spent.

The dentist stood back and fisted his hands upon his hips to admire the new display. Pride shone on his ruddy face, making him look younger.

"Beautiful," he declared.

It wasn't. The teeth gleamed, grimaces without a face.

Couldn't Mr. Thorpe feel the strange tension that had entered his shop? That sense of fury, abiding?

He clapped his hands together, as he had in the morning. "I'll draw up a sign and put it in the window. News will travel fast. Go get yourself some food and then we'll shut up for the night, Jim. Tomorrow is going to be a busy, busy day."

* * *

Jimmy dreamed of the battlefield that night. He knew it was Waterloo, as one *did* know these things in a dream, but he saw no distinct landmarks.

Everything was wreathed in grey smoke, which stuck to the back of his throat with a sulphurous taste.

A gun popped in the distance. Light flashed and a cannon boomed. Jimmy cast about, afraid of being shot, but he only saw smoke, moving, restless, like a living thing, as the gunfire played its deadly percussion.

Gradually, the clouds began to resemble shapes; here an arm, there a wispy leg. Jimmy watched, appalled, as human forms resolved out of the mist. Men with sunken cheeks and shadows dripping from their chins like blood. The soldiers whose teeth had been stolen.

Mutely, they advanced. Jimmy backed up, but there was nowhere to turn, no break in the smoke. Insubstantial hands reached out for him. One man threw back his head in a silent scream, showing the great yawning space where his teeth had been wrenched out.

Still the smoke drifted, cold and clammy across Jimmy's face. It was taking on a texture, a strength. Bitter tendrils teased at his lips, working their way inside his mouth and flooding it with bitterness.

He tried to cry out, but the smoke gagged him. Pain shot through his gums and his jaw as something began to tug. They wanted his teeth. They wanted his teeth in place of their own.

Abruptly, the scene dissolved. Jimmy slammed back onto his pallet in the corridor, curled into a ball. A foul flavour coated his tongue, but that was not what had caused him to wake up. It was the sound, pulsing with the same rhythm as the gunfire in his dream.

Click. Click, click.

His befuddled mind travelled back to the previous day, when he'd been awoken by a tapping at the door. This noise was different. Less hollow than a knock, more like a fingernail chinking against a glass. Slow. Decided.

Click. Click.

Wary, still shaken by his dream, Jimmy struggled up onto his elbows and listened. The clicking seemed to be coming from the opposite direction to the tapping yesterday – from the door which led into the shop.

Click click click, click click click.

The tempo had increased along with the urgency.

Throwing back the cover, Jimmy rose from his bed. Gooseflesh spiked on the back of his neck. The corridor felt colder than it had when he'd tucked himself into bed. He worried a thief might have broken the shop windows. After all, Mr. Thorpe had put out a sign advertising the costly dentures within…

Click click click click.

He should fetch the master. Yet instead he crept forward, in thrall to the sound.

Click click click.

Holding his breath, he opened the door to the shop.

The chattering stopped.

Jimmy blinked. One of the window shutters hung open. Streetlight puddled onto the stained floorboards around the barber's chair. There was no broken glass. No movement at all. Nobody had forced their way inside. There was just the shutter, folded back.

But he remembered securing it tightly before he went to bed.

The silence was somehow worse than the clicking noise. Although Jimmy saw no one on the street outside, he had the uncomfortable feeling of being watched.

Mustering his courage, he crossed the shop floor. He'd just drawn level with the barber's chair when the sound exploded like a thunderclap in the hush.

Click.

Jimmy spun to the right. There was nothing different about the denture display there, nothing that might have made a click; only the teeth, ghostly in the gloom.

With his pulse pounding in his throat, he turned back to the window and started to pull the shutter.

Click click click click.

His head whipped over his shoulder again. What he saw defied all logic. Four sets of dentures on the display had clamped themselves shut and grinned back at him.

Trembling, he stole closer to take a look. Were they… broken? Reaching out, he prodded the nearest denture set with the tip of his finger. It sprang open at once. Jimmy gasped, drawing his hand back.

"What on earth…"

Without warning, the teeth snapped shut again like a trap. There was a decided *click* as tooth knocked against tooth.

That was the sound he'd been hearing: dead men's teeth, opening and closing by themselves. Biting. Hungry for the life they'd left behind.

Jimmy spun on his heel and ran out of the shop, slamming the door behind him.

★ ★ ★

They were selling like hot cakes.

Jimmy stood gritty-eyed behind the counter, grinding tinctures with his pestle and mortar, while Mr. Thorpe ushered customer after customer over to the macabre display and spun them a tale.

"This brave captain died saving his brother-in-arms," the dentist said.

A lady with snowy curls edging around the rim of her bonnet took a set of dentures off the shelf to examine. She worked the sprung hinges, fascinated. "Poor soul," she lisped. "His teeth deserve a dignified mouth."

"Quite so, Mrs. Upton. Between you and me, I wouldn't let them go to just anyone who walked in off the street. But a lady of quality, like yourself, could give them a proper home."

Jimmy ran his tongue around his own gums and pressed down upon the ginger root in his bowl. How was it that nobody shared his qualms about taking dead men's teeth? They all seemed delighted, not horrified, to be wearing parts of a corpse.

Over by the display, Mrs. Upton parted her moist lips and slipped the dentures inside to try them for size. Mr. Thorpe presented her with a small hand mirror. Her reflection smiled, false and brilliant, a lunatic's beam.

"Stunning," Mr. Thorpe simpered. "They take ten years from you, madam."

Jimmy kept expecting the teeth to snap or gnash, to show some sign of their crazed behaviour from last night. He felt like he was going mad. It *couldn't* have been just a bad dream. Even by daylight there was that same pressure in the air, that same prickling anger lingering over the display. Every time he looked at it, his mouth filled with bile, the sour taste from the nightmare.

Wiping off the dentures on a handkerchief, Mr. Thorpe approached the counter. He placed the set of Waterloo teeth into a small box and tied it with ribbon.

"Do you wish the bill to be sent to you, madam?"

"Please. It will be settled at the end of the month."

Jimmy watched Mr. Thorpe pick up a quill and write the astronomical sum of fifty pounds into his ledger. That was more than Ma and Da had paid for his apprenticeship here.

Jimmy waited until the shop door tinkled closed behind Mrs. Upton before he ventured a word. "Sir..."

Mr. Thorpe tapped his fingers upon the ledger, satisfaction glowing from his face. "Didn't I tell you, Jim? That's four sets already. We'll be rich as Croesus by the end of the week."

"But something's wrong. With the Waterloo teeth."

Mr. Thorpe glanced up, alarmed. "Whatever do you mean?"

Jimmy didn't have the words to explain properly, but he had to try, he had to say something. "Last night they were... closing. On their own."

"That's simply not possible. You must have dreamt it."

"No, I didn't. At first I thought maybe the springs—"

The bell tinkled over the shop door, cutting him off.

Three top-hatted gentlemen sauntered inside. Mr. Thorpe's scowl smoothed rapidly into an expression of charm and good humour. "Gentlemen, how may I help you?"

Disconsolate, Jimmy returned to grinding his ginger. He was horribly conscious of the display opposite him while he worked. That feeling of being watched – although teeth couldn't *possibly* watch, could they?

* * *

He awoke to blood on his pillow. A splash of crimson, shocking to his bleary eyes. For a moment he just lay there, stunned. Something warm and wet oozed from the side of his lips. Jimmy wiped his mouth, swallowed a sickly sour taste. It hurt.

Fighting panic, he slipped an index finger between his lips and probed the throbbing area. One of his premolar teeth shifted beneath his touch.

That shouldn't be happening. He had all his adult teeth now and he took care of his dental hygiene, brushing each night with a badger-hair brush and tooth powder as Mr. Thorpe had taught him. But now there was something else that happened each night: he dreamed of soldiers, pulling at his jaw.

It couldn't possibly be related... could it?

A shriek sounded behind him. Starting up, he saw Sukie at the kitchen door, a shawl pulled over her nightdress. Her face was as white as a sheet.

"Blast me, I thought you'd been killed!" she cried. "What happened to you?"

Mr. Thorpe's footsteps sounded on the stairs. Before Jimmy had time to gather his wits, the master was upon them.

"Who screamed?" he demanded. The tassel of his nightcap flicked as he turned between Sukie and Jimmy. "Where did this blood come from?"

Jimmy clutched at his cheek, hoping somehow to hide his predicament. He didn't want to get into trouble – Mr. Thorpe insisted on his employees bearing perfect smiles.

"What have you done, Jim?"

"Nothing, sir."

"It doesn't look like nothing." He frowned. "Did you get in a fight with another boy? Did somebody break your teeth?" Jimmy shook his head vehemently, not daring to speak in case he dribbled blood. "Come and sit in the chair, let me take a look."

Reluctantly, Jimmy obeyed and followed him through to the shop. Early morning sun fell through the slats in the window shutters. Mr. Thorpe drew the bolts and pulled one slightly open, casting a spotlight on the high-backed barber's chair.

It creaked under Jimmy as he climbed up. The seat tilted him backwards with the head rest pressing hard at the nape of his neck. The thick wooden arms seemed to hem him in.

The Waterloo teeth grinned on mockingly from their shelf, as if this amused them.

Mr. Thorpe loomed over him. "Open your mouth." He did. Mr. Thorpe wrinkled his nose, poking and prodding. "The teeth themselves are healthy, but the gums…" He exhaled heavily, his hot breath washing over Jimmy's face. "How have you done this, Jim? You haven't been trying to practise dentistry on yourself, have you?"

"No, sir. I don't know how it happened. I just… woke up like this."

He could see that Mr. Thorpe didn't believe him. The dentist began to pack Jimmy's wound with gauze. "You'll have to keep your mouth shut today. It wouldn't do, to have my apprentice bleeding all over the counter. People would stop trusting me."

"Yes, Mr. Thorpe," he said thickly.

"And if you want to try drawing teeth, you've only to ask me. There's no need to butcher yourself like this."

"I didn't."

"So you say. But these gums are torn and scratched, like someone has been trying to…" Mr. Thorpe broke off with a troubled expression. For the first time, Jimmy noticed the dark marks beneath his eyes.

Like Jimmy, Mr. Thorpe had been working long hours to sell the Waterloo teeth, charming customers left and right, keeping the shop open past its usual times. But now Jimmy wondered if there was more behind his employer's tired appearance. Perhaps he wasn't the only one hearing noises and dreaming dreams.

"I… see them at night," Jimmy admitted quietly. Mr. Thorpe froze in place, a piece of gauze still in hand. "Soldiers. They're angry. They want their teeth back." Still Mr. Thorpe did not move. "I thought it was a nightmare," Jimmy hurried on, "but maybe… My gums… Do you think…?"

Mr. Thorpe shook himself back into action. "Well, that *might* explain this mess. You are acting out the dream without being aware of your actions. In your sleep, you are clawing at your gums."

But if that were the case, wouldn't there be blood on his hands and under his nails?

"How many Waterloo teeth are left now, sir?"

"Not many. Of those you see on the display, half are spoken for. I'm going to box them up this morning." Inserting the final wad into Jimmy's mouth, he stepped away from the chair and rinsed his hands in a bowl of water.

Jimmy sat upright, feeling like a stuffed turkey. The gauze was so dry it made him want to retch, and it was worse when he spoke. But he had to speak. He couldn't keep this all bottled inside.

"Have any of the customers… said anything? About the teeth being odd?"

"Odd how?" He noticed Mr. Thorpe was not looking directly at him as he dried his hands upon an apron.

"Sometimes, at night, I hear them chink… like coins. Opening and closing. I told you, didn't I, sir, that I saw that set shut all by itself?"

Mr. Thorpe heaved a deep sigh. "You did, Jim. But I think all this talk of soldiers and death has upset you. You're letting it prey upon your mind. Come, now. You're doing a man's job and it's time you put these childish ways behind you. You have to grow up. You wouldn't want me to send you back to your parents, would you?"

Jimmy trembled, aghast to think of how disappointed Ma would be and how much money Da had spent to get him this position in the first place.

"You've been doing so well up until now. I am hoping that once all these dentures are sold, you'll return to rationality."

Was it simply his imagination? Jimmy couldn't believe that. He'd never been given to extreme flights of fancy before. "I'm sorry, sir. I'm not trying to be difficult. It just… It feels very real. When I had that dream, I honestly thought the soldiers who lost their teeth wanted to punish me."

Mr. Thorpe regarded him from behind the counter. Jimmy couldn't define the expression in his eyes. Pity and sorrow were there, but so was something else. A hard glint like fear. "Punish *you*, Jimmy? Whatever for? Even the logic of your fantasy is at fault." Mr. Thorpe adjusted the angle of the ledger and moved the weighing scales, even though everything had been left neat and spotless the night before. "If there really were ghosts seeking revenge, they wouldn't come after you, would they? They would go for the person who interfered with their corpses. Or," he added, his voice purposefully calm, artificially casual, "for me. I am the one who has seen the profit, after all."

Jimmy's heart throbbed. His master had given himself away. He would bet his life that profit was not the only thing Mr. Thorpe had seen since the teeth arrived. He was being haunted too. But before Jimmy could ask questions, before they could have a proper conversation about what was happening to them, Mr. Thorpe abruptly quitted the shop and mounted the stairs back to his living quarters.

★ ★ ★

A deep chill had taken residence inside the shop. Jimmy balled his hands into fists, trying his best not to shiver; he wanted Sukie to see him as a man. But if he was alone, he would have been trembling long before now.

The corners were dark and the shadows stretched. His candle gilded the counter, which they both leant against, and allowed them to watch the display. Only a few sets of dentures remained upon the shelves. Somehow that was worse than the whole, grinning collection. Jimmy could study each tooth individually, make out the stains and uneven edges. All the canines looked sharper than he remembered them being this morning. More like fangs.

The candle flame swayed without a breeze. When Sukie exhaled, her breath looked like smoke. "Nothing's going to happen. You're having me on."

"I'm not! I promise. This is real." The teeth taunted him, stubbornly motionless now that he had someone to convince. "I've heard them every night since they arrived."

"Well, your ghosts are too slow for me. I have to get up at five o'clock tomorrow," she yawned.

"Just wait a bit longer. Please."

Sukie wrapped her shawl tighter around her shoulders and said nothing. Whatever she decided to do, Jimmy wasn't going back to his bed. He didn't want to dream of soldiers pulling at his teeth again. He needed to keep his eyes open.

There was a smaller set of dentures to the left of the top shelf. They glowed brighter than the rest: clean, pure and ethereal. Looking at them made Jimmy think of teething babies. He'd always imagined soldiers as muscular, grown men with mustachios, but he realised now that wasn't necessarily accurate. Some of the infantry who died at Waterloo would have been young men. Maybe only a few years older than himself.

Suddenly, something dropped to the floor. Sukie gave a start beside him.

He hadn't seen what fell, he'd been too focused upon the top shelf. But his blood chilled as the air rang with a familiar sound.

Click click click click.

Jimmy's gums throbbed with the same beat.

Casting his gaze to the floor, he saw a set of dentures clacking together. They inched forwards, propelled by their own motion.

Sukie's eyes met his in disbelief.

"I *told* you!"

She didn't scream as she had when she'd seen the blood. This time revulsion contorted her face. The teeth kept clicking, working their way slowly towards the counter. Jimmy swallowed. He'd never seen them move like this before.

"No," Sukie breathed. She seemed to be taking the sight of these teeth as a personal affront. "No, I won't have it."

Before Jimmy could stop her, she strode out from behind the counter and booted the dentures as hard as she could.

They flew across the floor. There was a crack as they collided hard with the wall and snapped into two separate pieces. The plates fell lifeless. But there was no pause, no intermission in the sound.

Click click click click.

Jimmy's eyes flew back to the depleted shelves. Nothing else moved. Whatever was making that terrible noise, it wasn't the Waterloo teeth, not now.

Click click click.

"I think it's coming from outside." Sukie moved to the window. Wood creaked a high note as she slid the bolts and began to fold the shutters back.

"Sukie, don't, we should go and fetch—" He stopped, his breath suspended.

A woman's face appeared behind the glass. Hair hung lank around her shoulders, pale as bone in the moonlight. Like Sukie, she wore only a nightgown. No expression animated her features. Unblinking eyes stared forward, apparently seeing nothing, as her teeth clacked together.

Sukie recoiled. "Who is *that*?"

"It's Mrs. Upton," he gasped. He ventured a step forward, trying to peer out into the darkened street. "Oh, God."

Figures were massing, just like in his dream. Bare-headed customers in their nightclothes, walking as if in a trance. Some already stood sentinel around the shop, no weapons except the inexorable gnashing of their Waterloo teeth.

"What the devil is going on down here?" Mr. Thorpe's voice boomed from behind them.

Sukie scuttled towards the master. "Oh, sir! Help!"

But Mr. Thorpe could not help. He made no effort to comfort Sukie as she clung to his sleeve. Every vestige of colour drained from his cheeks as he saw the figures outside. He looked like a spirit himself, in his nightshirt and cap, a candle trembling violently in his grasp.

Click click click.

Hands began to pat at the shop door. Jimmy didn't move from behind the counter. He didn't know what to do. He could still see Mrs. Upton outside the window, her palms pressed flat against the glass. A ghostly reflection of Mr. Thorpe overlaid her and blurred the two together.

The old woman gnashed her teeth slowly, with an air of menace.

Click. Click.

At last, Mr. Thorpe spoke. "By God, Jim. You were right. They've… come back for us."

There was no satisfaction in that. He'd rather be wrong, a stupid boy suffering from nightmares.

"Make them go away!" Sukie pleaded. "What do they want from us?"

Jimmy wracked his brains. He'd thought the soldiers sought the return of their teeth, but that was impossible. Even if Mr. Thorpe could find a way to sort the dentures back into individual sets, he had no idea where the corpses were buried. Somewhere overseas, perhaps in unmarked graves.

Yet if nothing could be done to appease the soldiers, why were they back here? There must be something he could give their angry spirits. Something to make them leave.

"Sir," Jimmy stuttered. "I think… I think we need to give the customers their money back. Collect all the Waterloo teeth and… and bury them. Somewhere decent. Hallowed ground."

"We can't let them inside the shop!" Sukie protested.

But from the way the hands were clawing at the door and rattling the handle, the sleep-walking customers would soon find their own way in. It was only a matter of time.

Mr. Thorpe swallowed, drew himself up. "Yes. Maybe you're right, Jim. I'll – I'll try to make amends." He nodded at Jimmy. "You stand over here with Sukie. Keep back from the door until…" He did not finish his sentence.

"Until you've told them we'll put it right."

"No, sir. Don't do it," Sukie pleaded. "I'll run out the back door instead. I can find help. A constable."

Mrs. Upton's palms thudded against the window. A pane of glass on the shop door smashed.

Mr. Thorpe winced. "I think it's too late for that, Sukie."

Jimmy dashed from behind the counter and sped towards the maid. She grabbed for his hand without hesitation.

"Please, kindly wait there," Mr. Thorpe called to the crowd. His voice was a high, quavering thing. "The account shall be settled. Just… wait."

The patting and the clicking ceased. In their absence, Jimmy could hear his own blood roaring in his ears.

Shaking, the master paced towards the door.

There was silence now. Jimmy must have got it right. The spirits wanted the dirty profit returned and a decent burial for their remaining body parts. If Mr. Thorpe could provide that, the soldiers would leave them all alone.

Mr. Thorpe's hands fumbled with the door chain. "You can all have your money back."

Sukie flinched as he turned the locks. "I still think this is a bad idea," she whispered.

The door tinkled open.

"I am so sorry for—" Mr. Thorpe's words died in a gurgle. The bell over the door clanged wildly, a cry for help.

They were swarming into the shop. Mr. Thorpe was overpowered, carried in a wave towards the barber's chair. He thrashed and screamed as the figures in white pinned him down. One by one, they bent to sink their stolen teeth into his flesh.

Wounds that looked like shrieking lips opened in the dentist's skin.

The children stood petrified.

Still unseeing, her face as impassive as an avenging angel's, Mrs. Upton straddled her withered legs over the chair until she was sitting in Mr. Thorpe's lap. Slowly, luxuriously, she dipped her head, biting hard into his jugular.

Blood spurted in a spray. The noise was indescribable. Not just the wet squelching but the tearing of flesh as the old lady shook her head, worrying her prey like a terrier with a rat.

"Go! Go!" Sukie yanked Jimmy towards the back door, which led onto the corridor where he slept. He wanted desperately to flee with her, but he couldn't tear his eyes away from Mrs. Upton. At last the old woman drew back, leaving her dentures firmly planted in Mr. Thorpe's throat. Nausea surged.

"Come on!" Jimmy's legs finally consented to move. Sukie pulled him backwards, out of the shop, and slammed the door behind them.

They panted, clinging to one another. There were no words.

Mr. Thorpe's screams ebbed behind the closed door, growing ever weaker.

Jimmy cursed himself. He'd been so stupid to think they could appease soldiers. They were men of battle; only blood would sate them. Now Mr. Thorpe was dying and it felt like it was all his fault.

He wondered, vaguely, what had become of the people who drew the teeth from the corpses in the first place, what horrors they were suffering. Could it possibly be worse than this?

"We're leaving," Sukie decided. "We're going to my parents' house. Hurry."

Jimmy had no argument left to give.

Hand in hand with his friend, he rushed towards the back door where the doomed barrels had first arrived, only one week ago.

Together, the children ran off barefoot, into the night.

THE PASSING PLACES

Ally Wilkes

"I just don't understand, okay," Adam looks in his rear-view mirror as he reverses down the narrow lane, "why you expected to be her Maid of Honour. After so many years away."

The mirror is smudged, making him look – momentarily – like a ghoul, smeared flesh and hanging skin. Then there's sunlight through the trees again.

★ ★ ★

Rewind to a summer's day in the late Eighties.

The sky is the blue of bubblegum ice cream; the leaves shine emerald like a mallard drake. Two little girls are wearing costumes, fantasy ballgowns in white lace with frothy skirts. Tiny pearlescent beads wink toothily in the dappled light. The path through the woods is twisting, and tree branches try to grab the flower crowns right off their heads.

Those ceremonial crowns are wilting in the heat. It's the type of summer's day which feels like it might go on forever, the sort of summer's day which characterises Ketchbury Away. June reaches up to adjust her crown, catching the sharp garlic smell of Jack-by-the-Hedge, with its tiny constellations of white flowers. She'd made it carefully: garlic, of course, is protective, for honouring death. But it's also for adding one or two cloves to spaghetti sauce, which is then dusted at the table with hard smelly cheese from a cardboard shaker.

Today, the girls have an important job: to get rid of evil. To postpone – however long – the death of the village.

June and April, the last two girls, walking solemnly through the woods.

★ ★ ★

"I didn't expect anything," June says tightly, laying her elbow against hot metal. Adam always takes every opportunity to open all the doors and windows, but this time having the convertible's top down is warranted; the day is glorious, not a cloud in the sky, the air warm and hopeful. They've been driving for hours, first grey London roads with their tumble of houses and dry cleaners, then the endless swoop of the motorways, then smaller roads, backed up with end-of-school traffic. And finally, the lanes, winding so deep through the valleys, so overstretched by trees, that sunlight is hard to come by.

"Are you kidding? You've been moping ever since you got the invite. Anyone would think she was marrying your childhood sweetheart."

"I didn't have a childhood sweetheart," June retorts, although she did: it was April, always April, and when the heavy cream envelope had dropped through June's door, she'd almost had a heart attack.

The *passing places*. Her skin prickles with anticipation. It had brought back memories of another world, streaked with soil. Damp fingers. Gouges in the mud, and a makeshift rope-ladder hanging limply like a noose.

"You haven't been back in, what? Ten years and three months?" It's maddening that Adam knows this precise detail. "Babe, it's normal that you've grown apart. You left. But this will be an opportunity to reconnect."

The idea had leapt into her own mind, as she'd stared at April's handwriting. Perhaps there was the possibility of a… reconciliation.

Homecoming.

June hadn't known how much she'd longed for it.

On the back seat of the car, June's newly woven flower crown flutters in the warm breeze: ribbons and roses, for celebration. A couple of sprigs of nettle, picked from the grey hard ground outside their flat, for sacrifice. Adam had seemed keen on the idea of the wedding, a trip back to the old country, but had refused to make one of his own.

It was rather rude, June thought idly; but then, he wouldn't need it anyway.

* * *

The tangle of roads approaching the village leaves only one way to get in, and satnav is notoriously no help. June had told Adam that he'd need to rely on local signposts; there's too much metal in the earth for GPS, or something like that. The hills are too tall, blocking off the signal. They're too far from the towns.

These places haven't quite made it onto Google Earth, with their hollows and culverts and sudden, strange, monolithic stones. The fields of oilseed rape are striking, hallucinogenic: a strip of shocking yellow, then the deep green of trees and hills, then a crowning strip of blue sky. It reminds June of a fancy cocktail, the sort they won't have at the wedding; it'll be cider back in Ketchbury Away, sharp enough to make your mouth pucker, effervescent enough to make the summer days seem endless.

"Shit!" Adam swings round a blind corner and they come face-to-face with a tractor. June's jolted out of her dreaming by the smell of pig manure, and for a moment she catches a similar smell rolling off Adam: damp and sweaty, as if he'd forgotten to put on his deodorant and aftershave. She stares at him in disgust, feeling something turn over in her stomach. Then it dissipates.

The tractor is close enough for the driver to eyeball them. He's a short man with a deeply lined, suspicious-looking face. He gives them a cautious nod.

"You need to go back," June says unnecessarily. "There's a passing place—"

Adam puts his arm on the car door and reverses like a lunatic to where the lane widens, temporarily, just enough to allow two vehicles to squeeze past side by side. For a moment the backwards motion makes June sick; she can see the summer lane with its high hedges, the cloudless sky, the sprays of white flowers in the bush. But she can also see Adam, her city boyfriend. The unreal and real world colliding.

★ ★ ★

It was a strange sort of story: she'd first met him in the rain, one of those London days where the traffic's roar is muted and the windows fog up.

He'd buzzed on her door, and when she'd opened it, he'd been there – soaking. Water running down his face, dripping off his hard nose and reddish beard, trickling down his neck. There was a pipe leaking above the doorway, cackling above them like a witch, but he hadn't seemed to notice. He'd just held onto the doorframe, saying, "Oh, sorry. It's just that I—"

"Who are you?" June had asked with a nervous laugh. He was very handsome, this stranger. A bit over-familiar, perhaps, with the way he leaned in her doorway. It was as if the rain had brought him to her; as if he might disappear at any moment.

"Wrong place, see," he said, and was that a faint Welsh accent, sanded off by living in the city? "I came to visit a friend."

He must have meant the previous tenant. His clothes were new, and clean, and quite expensive, but clinging to him like a second skin. She'd laughed again, a bit unbelieving, and said, "You'd better come in."

⋆ ⋆ ⋆

Now, it's past midday, and Adam is getting frustrated that they're no closer to the village. She can read it in the clench of his hands on the wheel.

Does he seem a bit too impatient? A bit too… eager? She hasn't really seen this side of him before. He normally lets everything flow around him, does Adam. He hasn't even noticed that she's confiscated his smartphone and Apple Watch.

June stares out of the car at the whipping hedgerows, trying not to look over-keen herself. It's all as she remembers: signposts leap out unhelpfully, too late to be followed. There's elder and ash and rowan hanging over the road, and the shrill chatter of birds amongst blossom. It makes June feel an unexpected abyss of longing for Ketchbury Away, for the dying village with its boarded-up church and faded ice cream vans, the old war memorial with graffiti carved in another language entirely.

She has no idea how she'll be greeted after so long.

People don't just leave.

They find themselves at a crossroads, the engine idling. To the right, there's a field with a single skeletal scarecrow. "Hello there," Adam says, and a blackbird lands on the scarecrow's head, gives them a beady eye. It makes June's heart beat faster, because she's sure there's a look of recognition.

But that makes no sense.

To the left of the crossroads is a signpost. White weathered wood, reading: KETCHBURY AWAY, 3¼ MILE.

"Ketchbury Away?" Adam repeats.

June shrugs. "It's the village's real name," she says, like it's obvious.

"Ketchbury Away…" he repeats.

Adam has been mispronouncing the name of her hometown since they met, and it had become a stone in her shoe, too small and too deeply embedded to be worth fishing out. Now, though – she notices him saying it right.

It crawls from his mouth, somehow. Like worms.

★ ★ ★

The *passing places* lie to the west of the village. Young June and April take turns carrying the doll, which is so old that its cheeks and forehead are smooth as marzipan, and it smells of hot wax and piss. April holds it as if it's a real baby; but April has always had that streak of whatever makes little girls pretend to be mothers.

There's always that sense of certainty about her. A sense more hard-edged since her father left. June is all hesitation.

The *passing places* are in the depths of the forest, a series of vast pits, inhumanly sized. The edges are unstable, held together by cat's-tail and primrose, and invite you to peep over the edge, into the abyss of brambles and stunted trees below. It's death to go down there, because the *passing places* are so secret and so sacred. All little girls understand that.

Two weeks ago, May Jenkins had eaten water hemlock and died. They'd been in the woods playing Troy Town, and her death – along with the rest of their bad luck – is now captured inside the doll, ready to be cast safely out.

★ ★ ★

Pollen falls from the trees above, great drifts of it floating through the air. "What the fuck, babe," Adam says, more cheerfully than she expects. Is he enjoying this? "We've been driving for hours."

The signpost says: KETCHBURY AWAY, 2 MILE.

"Are we gonna be the only people at the wedding who aren't from round here?"

Probably, June thinks.

"How's anyone meant to find the bloody place?"

"Careful," June says lightly. "No one can diss the old country but me."

She waves a hand through the drifts of pollen. As if through snow, they see another car approaching, a beat-up old Volvo full of dogs. "Get to the—"

"The passing place," Adam finishes. "Yeah, yeah." And he reverses into the little layby to let the larger car inch past with a crunch of gravel. Bobbing heads of cow's parsley peer into the car. He gives her hand a quick squeeze, but she's too busy batting the plants away to reciprocate.

Adam asks her who else will be there. June shrugs. Even when she was a child, the village was starting to contract: abandoned farmhouses on the margins, drives permanently blocked with barbed wire. There were fewer children round the maypole each spring, and when winter came, only a few gardens sprouted snowmen. The final straw was when May Jenkins had died, and suddenly April and June were the only two children in the village.

The last ones to carry on the ceremonies.

"Jesus, babe." He screws up his face against the sunlight. The day is as perfect as a ripe peach. "At least this isn't setting off my allergies." He claims to have hayfever, but June has never seen him so much as sneeze.

"Must be magic," June says simply, and flips her sunglasses down to cover her eyes. Adam becomes a blur of darkness in the corner of her vision. They drive another twenty minutes in silence. They cover eleven miles. They don't get to Ketchbury Away, but then, she hadn't expected to. Not yet.

* * *

The two girls pick their way to the point where the path stops.

"Let's play for it," June suggests, and April purses her lips, placing the doll down on an old tree trunk. They do three rounds of Rock-Paper-Scissors, from which June emerges victorious. Her heart is beating very fast when she picks up the doll. She's never done this bit before.

She has to get it right. Saving the village is a big responsibility.

Into the *passing places*, it's a steep unclimbable drop, then a carpet of summer foliage, the true depths unknown. June can make out ground elder, fat dock leaves, the starry blue of forget-me-nots. A small stream babbles somewhere out of sight. She wonders whether it's running clear, this time of year, or whether it's rusty-red with iron. The wind stirs the trees, and in the gleam of sunlight hitting the depths, she sees the matching gleam of a pair of eyes, staring up at them.

"Look!" June sounds squeaky as a whisper.

And then a man's voice. Hoarse.

"…is there someone up there?"

April puts her finger to her lips.

"Hello?" the man calls again. "Is there anybody there?"

June wriggles on her stomach like a worm, and reaches out to clasp April's hand when they're close enough to the edge to look over. Her hand is sweaty, clammy, and June realises they're both scared: that April is scared too. This has never happened before.

She can see scaffolding at the side of the pit, remnants of the shallow mining operations. A digger with its teeth still parted, sagging like an old dinosaur. At the bottom there's trampled-down foliage and a man, his face smeared with mud.

"Hello?" he yells. He hasn't seen them. The sides of the pit are gouged with his efforts to get out.

April squeezes June's hand, her own eyes gleaming. "Shh."

★ ★ ★

They're back at the junction with the scarecrow, KETCHBURY AWAY, 3¼ MILE, and in their absence a whole flock of blackbirds has gathered on the gates. June examines their lush, oily black feathers, the beetle-darkness of their beaks. Adam covers his face with both hands, as if he doesn't want the birds to see it. He exhales.

"I'm going to turn around," he says. He looks at her sideways. "Babe, are you sure you want to do this?" As if he's giving her a way out.

Mouth open, she laughs at him.

"Right," he says, tight-jawed, and reverses down the lane the way they'd come.

Three miles down the road, he pulls over again into one of the passing places and gets out. Seen against the hedgerows, his shape seems to… shift, weirdly, in June's shaded vision. He's not tall, and not bulky, but he suddenly becomes a stranger, like on that day in the rain.

That smell again. Things rotting.

A curious cow drifts over to examine him, its expression implacable. June fans herself with her flower crown, and wonders when he'll catch on: why there's no matching crown for him.

★ ★ ★

They encounter the wizened, stunted man driving his tractor again, and this time there are people on the back. "It's not far, you two!" one of them says cheerily, and waves. June self-consciously combs her fingers through her long, long hair, a bit dishevelled from the drive and the wind.

Not far now.

"Fuck Ketchbury Away," Adam says under his breath, then: "How long?"

The man shakes his head. "Oh no," he says. "No idea, sorry."

June looks at Adam and wonders whether she feels the tiniest bit guilty. He's not a bad man, just an average one. He thinks she belongs to his world, not the *passing places.*

But it's a big responsibility, to stop a village from dying.

★ ★ ★

They return three times to see the man in the pit.

He can't get out. And say what you like about Britain being a crowded island, about population growth, there are places out here where you can scream and scream and no one will hear you. Black spots when seen from the air at night. A darkness capable of swallowing up anything that isn't clever enough to run.

"How long d'you think?" June asks April, idly swishing a sycamore key around in her fingertips. They're lying on their backs at the cliff's edge, staring up at the green-and-blue sky.

"How long what?"

"Until… until he dies," June says. The word feels absurdly big.

April shrugs. "He needs water."

"It might rain. Or he could lick the rocks."

April rolls onto her belly and puts her hands to her mouth. "Did you hear that? She says you should lick the rocks!"

He tells them to get their parents, and April laughs and laughs.

The second time, it's been thanklessly hot all week, the village school holding lessons outside, and June is grateful to be back under the cover of the trees, dappled green and cool like a fountain. When they wriggle to the side of the pit, the man hears them.

He looks up, and the hopefulness on his face will *haunt* June. It's a horrible sudden grown-up feeling; this will be with her for the rest of her life.

He calls, very softly, "Little girls. Little girls, will you give me something to eat?"

June looks at April, who's shredding a silver birch twig with her nails, to make a flute.

"Please." His voice catches. It's rough and galled as an old oak tree. "I'm starving. I'm going to die down here."

June looks at April, a mute plea.

April sighs, and then they both shake their heads. What else are the *passing places* for? Better this man than the village.

★ ★ ★

On the third week, June is over at April's house for tea. The kitchen smells of jelly and ice cream, cloying, a bit too sweet, and there's a fussy tablecloth with blue gingham and ruffles. April's mum is doing the washing-up, her hands the yellow of Marigolds. April has popped up to her room.

"There's a man down there… in *those places*," June whispers.

"Oh?" April's mum says mildly.

Her throat is full of knives, and June blurts out the next bit. "He's been there a long time, since we did the ceremony."

The dishes and cutlery continue clinking; April's mum doesn't stop the washing-up. June is starting to worry that she doesn't understand.

"He's dying. He doesn't talk anymore, or stand up. Just eats the leaves and drinks the water and sicks them up again." They've watched him. He does it silently, like a dog. "April says we shouldn't tell anyone. That it's better that way."

Clink. April's mum goes still.

"She's got a knack for it all, that one," she says cautiously. June can see her throat bob as she swallows. "We're… lucky to have her, aren't we, pet?"

June doesn't answer. She knows April is the village favourite, which is unfair.

Then April comes into the room clutching a fistful of coloured pens, to make sigils to hang in the garden, keep Jack Frost away. "It's just a game, Mum," she says airily. "June doesn't know anything." But when she starts to draw, there are two little girls on the paper. Two little girls, one with her eyes crossed out.

"Why'd you have to talk about it? You ruin *everything*," she hisses at June.

★ ★ ★

Adam, June thinks, has stopped trying.

He'd done it back in London, bit by bit, long before the summons back to Ketchbury Away. He'd checked out, mentally and physically. Why else hasn't he reached for his phone, made any serious effort to avoid his fate? He's become untethered, taking turns – seemingly at random – and sweating.

He must be sweating, because of the smell.

June will never stop remembering the moment she and April had arrived, panting and flushed, at the bottom of the *passing places*. It had taken them a long time to tie knots in a rope, long enough to let themselves down, hand over hand, and step on ground never touched by anyone from the village. June had almost expected it to open up and swallow them whole.

The man had been silent for days, and neither of them had seen a dead body before.

April had poked at it with a stick, her eyes distant and beautiful. It was lying face-down in a tiny stream at the bottom of the pit, like the man had been trying to drink his way out. Three weeks is easily enough time to die, with no help, and June wanted very badly to turn the body over, to see whether he was still a man or whether he'd somehow become that waxen-faced doll, and it would mean no more deaths in the village, no more people leaving, for ever and ever. Whether this was still something sacred or not.

"No!" April whacks her with the stick. "You can't move him!"

Then how do we know he's really dead, June wants to ask.

She peers at the man, shading her eyes against the sun. The stream ripples and shimmers in the light, and her face is… hot… for some reason. She fixates on the details: the ragged clothing. The lingering smell of shit and rot. There's no chance that the water in the *passing places* is anything but death, and the man's curly hair is in clumps, reeking, like a ewe who's just given birth and is too exhausted to stand.

He must be dead. He has to be dead, or what's the point?

June can feel the hot prickle of tears behind her eyes.

"Baby." April pokes her. "Come on."

When they've both climbed up the rope, panting and – in June's case – crying, April is gleaming with self-importance. She knows they've done a good job. They'll be given sweets, and new clothes, when they tell the rest of them. She tears down the trail, glancing back at June with flashing eyes. "Hurry *up*, slowpoke. Get the ladder."

She doesn't wait.

June is left in the woods, at the *passing places*, with the body lying below, and the knotted rope leading down into nothing, that sinister and wetly vegetal world. Her heart is quivering like a hare's. She takes one last look at the pit, then follows April silently through the trees. What's the harm?

He's already dead.

★ ★ ★

"You must be excited to see her," Adam says, not looking around. "After so long."

"Yes," June says. "She was my best friend."

April had accused her of being weak, pathetic. She'd ruined everything. Muddy footprints in the *passing places*, and a lumbering path through the trees. Mr. Cowley's sheep had stuck its head right into the barbed wire and tugged; old man Diggory had coughed himself to death in his sleep. The village's death, creeping closer.

"One day you'll realise what you did," April had said, cold as the frost. "One day you'll want to make amends, and I won't let you."

June fixes her eyes on the next bend in the road. Her vision swims, and she stamps down, ruthlessly, on the tears.

"Thank you for coming," she says, keeping her voice steady. "Adam. Thank you."

He smiles. He has no idea.

And on one glorious final turn, Ketchbury Away opens up before them.

The war memorial, with the names of The Honourable Dead scratched out. The village pub, where Mrs. Jenkins had hung herself in the back garden among the geraniums. The boarded-up church that has had no vicar since Jane Howlett crashed her Jeep straight into the lych gate: this isn't a Christian place. The whole street has been done out in ribbons, fluttering everywhere in the gorgeously warm breeze. They hang from the signposts, from the village's single lamppost, from upper windows and weather vanes. It looks just like the old days.

June presses a fist to her chest. She's made it. They're here.

And now they'll *have* to take her back.

Adam stops the car abruptly – probably because the villagers are flocking out to meet them, doors and windows winking in the sun. Each one wearing a flower crown. June opens her mouth, turning to her oblivious boyfriend in the driver's seat; her hand reaching behind, into the back, to pick up her own crown.

She screams.

Adam is a drowned thing, long dead.

He's hairless, slippery as an eel, his nose the deep black of melted asphalt. No eyelashes, and bloating; he's become shapeless and slimy, and she knows if she were to touch him, her hands would slip right off.

There's a knock on the side of the car, and June screams again.

"Silly," April says. "Only me. Just look at you!"

She's not much taller, spry and sharp-boned as a little elf. She reaches for June with lily-white arms, her fingers covered in rings and her wrists with ribbons, so many ribbons. The dress is white, of course: white and perfect and subtly odd, like the princess dresses they'd worn when they were the last little girls in Ketchbury Away, charged with making sure *something* suffered in the village's place.

June glances back at Adam, and he's normal again. But that smell, that rotting smell – the smell of something left in water, left to bloom and grow soft and soapy, like Play-Doh in the bath – doesn't abate.

April smells of flowers, and her bare arms are warm. June wants to sob with the relief of it; she's been let back in. She hasn't been cast out.

"It's so good to see you again," April is saying, stroking her hair. She shades her big green eyes. "Have you come far?"

"A long way," Adam's voice says. "Practically *years*."

It's a weird thing to say. June feels something crawling up her neck, like a centipede. The villagers surrounding them are all decked out for the wedding, but it's a silent crowd. Somewhere, a child cries, hot and fitful. Maybe there's measles going round again. There's always fucking something, in Ketchbury Away. The countryside can be a dangerous place.

"Well, come on then," April claps her hands. "Get out of the car!"

June does as she's told. The diminutive man from the tractor is there, his sleeves rolled up, holding a rake that's so old and rusty it might fall to pieces any moment. She also spots the Volvo driver, a handful of dogs straining on their leashes. The other villagers have pitchforks, and scythes, and other farming implements whose uses have been long-lost in June's memory. Still, that silence; the silence of the ancient ceremonies.

"We're so glad you could make it," April whispers.

The scythes gleam, sharp and deadly, in the sun.

"I brought you something."

"I know," April says, squeezing her fingers to the bone. She doesn't give June the chance to retrieve her flower crown.

But then, why would she? June won't need it.

Adam reeks of rot, muddy water, the smell of the *passing places*. Numbly, June knows that – if she turns – he'll once again be the dead man from the pit. The drowned body, the death of the village. Somehow crawled up to find her, after so many years.

THE GHOSTS WE CREATE

David Farrow

See, here's the thing: when you grow up in a haunted house, you get so used to 'weird' that it becomes your new normal. That door swinging open on its own, those lights flickering for no reason, that shadow lurking in the corner of your eye? That's just how it is. The things you see every day would drive men twice your age insane, but for you, it's all you know.

That's why I wasn't scared of the eyeless lady, even though her face was all wrinkled and cracked – just like my nana's, except without any colour. She only came in the middle of the night. I'd open my eyes, and she'd be sitting on the end of my bed, running her withered hand along the blanket. She always wore the same blue dress and flowery hat. She'd stare at me and smile, except she couldn't really stare, because she had two voids where her eyes should have been.

I asked my parents who she was one day, and it scared my mother so bad that she shattered her coffee mug on the kitchen tiles. That set my dad off, like so many things did back then, and he started shouting and she started crying and I was cowering by my bowl of cornflakes, hoping they'd ignore me. My sister Bethany hightailed it into the den the second the volume got too loud. She was two years older and used to this ritual by now. I wanted to join her, but I was afraid they'd start shouting at me too, so I sat there and kept my eyes down and waited it out.

Bethany never saw the eyeless lady, but she had a ghost of her own: a boy with no hair who would stare into her bedroom sometimes. She never told Mom and Dad because she knew better. But when it was late at night, and neither of us could sleep because of the house creaking and moaning around us, she'd slip into my room and tell me stories about her personal ghost.

"His head is like an egg," she said. "Big and grey and round and cracked at the top, with a little blood seeping out of the crack." She whispered these details in one quick, nervous breath, as if mentioning the boy was enough to summon him. Bethany insisted on keeping the curtains drawn when she visited, so we sat there in the dark, our clammy hands clutching each other.

"He doesn't have ears and his nose is a little nub. He stands outside my window and puts his hand on the glass and just *stares* at me, and sometimes he taps, once or twice—" She demonstrated on the bedframe, her nails rapping like a woodpecker on a tree trunk. "But he never tries to open the window or get inside. I'm scared of him. I can't sleep with him standing there, and when I do sleep, I have nightmares about him."

"Everything's gonna be okay," I told her. "If your ghost gets inside, the eyeless lady will take care of us."

"You're stupid," she said. "God, you're so stupid, Gordon. No one's coming to help us." She let go of my hand and glanced towards the curtains. "I'd run away, you know. If I weren't so worried about what would happen to you without me."

"Don't go," I said, panic tightening my chest. "Please, *please*, don't go. The boy with no hair is out there. You're safer in here with us."

She stared at me, slivers of moonlight streaking her face. "It's not safe in here, either."

But she left before I could ask what she meant.

There was another ghost, too, and this one was everybody's ghost. I couldn't tell you if it was a man or a woman, a child or a grown adult; it was always in your periphery, so you'd never get a real good look at it. The air felt hot with it around, and lights would blow out with no warning. Tempers got fiery too. You could tell the ghost was nearby because Mom had a tendency to get all sweaty and snap at us for no reason.

Dad thought it was a home invader at first, so he took a fireplace poker and stormed through every room in the house, looking for an assailant that wasn't there. But of course he never found a thing. The shadow ghost, as I called it privately, became an obsession for him. Sometimes I'd wake to find him wandering down the hall in his pyjamas, a kitchen knife or a beer bottle or a baseball bat clenched in his hands. I never let him know I saw him. I was too afraid of having those household weapons turned on me.

"Your dad is scary," Rudy told me once. He was the quietest kid in our class and my only friend, and we'd walk home from school together, backpacks loose on our shoulders. Rudy had this illness, and we weren't supposed to talk about it, but of course the other kids did anyway. They laughed at him for being sickly and weak and called him names like 'pussy' and 'faggot'. I was used to these names; they came spilling out of Dad's mouth whenever he saw me cry or whimper or caught me reading superhero comics. I couldn't bring myself to stand up for Rudy in school, but at least I could be his friend.

"Dad's not so bad," I lied. "He's just got kind of a temper." We kicked through the autumn leaves together, our sneakers crunching on the blanket of brown and orange.

Rudy looked sceptical. "Be careful, you know?" he said. "I don't want you to get hurt."

He never came inside, never went further than our driveway, and I'd watch him out the window as he trudged his way home. When I wasn't doing homework or reading in one of the house's many hidey-holes, I'd sit in my bedroom and think about Rudy. Sometimes I lost track of time when I did this, drifting into a dreamlike haze. The eyeless lady was always waiting for me when I came back to myself. Hand on the blankets, flowery hat tipped like a movie star. She'd smile and whisper words I couldn't hear, and I'd curl up on the pillow, her sweet susurrus lulling me back to sleep.

★ ★ ★

The four of us lived in that house for most of my childhood, but everything changed when Bethany found Dad dead in the kitchen one morning. He had a knife in his left hand and black, charred marks all the way down his arms and neck. He'd always been a big man, but he looked small in death. Fragile. His eyes were open and scared and bloodshot, as if he'd died of fright.

That wasn't the real cause, of course. Forensics thought it was a suicide – that he'd stuck the knife into a wall socket and electrocuted himself. Bethany and I knew better. Dad had antagonised the shadow ghost one too many times, and it had finally turned on him. The scorch marks told me everything I needed to know.

Mom was understandably shaken, and her first step was to get us out of the house. She made us pack our bags and leave as soon as the coroner had taken the body and the cops had vacated the scene. She told us the wiring in the house was faulty, and we couldn't stick around or we'd get shocked to death too. Bethany and I knew she was really afraid of the shadow ghost. Its presence had taken a toll on Mom over the years, worn her down physically and mentally; it had wrinkled her skin with worry lines and placed permanent bags under her eyes.

I knew, of course, that the ghosts weren't the only things to blame for Mom's transformation. But Dad was gone now, and even though I could see how much that rattled her, there was something else buried in all her grief. Relief, maybe, that his presence had been exorcised. Losing him loosened some of the shackles that had kept us trapped in that house. So, we left. Took our things, found a cheapo motel out of town, and stayed there until Mom could sell the place.

Rudy showed up the day after we checked in, and he waited nervously below the balcony, rocking his bike back and forth. He rested it against the wall and ran forward to hug me, holding me tighter than anyone had before – even Bethany, even my own mother. We melted into the shadows by the vending machine. He gripped my steady hands with his trembling ones.

"Is he…?" he started, then swallowed. "Is he gone?"

Out of the house, away from its darkness, I felt serene for the first time in my life. I felt a heaviness lift from me that I'd never even realised was there. "Yeah," I said. "He's gone."

Rudy leaned forward and kissed me on the cheek, then found his way to my mouth, his lips chapped and dry. It was a gentle thing: chaste and fleeting. "I've wanted to do that for so long," he said, out of breath. We stood there, foreheads touching, and shared a hesitant smile.

"I know," I said. "Me too." And I kissed him back.

I kept waiting for the eyeless lady to appear at the foot of my bed, but she never did, and over time I almost convinced myself that I'd imagined her. Bethany slept much easier without the hairless boy staring in through her window. Even my mother, who'd become an insomniac over the years, was able to find her moments of rest. By the time we found a new house halfway across town, the phantoms that had surrounded us our whole lives seemed like something out of a dream.

The new house was closer to Rudy's, and we'd go biking together, our tyres clattering along the uneven streets. He knew all the best spots in the woods to hang out and watch the sun set through the trees. We sat together, holding hands, far away from the wary eyes of town, and sometimes he'd rest his head on my shoulder, and sometimes I'd rest mine on his, but always, *always*, we were happy. Being with Rudy felt like home. A home without any ghosts to haunt it.

⋆ ⋆ ⋆

The years passed, and we grew up. Bethany aced her classes and disappeared off to college somewhere across the country. I still had a few years of high school left in me, so I took up some odd jobs here and there, hoping to save up for my own college tuition. None of the jobs lasted very long. I had a hard time sitting still, always wanting to move on to bigger and better things, so I'd collect my pay cheques and put in my notice and find something new to carry me forward.

Eventually I took up a morning paper route to make a little extra cash. It was a simple job, but I liked it. There's something freeing about zooming down the streets with the wind in your hair and the wagon full of papers clattering along behind you. It took me all over town, too. I liked getting the chance to explore all the nooks and crannies I might never have noticed otherwise: the places Rudy and I tended to overlook.

One of those nooks, though, I knew all too well. It was our old house. The place had sat empty for years, as if its reputation had cast a shadow over the building, warning visitors to stay away. The FOR SALE sign had disappeared a long time ago. Someone must have bought the place, but I'd never asked who, and it seemed like I might never learn.

So, the house sat there, growing dust, a hollow, vacant home – until one day it suddenly wasn't. I pedalled past it on my paper route and saw a moving van parked in the driveway. A redheaded man in a garish maroon scarf directed the movers up the steps and into the house. In the second-floor window, a woman's shadowy face stared out at the procession. I assumed it must have been his wife, at least until another man came out of the house and kissed the redhead on the lips. The dark woman was gone when I looked up again.

I was pleased at first, happy to see another gay couple moving into the neighbourhood, but Jim and Rodney Fisher were hardly the beacons of progress I'd been hoping for. The Fishers were notoriously reclusive.

Anyone who tried to be friendly to them at the supermarket got the cold shoulder, and they'd ignore you if you waved to them on the street. Their next-door neighbour said they never answered their doorbell, even though she'd come over several times with a 'welcome to the neighbourhood' casserole.

I saw them once or twice around town. They were on the scrawny side, almost a little sickly, and I wondered how much of that had to do with the house. Did the eyeless lady come and sit on their bed at night? Did the boy with no hair stare in through their window? Did the shadow ghost stalk their halls, bringing hot tempers with it?

Rudy and I talked about them sometimes, on the rare occasions we could make it to our woodsy rendezvous. His illness was getting worse in his teenage years. Just riding his bike took the energy right out of him, and he had to find a bench to sit and recuperate before attempting any sort of nature walk. We still hadn't told anyone in town we were seeing each other, and with the Fishers making such a poor impression, we were afraid to even try.

"It's not fair," Rudy griped. He turned a leaf over in shaky hands, threatening to crumple it. "When you're out, you have all these eyes on you. You have to be perfect or you're making every last gay person look bad. If you're not perfect for them, you don't deserve their respect. Maybe you don't even deserve the same rights. You know?"

I sat beside him and rubbed his shoulders and said nothing, because his defeatist talk just reminded me of my father, drunk and rambling and lamenting the 'liberal brainwashing' turning all the kids these days into queers. I could feel his presence, sometimes, when I touched Rudy; how easily my firm hands could damage him, bruise his skin, scar him in ways I'd never be able to take back. Maybe I hadn't exorcised Dad's ghost completely. Maybe there was still a piece of him haunting that house, haunting *me*, keeping me under his shadow.

I worried about the Fishers, despite the aloof face they put on for the townsfolk. Jim had arrived in town wearing brightly coloured clothing that almost made your eyes ache, but after two months in the house, his wardrobe had shrunk to a few black shirts and a pair of washed-out jeans. Clean-shaven Rodney developed patchy stubble on his face and deep bags under his eyes. I'd seen my parents slip into funks like this, and I didn't want the same thing to happen to the Fishers. But it wasn't my house anymore. There wasn't much I could do.

The last time anyone saw the Fishers together was a morning in late April. They had stopped by the hardware store and picked up twelve cans of black paint before returning home. Their neighbour said she heard their front door closing, but by the time she walked onto her porch, the men themselves were nowhere to be seen. She didn't think much of it then. By the next morning, that opinion had drastically changed.

She was waiting outside that day when I pedalled by with her paper. She cradled a cup of coffee in her hands and stared in bewilderment at the house next door. When I passed by it, I understood. Overnight, the Fishers had painted over every single window in their home with thick layers of black paint. The building, which had already been fairly grim before, now radiated darkness. Looking at it for too long made my skin crawl. I couldn't shake the sense that something was staring out at me from behind all that blackness.

"They've finally snapped," said a woman at the supermarket the next day. "I knew there was something off about those two."

"I bet it's some freaky sex act," said her loud, gossipy friend. "Like blackout curtains, but more extreme."

I lowered my face and tried to shrink away, but a third voice joined the discussion. "It's symbolic, if you ask me. Those folks never wanted anything to do with the rest of us. Now they're out of sight, out of mind. Just the way they like it."

Everyone had a lot to say, but I didn't agree with any of their theories. They didn't know that house like I did. They hadn't grown up there; they hadn't seen the things I'd seen. They didn't know about the actual phantoms that haunted the property.

The Fishers had painted over the windows from the *inside*. Which meant that they were afraid of someone looking in.

⋆ ⋆ ⋆

For the first time in years, I started having dreams about the eyeless woman. She would appear in the doorway of my bedroom, her blue dress flowing around her, and reach out a withered hand towards me. Her smile was as wide as ever. She never moved her lips, but I could hear a voice in my head: soft, whispery, like wind blowing through the trees.

Come home.

I tried calling Bethany to talk about the dreams, but as soon as she heard me mention the old house, she hung up on me. I guess her own nightmares of the place were a little too fresh. Rudy and I made a point to never discuss the house while we were together, and I didn't want to mention the dreams to my mother, either. She'd moved on over the years, but still had this fragility to her, like she was one glass of wine away from slipping back into her old traumas. So, I kept the dreams to myself. There wasn't much else I could do.

It became clear that the Fishers weren't bothering to pick up their papers, as the stack on their front porch grew larger and larger with each passing day. Sometimes I'd stop and ask the neighbour if she'd seen them yet, but I always got a shake of the head. She was worried. I could see it in her eyes.

One morning the neighbour wasn't out and about, and her car was gone from the driveway when I pedalled by. I should have kept on going, but something made me screech to a halt outside the house. The black windows stared down at me, like a whole slew of empty eyes. My skin prickled with goosebumps.

Come home, the eyeless lady whispered in my head.

I left my bike leaning against the mailbox and approached the porch. Even the little window slits on the front door were painted over. For the first time, I noticed another blot of paint smearing the surface of the door: a few angry black streaks that looked almost like an eye.

I reached out a hesitant hand, but the door clicked open before I could touch it, like someone had pulled it from the other side. My stomach clenched. I thought about Rudy, how he would lay into me for even *thinking* about going back in this house. But he didn't know the place. He'd never been inside. He couldn't hear the whispers I could; he couldn't understand that I'd never really left the house, that its memory had been living in me all this time. I pushed the door open all the way and stepped inside.

"Hello?" I called. "Is anyone here?"

Walking into the front hall brought back such a rush of memories that I almost staggered. All the times Mom would kiss me on the forehead as she sent me off to school; all the times I'd kicked off my shoes on the welcome mat before running off to play in my room; all the times Bethany and I would hide under blanket forts and whisper scary stories to each other. There were new pictures hanging on the walls, and the Fishers had changed the wallpaper to a garish floral design, but somehow it still felt like home.

The lights were off, and when I tried the switch there was a brief pop, then nothing. I flicked it a few more times before giving up. A pervasive heat had crept into the air, as if the Fishers had cranked up the thermostat, and it made me tug nervously on the collar of my shirt. Power outages and surges of heat, in this house, could mean only one thing: the shadow ghost was nearby.

I continued down the hall, my footsteps creaking, and saw another painted eye. Then another. There were several of them, smeared at various heights along the wallpaper. I reached out and brushed my hand along one of them. My fingers came away with little flecks of dried paint. The wall itself was hot to the touch, and I couldn't help but remember my father on the day we'd found him, with those scorch marks crawling up his skin like patches of spreading mould.

The cluster of eyes grew thicker as I walked further into the house, forming an archway above the entrance to the den. There was no sunlight coming through the painted-up windows, so I could only rely on the light streaming through the front door to guide me. A faint smell reached my nostrils: a cloying odour, like roses mixed with sewage. I stepped into the den and waited for my eyes to adjust to the darkness.

All the furniture had been removed, leaving the hardwood floor bare and empty. At first I thought the inner walls had been painted over completely black. But then shapes emerged, and I saw that every square inch was covered with those angry painted eyes. They coalesced in a pure black patch at the far end of the room, the paint smearing together into the loose shape of a doorway. There was a figure slumped on the ground in front of it.

I should have left, I should have listened to that inner voice of reason that sounded so much like Rudy, but I drew closer anyway. The cloying smell grew stronger. In the darkness, I saw Jim's body slouched in a heap on the floor. His limbs were tangled together, and his eyes had been plucked from his skull, leaving two bloody gaps that stared up at me vacantly.

The air grew thicker; it almost seemed to coagulate. I had a hard time breathing in the sudden wave of heat. When I looked up from Jim's body, I saw a hallway stretching out before me where the painted doorway had been just seconds before. The walls were a solid ashen grey, and there was a figure standing at the far end. Her blue dress fluttered in a wind I couldn't feel. The two little voids in her face pierced into my brain, and I knew, despite her blindness, that she could see me in my entirety. All my shameful secrets, all the darkness and rage and resentment I'd been holding on to, ever since I'd learned the world could hurt me; the parts of me that even I didn't want to see. She reached out an ancient hand, like an old woman scattering crumbs to pigeons in the park.

Come home, the eyeless lady whispered.

My skin prickled with sweat. When I looked behind me, I saw a dark shape lurking in the entrance to the den, heat radiating from its outline in shimmery waves. It was the shadow ghost. It didn't step inside, didn't make any threatening moves towards me, but I could feel every cell in my body burning in its presence. I couldn't look at it for long. There was nothing else to look at, though, nothing except Jim's slumped body and the wall of eyes and the long hallway with the beckoning woman at the end. I wondered if the hairless boy was here too, staring in at me through layers of thick black paint.

I had the void before me and fire at my back; there was no way out of this room that didn't end in some horrible fate. I closed my eyes. Behind the safety of my eyelids, I tried to picture the house as I'd known it growing up: a dark place, a haunted place, but a home. A place where I could curl up in a cosy nook with my comic books, where Bethany could study at the kitchen table, where Mom could knit endlessly by the windows, where Dad could sit on the sofa and watch his favourite game shows. I latched onto that image like a lifeline. Then, with my eyes still pressed shut, I turned and ran.

I couldn't see the shadow ghost, but I could feel it as I ploughed through the doorway, and for a horrible moment I felt engulfed in flames. The peaceful images in my head were shoved aside by vicious memories: of Dad smashing a beer bottle against the counter, of my parents shouting over each other from downstairs, of Bethany and I cowering together and crying in my bedroom. I could blame a phantom for those memories, but I knew, deep down, that the worst ghosts in the house were the ones we'd created ourselves. Spectres of hate and fear and sadness that would haunt these halls long after we were gone.

The memories threatened to consume me, to drown me in their endless fire, but I clung to that one desperate image: of my family at their best, just *existing*, just living together in that rare, precious moment of peace. And the tug of the shadow ghost lessened. I wrenched myself free and staggered down the hallway towards the light of the front porch. The air outside rushed into my burning lungs, cooling them, and I let out a strangled laugh of relief.

I didn't look back. I just picked up my fallen bike and pedalled away, my legs rising and falling, my heart thumping erratically. I could feel the house's hold on me waning with each mile I put between us. I knew I couldn't escape it forever. I knew it would always be waiting for me, black windows looming, hiding the spectres within. But for now, at least, I was free.

★ ★ ★

Jim's death was ruled a murder; a ritualistic one, judging from the painted eyes smeared everywhere inside. The police weren't able to find a single trace of Rodney. The prevailing theory around town was that he'd fled the state after murdering his partner. I suspected differently. I thought the house had gotten its hooks into him – that when the eyeless lady had appeared at the end of her impossible hallway, Rodney had followed her beckoning hand, and the house had simply swallowed him up.

If I'd been a little weaker, I might have joined him.

For months after the incident, the house remained empty. The grass was overgrown and filled with all sorts of tangled weeds, and flecks peeled from the outer walls. Its windows were still painted over. The black eye on the front door stared at me every time I rode by, like the house itself was watching me, waiting for my defences to slip, so it could beckon me back inside.

Last week I passed the house again, and this time I saw another moving van in the driveway. A harried-looking mother and father carried furniture up the front steps while two small children laughed and darted through the grass. There was a third face peering out from around the corner of the house – a young boy with no hair and a round, egg-like skull – but he ducked away when he saw me looking.

The new family has already started tidying up the place, scraping the windows clean and trimming the untamed front lawn. They've even put out Halloween decorations. There are huge cobwebs stretched across the front porch, and a stuffed scarecrow sits on a rocking chair in the yard. It's wearing a black dress and a witch's hat. I don't like that it doesn't have eyes. I can hear the faintest of whispers every time I bike past it.

The new occupants of the house may be settling in, but its old occupants, the ones that haunted me my entire childhood, are still there too. I know it's only a matter of time before the son starts seeing an eyeless lady perched on the foot of his bed, before the daughter starts complaining of a boy with no hair peeking through her window. Even the parents will notice the shadow ghost before long.

"I want to warn them," I told Rudy one day, and it all came pouring out of me: the ghosts, the hauntings, the residue of that place. "I couldn't save the Fishers, but maybe I can actually do something this time. Get those folks out of that house before it destroys them."

Rudy sat there quietly. I thought he was taking in the whole story, digesting what I'd told him, but he didn't seem all that surprised. His cheeks were exceptionally pale, and his knees knocked together in the October chill, like a strong gust of wind might blow him right off the bench.

"I don't think you can save everyone, Gordon," he said quietly. "And I don't think ghosts ever really go away. At some point you have to learn to live with them."

I sat with him and fought back the fears that were rising to my mind, stronger than ever these days: that someday my father's echo would shape me into the kind of man he was; that the shadow ghost would fill me with a hateful fire I could never put out; that the eyeless lady would beckon me down her hallway one last time, and I would give in, take her hand, and follow her. I knew I wouldn't have Rudy forever. We were taking it day by day, but his days were dwindling fast. Then he'd be just another ghost. Another shadow I had to carry.

"I'll try," I said finally. "To live with them, I mean."

Rudy's lips cracked into a smile. "I know you will."

The wind whispered through the leaves, but this time there were no voices buried in the sound. It was just the two of us, huddled together, waiting in the autumn dusk for the darkness that always comes.

THE FINAL SLIDE

Ramsey Campbell

As Jake climbed out of the foremost limousine his cousin Claudine's leg stretched forth from the next hired car. A tempting length emerged in what he would have liked to fancy was an invitation of some kind before she pulled her black dress down and stepped onto the pavement, prompting Jake to pretend he'd been gazing at the church. When she followed Aunt Bee and Uncle Chuck to join his parents and his grandmother he risked sending her a grin, which collapsed under his suspicion that you weren't supposed to smile at funerals, unless you were miming bravery like the three women. "Claudine," his mother said. "You're looking so grownup."

"And look at Jake in a suit," Aunt Bee enthused. "You'd never think they were thirteen."

Uncle Chuck's inevitable quip sounded untypically dutiful. "Lucky for some."

Jake sensed his father felt bound to contribute. "Lucky for us we've got such good kids."

Jake thought all four parents were determined to ignore his grandfather and the box he came in, a bid that simply made the old man's absence painfully insistent. He wasn't going to blub; above all he mustn't let Claudine see him blub, even when he glimpsed how his grandmother kept not quite touching her face as if she was searching for tears or preparing to stem some. He might have liked to take refuge in the church, a long concrete bunker decorated with multicoloured abstract jigsaw windows and topped with a cross that looked plastic. Must the family wait until the last of the audience were seated? They had by the time the priest came to the churchyard gate and raised a discreet hand to activate the undertaker's men.

The family stood back as the man in charge lifted the tailgate of the hearse. Jake expected the bearers to hoist the coffin on their shoulders while respectfully suppressing any sounds of exertion, but as they slid the casket out it sprouted an undercarriage like a plane preparing to touch down. "That's what I call travelling in style," his uncle murmured. "He's got more wheels than ever."

Jake wasn't sure if he was meant to laugh, particularly when his father emitted a noise not quite like a tut before taking the widow's arm to usher her in the wake of the coffin. Its trundling turned hollow as the men guided it into the church, where it was echoed by a widespread muffled rumble – the congregation standing up like, Jake thought, children acknowledging a teacher. The advance of the casket set off a song exhorting listeners to look on the bright side of life. He'd seen the film it came from, and it contained a word you surely weren't allowed to say in church. Would the coffin reach its goal – the space beneath a screen filled with a photograph of his grandfather – before the word showed up? He could imagine the men yearning to accelerate the coffin but forbidden to do so. Part of him wanted the word to overtake them, except how might it affect his grandmother? He never knew, since the coffin gained its destination as the song urged someone to forget their sins and grin instead, then fell silent. "By gum, that was close," his uncle muttered behind him.

Was the priest hiding a wry smile? She bowed her head while the family sidled along the front row flanked by twin aisles. Jake found himself next to Claudine, more than close enough to touch, and sought distraction by grabbing the memorial booklet from the ledge in front of him. The cover displayed Albert Bancroft decades younger than Jake had ever known him, his eyes competing at width against his plump comfortable grin. Having waited for the family to finish shuffling sideways, she raised her head and a measured sympathetic smile. "Please all be seated. We have got together here today to celebrate the life of Albert Bancroft…"

Jake was suppressing an image of his grandfather riding the coffin with the glee he'd shown his wheelchair, scooting along in the casket with a child perched on the lid, just as he'd taken the grandchildren for speedy wheelchair jaunts. The priest's assertion that Albert Bancroft had been full of fun didn't help. "I see many of his pupils from the schools he taught are here with us today," she said. "They've told me how much they looked up to him, and he used to say he looked up to them." But his first love had been his family, and "he liked nothing better than feeling close to them." Jake might have preferred not to be reminded how close Claudine was, since every movement she made felt like an omen of presumably inadvertent contact – of the likelihood that his mind and some of the rest of him would start acting in a fashion inappropriate to the occasion – and he could only strive to clamp his attention on the priest's next reminiscence. "Towards the end of his time on earth he joined our congregation and was active in the choir. He told me it gave him a new lease of life."

By now Jake's grandmother had begun to sniff. He felt the reaction closing in as his mother echoed it beside him and Claudine did. To avoid appearing heartless he dealt his eyes a brace of manly dabs. At first he was relieved to see the priest had finished reminiscing about his grandfather. "And now please all stand while we sing a hymn," she said.

He wasn't going to expose the antics of his newly unruly voice to his cousin. He tried just reading the lyrics in the booklet until he sensed his mother's gaze, reproachful if not uncomprehending. The congregation was apparently expected to applaud its own performance at the end of every verse, but complying with this and simply pronouncing the verses aloud failed to placate his mother much. He found the lines about the little tiny baby in some unidentified person's hands too embarrassing to utter except in a mumble. Did whoever had hold of the baby prefer to remain unnamed? Supposedly everyone there was in his hands, which left Jake wondering why he'd never felt them. "That was Albert's favourite hymn," the priest said. "I don't think I ever saw him happier than when he was teaching it to our children in the choir. Now I believe that's our cue to see more of him."

Of course she didn't mean he was about to clamber out of his box. He was already above it on the screen, where the chubbiest stage of his face was bestowing a grin on whoever he had his eye on, presumably the family member who had photographed him. His face must have looked as huge as that to babies, and Jake thought he recalled it looming over him, or was this because it was doing so now? In a moment it was ousted by a portrait of a slender youthful couple in prim suits. As Jake grasped they were his grandparents the priest said "I hope these will bring back happy memories for everyone."

The young couple emerged from a church in a flurry of confetti, an image Jake's grandmother gave another sniff, which he had to assume denoted happiness – you were meant to tell the truth in church, and he couldn't imagine the priest risking a fib. He could only hope the truth of his ungovernably lively feelings for Claudine wasn't visible to anyone; it felt as if his body was owning up to thoughts he didn't dare admit. At least he wouldn't figure in the pictures on the screen for a while yet, if at all, and he hoped that absence let him hide from everyone around him – let him elude their attention, at any rate.

The couple aged as they went on their travels, posing among snaggletoothed columns robbed of a roof, raising glasses at a table outside a waterfront taverna, prancing among costumed dancers to the vanished tune of a bouzouki. The man's face expanded from shot to shot as if his body was pumping it wider while his smile did its best to keep up. Each photograph earned a grandmotherly sniff, emulated by Claudine and the women. When Uncle Chuck cleared his throat and was imitated by his brother-in-law Jake felt prompted to make it a trio, only for Claudine to dart him a glance suggesting he was trying too hard to impress whoever he'd had in mind. He was glad when the slide show incorporated school photographs that showed his grandfather the teacher behind lineups of various classes, his hands around the shoulders of whichever child sat in the middle of the row. The image roused reminiscent murmurs further down the church, but for the moment the front row was refraining from audible grief. Soon the screen showed his grandfather with his eyes raised heavenwards, or rather to the little girl he must have launched into the air, her skirt blooming like a white flower as she plummeted towards his outstretched hands. "That's me, Claudine," Aunt Bee whispered.

Jake was anticipating another round of sniffs, but his grandmother sounded oddly disconcerted. "Who took that?" she said, not as low as he might have thought proper.

"Someone must have," his father murmured. "Perhaps you've forgotten you did."

"I'd remember if I had. I don't want to forget anything about the family."

Her husband reappeared with his hands held high. Jake thought he looked as if he was miming a confession, but the eager hands were poised to grab another tumbling toddler. "Well," his father said, "there I am, but now it's me who can't remember."

"Then this time it's both of us."

"I mean I don't remember putting it in the show, or the other one either."

"Then as you told me just now, someone else did."

Presumably the next photographer had been a helpful tourist. The family so far were seated on rocks by the sea. The father had his arms around the children, his fingers splayed on their naked midriffs, while his wife draped an arm across his shoulders. Some or all of this satiated his smile, which maintained a proprietary contentment as the years widened his face and slimmed his wife down besides heightening their children, until it was seized by the first of the strokes he'd experienced. The condition skewed the left side of his mouth, tugging that corner high to indicate a permanent sleepy wink, as if he was owning up to some sly aspect of himself. As Jake attempted to grasp what if anything the notion might imply, his mother murmured "He was so happy when he had you two to play with."

She meant Claudine and Jake. He was the latest airborne toddler, his grandfather having devoted a series of exercises legendary throughout the family to regaining the use of his left arm. Jake couldn't recall being flung, unless the hollowness that lurched into his stomach was a kind of memory, a trace of the apprehension he might have felt at his helpless flight or at the prospect of being caught, although why should his grandfather's clutch bother him? Surely he was just uncomfortable with Claudine viewing his infant self. The next image rejuvenated her in the same fashion, and he could have thought it had done so to his grandfather, whose visible delight almost did away with his fixed wink. His elevated gaze and lopsided smile were waiting for Claudine to fall into his eager hands. Should this have been what the priest meant by looking up to children? Claudine's skirt had flown above her waist, and Jake assumed this was why someone further down the church loosed a shrill disapproving cough, certainly not because they suspected Jake couldn't help imagining his cousin in that state at their present age. His grandmother twisted around to glare. "What nasty ideas some people have," she muttered.

She couldn't mean him. Surely his face wasn't admitting to them, but he gave his eyes a pair of pronounced dabs to feign propriety. Meanwhile the onscreen family aged several years and exhibited the evidence in swimwear on another beach, where he and his cousin were the subjects of their grandfather's embrace. The old man was arrested in caressing their six-year-old midriffs, perhaps in a bid to prove he could still wield all of himself. The lowest outspread finger of each hand pointed downwards as if describing a secret sign. Jake remembered the Spanish holiday but not the moment, let alone any secret his grandfather's skewed smile might have been withholding. Had the image made someone restless? The acoustic was so generalised Jake could have thought the muffled shifting was in front of him.

Now his grandfather was in a wheelchair, having suffered another stroke. His left eye was almost shut, covering whatever thought the wink might imply, and the stroke had fixed more of his smile, pinching it inwards. While this might look secretively introverted, for the moment it appeared to be relishing the speed of the electric vehicle if not inviting a rider. Perhaps it had enticed Claudine, about ten years old by now, since the next shot found her perched on his lap. The acceleration of the chair had sent her skirt high on her bare thighs. The old man's left hand on her waist hardly could have, even if the fabric was bunched around it. Jake saw the priest growing uneasy in a different way from his. "Who'd take a picture like that?" Aunt Bee protested, not even under her breath.

"I don't know, mum. I don't remember it."

"Who'd put it up for everyone to see, and in church as well?"

"I promise you I didn't," Jake's father said along the row. "I've never seen it before."

Jake would have said the same about the next photograph, which reduced him to ten years old or so. His shorts were absurdly brief, presenting all the flesh they could on his grandfather's lap. The old man's hand lay low on Jake's midsection, really quite uncomfortably low, and how could Jake have forgotten that when he felt so mortified now? Surely the hand had been out of the old man's control. Before Jake could confirm it was the left hand the image gave way to another, in which his cousin had taken his place. She appeared to be close to the age she was now, and was wearing the same outfit. Whether or not the chair was in motion, her skirt stayed tugged down to her knees, on which the old man's hands were resting. A doubtful mutter somewhere in the front row appeared to enliven the image, and then Jake saw it had been replaced by its sequel. Perhaps a convulsion of some kind had shifted his grandfather's left arm, since the fingertips had scaled Claudine's knee, vanishing under the black hem. "That never happened," Claudine whispered urgently. "Mum, it never did."

Her voice faltered as the image changed again. The rest of the old man's hand had followed the fingertips. Jake heard gasps and other expressions of outrage, not just on the front row, but his grandmother's reaction was most pronounced. "No," she said so loud she might have been confronting a malefactor. "That's very much more than enough."

Before anybody could respond she lurched into the aisle and strode to the coffin. Bright rage had dried her eyes. The priest made a timidly respectful move towards her, but the words she started murmuring proved just as ineffectual. The widow thumped the coffin with both fists, an assault that propelled it towards the altar. Its readiness to travel prompted her to dart to the far end, clutching at it with both hands as if she was striving to dislodge the lid, and send it away from the altar. The spectacle of her racing the casket down the aisle appeared to paralyse the congregation, and Jake felt as if she was enacting his notion of the speedy coffin. Could any of the images on the monitor have been somebody's fantasy too? As his grandmother sent the coffin past the front row the screen turned emptily black. "Isn't anybody going to stop her?" Claudine pleaded.

Jake wanted to feel she was appealing to him. He scrambled over the ledge in front of the pew, wishing he'd vaulted instead to impress her, and sprinted after their grandmother. He couldn't tell whether she was shoving the coffin or being dragged by it, but she was already almost at the exit from the church. From gaping at her progress or otherwise falling short of intervention the mourners transferred their attention to him. He felt delegated to act on everyone's behalf without being lent any of their authority. By the time he reached the door his grandmother was speeding the coffin out of the churchyard.

As he dashed to the gate the coffin trundled bumping off the pavement. His grandmother might have floundered after it into the traffic, having tripped over the kerb, if two of the undertaker's men hadn't caught hold of her. A hulking truck swerved to avoid it but collided with its last few inches, tipping up the casket on the opposite side of the road. Another truck was next to ram it, demolishing so much of it that the lid flew off. Its occupant toppled forth like an enervated jack-in-the-box. As the figure tottered stiffly on the tarmac the impact seemed to loosen the arms folded on its chest, so that it jerked out its hands to ward off an oncoming car. Jake had a moment to glimpse the secretive lopsided grin that death appeared simply to have emphasised. Then his grandfather fell on his back, and a wheel of the car removed the grin along with much more of the face, and Jake could only hope that everything the screen had shown was gone the way of the erased head.

THE MAN WILL CREEP

Angela Sylvaine

Vera rushed through the door of the girls' bathroom, calling, "Gotta go, Kent." She slumped against the door. Why couldn't he just take no for an answer and leave her alone? She used to spend her free period grading and catching up on emails before Kent set his sights on her.

She slipped into the last stall, her normal hiding place, and closed the door. Exhausted, she leaned her head against the wall, trying not to doze like she had yesterday, despite the scent of ammonia and stale urine that permeated the stall. More than anything, she needed a good night's sleep free from nightmares of *him*.

Her eyes roamed over the graffiti marring the painted metal surface of the stall door, mostly innocent stuff.

Stacy + Bobby

Jill & Marcy BFF4EVA

Victor is a nose picker

There were others that made Vera cringe and wish she'd gotten a job in elementary education instead of middle school.

Debbie is a slut

Felicia sucks dick

Phillips jerks off at his desk

Her gaze caught on a crude drawing – a face with a gaping jaw and long, sharp teeth. She sucked in a strangled breath, and leaned close, seeing *him*.

No. It couldn't be. She rubbed her eyes and looked again, the image blurring, then coming back into focus. Still there.

Giggling spilled into the room as the door opened, then closed.

She froze.

"Read it," a familiar voice said. Nicola.

Vera peered through the crack above the door's latch, saw three girls standing before the row of individual sinks looking into the long mirror that spanned the wall. A short girl stood between Nicola and her sidekick Kimber.

"But I don't want to," the middle girl said. Anya? No, Ina. The sixth grader who wore clothes several sizes too big for her and came for the free breakfast Vera supervised most mornings.

"It's that or we take your skirt. Then everyone sees your shit-stained underwear," Kimber said.

A hot flush crept up Vera's neck. Suddenly, she was back in another bathroom, hiding, praying she wouldn't be found. She pulled up her feet, wrapped her arms around her knees.

"No," Ina said, the word almost a moan.

"Guess it's the skirt then." A scuffle sounded.

Stand up. Help that poor girl, Vera told herself. But she couldn't make herself move.

Paper crinkled.

"He appears, all dressed in black, his jaw unhinges with a crack," Ina said, sobs punctuating her words. "Watches you with blood-filled eyes, grabs with fingers sharp as knives."

Noooo. Vera stared at the drawing scratched into the stall's paint. The jaw seemed to open wider, mouth yawning and teeth lengthening. *Shut up!* she screamed, but only in her mind. Her throat locked tight.

"Late at night, the man will creep, eats the bad ones while they sleep." Ina's voice rose to a high whine, the words coming out in a rush. "Sing this song, again and again, say his name, invite him in."

Vera closed her eyes and covered her face with her hands to blot *him* out, but he followed her behind her eyelids, his face floating in the darkness. The jaw snapped closed, and she flinched, as if he were there, his hot breath singeing her skin.

"Finish it," Nicola commanded.

More crying, then, "Careful, careful, what you dare, not all survive his bloody stare."

Don't say it! Vera begged internally.

"Mr. Chew, Mr. Chew, Mr. Chew," Ina said in a rush, the words running together. "I summon you."

Something sharp scraped down Vera's cheeks, a stinging sensation dragging over her skin, and she imagined pointed fingernails caressing her face. Her eyes popped open. She was alone in the stall. Of course she was. It was just a stupid rhyme.

One she thought had died two decades ago.

She lowered her hands from her face, saw several of her fingers tipped with blood where she'd clawed through her skin.

"Mr. Chew," she whispered, then slapped her hand over her mouth to silence herself. After that terrible night, she swore she would never, ever say that name again.

"I did what you said. Please, just let me go," Ina begged.

Please. Vera had begged too, but that never worked, only made things worse, only fed that dark pit inside monsters like Nicola. Monsters that weren't from some stupid rhyme. Monsters that were real. Monsters that preyed on the weak, the helpless.

Anger flamed in Vera's chest, burning away just enough of the fear to make her stand. She was not weak or helpless. Not anymore. She slammed open the stall door, leaving a set of bloody fingerprints on the surface as it smacked into the wall.

The three girls gaped at Vera, Nicola maintaining a tight grip on Ina's upper arm.

Vera's own arm throbbed where the bone had snapped under a similar grip. "Leave her alone," she said, wishing her voice sounded more commanding.

Nicola released the girl. A piece of paper fell from Ina's grip, drifting to the floor, and she took her chance to run out the bathroom door, her footsteps echoing in the hallway as it closed.

"Hey, no running," a voice called. Kent. Waiting for Vera.

"What the hell is wrong with your face?" Kimber asked.

In the mirror, Vera saw both her cheeks were marred with vicious scratches that trailed from beneath her eyes to her jaw, a few of them seeping blood. She stepped up to the closest sink, splashed water on her face and hands, then wiped at her cheeks. "Nothing."

Nicola glanced at the open bathroom stall; her mouth twisted in a sneer. "Were you hiding in there, Ms. Bradley?"

Vera picked up the discarded paper – a completed English quiz from her eighth-grade class, which Nicola was in. But someone had written on the back, scrawled that awful rhyme in pencil. "Where did this come from?"

"Don't recognise your own quiz, now?" Nicola scoffed.

"I meant this on the back, who told you this?"

"I don't know." She crossed her arms. "It was on there when you gave it back."

"That's not possible." Vera gripped the edge of the sink.

Kimber giggled. "Aww, I think she's scared."

"Is that true, Ms. Bradley?" Nicola asked, stepping up behind Vera. "Are you scared of Mr. Ch—"

Vera whirled around, grabbing the girl's arm. "Don't you say that name."

Nicola frowned, eyeing Vera's grip.

She let go.

"What name?" Nicola asked, batting her eyelashes in feigned innocence.

"I think she's talking about Mr. Chew," Kimber said, giggling again.

Laughing at Vera.

She crumpled the paper into a ball. "I'm reporting you to Principal Phillips for bullying. And I don't know where this came from" – she shook her fist that held that awful rhyme – "but it ends now."

"I actually think we should go talk to Phillips, tell him we caught you hiding out in the bathroom and spying on us." Nicola gave a pout and clutched her arm. "Then you assaulted me."

Shit. Vera knew better than to grab a student like that.

Nicola turned to her friend. "Let's go."

Kimber groaned and said, "Do we really have to talk to Phillips? His breath smells like boiled eggs."

"Yes, now shut up and go." Nicola shoved her friend toward the door, flipping Vera off before following.

"Wait." Hoping to talk them out of reporting her to Principal Phillips, Vera lunged after the girls, tripping over her own feet and stumbling into Nicola, shoving her between the shoulder blades. Nicola crashed into Kimber, whose face smacked into the bathroom door.

She staggered back, clutching her bloody nose. "What the fuck, Nicola?"

Vera backed up several steps, shaking her head. This couldn't be happening.

Nicola whipped around to glare at Vera, who brushed past her and led Kimber to the closest sink. "Are you okay? Here." Vera tore a paper towel from the dispenser and wet it, handing it to the girl to stem the flow of blood, which was minimal. "It doesn't look broken."

"You pushed me." Nicola jabbed a finger at Vera.

"I... I did not, I wouldn't do that," she said, the lie raising bile in her throat. She couldn't afford to lose her job over this, not when she'd finally started building a new life for herself.

The bathroom door cracked open, and Kent peeked inside. "Everything all right in here?"

At that same moment, Nicola said, "You liar," and strode forward to shove Vera backward. Caught by surprise, she didn't brace or try to stop herself from slipping between two sinks and smacking into the mirror. Her head hit the glass with a crack, and she slid to the floor.

Anger flared through her veins. She'd sworn she would never let anyone lay their hands on her again, and she tried to get up, to give that little bitch a taste of her own medicine, but her vision blurred, and dizziness weighed her down.

"Hey!" Kent roared, barrelling into the room and grabbing Nicola's arms, pinning them behind her. "Security!"

Vera's head slumped to her chest, hair falling forward to cover her face. Blood dripped down her forehead and turned her vision red.

★ ★ ★

The paramedics fastened the straps around Vera's body and raised the gurney to waist height. They'd already bandaged her head but wanted to take her to the hospital for a full examination and X-rays. Her gaze landed on the mirror. Cracks spread above and below the circular imprint of her head to form craggy shards. Like two clawed hands reaching out for her.

A strangled gasp caught in her throat.

"Take it easy, we'll get you some pain meds as soon as the doc checks you out and makes sure it's safe," one of the paramedics said.

He is not real. He's just a product of your imagination. But someone had written that rhyme on Nicola's paper, maybe the girl herself. There was no way she could know it, though.

First, he'd showed up in Vera's nightmares again, now he'd infiltrated her classroom. Almost as if he were following her, pursuing her.

Could he be real? After what happened to her grandfather – *blood, so much blood* – all the doctors convinced her he wasn't real, but what if they were wrong?

The paramedics wheeled Vera into the hall, where kids stood clustered in groups, watching and whispering.

Kent caught up as they travelled the length of the hallway, gripping her fingers in his sweaty hand. "It's going to be okay, Vera. You're lucky I heard the commotion."

She wiggled her hand free of his grip, curled it into a ball. "Yeah, lucky." When asked what happened, he'd claimed to hear shouting coming from the bathroom as he walked by. Only Vera knew he had been waiting for her.

They passed the front office, where a large window offered a view inside at the waiting area reception desk. Nicola sat in a plastic chair beside the school security officer. She saw Vera and charged toward the window, smacking the glass and yelling, "You won't get away with this!" The security officer grabbed her arm, pulling her back.

Vera turned away, couldn't look at the girl. Nicola may have been the one to push Kimber into the wall, but it was Vera's fault, and they both knew that.

"That girl has always been a menace," Kent muttered. "Maybe she'll finally get what she deserves."

A spike of pain pierced Vera's skull, and she bit her lip to keep from crying out. That little bitch *was* a menace. One who preyed on those weaker than her and terrorised girls like Ina.

Maybe a white lie was okay, then, to stop Nicola from hurting anyone else.

To give her what she deserved.

The gurney's wheels thumped over the lip of the front doors as the paramedics steered her toward the ambulance. "We'll take good care of her, I promise," one of them said, and she was glad Kent stayed behind. She'd been worried he'd convince them to let him ride along.

"I'll be by to visit you as soon as it's allowed," Kent called.

Of course he would.

* * *

Vera pulled into the teachers' parking lot and stepped out of her hatchback, the door giving a screech of rusty hinges. She stood and braced herself against the roof, head throbbing. Though the incident had happened almost a week ago, the effects of the head injury lingered. She'd been sleeping worse and worse because of those damn nightmares. Even doubling her Ambien hadn't helped.

That smile, too big for his face. A jaw hinged wide to open a mouth lined with razor-sharp teeth. And those unblinking eyes – bulbous, white orbs with blood-red irises pitted by black pupils. She woke whispering his name.

Mr. Ch—

She clenched her eyes closed. *Don't even think it.*

Vera slammed her car door, gave a startled gasp when she turned to find Kent standing behind her.

"I told you I'd pick you up." He grabbed her hand and forced it into the crook of his arm, pinning it there. "You shouldn't be coming back so soon."

Vera struggled to control her breathing, to remain calm even though she wanted to yank free of his grip. She didn't have the energy to fight him today, allowed him to lead her across the lot. "I can take care of myself."

Kent gave her a condescending look and patted her hand. "Nicola's back today, too. Should have been expelled, if you ask me."

"Everyone deserves a second chance." Vera had actually lobbied for a lesser punishment for the girl, guilt over blaming Nicola for Kimber's injury getting the best of her.

"I'll be keeping an extra close eye on you, today. And the investigation should go quickly, especially with my eyewitness account."

"I'll be fine." She might not be, though, not if Nicola was able to convince them Vera had lied. The school board would be conducting a misconduct investigation, since Nicola was claiming self-defence. Her father was on the board.

"That other girl, Ina, the one they were bullying, she's saying they were just having fun, even though I saw her running out of there. Seriously, I don't know where you'd be if I hadn't witnessed the whole thing."

Now he thought she owed him. Her stomach twisted, threatening to send up the instant oatmeal she'd had for breakfast. "Ina's probably just scared of Nicola."

Kent stopped on the sidewalk. "So, what're you making me for dinner tonight? Now that you're feeling better, I figured you'd want to thank me properly." He gave a lopsided grin that many would think was charming, but she saw the predatory gleam in his eye. Her ex, Derek, had that same gleam.

"I appreciate everything you've done, really." She tried to extract herself, but he kept her hand gripped in the crook of his elbow. "I'm on breakfast duty, Kent."

He narrowed his eyes, then let her go. "All right. I'll take a raincheck on dinner, then."

She forced herself to walk, not run, through the front doors of the school and made her way to the cafeteria. First Kent, now *him* coming back, it was almost enough to make her move again. Vera had slipped from her hospital bed while Derek was at work, leaving all her belongings behind except the clothes on her back. Thanks to some cash from a sympathetic nurse, she was able to make it to a women's shelter the next town over. That was almost a year ago. A year of sacrifice and hard work to rebuild her life from scratch.

Vera would not let man or monster take that life from her.

There were about two dozen children scattered around the rectangular dining tables, most munching on breakfast and a few busy with homework. She normally made the rounds, checking in on each of them, but today she made a beeline for Ina, who sat alone in the back corner.

"How're you holding up?" Vera asked, sliding onto the bench seat beside the girl.

"Fine, Ms. Bradley."

"I wanted to talk to you about what those girls did."

"They're my friends, we were just goofing around." Ina wrapped up her half-finished granola bar and shoved it in her backpack.

The flap was open, and Vera caught sight of a little doll with its eyes cut out and a rope wrapped around its neck. A note was pinned to the chest that said *snitch*.

Ina zipped her backpack shut, not meeting Vera's eyes.

Vera clenched her teeth. She'd convinced the principal to take it easy on Nicola, and the girl was already terrorising Ina again. "Those girls don't come to breakfast, it's safe to talk here."

Ina just nodded.

Vera crouched so she was at the girl's eye level, not wanting to ask the question but needing to know. "So, everything's okay since you played that game with them? Nothing's different? No nightmares?"

"How did you know that?" Ina's breath hitched in her chest. "I got freaked out, but he's not real. My mom, she says I have an active imagination."

That's what Vera's mom had said too. Even after what happened – *so much blood.* Just an overactive imagination and coincidence.

Maybe that was true.

But maybe not.

"You're friends with those girls now, huh?" Vera said. "No hard feelings toward them, or anyone else that might've, uh, hurt you?"

Ina rubbed her arm where Nicola had gripped it. "Nah, it was just for fun. Friends scare each other sometimes, right?"

Vera's heart broke for the girl. "Okay. Well, maybe try to steer clear of them. And if you do sometimes feel mad or think about bad things happening to them, just try to forget about that and focus on happy thoughts. Like horses." She pointed to the horse pictured on Ina's T-shirt. "You like them a lot, right?"

"Yeah." Ina's face lit up with a smile. "At my church camp last summer, we got to ride every day. My favourite was Cocoa. Like the drink."

"That's perfect." Vera stood. "When you feel mad, you just think about riding Cocoa, okay?"

"Okay. Thanks, Ms. Bradley." Ina hitched her backpack up on to her shoulder and left the cafeteria.

Vera sighed in relief. If *he* was real, and that wasn't a fact, Ina should be okay.

The remaining breakfast period passed quickly, and the pain in Vera's head receded a bit. She made her way to her first period English class, the one Nicola would normally be in. Not today though. Principal Phillips had moved the girl to another class.

The chatter died down as Vera entered. She set her bag beside the desk, saw the substitute had left a folder of the class's completed homework and stuck it in her bag to grade later.

She cleared her throat, readying the little speech she'd prepared. "I know you're all aware I was injured last week, but I'm doing fine, and I won't be answering any questions about what happened. And thank you to those who sent cards and flowers. That was very sweet. But don't think that means we won't be having our normal Wednesday quiz."

The kids groaned, several objecting with cries of "C'mon Ms. Bradley" and "Give us a break."

"Please write out a summary of the first chapter of *Lord of the Flies*. What instances of foreshadowing occur, and what can you predict might happen? What do the boys' attitudes reveal about human nature?" Vera turned and pulled the string on the projector screen, raising it so she could write the questions on the marker board.

She froze at the sight of the words already written on the white surface.

He appears, all dressed in black

His jaw unhinges with a crack

Vera whipped around, not needing to read the rest. "Who did this? Who wrote this?"

The kids stared back at her, started whispering to one another.

She turned and wiped at the awful rhyme with an eraser. "Just forget this, you hear me. Do not say it."

Someone giggled, and she caught Nicola peeking into the classroom doorway. Tormenting Ina, now Vera.

"You," Vera said, rushing through the door and down the hallway after Nicola, who was running away.

You little bitch.

Heat flared up Vera's chest and neck. She raised the eraser in her hand and chucked it at the girl's back. Nicola cried out and stumbled, as if hit by a brick instead of a chunk of felt, then spun around, a victorious smile on her face.

Nicola quickly schooled her expression, adopting one of fear. "Please, don't hurt me," she cried, falling to her knees at the end of the hallway.

Something caught Vera's elbow.

Kent. "We're going." He pulled her in the opposite direction from Nicola.

Vera struggled against his grip. "Let me go. I have to make her stop this."

He got within an inch of her face. "She's baiting you. Trying to get you to mess up and prove her right."

Vera sucked in a breath, looking around her. Several teachers had come out of their classrooms and were watching what was happening. One of them rushed over to Nicola and knelt beside her. The girl was pointing at Vera and crying.

Kent hustled her toward the front doors, stopping at her classroom to grab her bag. Vera kept her head down, refusing to look at the students, the other teachers.

They made it outside and Kent stopped. "What were you thinking?"

That he's back. That I have to stop him.

He couldn't be real, but there was no other explanation for that rhyme showing up on Nicola's paper, the worst possible place. That girl would continue to spread it just to spite Vera.

Unless she was gone. Then Nicola would have no reason to keep up with the rhyme.

When she didn't answer him, Kent said, "I told you it was too soon to come back."

"You're right. I'm going home, at least for today." She walked toward the parking lot, Kent keeping pace beside her. It wasn't a long-term solution, but it would work for now. Give her time to think.

He looped an arm around her waist, steered her toward his car. "I'll drive you."

"That's not necessary." She rushed toward her car, pulling the keys from her purse and holding them in her fist so they protruded through her fingers.

"I'll call over lunch to check on you," Kent called.

Of course he would. The sun emerged from behind a cloud, sent a spike behind her eyes that started her head throbbing again.

⋆ ⋆ ⋆

Vera stood shivering before her bathroom vanity, scrubbing the blood from her hands and arms where she'd scratched herself in her sleep. He'd invaded her dreams again, filling them with clawed fingers dragging along skin. Copper tainted her mouth from where she'd bitten her tongue, and she rinsed again and again.

The taste of the blood in her mouth woke the memories she worked so hard to suppress. Vera huddling in the bathtub in their apartment while her grandfather pounded at the door. Hiding made the beating worse, she knew that, but she kept trying. *Mr. Chew, Mr. Chew, Mr. Chew, I summon you,* she chanted, again and again, until her grandfather broke through. He'd smacked her so hard her head hit the wall, and she'd passed out.

She woke to her mother's screams.

Vera was beaten bloody, her body blooming bouquets of bruises over every inch of her skin, and her mouth oozed copper, some from cuts, some vomited up from her stomach. There was so much blood she'd had to swallow it or drown.

Her grandfather was worse though, because he didn't wake up. Couldn't. He'd been ripped to shreds.

Vera screamed then, too, her terror eclipsing her mother's. Because this was Vera's fault, and she was sorry, so sorry she'd called *him,* so sorry she'd begged *him* to punish her grandfather. They eventually convinced her a real live person killed the old man, that she wasn't to blame. The creature she'd drawn and the rhyme she'd written were just the coping mechanisms of an abused and traumatised little girl. Even so, she swore to never ever say *his* name again, destroyed all evidence of *him.*

Her phone rang, wrenching her from the past, and Vera rushed to her bedside table to see the name on the screen. Kent. "Leave me alone," she yelled, chucking her phone at the wall.

He'd kept his promise to call her over lunch yesterday, then showed up in person after school. She didn't answer the door, and when he texted, she claimed she was sleeping. Now, he was calling her at six o'clock in the goddamn morning.

Still shivering, she put on a long-sleeved shirt and sweatpants.

Pounding sounded at her front door, and she let out a little yelp. She crept down the short hallway that led to the front room of the house, a small open-concept living and dining room. The pounding sounded again.

She tiptoed across the darkened room and slid open the peephole. Kent. Shit. She pressed her forehead to the door.

"Vera, open up. It's Nicola, someone attacked her."

Good. No. She grimaced at her vindictiveness. Vera could not allow herself to relish the girl's suffering, no matter what she'd done.

Vera flipped the deadbolt, swinging open the door. "What happened? Is she okay?"

Kent pushed past her, the thud of his boots striding across the wood floor making her flinch. He took a seat on her thrift store couch, and she froze at the sight of him there, invading her space. Her home.

"No, she's not."

Closing the door, she asked, "What happened?"

He reached to click on the lamp on the end table, then took off his jacket and tossed it over the back of the couch. As if he belonged here. "The police found her about an hour ago. Really gruesome scene. Don't know what kind of monster could do that."

"Wait." Her legs went weak, and she slumped onto the edge of the rocking chair that sat beside the couch, the movement causing it to rock forward with a creak. "She's… dead?"

"Yeah." He scrubbed a hand over his face. "She was found in her bedroom; parents didn't hear a thing."

"Oh, God." Vera covered her mouth. *Ina, no. You were supposed to think of Cocoa.*

Kent leaned forward, bracing his hands on his knees. "I know you're not capable of anything like that, but you realise you'll be a suspect, right?"

Vera stood. "I could never hurt her."

He sighed, giving her that look again as if she were a child. "I know, but you have a motive, and you attacked her at school yesterday. You have to be prepared."

"Okay." She clutched her stomach, feeling sick and hollow. "I don't have anything to hide." *Except that I think a monster did this.*

"I walked over here, made sure no one saw me. We'll say I spent the night. That'll give you an alibi." He got up and approached her.

"No." She backed away, bumping into the dining table, then manoeuvring around it to keep the expanse of wood between her and Kent.

"It's okay." That crooked smile again. That predatory gleam. "I won't abandon you."

A shudder shook her body. "I just… this is a lot. Maybe you should go for now."

He gripped the back of one of the dining room chairs, curling his fingers around the wood and squeezing. "You still have your job because of me, and now I'm going to keep you out of jail. A little appreciation would be nice."

Heart hammering in her chest, she said, "Thank you, really, I just don't want you to have to lie for me."

Kent moved toward her.

With the table on one side and the kitchen peninsula counter on the other, Vera was trapped. She held herself perfectly still as he approached.

"I can see that you need me. I'm not leaving." He reached out and cupped her jaw, the feel of his slick palm on her skin sending a wave of revulsion through her.

"Okay." Vera eased away from him, busied herself piling up the school papers strewn across the dining table. She didn't even remember taking them out. "I'm sure you're hungry. Why don't I make you breakfast as a thank you?"

Kent patted her butt. "That's a start." He went back into the living room and stretched out on the couch, grabbing the remote.

Tears stung Vera's eyes and she blinked them away, but one escaped to land on a student's homework. The liquid created a splotch, and she went to brush it away with her thumb, but stopped at the sight of what was written there.

He appears, all dressed in black
His jaw unhinges with a crack
Watches you with blood-filled eyes
Grabs with fingers sharp as knives
Late at night, the man will creep
Eats the bad ones

Half-finished. A pencil complete with her tooth marks lay across the page, waiting to write the rest. She flipped through the pages in her hand, found the rhyme written across the back of every sheet. Several pages also featured a name.

Nicola
Nicola
Nicola
Nicola

A sob hitched in her chest and broke free, but she turned it into a cough.

"You okay out there?" Kent asked.

"Fine," Vera managed.

She was not fine.

It was me. Not Ina.

Me.

Vera must have been the one to write the rhyme on Nicola's paper too, but that was before she'd ever had a real reason to wish the girl harm. Why had Vera started all this? Why had she called him back after almost twenty years?

Kent laughed at something on TV, and she stared at him lying there on the couch that was her first piece of furniture here after running from Derek with nothing. Watching the TV she'd saved up for months to buy herself. Soon he'd be eating her food. And that was just the start, he'd said.

He had her trapped now. Nowhere to hide. No way to run.

She stepped into the kitchen and stood at the sink. The window showed only darkness, the sun not yet starting to rise. Vera turned on the water, closed her eyes, and whispered, "Mr. Chew, Mr. Chew, Mr. Chew, I summon you." Her body quaked, and she wrapped her arms around herself, the fabric of her shirt snagging on the fresh scratches that marred her arms. Scratches she knew now weren't self-inflicted. Nicola had put up a fight.

Gasping, Vera opened her eyes to face her own reflection in the window above the sink. Mr. Chew stood behind her, a semi-transparent apparition whose head nearly brushed the ceiling. His mouth stretched wide in a ravenous smile, and her lips followed suit, as if tugged by invisible strings. When he raised his clawed hands, hers rose too, flexed with the need to rip and tear. They turned from their reflection and crept toward the living room, teeth gnashing in anticipation.

THE LINNHE QUEEN

Sally Hughes

It took them three hours to find the line. Three hours of plunging the old, rusting hook into the salt black water of the loch, scraping through silt and weeds and shingle, finding nothing. On Hogmanay night, too. Well, there was nothing to be done about it.

When the storm blew up on the 29th, Callum was gripped by fear. Two days and nights of howling winds and surging tides, and all he could do was stand at the window, wiping away condensation, peering out into the gloom. That afternoon the weather finally roared away back into the Atlantic, and Callum went down to the shore in the early dusk. A line had sunk. Years of work and a mountain of mussels had plummeted into the loch's depths, and lay spoiling amongst the grit and grime.

He hadn't even needed to phone his grandpa. Five minutes later Callum heard the clip of boots on the road, saw the acid yellow gleam of the old man's jacket. Sandy showed neither surprise nor dismay at the sunken line. "It could have been worse," was all he said. He had been working this loch for forty years. He knew its ways.

As they eased the *Linnhe Queen* out into the bay and began searching, an unholy silence fell over the water. Even the eider ducks and gulls on the island were hushed. The tide was a slow murmur beneath the gentle rocking of the boat. Unlike Callum, Sandy was a bletherer but tonight he was oddly quiet too. Perhaps it was simply that he knew what was at stake. Only when the hook finally caught, and they knew they had the line, did the men look at each other. "Ach, well," Sandy said. "It's just a question of time, now."

They had the line, but a night of work was ahead of them. The knackered old crane at the stern ground into life, lifting the line metre by painful metre. It came up like some bloated monster of the deep, fat with mussel shells and kelp and strands of drifting algae. The men tied on floats with frozen hands, praying they could finish the work before the tide really began to run and pulled the whole line back down to the seabed. There was no question of pausing or resting. Once you began lifting the line you could not stop.

Callum was not sorry that the grind of the crane's engine made talk difficult. He was in no mood for his grandpa's tales of battles, treasure, demons. He didn't want to hear again of the Each Uisge who haunted the loch, coming out of the water in the form of a man who lured lasses down to the shore with the eerie blue light of his lit cigarette, pulling them in to drown after a kiss from his cool, wet lips. Callum had no time for such stories, even in play. There were horrors close enough: a bad harvest, a scuppered boat. The small, warm bodies at home growing thin and cold.

As Callum worked, saltwater splitting open the barely healed sores on his hands, his anger rose. It didn't have to be this hard. If Sandy would only sell some land, use the money for new lines, a better boat... but Sandy would never retire the *Linnhe Queen*. She was named for Sandy's wife, Callum's granny, a woman he'd never met. Mhairi Campbell, the first woman to climb the Ben. Mhairi Campbell, who loved the loch so much she swam in it each morning, until the morning she didn't come out. And her such a strong swimmer too. They never found her body. It was as though she'd been taken by the Each Uisge himself.

She wasn't the first woman to disappear. Before Mhairi, it had been the girls with sad eyes and restless hands that vanished; girls who wanted more than seven days of work a week and the occasional WI meeting as a treat. Callum had heard of at least a half-dozen of them: a parade of Bettys and Floras and Isabels, leaving on the first train to Glasgow, faded hats pulled low over their worn faces. But Mhairi had not been like that, folk said. She loved this place in her bones.

The crane gave a sharp cry and snapped Callum out of the strange dream he had been falling into. He paused in the middle of tying a knot. "What's wrong?"

Sandy shook his head. "I don't know," he yelled over the whine of the engine. "Sounds like something's gone." He slid to the crane, peered into the water. "Aye," he shouted over his shoulder. "It's got caught on something. Give me a minute."

Callum nodded, cold sweat beading his forehead. When Sandy switched off the engine, the silence was oppressive, as thick as if they lay at the bottom of the loch, swallowed up by the saltwater. Sandy leant over the side, cursing under his breath.

Callum gave the knot a savage twist and felt the rope sear his palms. Tying the floats tightly enough took all his strength. They had barely a third of the line up, and already his shoulders were aching with the strain. He wanted nothing more than to say to hell with it, and let the whole line go plunging into the depths. To distract himself he looked back at the hillside where his small house lay. A constellation of faint orange lights showed where the crofts were scattered amongst the peat and rushes. High above, the line of the hills shone white in the black sky.

Sandy eased out something caught in the rope with a grunt, then showed it to Callum with a smile: a long, thin piece of driftwood, crooked as a broken finger. Sandy tossed it away into the water, then straightened up. But he made no move to return to his work. He stood absolutely still, staring into the darkness, towards the shore.

"Sandy," Callum murmured, then when his grandfather showed no sign of hearing him, "Papa!"

Sandy flinched. "Sorry, wee son," he said, slipping into a long-abandoned nickname. "Sorry. I thought I saw something – a light on the shore." He came to Callum's side, peering out across the water. "Can you see it?" he asked softly. "Over there?"

Callum gazed in the direction of Sandy's pointing finger. "What am I supposed to be looking for?"

"A light, on the beach, beside the slipway."

"It'll be some drunk tourist," Callum said. "It's almost time for the bells."

"No… no." In the merciless glare of the boat's floodlight, Sandy's face was tight with tension. "It's blue. It looks like a blue fire. Can you really not see it?"

Callum sighed, and looked again. There was a quick spark of something, fleeting as a salmon's splash. Then nothing but the faint, warm lights of the houses and a thin, knife-sharp moon above. "I can't see anything, Sandy."

Sandy looked at him sharply. There was a sudden swirl of water underneath them that sent the *Linnhe Queen* listing to the side. Callum reached out automatically to steady his grandfather, until the boat righted herself.

"Must be the kelpies out for a ceilidh," Sandy gave a shaking laugh. "They should be out on the islands tonight celebrating."

"And we should be at home with a dram in our hands," Callum said. "We won't get this done looking for kelpies, or faeries' bonfires."

Sandy nodded, but still made no move to the crane. "She loved this night," he said. "Mhairi – your granny. She said it was the most special night of the year. Each Hogmanay she'd roast a joint, and afterwards we'd eat black bun she'd made in November, with a slug of brandy. I've not tasted the like since she… went away. She left a piece on the doorstep for the faeries, and in the morning, when she went out for her swim, it was always gone." Callum shifted, uneasy. There was something unfamiliar in Sandy's voice. Usually his stories meandered easily from anecdote to joke to digression. Tonight, he spoke seriously and simply, as if he were bearing witness.

"Sandy!" Callum snapped, his voice louder than he had intended.

Sandy shook his head. "Don't mind me, lad." His steps back to the crane were uncertain.

They worked on, but their progress was slow. Sandy's gaze was drawn, again and again, to the light that only he could see on the shore. At this rate they would still be lifting the line when old New Year came on January 13th. Callum tried to beat down his anger, concentrating on lifting and bending and tying, the stink of mud and fish in his nostrils.

When the noise of the crane was stilled once more, he whipped his head up, ready to throw an accusation at his grandfather. But then he heard the faint pops and bangs, saw the spreading flashes of green and yellow light blooming above the town.

Sandy crossed the glittering deck. "Happy New Year, wee son," he said, offering his hip flask, a lit cigarette between his lips.

Callum accepted the drink, the grip of his anger loosening. "Happy New Year," he said and took a large mouthful of whisky, savouring the hot tingle on his tongue. His head was still tipped back, the hip flask at his mouth, when he heard Sandy spit out the cigarette. "In Christ's name, what's that?"

Callum dropped the hip flask. It clanged onto the deck, skidded into some dark corner. Sandy had his hand at his mouth, staring out over the water. "No!" he said. "Get away!"

Callum turned his head to where Sandy was looking. Was that some movement in the loch? A shape of something, coming towards the *Linnhe Queen*? Callum braced himself against the side, leaned out as far as he could and tried to see. Was it the wake of a seal? The sleek head of an otter? No – it was something else. Something flickering, insubstantial, that he could not quite bring into focus—

There was a clattering behind him. Sandy was stumbling backwards, his boots slipping on the deck's frosted grime. "It can't be," he whispered. "Get away!"

He was lurching towards the starboard side, mad with fright. Callum saw him slip, and topple back into nothing.

Callum leapt with all the strength in his legs, slid across half the width of the boat, and grabbed Sandy's fluorescent collar with his frozen hands. He hauled him forwards, yelping at the pain in his shoulders. His grandfather's head barrelled into his chest, sending them both sprawling onto the deck.

Callum coughed out a painful breath. "Jesus, Papa," he croaked, when he could speak again. "What the hell?"

Sandy rolled off him, then crouched against the bow, his head in his hands. "I'm sorry, lad," he burst out. "I thought I saw—"

"Aye, I saw it too!" Callum thundered. "A seal. A dolphin. Maybe even one of your blasted kelpies. But nothing worth throwing yourself in the loch for! We could have both been for it if we'd gone in!"

Sandy still wouldn't look at him. "I'm sorry," he babbled. "I'm sorry."

Callum hauled himself up, and stood for a moment above his grandfather's rocking figure. He saw suddenly how Sandy had grown thin this winter, how his hair was a faint wisp of white.

It was not his grandfather's fault. It was too much for him, that was all, working through the night. It was almost too much for any man.

Callum reached down, grasped Sandy's forearm, and got him to his feet. "It's okay," he said. "You just need some rest, is all. Let's get this bloody thing finished, alright?"

But it was hard to get it finished. Now the line seemed more reluctant to come up than ever. They had to work the crane until it came belching to the surface in a swirl of silt and foul-smelling air. The crane's roar was low and threatening, an animal growl of warning. Callum's home, his warm bed, seemed further away than ever. He looked back at the floats they had already tied on. They glistened in the darkness like the upturned bellies of dead whales.

Then the line was stuck, snagged on debris or a submerged branch. It took five minutes of repositioning the crane, sweating and swearing, before the section came loose. Something came with it – something that shot up from the bottom of the loch, and floated at the boat's side with a grey gleam. "Sandy! Come and look at this," Callum called.

Sandy switched off the crane and walked over slowly.

"What do you think that is?" Callum pointed down. It was difficult to see. It was something long and silver and sinuous, decorated with strands of kelp, and the dagger-like shells of razor clams. Sandy did not answer.

It was already sinking. Without thinking, Callum leaned down and grasped it, ignoring the sting of saltwater on his sore hands. As soon as he touched it, his stomach lurched. It was smooth and slippery and horribly solid. Sandy had an arm on his shoulder, trying to pull him back. Callum shook him off and jerked the thing into the boat and onto the deck.

When he saw what it was, he clutched his stomach, afraid that he really would be sick. It had once been a person, but it had become something else – something claimed by the loch. A body picked clean, and then rebuilt. The bones were plated in mussels and cockles and oysters. It had thick strands of bladderwrack for hair. The needle-sharp legs of a crab waved from one of the empty eye sockets. In the boat's yellow floodlight, it glowed like a rare pearl, repulsive and beautiful.

Callum took a step towards it.

"No," Sandy said, his voice very quiet. "It's her. Don't touch her."

Her? Callum looked again. The hips were narrow, the three remaining fingerbones were delicate. Sandy was right, it was a woman – a woman wearing a crown of mussel shells. The Linnhe Queen.

He looked quickly at his grandfather. Sandy's face was working with terror. "Sweet Jesus," he whispered. "Mhairi!"

Callum tried to speak calmly, tried to soothe his racing heart. "It's not Mhairi, Papa. Look at it – it could be anyone. A tourist. People have accidents here all the time." But he knew as he spoke that it wasn't true. Tourists got lost on the Ben, or in Glencoe in bad weather. They didn't wander into the loch and drown.

"She's come." Sandy collapsed onto his knees in front of her. "She's come for me. I knew she would."

"Papa." Callum crouched down, hugged Sandy's shuddering body to his chest. "Hush, now. Hush. It's not Mhairi."

"I didn't mean to," Sandy moaned. "I only wanted to frighten her."

Callum's back stiffened with a sudden cold fear.

"I only wanted to frighten her. Make her listen. She wouldn't listen to me. New Zealand, and the chance of a new start, a new life. No more scrabbling to get through the winter. No more worrying about keeping warm, or the boat breaking down. But she wouldn't even think about leaving. She said she couldn't, it would kill her."

"Stop," Callum said into Sandy's ear. "Please, stop."

"She wouldn't listen," Sandy's voice streamed on. "She loved it here so much. She loved it more than she loved me. She'd have let me go by myself if I hadn't have done something. It was a foggy morning. I followed her, in the wee boat. I just wanted to frighten her. I wanted to make her need me as much as I needed her. I never meant this." He lurched forward out of Callum's grip and grasped her hand of bone and shell. "Do you hear me, Mhairi? I never meant this!"

Suddenly Callum understood. He understood why Sandy had worked this water for decades, why he kept a boat that was not fit for purpose, why he made a life that was harder than it needed to be.

It was not love.

It was penance.

Sandy lifted his head and looked at his grandson. A light flashed in his eyes, a strange blue flame. His thin lips were wet and dark. "You believe me, don't you, wee son? You know that I never meant this."

Dread seeped through Callum's body as he held that awful gaze. He thought of the stories Sandy had told him of his grandmother, the same stories, over and over again. *She loved this place in her bones.* He thought of the stone without a coffin in the graveyard, and the glow of Sandy's cigarette as he walked these shores after nightfall. "Each Uisge," he whispered.

Sandy's thin mouth twisted. He raked his long white fingers over his scalp.

A sudden bang hammered through the silence and Callum cried aloud. The rope holding the grapple hook on the crane, the rope straining under four tonnes of mussel line, had snapped.

"Oh God." Callum ran to the stern. The floats they had spent all of this hellish night tying on were not enough to support the weight of the line. It was already sinking.

"Help me," he choked out, trying to forget the skeleton on the boat, the words he had just heard. All that mattered was saving the line. "Find a new rope for the crane, I have to get it back—"

"No, Callum." Sandy's voice was deathly soft. Callum turned slowly. His grandfather was standing up straight, the same vivid blue flame dancing in his pupils. "You don't need to do anything, my wee son."

Swift as a sudden breeze, he threw himself into the loch, following the line.

Callum heard a scream from far away. It only took a moment for him to rip off his jacket and throw the lifebelt overboard, but the moment was enough. When he plunged into the water, his grandfather's coat was only a faint yellow shape, being swept downwards. Moving fast, too fast. Faster than Callum could swim. He stretched out his arms, but Sandy was far beyond his grasp, as though some monster had pulled him into the depths. Callum surfaced, the taste of blood in his mouth, his lungs heaving with the fierce bite of the cold. He dove again, and it was harder this time. His limbs were seizing up. He could see nothing in the black water.

Sandy was gone. The line was gone.

Callum's hands were bleeding when he hauled himself back on board, his body exhausted. He pressed his arms around his chest, trying to still the violent shaking. He had to get dry quickly, but he was unsteady as a drunk, and as he staggered towards the cabin, his feet caught on something. He crashed onto the deck, coughing up a red-flecked foam of saltwater and snot. His eyes were streaming. He wiped his face with one sticky palm and looked again at the skeleton.

She shone in the sickly pool of light, so monstrous, so beautiful. Her broken body given new flesh and new life by the strange creatures of the water she had lain amongst for so long. Callum swallowed a sob and crawled towards his phone. He kept his back to her as he called 999 and wrestled off his clothes. He could not shake off the sense that somewhere in the mouldering remains of bone and shell was a mind and a will. Deep in the blind eye sockets, there was a spark that saw again the quiet loch and the hidden hills. That saw him.

CLOSED CIRCUIT

Eliza Clark

S can see right into her apartment, he watches her while he smokes, leaning out of the window of his studio apartment. Her window a stone's throw from his because part of the city is cramped and overdeveloped and claustrophobic and miserable. His apartment is two floors higher than hers, the top floor, he calls it *the penthouse* even though it's a shithole. The layout of her place is almost identical, but her studio is cleaner, cosier, looks like a girl lives there. She's never noticed him before. She never looks up. She never sees him.

S got to know her routine on account of how it lines up with his cigarette breaks. 7 a.m. – his first cigarette of the day, she is eating breakfast, getting ready for work. When he has another cigarette before lunch, she's gone. Gone till the 6 p.m. cigarette, which he has just as she arrives home. He watches her take off her coat and her shoes – then she'll go to the bathroom and drink a glass of water. Then he'll stub the cigarette out. She goes to bed around 11 p.m., when he has his final cigarette of the day. He watches her patter around in her robe and her slippers, picking up after herself while the TV is on. Cups and glasses gathered and dropped in the sink before she pulls the curtains. Weekends vary. Usually she's out in the afternoon, sometimes she hangs out all day cleaning and doing laundry. Rarely out at night. Never brings anyone home. Always on her own. One time he thinks he sees a guy in her apartment – scares the shit out of himself, thinks there's some creep looming behind her while she sits on her couch with her laptop. He blinks hard and realises it's just a coat hanging behind her, that his eyeballs are so dry they've started to fuck with his vision.

He does not seek to arrange his cigarettes around her life. But he does watch her. He watches her because she is there, the window of her apartment like one of those ancient web 1.0 streams; just some bitch and her webcam and her boring life. He smokes and she exists within his eyeline. The apartments around her are empty because they are not nice apartments; this is not a nice neighbourhood.

He lives here because it is cheap and easy to live in this neighbourhood on a meagre income. He lives a life of extreme isolation. Never leaves his apartment. Works in remote tech support. Everything he needs ordered online and delivered to his home. He chats to strangers on forums, he downloads films and television shows and pornography. And he watches her.

* * *

HI THIS IS YOUR REMOTE TECH SUPPORT, S, HOW CAN I HELP YOU TODAY

hi
computer broken

CAN YOU PLEASE PROVIDE MORE INFORMATION

my computer broken

PLEASE ELABORATE

fix computer

OKAY. PLEASE GRANT MY PERMISSION TO ACCESS YOUR SYSTEM

yes fix computer
grant permission to fix computer
are you fixing
mouse is moving
stuff happening on screen is that you

YES

thank u

☺

is fix

Ticket #011749 is closed.

★ ★ ★

On Saturday night she takes off her robe in front of the window. Lights on, curtains open. Something she's never done before. She stands in profile, maybe looking at a mirror. Looking at her body. She cocks her head, weighs her breasts in her hands – moving them higher on her body. She drops them again, sighs in dissatisfaction. She twists to look at her side profile, twists her body to face the window, head still turned to face the mirror. He doesn't know, exactly, what to do. S is hanging out of his open window; his lights are on. He's obvious. He was already hanging out here when she started doing this.

Sort of exciting. Never really felt any type of way about her when he was watching her go about her day. Clean her apartment, put on her coat, put a kid-sized pizza in the oven – she was just like this moving thing his eye was drawn to. He watched her the way he'd watch a fly buzzing around his room. He looks at her breasts, the way they sit on her ribcage. He follows the line of her ribs to the curve of her stomach to the top of her pubic mound, cut out of view by the window frame, like a censor bar. Her body is okay, her face is sub-average. Not the kind of woman you'd pay to see, not the kind of woman you'd *subscribe* to, but he's happy to look at her for free. He gets hard and he gets embarrassed – something juvenile about it, all hot and sweaty over a regular looking woman just because she can't see him.

Would it be better if she could see him? Or worse. He slips his hand below the waistband of his sweatpants, takes a drag on the cigarette, palms his dick through his underwear.

Then she turns her head toward the window. Then she glances up at him. A doubletake, she *looks* properly at him, as if noticing him for the first time. Maybe this is the first time she's noticed him.

After a moment, he waves. He takes his hand out of his pants and waves because he cannot think of what else to do. He was out here first. She should have closed her curtains.

He expects her to glare at him, to startle. To pull her curtains closed. But she just stands there. Naked and staring up at him. Reminds him of making eye contact with an animal at the zoo, a thing which exists to be looked at, now looking back.

She stands there until he finishes his cigarette. He stubs the cigarette out on the window pane and steps back, holding her gaze, closing his curtains before she does.

* * *

HI THIS IS YOUR REMOTE TECH SUPPORT, S, HOW CAN I HELP YOU TODAY

Hi S
I have a problem
Maybe you can help

LET ME KNOW HOW I CAN HELP

Could you remotely connect to me
Will be easier to show than typing it out

SURE

I can't get this video to play

S plays the video. It is a video of a person flinging themselves from the high window of an apartment building, then hitting the roof of a car with a thud. Happens in a few seconds. There's no crowd, no fanfare, but the camera is trained on the jumper like they knew this would happen in advance.

What do you see
Is it working?

Ticket #011768 is closed.

★ ★ ★

Next 11 p.m. cigarette break, she opens the curtain, still fully clothed, and then she strips, slowly, like she's putting on a show. She doesn't look up at him. Doesn't acknowledge him at all. And she's all shy and awkward with it. He imagines what a woman in a porno in the same scenario would do and he's kind of embarrassed for her, mostly hard for her. He finds a couple of girls (much hotter girls) on OnlyFans who do this fake voyeurism shit – film themselves from their own closets or backyard but it's not as good as the real thing, even if the real thing is much older and plainer than they are.

She closes her curtains, and he jerks off and he looks at the semen on his hand and the window and wonders what they are doing with their lives – the two of them. He looks around his musty studio apartment, the hum of the fridge, the hum of the PC tower, the hum of an overloaded power outlet, too many devices stuffed into the crackling sockets of a giant multi-plug adaptor. The air in the apartment is stuffy and damp, sizzling with static electricity. He washes his hands and wipes the window and lies awake for half the night. 7 a.m. rolls around and it is time for another cigarette and a coffee and another day of remotely resetting the computers of office workers who have not thought to switch their machines on and off again, or who have lied to their boss about clicking on links in phishing emails, downloading garbage, or spilling soda on their hardware.

11 p.m. showtime becomes a regular thing, at least. Something to look forward to, some cheap IRL thrill inside of a long beige day – the only other excitement buzzing from the intercom. Groceries. Socks. A set of dumbbells. High strength vitamin D supplements. Clock strikes eleven and she's always there waiting. After a week or so of stripping for him, she starts touching herself. Maybe another week before she masturbates all the way to climax, her forehead pressed up against the glass. She never looks at him. Not the way she did that first time, she never looks at him. He's not sure he wants her to.

He scares himself again, thinking her black coat on its rack is a guy – a murderer, a robber, a rapist. Could even swear it has a face, could swear it was looking back at him. One long blink and it's just a coat.

* * *

HI THIS IS YOUR REMOTE TECH SUPPORT, S, HOW CAN I HELP YOU TODAY

Got a virus I think

PLEASE GIVE ME PERMISSION TO ACCESS YOUR SYSTEM
I'LL SEE WHAT I CAN DO

Depends is this a person or a computer

I AM A PERSON

Hmm
Okay
Do you have a computer or automated service instead

NO

Well I don't want some guy going thru my computer
No offence

OKAY
I CAN ADVISE WITHOUT REMOTE CONNECTION

Sure
I downloaded a file

OKAY
WHAT KIND OF FILE

Video

FROM WHERE

It was a torrent

I CAN'T HELP WITH THAT

Why

I CAN'T HELP WITH TECH ISSUES CAUSED BY ILLEGAL ACTIVITY

Not all torrents are illegal

OKAY
WAS THIS ONE LEGAL?

Fuck off man

Ticket #011773 is closed.

★ ★ ★

One Sunday, she's gone all day. Then she reappears around 6 p.m. with a man. A man who is kissing her and groping her the moment they step through her front door. He unbuttons her shirt and she settles her hands on the windowsill, bends over for him, for this guy.

S wonders if they know each other, or if she found him at a bar or a party or something. She's been living here for maybe a year, and this is the first time she's had company, and it seems to be for S's benefit.

He, the stranger, pulls up her skirt and pushes inside of her, pressing her up against the glass. Now she looks. Looks to see if S is watching her. And they lock eyes for the first time in weeks since this whole thing started. She smiles at him. She waves. He understands the message – or he thinks he does. *This could be you, you wish this was you, what if it was you?* And if it's supposed to turn him on, it doesn't work. Pisses him off, actually, because now he's embarrassed. Makes him feel like some kind of freak in his cucked little apartment watching what he can't have because he's too much of a bitch and loser to take himself and his dick outside. He swipes his curtains closed, petulant, but jerks off anyway. Pissed off and lonely and pathetic.

Takes a steaming hot shower afterward, scalds himself raw and scrubs till he's taken the nasty, filthy outer layer of his skin off. He shaves and he buzzes his hair short, and he looks clean and decent and less like the ragged and pale streak of filth that had occupied the apartment a moment ago.

Then he cleans. Takes all of his clothes and his sheets and his towels down to the laundromat in the building. He vacuums and scrubs till the place looks sterile and not like the neckbeard nest it had been a few hours ago.

Tomorrow, I get my shit together, he thinks. *Tomorrow I quit smoking and jerking off. Tomorrow I quit being so fucking weird.*

* * *

HI THIS IS YOUR REMOTE TECH SUPPORT, S, HOW CAN I HELP YOU TODAY

Hi S
Can I ask you a question

I'M HERE TO ANSWER QUESTIONS

Do you like to watch

IS THERE SOMETHING I CAN HELP YOU WITH

IS THERE SOMETHING I CAN HELP YOU WITH sits unanswered on the screen for minutes. S waits for a response. But the client logs off. Ticket #011788 closes automatically. He picks at the skin on his thumbs and swallows. He's itching for a cigarette, but the apartment still smells of clean laundry and soap and bleach and he doesn't want to fall at the first hurdle. He picks up his current pack of cigarettes and tells himself: *You can have one if you go outside.*

He opens the door of the apartment, looks into the hallway. The hallway's not a problem. The *building* isn't a problem, he knows the building. This hallway and the elevator and the laundromat are all safe spaces. It's outside. Outside is the problem. People scurrying around their sad little lives, looking at him – seeing through him, judging him.

Clutching the cigarettes he calls the elevator, and descends, trembling to the ground floor. He checks his keys are in his pocket (they are) and he squints at the harsh daylight flooding through the glass door of the building.

One step and two steps and three steps and he's a few feet from the door when he sees someone across the street maybe heading toward his building and no, nah, no, that's it, he's done, this experiment is over. He's nauseous and breathless and lightheaded and it's probably the lack of nicotine so he should just head back upstairs, and smoke first and then maybe just *step* outside and that works, doesn't it? *You can have a cigarette but then you HAVE to go outside*, he decides, scuttling back to the safety of the apartment.

He opens the window and lights a cigarette and feels better. Safe and fixed for nicotine and having a moment of perfect peace, disrupted by a note on her window.

Taped to the glass on an A4 piece of paper, she has written WHAT IS YOUR PROBLEM? in thick, black pen. He squints, trying to see past the paper but she isn't there. The apartment is empty – it's a weekday, she's at work. The black coat that scares the shit out of him is gone.

In the spirit of self-improvement, he has two apples and a chicken breast for lunch. He follows an at-home workout he found on YouTube. He showers. He makes coffee. He closes three regular-bullshit tickets and three giga-bullshit tickets and receives an email from the automated bot that 'supervises' him congratulating him on closing more tickets than average today.

He opens his final ticket of the day, #011794.

HI THIS IS YOUR REMOTE TECH SUPPORT, S, HOW CAN I HELP YOU TODAY

Hi S
Could you connect to my system
Will be easier to show than to explain

SURE

S remotely accesses #011794's system – he's greeted with a plain desktop, a single .mov file on the screen. He goes back to the chat.

I'M ON YOUR SYSTEM
GO AHEAD AND SHOW ME THE ISSUE

Sure

S looks at #011794's desktop again. Watches the mouse move from the centre of the screen to the .mov file. S sighs, figures #011794 has a screen recording of whatever their problem is.

Not a screen recording. A crackly video shot at night by a camera not-quite-good-enough to film in the dark. Mostly black with a dim yellow square at the centre of the screen, a man in shadow leaning out of the light. Smoking. Jerking off. Enough of his face visible and illuminated that he can easily identify himself and it'd be plain to anyone watching that he's yanking his dick. Her fucking window, shot from her fucking window, he's sure. He goes back to the chat and #011794 says:

You know I asked earlier if you like to watch
But I already knew

And then they disconnect, closing the ticket, yanking the video before he can ask or abuse or otherwise freak out.

⋆ ⋆ ⋆

He waits at the window till six. He has an apple in hand which he intends to toss through the glass the second she walks into the apartment. He smokes, stares at her little note WHAT'S YOUR PROBLEM? *What's yours, bitch.*

She doesn't come back at six. But at six fifteen there is a knock on his door which startles him. He looks through his peephole and there she is. Eyes teary and makeup smeared, face pink and ugly with anger.

"Open up," she says. And when he doesn't answer, "*Open up*," followed by "I know you're in there! You don't leave!" Her voice is shrill. Been forever since he heard a woman's voice IRL. Speaking normally and upset; no nasal porn voice, no *yeah daddy* or anything like it.

He opens the door, chain still on. And it's weird to hear his own voice, weird to hear himself say: "Why are you fucking with me?" This thin, sad sounding thing. "I get the message, just leave me alone." Thinks about how he was all geared up to break her window a moment ago – yeah, fucking right.

"What do you mean leave *you* alone?" she asks. Her laptop is wedged under her armpit.

"You know what I mean," he says. "I don't know how you found out my address or my work—" but she cuts him off, scoffing.

"I don't know where you work," she says, incredulous. "I should be asking you how you got my email address."

"I don't have your email," he replies. "I don't even know your name." She seems to believe him, and her face softens. She looks even older than he thought she was. Figured she was mid-thirties but she might even be in her early forties. Her clothes are professional and put together, maybe the office-lady look is ageing her. He wonders if she's divorced or if she's just a spinster.

"What did you mean – *leave you alone, why am I fucking with you* – what happened to you?" she asks.

"I got shown a video of myself," he begins. He clears his throat. "At the window."

"Yeah?" she asks.

"It looked like it was filmed from your apartment," he says. She sighs. Asks if she can come in, if they can talk. He nods, closes the door and unhooks the chain, opens it all the way and lets her in. The apartment is clean, at least, but it's still pretty shitty. Undecorated, unloved – the most personality on display is the three-monitor PC setup in the corner of the room.

"Show me what you got," she says. She puts her own laptop down on his bed and looks at him, expectantly. Still hasn't told him why she's so upset but S can take a guess.

"It was on a client's desktop – I do remote tech support – I don't have access to it," he says. She clicks her tongue, her patience for him wearing thin.

"You can't hack back into it?" she asks. He does his best not to repeat her, not to mock her for that, *hack back into it*, Jesus Christ, what a moron. "Why should I believe you?" she asks. So he does his best to describe the video, the circumstances leading to seeing it. He shows her the chat logs, which do a lot to back his story up.

She received a video of herself masturbating, apparently filmed from the window of his apartment. Sent to her personal email today with the subject line *whore* and no text in the body, just the video. She shows it to him. It looks a lot like his video. It is grainy, the quality isn't great. He rubs his eyes because he starts seeing faces in the static, weird, bug-eyed figures. They go away after a long hard, blink.

The angle's too high, *way* too high, to be his apartment. He tells her as much.

"This wasn't filmed from my place," he says. "Go look out the window, the angle's wrong."

She is suspicious, but she looks out of the window.

"The roof," she says. "It was filmed on your roof."

"Everyone in the building has roof access," S says. "It's feasible," he adds. *You weren't exactly subtle*, he thinks.

"And your video?"

"I mean it looked like it was from your apartment, but…" he shrugs. "I guess it could've been next door." He joins her at the window, looks down at her apartment. WHAT IS YOUR PROBLEM? has come partially unstuck from the window. "Maybe I could—"

"You're not coming to my apartment," she says, before he can even finish. She steps away from him, glances around the bare apartment, looks for a while at the computer. He opens the window, leans out and looks at the apartments beside and above hers. Could've been one of them. Maybe even the apartment below. "How old are you?" she asks, suddenly. *Younger than you*, he thinks.

"How old are *you*?" he asks. She smiles, face sour. Her lips are kind of thin. He's not into that over-filled look but maybe she could use a little of it, to look younger. Her mouth droops at the corners and he can see greys at the roots of her hair.

"Fair enough," she replies. "Do you know anyone else in the building? No enemies?"

"I'm pretty quiet," he replies. She looks at him for a while – tired eyes looking him up and down. He wonders if she's tired from fucking that strange guy all night. Wonders if she still feels it, if she's sore, if she has any bruises.

"Are you attracted to me?" she asks. "Up close? Are you attracted to me?"

"This feels like a trick question," he says. Because it does. But he knows what his answer is supposed to be when she starts looking wounded and embarrassed. "Yeah," he says. Resists the urge to shrug, because the more he looks, the less he likes what he sees. Her body looked good from far away but what if it looks different up close? What if she's saggy? What if she has rolls? And hair? She sits on his bed and starts unbuttoning her shirt.

"Do you like to watch in general? Or did you just like watching me?" she asks.

"I've never done it before you," he says. "And that first time was an accident, I'm not a creep," he insists. She pats the bed.

"Sit down," she says. "Don't touch me," she adds. Unbuttons her shirt down to her bellybutton and touches her breasts through her bra. "Just watch," she says. He nods. He doesn't really want to. Without two layers of glass and a couple of yards for air this is nothing, it does nothing for him. She unbuttons her pants and shoves her hands in her underwear and bites her lip and looks at him and she just makes his fucking skin crawl.

He looks at her still-open laptop and the creepy, grainy video up on the screen. Again, he sees faces, sees eyes in the static. He looks back at her but for what? Her rubbing her used-up cunt like some sad, old whore – so lonely and so desperate for validation she's turning to a loser like him.

"I don't want to do this right now," he says.

"Fine," she replies. She takes her hand out of her underwear, clears her throat. Buttons her shirt, gathers her laptop and goes to leave.

"I'll be at the window at eleven tonight. You don't have to come but I don't want to change our routine," he says. "Maybe they'll be watching."

"Fine," she replies. And she leaves, slamming the door behind her.

* * *

Opens his curtains and his window for the 11 p.m. cigarette. Sees her apartment in darkness, paper sign removed from the window. Pitch black in there, no lights, no sign of life. He wonders if she's gone out, gone to stay with someone else. He lights the 11 p.m. cigarette and looks at the apartments around hers – also pitch black. Wonders if they might be empty when he sees *her*, panicked and pounding at her own window. She looks behind her, and then to him, and scrambles to open the window. He watches her climb out on the ledge and calls *hey, hey, what are you doing?* She doesn't reply, too preoccupied with what's in her apartment, looking back into it again, and then again before shuddering, startling, and facing forward.

She takes a breath. She looks him dead in the eye (ignoring him yelling *what's wrong?* Ignoring when he says *just wait there, I'll get a ladder or something*) and jumps.

She sails toward the ground. Lands on the roof of a car with a smash. He looks down at her, watches a small crowd gather, hears screams from the ground. He scrambles over to the landline and calls the police and is told *we're on the jumper*, and when he tries to say *no no there's someone in her apartment*, he's told *we're on it we're on it*. But he watches the apartment, and he watches the street and cop cars pull up and no one enters her building.

He leans as far out of the window as he can – there's been no movement in her room, no light indicating the opening or shutting of the front door.

He looks and he looks, and waits for the cops or to see somebody run out of there. And then, in the darkness, a ghoulish face grins back at him. White skin, eyes the size of fists stare up at him. It stands in her window, unblinking, smiling. He stumbles back into his own apartment – his PC clicks on. He turns and sees footage of himself staring out of the window, backing up, the PC clicking on behind him, him turning to look at the monitor. A delay of thirty seconds, maybe a minute.

The footage changes. The camera – the thing in the apartment, turns and heads for the door. S watches, watches it scuttle down the hallway, low to the ground like an animal. It seems to drop through the floor. S sees carpets and floorboards and crawl spaces, rat bones and people watching television, until it's at the ground floor lobby and comes out into the street. S tries to turn the PC off at the wall but an electric shock knocks him to the ground.

Pounding on the door then, a heavy thud, the door opening and stuck on its chain as one bulging eye peers around the frame, watching and watching and waiting to *see something*. He crawls to the window, goes to open it when the thing, the eye, begins rattling the door, the chain struggling to hang on. He stops. The thing stops.

"What do you want?" he asks. And it replies. Not aloud, but he hears it.

I like to watch

LOON VOICES

Michael Rowe

Kaley said, "Mum?"

"Yes, buddy?"

"Mum, I saw someone on the lake last night." Kaley paused, taking a bite of toast. He chewed for a moment. "I think it was Jesus."

"You saw Jesus on the lake? *Our* lake?"

"He was walking on the water, just like in the Bible. Nobody else can do that, right?"

"What did he look like?"

Kaley sighed. "He looked like *Jesus*, Mum. He wanted me to go swimming, but I told him it was nighttime. I told him it was too dark to go swimming."

Julia O'Neill laughed and ruffled her son's hair. "That must have been some dream, buddy." She looked out the window at the lake. The family of loons she'd watched every day since their arrival bobbed past, riding the waves. "Kaley, look! The loon family is out for a morning swim with their baby!" She opened the window and tried to imitate a loon call, failing miserably and knowing it.

From behind her Kaley sighed again, a great condescended-to seven-year-old's sigh this time. "It wasn't a dream, Mum."

⋆ ⋆ ⋆

After breakfast, Kaley announced that he was going to find Jesus.

He said it the same way he might have announced he was going blueberry picking or hunting for garter snakes. Julia snorted, then gasped. Once she started giggling, she found she couldn't stop.

Kaley finds the Lord, Julia thought. *Hallelujah!*

"What's so funny about that?" Kaley asked, frowning.

"Nothing, nothing. You go and find Jesus." Then, remembering that Kaley had said he'd seen Jesus walking across the water, she warned, "Stay away from the lake unless I'm with you."

She'd almost said *unless Dad and I are with you.* Two years after Patrick's death she was fine in the city; but out here, up north, on Devil's Lake, she felt Patrick's absence like a papercut that never healed. It had been time, though, to come back to the cottage outside Alvina. *For Kaley,* Julia told herself, knowing it was a lie, albeit a good-mother lie. *Not for me.* She pushed back the tears that always seemed ready to flow in these unguarded moments.

"I think Jesus must live there." Kaley pointed out the window, across the lake to where the granite shoulders of Blackmore Island shrugged out of the water two miles offshore, draped in a dark green summer mantle of windswept eastern white pine. "That's where he was coming from. How am I going to find him?"

"You figure it out, buddy," Julia said, already thinking of other things. "I have to wash up these dishes."

"I'm bored. There's nothing to do out here. When can we go swimming?"

Julia sighed. "I don't know, Kale. I must finish these dishes." She caught the impatience creeping into her own voice. *What was the point of normalising, of coming back up here for the first time since he died, if I'm still as tense as if I was back in the city? Damn it.* "When I'm finished, we can go swimming. Would you like that?"

"Yay!" Kaley shouted.

⋆ ⋆ ⋆

Julia and Kaley swam in the lake all morning.

When she grew chilled, Julia arranged herself on a towel in a Muskoka chair and read a paperback novel in the sun until she was warm again. At intervals, she called Kaley out of the water and reapplied sunblock to his face and body before he ran back into the water, diving in as neatly as a young seal.

Floating on the surface of the water, just at the point where the waves blended into the overall grey-blue of the lake, the family of loons – two adults and a chick riding his mother's back – glided past. *The only other family on the lake this early in June*, she thought. *It's come to this: my primary adult companionship is loons.* The thought made her smile. *The baby is so cute. Kaley used to ride my back like that when he was learning to swim.* And then, painfully: *Loons mate for life.*

"Kaley, look! Look at the loons!" She smiled, and half-waved at them as they bobbed past. "Kaley, can you see them? Look! Oh, they're so pretty!"

"I'm swimming, Mum," Kaley shouted back, not irritably, just to be heard. He dove under the water and vanished beneath the waves.

My little porpoise. And Patrick won't ever see his son swim underwater.

At 1:00 p.m. Kaley said he was hungry. Julia realised she was hungry too.

"How about a sandwich?" she asked. "Some nice cold chicken? With tomatoes and mayo?"

He was sitting on a log, his back to her, staring at the lake. Without turning he said, "Yes please, Mum."

Julia frowned slightly. "Kale, you can play on the beach if you want, but do not go into the water. Do you understand? Stay out of the water until I come back down. Or you can come up to the cottage with me." She waited, hands on hips. "Do you hear me, Kaley O'Neill?"

His back still to his mother, Kaley said, "I promise, Mum."

Julia turned her head in the direction Kaley was staring but saw nothing. "Buddy, what on earth are you staring at?"

He pointed across the water towards Blackmore Island.

"There," Kaley said, as though it were the most obvious thing in the world. "He's coming. Can't you feel it, Mum?"

* * *

At two in the morning, Julia woke in complete darkness to the sound of screaming, accompanied by frantic splashing, as though the lake itself had woken up and begun to drown.

Kaley's going under, she thought calmly, still half-asleep. *Kaley is screaming and dying and he's out there in that black water. Jesus came for him and dragged him into Devil's Lake. The last sound I will ever hear from my son is the sound of his screaming.*

She sat upright as though spring-loaded, instantly awake in the torpid heat of her bedroom. In one balletic movement she swung her legs over the side of the bed, switched on the bedside lamp, and stood up.

"Kaley!" she shrieked. "Buddy, where are you? Kaley! Answer me! *Kaley*!"

Julia ran down the short hallway to Kaley's room and wrenched the door open. In the moonlight, she could see that his bed was empty. The window was closed, and the room was stiflingly hot. Whimpering softly, she crossed the hallway to the living room in the dark and cracked her shin against the edge of the coffee table. The emptiness of the house pressed closed around her, as oppressive in the summer heat as a wet Shetland wool sweater.

The screen door to the outside, to the lake path, was wide open.

Please God, she thought. *Not my Kaley. He's only seven. You took my husband before his time, and he left me alone with a boy to raise. Please don't take my baby too.* Julia crossed her arms across her belly. She felt a fluttering phantom ache in the place where the faded smile of scars was hidden by the cotton of her nightgown.

The path to the lake was clearly delineated by the moonlight. Something in the dirt cut into her feet as she stumbled towards the water, calling Kaley's name. The sound of splashing was fainter now, though the disconsolate screams, having seemingly reached a new pitch of ragged despair, still echoed across Devil's Lake.

When she saw Kaley, he was standing motionless in the lake just past the shoreline, as though testing the temperature before diving in. The water lapped at his ankles. Spinning in a lazy circle above his head, a thick cluster of moths flickered in and out of the moonlight like a corona of sparks.

Julia's world turned bright and dark at the same time, and the night sky seemed to tilt, folding in on itself in star-shot spirals. She steadied herself, then took two faltering steps into the lake, wading out to where he was, soaking the hem of her nightgown.

"Kaley?" she whispered. Carefully she half-pulled, half-lifted him out of the water and set him down on the beach. "Kale? What are you doing down here? What happened?" She shook him gently, and he moaned softly. The moonlight fell on his face and she saw that his eyes were closed. "Kaley? Are you okay?"

"Don't want to go swimming," he muttered. "No, Jesus. No swimming at night."

She reached down and touched his leg and found the fabric of his Scooby-Doo pyjamas drenched. She touched her damp fingers to her nose and smelled urine. *He hasn't wet himself since he was five,* Julia thought. *Not since the week before Patrick was killed.* She shook him again, whispering softly, trying to remember everything she'd ever read about sleepwalkers.

"Kaley, wake up, honey. It's Mummy. Wake up. You're all right. You're safe."

"Mum?" His voice was thick with sleep. "Mum, listen."

"Wake up, Kaley," Julia whispered softly. "Honey, you're dreaming."

"Mum," he said, eyes still closed. He reached for her hand. His own was slick with sweat. "If you listen, you can hear Jesus creeping up on you."

From the lake, that terrible lamentation came again, and another splash, far out on the water. Then the night silence planed over Devil's Lake and swallowed all sound.

Kaley shivered. "Mum, I'm cold."

Julia led Kaley back up to the cottage. She wiped him clean and changed his pyjama bottoms, then tucked him into her own bed. She stayed awake until just before dawn, watching her son breathe.

* * *

The next morning, Julia asked Kaley if he remembered walking in his sleep down to the lake. He looked at her as though she were crazy, and said no, of course not.

"Did you have any funny dreams?"

"Something," he said, shrugging. "Maybe. I dunno."

"Kaley, how could you not remember something like that?"

"Mum?" He tapped his spoon absentmindedly against the table. "Mum?"

Julia stared at him. The kitchen suddenly seemed unpleasantly warm in the morning sunlight. Outside the closed window over the sink, a wasp thudded with murderous implacability against the glass. "What is it, honey?"

Kaley hesitated. "Can I have Lucky Charms for breakfast?"

* * *

Later that morning, Ernie, the handyman from town, drove up to look at her roof. Standing by his truck, Julia told him about the tumult on the lake. "It was horrible," she said. "Like nothing I've ever heard before." She didn't add that Kaley had walked in his sleep, or that she'd found him ankle-deep in the dark water at 2:00 a.m.

"Oh, a Northern Pike or a Muskie probably got one of the loon babies, for sure," Ernie said. "Mean fish. That's what the screaming you heard was. One of the little ones. One of the babies." Julia thought he sounded almost cheerful. "Hey there, Kaley!" Ernie waved at Kaley through the open door of the cottage. Kaley looked up from his bowl of Lucky Charms and waved back.

When Ernie saw Julia's horrified expression, he softened his tone. "It happens, you know, Mrs. O'Neill. This is the wilderness. Them Muskies get to almost forty pound, and the little loon babies are no matches for 'em. They come up from under the water, and they got jaws like this" – Ernie made a scissoring movement – "and a mouth of mean, sharp teeth. Take one of them loon babies right under the water. Mean fish," he said again. "Mean as hell. You're way up north, Mrs. O'Neill. This is the wilderness. It's a hard place."

"So, the screaming I heard," Julia said, "was what? A baby *loon*? A baby loon being..." She almost couldn't bring herself to finish the sentence. "Being *eaten*? Being eaten in front of his *mother*?"

"The baby would have gone right under," Ernie said kindly, as though Julia should draw comfort from that. "What you heard was probably the mother. They're just birds, you know, but they... well, they *know*, you take what I mean?"

"Yes," she said, remembering the moonlight. "A mother knows."

"I'm sorry, Mrs. O'Neill. Must've scared you something awful. But it's the way of nature, I'm afraid." Ernie turned towards the ladder in the back of the pickup.

"Ernie?" Julia said. "Out of curiosity..."

"Yes, Mrs. O'Neill?"

"What's out there?" She pointed towards the island. "When Patrick was still alive, we never asked. Is there anyone on that island? Any cottages or summerhouses? Does anybody live there?"

Ernie stopped and turned around to face her. His expression was a study in small-town Ontario neutrality, the polite blankness that year-rounders show to summer people who are crossing lines they're not entitled, or invited, to cross.

"Why do you ask, Mrs. O'Neill?"

"No reason," Julia said. She felt foolish, suddenly, in the face of his bareness. "It's just – oh, I don't know. Kaley's been having some odd dreams the last couple of nights. He said he saw Jesus walking on the water out there. Isn't that silly?"

"Nobody lives there now, Mrs. O'Neill."

"But someone did?"

"Ages ago," Ernie said. "A family in the 1800s, name of Blackmore. The island's named after them. There was a house out there. A big old house, a ruin now, probably. There are lots of stories about it – it's the local 'haunted house' in Alvina, more or less. We heard them as kids. Spook stories. Every town has someplace like it."

"Spook stories?" Julia frowned. "What sort of spook stories?"

Ernie looked away. "Oh, you know. Lots of 'em. Stories about a couple of kids drowning out by the island in the 1960s. Other stuff, too. Ghosts, strange lights. Witches, too, if you can believe it. People talk, you know, but it's all a lot of old wives' happy horseshit." He looked at her, embarrassed. "If you'll pardon my French, Mrs. O'Neill."

"I've heard worse," Julia said. She waited for him to go on.

"It was a long time ago. No one goes out there," he added pointedly. "No one. Never."

"Could anyone be living there now? Kaley says he saw someone—"

Ernie cut her off. "Mrs. O'Neill," he said, almost brusquely. "Your boy was *dreaming*. And if he wasn't dreaming, whatever he thinks he saw, it sure as hell wasn't *Jesus*. Jesus didn't eat that loon baby. You're way up north, Mrs. O'Neill. Strange things happen up here sometimes." His voice softened, though it was still gruff. "That's all I mean, ma'am. You can read into that anything you like. Now, if you'll excuse me, I'd better check your roof." Ernie looked up into the cloudless blue sky. "Looks like rain," he added, turning away from her and reaching for the ladder.

* * *

Julia turned and walked back towards the cottage. Then she stopped short.

Kaley was standing motionless in the living room window, staring out at the lake. His arms were spread wide, palms pressed against the glass in a gesture of benediction, or welcome. From where she stood, Julia could see that his eyes were closed, and Kaley's mouth was open, the way it was when he was dreaming, the way it had been since he was a baby.

She hurried up the path, feeling very cold despite the heat from the sun that was even now climbing higher and higher into what was undoubtedly a perfect blue Ontario summer sky. She abruptly felt Patrick's loss break over her, this time with the force of a tidal wave that left her marooned and parched and alone.

At her back, the two adult loons skimmed across the water in a zigzag pattern, their wings beating furiously as they swept back and forth across the surface of Devil's Lake, searching for what they had lost.

To Julia's ears, the female loon's keening cry sounded almost human.

BLURRED AND FROZEN

Carl Tait

Ashley pulled on a tired pair of grey sweatpants and reached into her closet for a dressy blouse. The mismatch was intentional; a comfortable pairing she often wore during video conferences on work-from-home days. She was looking forward to her 9:00 a.m. call and had never understood why so many people found video meetings objectionable.

Settling into her favourite spot on the living room couch, Ashley opened her laptop and clicked on the link for the meeting. After the expected parade of popups and whirling icons, she arrived at a screen checkerboarded with the faces of her colleagues. They greeted her with quick hellos before immediately going back on mute while waiting for their manager to arrive.

Connor's ruddy face sprang into view a couple of minutes later. He gave the team a maniacally cheerful smile that only a morning person like Ashley could appreciate, then cleared his throat.

"Good morning, everyone. I'd like to go over our progress on the Medford project, but I want to start with the fun stuff. Has everyone received their 3D augmentation kits and installed the driver software?"

There were nods all around. Ashley and two of the others held up blue helmets with odd protuberances.

"Great, great. Why don't we give them a try? We always want to stay on top of the newest technology."

The screen filled with images of people slipping the strange devices onto their heads. As Ashley's helmet settled into place, she felt a low hum against her skull. She had expected magic but was disappointed. The visor now covering her eyes provided no apparent difference in video quality, other than making it appear her colleagues were not wearing helmets. Had she done something wrong in the setup? She was relieved to see the apprehensive looks of her coworkers, suggesting she was not alone in her failure to observe any improvement.

Connor laughed. "You all look concerned. Don't worry; it doesn't start working until I enable it on my side. Here goes." He clicked the mouse on his computer.

The faces on the screen shifted and solidified around a conference table. There were audible gasps.

This isn't just 3D, Ashley thought. *It feels so realistic. We're all here together.*

She looked across the table at her friend Doreen, whose mouth was agape with childlike wonder. Both women raised their right hands and reached out towards each other. Ashley stopped when her fingers hit an obstruction.

Connor shook his head. "You're both ramming your fingers into your computer screens. That's as far as you can go. But isn't the effect incredible?"

There were awed nods around the table.

"All right, on to the Medford project. Doreen, how's your analysis going?"

Doreen answered, but Ashley's attention was elsewhere, her eyes roving the simulated conference room. She refocused when Connor began his reply.

"Well, of course the important thing is…"

Silence. Her boss's face was frozen in a disconcerting blur, like a sculpture inspired by a Francis Bacon painting. Ashley understood this was nothing more than a networking glitch, but the fact did not allay her unease.

Connor's head jerked back into focus. "…and that should do it," he continued.

Horrified faces around the table stared at him.

"Oh, did I drop out? We're all used to that in regular video calls, but I know it must be weird in our brave new 3D world. You'll get used to it. Ashley, can you fill us in on your progress?"

★ ★ ★

The adjustment period was remarkably brief. Over the next few days, Ashley donned her humming blue helmet several times to join video calls in eerily lifelike fashion. She was amused to see that even some of her video-hating colleagues started coming to meetings on time and with enthusiasm. The occasional freezes still occurred, but they became tolerable irritations.

On Thursday morning, Ashley had just seated the device on her head when she felt a tap on her shoulder. She removed the helmet with a start and looked up at her husband, who was shifting from foot to foot.

"I'm sorry to interrupt," Rick said. "I know how much you love your new sci-fi video stuff. But I wanted to remind you I'm home early tonight. I can pick up dinner."

Despite the early hour, Ashley felt her stomach gurgle. "Great. Mexican? Indian?"

Rick considered the question in silence for an unusually long time. His indecisiveness was a long-running joke between them.

"Okay, Indian. Yum. Should I get your usual order?"

"Yeah. Sorry, I've gotta jump on this call."

Rick raised a hand and nodded. "Right, right. I'm gone. See you tonight."

His wife's helmet bobbed in assent as she joined her conference.

Doreen was telling a story about her golden retriever that Ashley had heard more than once, but she managed to laugh at the right places, along with her coworkers. The hyper-realism added to the humour as Doreen pantomimed her interactions with the misbehaving dog.

Connor arrived even later than usual. His 3D image finally popped into place, hands clasped tightly in front of him on the conference table. His normally immaculate necktie was slightly askew.

The laughter from the dog story died down.

"Please don't be alarmed by what I am about to tell you," Connor said.

Ashley was sure she was not alone in feeling intense alarm following that statement.

"We need to exit this conference immediately," her manager continued. "We'll have an in-person meeting tomorrow morning at 10:00 a.m. in the office. In the meantime, please do not use your helmet for any reason."

"Why?" asked Ashley.

Connor's image blinked out.

Ashley exchanged a puzzled look with Doreen before logging out of the call.

The rest of the day was relatively normal. Aside from background worry about her boss's mysterious comments, Ashley had a productive afternoon. She was rewriting a difficult paragraph mired in statistical analysis when she heard the scrape of a key in the front door.

"Chicken tikka masala!" sang Rick as he entered the apartment. "With fresh-baked naan. Hurry up or I'll eat the whole thing."

Ashley laughed and closed her laptop as she stood up. She gave Rick a hug and took one of the warm bags of food. Within minutes, the table was spread with an Indian feast. Ashley filled a plate with aromatic chicken and speared a piece with her fork, sighing as she savoured the richly flavourful treat.

"This is delicious, hon. Thanks so much for picking it up."

Rick made a mock deferential gesture with his hand. "Certainly, madam. Didst thou enjoyest thy day?"

"Muchly, sir. Can I interest your nobleness in a piece of naan?"

Her husband smiled but didn't answer. Ashley hadn't expected such a simple question to trigger his hesitancy.

"Rick?"

Another moment of silence, then he spoke at last, a touch of irritation in his voice. "Well, I'll get it myself if you don't want to hand it across the table."

Ashley was hurt. "I'm glad to give it to you. I was just waiting for an answer."

"I said yes, but you sat there staring into space."

"Sorry. Here you go." She tore off a generous hunk of the steaming flatbread.

You didn't answer me, she thought. *Why would you lie about something so silly?*

She finished her chicken tikka masala with reduced joy.

* * *

The conference room in real life was a nondescript, low-budget affair. The particleboard furniture was a perfect match for the ageing chairs with frayed cushions. Ashley picked idly at a chip in the veneer of the conference table while she waited for her colleagues to arrive.

Doreen entered the room clutching a pile of blue binders. She chose a seat across from Ashley and released the binders onto the table with a plop. Ashley briefly wondered if the table would survive the impact.

"What's this all about?" asked Doreen. "Do you have any idea? I was in the office yesterday when they announced this meeting, but no one would give me any details."

"I don't know," Ashley replied. "Connor is usually so upbeat about everything, but he looked kind of freaked out yesterday."

"Well, I guess we'll find out soon." Doreen looked up and smiled as several more coworkers entered the room.

Connor was the last to arrive. He strode in stiffly, gripping a blue binder of his own in one sweaty hand. He seated himself at the head of the table and began to speak.

"Thank you all for coming into the office today. I'm sorry to announce we have a problem with our new 3D conferencing system and I emphasise you must stop using it. We have already disabled and uninstalled the system internally."

"Why?" Doreen asked.

Connor toyed with the corner of his binder. "It seems that the system can trigger undesirable side effects in some people." He looked down at the table.

A man whose name Ashley had forgotten spoke up. "Are you going to tell us the whole story, or do we have to pry it out of you one question at a time?"

Their boss looked up, his eyes sharp. "Okay, that's fair. I'm sorry for being cryptic. We're hopeful this isn't too serious, but it turns out those video freezes are so realistic that they can cause problems for people in the real world."

Ashley's fingers threatened to claw a hole in the particleboard of the table. "What do you mean?" she asked.

Connor opened his blue folder and began to read from a memo.

"'Some subjects report their perception of the world freezing for several seconds at a time. During this period, the subject will appear to be in a trance-like state to observers. The frozen period typically passes quickly but may increase in duration over time.'"

"Oh, crap," said Doreen.

Ashley's lips were numb. "What can be done?" she asked.

"That's the good news," said Connor, closing the folder. "Most people won't be affected at all. For those who are, there is already a workaround for the problem. We are offering neurological exams at no cost for all employees who used the new system."

"Well, thanks a bunch," said the nameless man. He turned and left the conference room.

Connor flushed. "Look, I'm really sorry about this. No one knew there were any issues until we got the shutdown notice yesterday. I hope it won't actually be a problem for any of you."

Ashley thought back to the odd conversation with her husband the previous evening and suspected her manager's hope was forlorn.

★ ★ ★

Dr. Kepler was nothing like Ashley had imagined. She had pictured the neurologist wearing peculiar headgear and sitting behind a desk that featured a human brain in a jar. In reality, Dr. Kepler was a genial man with a bald head and nothing more remarkable on his desk than a letter opener. His face wrinkled in a friendly smile.

"Ms. Horton, you may well have nothing to worry about. This headset induces a neurological problem in a very small percentage of people, and I'm told you only used it for a few days. Have you experienced any problems since then?"

Ashley told him about the strange conversation with her husband. Dr. Kepler's smile faded slightly.

"I see. Well, let's run a few tests."

Ashley envisioned a fleet of robots pinning her down while needles were rammed into her brain. She drew in her breath sharply.

The doctor regained his smile. "The tests will not hurt, I promise."

He was correct. The assorted tests for reflexes, reaction, and co-ordination were almost childishly simple and Ashley's worry began to ease.

"Just one more thing," the doctor said, starting to turn away. "We need to..."

His rotating head became a frozen smear of flesh; a nauseating blur that no longer resembled a human.

Ashley screamed, or tried to. She found it difficult to move. With effort, she lifted a hand and reached toward the unmoving monstrosity that had been her doctor moments earlier. She forced her arm through the suffocating air, which had become a thick, gelatinous mass.

She blinked. The smeary flesh of Dr. Kepler's face rearranged itself into a look of concern. Ashley was startled to see a nurse now standing at his side.

"Are you back with us?" the doctor asked.

"Yes," Ashley said. "What happened?"

Dr. Kepler frowned. "You were completely unresponsive for over a minute. I called my nurse for assistance."

A tear rolled down Ashley's cheek. "So, what can we do?"

The doctor nodded to his nurse, who left the room quietly. He sat down behind his desk, his hands flat on the surface.

"Describe what happened from your perspective."

Ashley told him, and he nodded thoughtfully.

"Yes, that fits the pattern. But I must correct you on one point: you did not move at all. Your actions occurred only in your mind."

"I don't know if that's better or worse."

The doctor shrugged. "We need not speculate."

"What can be done? My manager said there was a treatment. Is it some sort of medication?"

Dr. Kepler ran a finger across his eyebrows. "No, not a medication. Let me tell you about the implant that can help you."

"Implant."

"Yes, I'm afraid so. The neurological anomaly that the infernal 3D device has awakened is not easy to reverse. The best solution we have at the moment is an implant that triggers the brain to compensate during the mental freezes."

"That sounds terrifying."

The doctor turned up his hands. "I understand the idea is uncomfortable, but it seems to work well. It prods your brain with available stimuli and your mind fills in the gaps. You will also be able to speak and move in response, but everything will be a bit sluggish until the episode passes."

Ashley's hands were shaking. "I need to think this over."

"Don't take long," said the doctor. "That was an unusually long period of catatonia and it may get worse."

★ ★ ★

The light was too bright. It hurt. Ashley began to panic, her arms and legs flailing weakly.

"Ashley. Ashley. You're okay. The surgery went fine. Try to relax."

Dr. Kepler's voice was reassuring. The implant was in. The light was still too bright. Ashley forced her limbs to behave and managed to lie quietly.

"They'll take you to the recovery room now. You can see your husband shortly."

A vague sense of movement as the gurney began to roll. Flickering consciousness. Rick's concerned face. Terrible nausea. Not from Rick, from the anaesthesia. Or from the implant. She didn't know. She couldn't think.

Sunlight through the window. She was in a hospital room. She realised it must be the next morning. She turned her head with an effort and saw Rick dozing in a padded chair.

"Hey, hon," she croaked.

His eyes flew open and he smiled. "How are you feeling?" he asked.

Ashley grimaced and reached instinctively to the sore spot behind her left ear.

Rick gently stopped her hand. "You're not supposed to touch it. Just a little bump under a bandage. They said it'll heal quickly."

She nodded and promptly fell asleep again.

Back at home the next day, Ashley marvelled at the speed of her recovery. A small achy spot and a mild headache; that was all. She silently thanked Dr. Kepler for his surgical skill and hoped the implant itself would be equally successful.

She had long conversations with Rick, trying to trigger a freeze or an unexpected pause. Everything was blissfully smooth for most of the day, but in the evening during a long talk about nothing in particular, Rick gave her an odd look.

"There. Did you feel anything?"

"No. What happened? Did my head explode?"

He laughed. "No, you were a little slow to respond, and you didn't talk as fast as usual. But only someone who knew you well would have noticed. Now you're back to normal."

Ashley nodded thoughtfully. "Weird. It all felt the same to me."

"It's strange you can't tell when the implant is working its magic."

"Dr. Kepler said it's active all the time, providing little nudges. When a freeze happens, those nudges get me through it."

"And it only lasted a few seconds. Right before the surgery, you had a couple of long, terrible episodes that scared the hell out of me."

Ashley grimaced. "Just be glad you weren't living them from my side."

Rick clasped her hand.

★ ★ ★

The cheaply outfitted conference room seemed almost cheerful in its banality when Ashley returned to the office the following week. Her team's morning meeting around the battered table was filled with tentative smiles and is-she-really-okay looks. Ashley took care to answer every question crisply and precisely, speaking a bit more slowly than usual to cover any gap filling that might occur. Her colleagues gradually relaxed, and by the end of the meeting, Connor's relief was palpable. He adjourned the discussion with a quiet but emphatic sigh that Ashley was certain she was not supposed to have heard.

As the room emptied, Doreen remained behind and signalled her friend to stay.

"It's great to have you back," Doreen said. "Forgive me for asking so bluntly, but are you really all right?"

"I think I'm fine. No more blurred and frozen craziness. The world and I are back in sync."

Doreen let out a sigh of her own. "I'm glad. People around here were so worried."

"By 'people', do you mean Connor?"

"I mean everybody, but with him, it was the most obvious."

"Of course. He was the one who was pushing for the 3D video conferencing."

Doreen's face hardened. "Maybe I shouldn't say this, but I think he was way more concerned with himself than with you."

"I'm sorry to hear that."

"It shouldn't come as a surprise. You know he's never liked you."

Ashley knew no such thing and was hurt by the suggestion.

"What makes you say that?"

"Oh, come on, everyone knows you're the one he sees as a threat. He was glad that something bad happened to you. He was hoping you'd never come back."

Ashley was too shocked to answer.

Doreen's smile returned. "Anyway, I'm happy you're better now. See you later." She picked up her pile of blue folders and left the room.

The happy glow of the return to work was gone, replaced by a cold indifference. Ashley made it through the day with difficulty, avoiding people as much as possible. Uncharacteristically, she left the office at precisely 5:00 p.m.

When she arrived home, Rick was already there. She fell into his arms and cried. He held her tightly, caressing her hair and not pressing for an explanation. As her tears subsided, she described sharp fragments of her painful day.

Rick was confused. "Wait, you never told me your manager dislikes you."

"I never knew it until today. I still can't believe it."

"Are you sure it's true?"

"I was told that Connor is glad this awful thing happened to me."

Rick stared at her. A malicious grin spread across his face.

"Is that all?"

"All? My boss is delighted I went through this horrible experience. Isn't that enough?"

Rick's jagged laughter cut Ashley even more deeply than her manager's betrayal.

"I'm not surprised he was glad to see you punished. I was pretty happy about it myself. You needed to learn a lesson."

Ashley stepped back, her face pallid. She closed her eyes.

"How can you say something so awful?"

"Awful? In what way?"

Her eyes flew open. Rick's venomous grin was gone, replaced by a look of puzzled concern. "I said I was sorry your manager turned out to be a nasty jackass. I was sympathising with you."

"That's not what you said."

"Yes, it is!"

"Well, it's not what I heard."

The implication was a painful epiphany. Ashley looked at her husband in horror.

"Oh, my God," she said. "I need to call Dr. Kepler."

* * *

The neurologist drummed his fingers on the desk in an irritating repeated cadence.

"The gap filling is not perfect," he said. "The implant boosts the incomplete sensory data and passes it along to your brain, which papers over the holes. The accuracy is generally remarkable."

"So you think it's remarkable that I'm prodded into thinking my husband is making vile remarks while grinning like a scary clown."

Dr. Kepler's fingers halted their rolling. "No, I do not. Your case presents unusual and disturbing anomalies."

"What went wrong? How can we fix it?"

The doctor rose from his chair and began to pace as if giving a lecture in a large hall. "Let me focus on one positive aspect. You say these interludes are fairly short, yes?"

"I think so. My husband said my sluggish moments pass quickly, and we assume that's when the implant is helping to melt my freeze-ups."

"Nicely put, and correct. Considering that your episodes were getting longer before the surgery, this is a very good sign. The appliance is teaching your brain how to behave correctly again."

"Thrilling."

"I sense sarcasm, but the point is that we may be able to remove the implant in the near future."

Ashley raised her eyebrows. "How soon?"

"Perhaps within two months."

"How am I supposed to deal with my random horror-movie vignettes in the meantime? And how can I do my work when I have illusions of colleagues confirming paranoid fantasies about my boss?"

Dr. Kepler stopped pacing.

"Paranoia. I believe that's the key. You are an imaginative person, and you seem to envision worst-case scenarios as a matter of course."

He knows my secret and he's out to get me, thought Ashley, suppressing a laugh.

The doctor returned to his desk and began typing.

"There is an unusually good medication that may help reduce the darkness of these interpolated thoughts. But it doesn't always work with incorrigible sluts like you."

Ashley's heart spasmed. "Excuse me?"

"Don't you remember your last visit? You wanted us to do it on the desk. You said we should put the brain jar on the floor and go at it like dogs."

Atop the left side of the desk stood a large glass jar, the kind that might have stored jellybeans in an old-fashioned candy shop. But there were no cheery confections in this jar, which instead housed a knobbly human brain preserved in a viscous liquid. Small bits of detached flesh drifted in the fluid.

"Ms. Horton?"

The doctor's sharp tone caught Ashley's attention and she looked up at him.

"I've transmitted the prescription to your pharmacy. Please let me know how the medication works out for you."

Ashley looked back at the desk. The brain jar was gone.

* * *

The smell of garlic filled the kitchen. Rick was standing at the counter, mincing a clove with his usual fastidious care. Ashley sat at the table, watching her husband while enjoying the aroma and the sense of comfort.

Dr. Kepler's medicine seemed to be working. There had been no paranoid interludes for two days. Ashley was hopeful her dark fantasies would remain at bay until her brain was healed and the implant could be removed.

Rick turned. "Hey, can you get me one of those nice red tomatoes from the fridge?"

"Sure." She pushed back the chair with a squeak and walked to the refrigerator. Opening the door, she half-expected to see bags of severed fingers, but was greeted only with the bright colours and scents of fresh vegetables. She smiled and selected the plumpest tomato, handing it to her husband.

"Thanks," he said, continuing to mince the garlic.

Ashley kissed him on the cheek. "And thank *you,*" she said. "I know this has been a hard time for you as well."

Rick put down the knife and turned his head, giving her the lopsided smile she'd always found endearing.

"You're the one who's had to endure this hellish garbage with your brain locking up. I'm here to help you get through it. I'll always love you and always be looking out for you."

Ashley sighed with contentment. "In a couple of months, I'll be able to get this implant removed and we can get back to normal life."

"What if you have more of those terrible episodes in the meantime? I can't stand to see you suffer like that."

Ashley caressed his shoulder. "The medicine is working. I'm fine."

A shadow crossed Rick's face. "Two months is too long. The implant has to come out sooner than that."

"I trust Dr. Kepler."

"Yeah, the guy who told you everything would be great, and then it was awful. Nope, sorry. That thing has got to come out now."

"What?"

"It's okay. I'm good at this. Won't hurt much." He grabbed her by the arm, picked up the knife, and raised it to her ear.

Not really happening, not really happening, thought Ashley. *Just another trip to Crazytown. It will be over in a few seconds.*

Then she felt the searing pain as the knife tore into the flesh behind her ear. She saw her red blood dripping onto the freshly minced garlic.

Frantically, she grabbed Rick's hand and struggled to force the knife away. She lashed out while screaming, her eyes squeezed shut in terror.

The pain vanished. Was the paranoid episode over?

Eyes still closed, Ashley touched the area behind her ear. She felt the gentle bump of the implant, safely covered with healing skin. Relieved, she opened her eyes.

The countertop was spattered with blood. She turned away in disgust, and saw more blood, a thick, dark pool of it, expanding rapidly across the floor.

In the middle of the pool, still jerking, was Rick's foot, clad in his familiar but now blood-soaked sneaker.

The rest of his body was out of sight, behind the counter, but Ashley didn't check on his injuries. Instead, she crouched down, wrapped her arms around her knees, and closed her eyes tight.

"It's not real," she whispered, and tried to make herself believe it. She said it again and again, a desperate incantation to dispel the nightmare.

"It's not real, it's not real, it's not real..."

THE BALCONY

Robert Shearman

The balcony wasn't that high off the ground, not really. Billy couldn't even be sure that the fall would be enough to kill him. It wouldn't be a good thing if he *did* fall, of course, he knew that. He'd probably end up with a broken arm. Or a broken leg, maybe – and he wondered which one would be better, and he decided definitely the arm, especially the right arm, then he wouldn't be able to do any homework when he went back to school. Billy leaned hard against the grubby Perspex barrier and peered over the edge; he wanted to look straight down, and he stood on tiptoe and tucked his chin against the other side to get the angle just right. Maybe he was wrong. Maybe the fall *would* kill him. Especially if he tipped himself right over so he'd fall on his head. He'd have to ask Mummy. Or George, even. George said he knew ever so many things, and he was always jabbering away, jabbering was what he liked to call it – he'd been jabbering at Mummy all the way down in the car and Billy hadn't minded at first, but after a while he'd had to bunch up on the back seat and jam his fingers in his ears and count all the cars on the motorway to distract himself. Yes, he'd ask George whether the fall from the balcony would kill him or not. George would know.

Billy knew that if the barrier gave way that very second he'd topple over the edge, there'd be nothing to save him. He pushed at it even harder with his whole body. He stood back and rattled it fiercely with his hand, but it wouldn't break.

When they'd first seen the hotel room, Mummy had wrinkled up her nose in that way Billy didn't like, and she'd said, "Not very big, is it?" And George had laughed, and said, "Big enough for what we need!" There was a double bed for Mummy and George, and a little roll-up bed for Billy, and there was a little television set and a kettle, and there was a bathroom and a balcony. "Why don't you go play out on the balcony for a bit?" George had asked Billy. "It's been a long drive and your Mummy and I need to lie down and do bed things." So Billy had taken his things and gone out on to the balcony, and Mummy had smiled through the window at him and closed the curtains.

It wasn't a very big balcony, and it wasn't very clean. There was a plastic chair in the corner and Billy sat on it for a while but it didn't have a cushion and it made Billy's bum feel cold. Billy had brought a book with him and he liked the book but he didn't want to read his book again just now, he was on holiday. He had a couple of little toy cars and he raced them against each other on the stone floor, but they were the same cars he played with at home so that wasn't very exciting. He had asked Mummy whether she could buy him a new car to play with on holiday but she'd said, "I'm taking you on holiday, isn't that enough?" And now he was on holiday and it wasn't.

There wasn't much of a view from the balcony. Billy knew the sea was out there somewhere, and he thought he could hear people having fun on the beach, but he didn't know which direction that all might be in. Where he wanted the sea to be was filled instead with a shopping centre and a car park. The hotel was built in an L-shape, and Billy could see all the balconies in the adjacent wing. He counted how many floors the hotel had – nine floors, and if you fell from a balcony on the ninth floor you'd definitely be dead, and he felt a little stab of jealousy for all the holidaymakers who had that option. Most of the hotel rooms had their curtains drawn just like his, and he supposed behind each and every one of them other Mummies were doing bed things with their Georges.

On a balcony two floors beneath his and a little round the side, Billy watched a woman step out wearing a bikini. She had long blonde hair and her bikini was red and she was carrying a towel and she was smoking a cigarette. Billy thought she looked nice. She lay the towel down on the floor, and then walked over to her own Perspex barrier, just as Billy had done. Billy wondered whether she too was trying to find out where the sea might be, or calculating whether the fall would be fatal if she jumped over the edge.

And then, quite suddenly, she turned her head and looked straight at him. Billy didn't know why – he hadn't made a noise; he was a good boy – Mummy and George had told him to play quietly and he had been as quiet as could be. The woman had caught him staring at her and now she was staring right back. Billy wanted to duck out of sight, or at least look away – and yet he didn't. From a good twenty metres away, across the unlovely expanse of breeze block, she looked into his eyes and he looked into hers. She didn't smile. She didn't even give the hint of a smile. And after a long half-minute of all this staring and not smiling, never once breaking eye contact, she slowly raised her hand. It was the hand that held the cigarette, and Billy thought she was going to put it between her lips, but she didn't, she just held the hand up and the smoke drifted across her face. And then the hand moved back and forth. Two, three times. Billy realised it was a wave. She was waving at Billy. Still unsmiling, and still waving, five times, six, and there was nothing friendly in that face and the eyes seemed hard like pebbles.

Billy hesitated, and then he waved back.

The woman gave a single nod to that, and Billy didn't know what that nod meant. And then she turned her head away as if he were dismissed, or as if he were already forgotten, or as if she had never even noticed him in the first place. She took a single puff at her cigarette and then flung it away over the barrier. Billy watched the cigarette fall, and soon it was too small for him to see. And Billy thought that had the cigarette been a person, had that been the scale so that the cigarette was person-sized, then it would have been like the person had fallen from an aeroplane, there would have been such a long way to fall, there was no way anyone could survive a fall like that. Billy thought the cigarette would have screamed and screamed! The woman turned her attention to the towel.

And Billy turned *his* attention to his toy cars. They took part in an epic race over the entire balcony, and at one point the red car was chasing the blue car across the rim of the barrier itself, and Billy wondered what it would be like if the car suddenly skidded out of control over the side and into oblivion – the passengers would scream and scream like the cigarette had as they plummeted down towards certain destruction. He even came close to putting it to the test, to throwing the blue car as far as it could go, and then the red car too, to find out which bits of the cars would smash off when they hit the ground. But he didn't when he realised he'd then have no cars left to play with and he'd be bored.

At one point a seagull flew on to the balcony and watched him beadily. Billy didn't move, he didn't want to scare it away. "Hello," he whispered, "please don't go" – but then the seagull took flight anyway.

He hadn't even thought about the woman for ages and ages, and then he remembered her and that gave him a sudden thrill, it was something else for him to look at! He saw that she was now lying on her towel sunbathing. The bikini was off – she lay there entirely naked, face down. And Billy had always known that everyone else was covered all over with skin just the same way he was, but he'd never seen so much of it before.

Because she was lying on her front Billy couldn't see her boobs, and Billy was old enough to know that the boobs were meant to be the most exciting bit. So that was a little disappointing, but also a relief, because he wasn't sure he was quite ready for the full reality of boobs just yet. What he was being given already was exotic enough. And as Billy gazed down at her he felt that he was no longer being a good boy, this was properly *naughty*, and he would get in trouble if he were caught. But the woman didn't see him. She never stirred. She was fast asleep. He looked at the way her hair was draped casually over her shoulders and masking her face. The arms out in front, as if she were swimming and hadn't realised there wasn't any water there. The bottom raised slightly in the air, or maybe it was just a fat bottom, or maybe all bottoms were fat once you took the pants off and the cheeks were no longer strapped in. Still looking for a hint of boob, he gave special attention to the little crack between towel and chest, and he thought maybe he'd caught a glimpse of one of them propping the rest of the body up. But he really couldn't be sure.

The seagull landed on her balcony. Billy didn't know whether it was *his* seagull, but he pretended that it was. The seagull stared at the woman too. And it looked up at Billy, and Billy thought they shared some little bond of complicity. Then the seagull gave a single flap of its wings, and hopped up, straight on to the woman's bottom.

Billy held his breath, not sure whether to laugh or to cry out. Waiting for the moment when the woman would wake up and shoo the bird away. And when she did, would she see Billy staring down at her too? He didn't want her to catch him. He wanted her to catch him.

But the woman didn't react. She didn't so much as move the slightest muscle. Even the seagull looked surprised. It prodded at the naked bottom harder, seemed to huff. And then it started to parade across her spine.

The balcony door opened with a clatter, Billy looked around. "So, this is where you've been lurking!" said Mummy. "Do you mind sharing your balcony with the rest of us?" grinned George. And Billy felt guilty, as if he'd been hogging it to himself.

George looked over the edge. "Aye, aye," he said. "I can see why Billy likes it out here!" And he chuckled and pointed.

"Disgusting," said Mummy. "Where just anyone can see!"

"Well, I'm not complaining," said George. "They promised us a room with a view, didn't they?" And Mummy's nose wrinkled and Billy knew she was annoyed, but she laughed anyway.

"Come on, Billy," said Mummy. "We're going to the beach. Do you want to see the beach? Do you want some fish and chips?"

"Yes," said Billy. "Uncle George, if you fell off the balcony, would it be high enough to kill you?"

"'Spect so," said George. "Fish and chips, yum yum. I've worked up an appetite!"

* * *

"I know you've been to the beach before," Mummy had said. "But pretend it's your first time for George, it would mean such a lot to him." That was easy, Billy didn't remember ever having gone to a beach, it must have happened when he was very small. "Do you like the beach?" George now asked, displaying it with his arms out wide as if he owned it, and Billy said, "Yes." Billy didn't much like the beach. He liked the sea part fine, and he liked the sand part fine, although he didn't like the way it got between his toes, Mummy had told him to take his shoes and socks off and that had been a bad idea. It was the people part of the beach Billy didn't like, and there were so many people. Billy asked Mummy what all the people were doing there, and Mummy said, "They're all here to have fun, just like we are!" Billy thought that sounded rather unlikely.

George bought fish and chips, and they ate them sitting on a large rock. Seagulls flew down, and Billy fed them a few of his chips. "Don't waste those chips, I paid for those chips," said George. "Seagulls are just flying rats." "That's pigeons," said Mummy, and George said, "They're the same thing." The breeze turned chill; it began to drizzle.

Mummy said they could have ice cream for afters, and they went into a café. The three of them sat down at a table as if they were a proper family. A waitress came up to serve them. She had long blonde hair and

Billy didn't think it was as nice as the long blonde hair of the woman on the balcony. "I fancy a knickerbocker glory," announced George. "Would your establishment happen to sell a knickerbocker glory? What's the knickerbocker glory status?" The waitress said they did indeed serve knickerbocker glories. "Well, I will be taking the knickerbocker glory, and the boy here will have a knickerbocker glory. Do you want a knickerbocker glory?" – and at that he nudged Mummy and Mummy said she was fine without. The waitress giggled, then she said she would bring them two knickerbocker glories. "My girlfriend will be sharing my knickerbocker glory," George said to the waitress, "unless you'd like to share it with me instead?" The waitress giggled again, just the same giggle as before, and said the knickerbocker glories would be right over. "Toot sweet," said George. Billy asked what a knickerbocker glory was. "Ice cream," said Mummy, shortly.

Then the ice creams arrived, and Billy thought they were the biggest ice creams he had ever seen! He wasn't sure whether to be pleased or not. Frankly, he felt a little intimidated by them. He stuck in his spoon and churned the froth around a bit. George jabbered some more to the waitress about knickerbocker glories and their impressive size. "That's enough now," said Mummy, and the waitress didn't know what to say, so she giggled one last time and fled. "I'm just having a bit of fun," said George. "Want a taste of my knickerbocker?", and Mummy didn't say anything. George smiled. He took her hand, and he gave it a squeeze.

"That hurts," she said.

"Come on, 'Chelle," said George amiably, "don't be a cunt."

Billy and George ate their ice creams for a while, and George jabbered away the whole time. But he wasn't speaking to Mummy, he spoke only to Billy, and Billy found that rather disconcerting. It made him feel a little sick. He couldn't finish his ice cream, but George didn't seem to mind, as soon as his own bowl was empty he slid Billy's across the table towards him and tucked into that one too. "Do you like the beach, Billy?" he'd say again. "Is this the holiday you dreamed of, Billy?" Billy knew Mummy's nose would be wrinkling with displeasure, but he dared to look at her, and was surprised to see instead that she was blinking away tears. And then it was as if she could stand it no longer. She pulled the spoon out of George's hand; it clattered to the table. George turned to look at her. She whispered to him, "I'm sorry, I'm sorry, I'm sorry." She reached out and stroked his chin with her finger, slowly, as if she were exploring it for the first time. Then she kissed him on the mouth. She used her tongue and everything, Billy had to look away. He wished he still had his knickerbocker glory to play with.

They went straight back to the hotel. George said to Billy, "Do you fancy staying here in the lobby for a while?" Mummy protested – Billy wasn't old enough to be left alone in a hotel lobby, the idea of it! "Then it's either the balcony or the bathroom, champ," George said. "It's your choice." Billy chose the balcony.

They shut the door on him and pulled the curtains, and there was a strange greyness out there that seemed to swallow the sky, and Billy suddenly felt more properly alone than he'd ever been in his entire life.

The woman was still lying on her towel on the balcony below. The sun had long ago vanished behind the clouds, she wouldn't be getting much of a tan any longer. The drizzle had turned into rain, proper hard rain with proper hard raindrops, and though there was some shelter on the balcony, the wind was blowing it over the barriers. It spattered her body.

Billy thought the naked woman no longer seemed so naughty or forbidden. Of all the people staying in this huge hotel, Billy and the woman were the only ones out in the gloom and in the wet. He felt a new affection for her. It was as if all the afternoon she had been out on her balcony just for Billy, waiting for him to come back to her.

At once a whole flock of seagulls descended upon her. And Billy felt a sudden rage – he'd never wanted to protect anyone before, not even Mummy, not even during the really bad times last Christmas. But now he knew this woman was his responsibility, and he alone could save her. And the seagulls were swarming all over her body now – on her skin, in her hair, nuzzling into that gap where Billy had once tried to see her boobs – there was no part of her they didn't claim as theirs, and there must have been a dozen of them, all nipping at her savagely with their beaks.

Billy wanted to scream out, but he knew he mustn't make any noise, he'd promised Mummy he wouldn't do anything to disturb George during the bed things, he didn't like it. So he hissed at the seagulls under his breath – "Shoo!" It was really little more than a whisper. "Leave her alone!" Hoping they would hear but that George wouldn't, and shaking his fists at them for good measure.

It shouldn't have worked. But as one the seagulls took fright. Cawing in protest, they streamed off the balcony and into the air.

Only one seagull was left behind. And in an instant Billy saw it was *his* seagull again, he knew it with absolute certainty. It was in its favourite position, once more perched upon the woman's naked bottom. Billy wondered why it hadn't flown away with all of its friends.

And then he realised. The seagull was stuck fast! Its legs had somehow got trapped within the crack between the two arse cheeks. Billy watched as it tried to pull itself free; it flapped its wings, it strained to heave itself out. But it was no good. The more the bird struggled, the more the folds of the woman's bum seemed to tighten their grip.

The seagull at last turned its head and looked straight at Billy. It gave a desperate cry. But it was drowning in quicksand, Billy could see that it was sinking ever deeper, past its breast, past its flank. It could no longer move its wings. Its head was soon the only part of the bird that was peeking out of the greedy buttocks; and still, the seagull refused to believe that all was lost, twisting its little neck from side to side in search of some salvation.

Then the bottom spasmed. It was as if the woman was releasing a colossal fart. The deadly arsecrack widened. The seagull gave one last squawk that sounded more bemused than frightened, and then was sucked under. It was swallowed whole. It was gone. The woman's entire body seemed to lurch with the effort of the kill – the expanse of bare tanned skin rippling right up her spinal column. And when the convulsion was over, the body was left splayed in a slightly different position. Billy could see a flash more thigh, a flash more boob. A flash more face, too – the long blonde hair was now parted, and her cold dead eyes were open and staring straight at him.

Billy rushed to the balcony door and tried to slide it open, but it didn't move, it wouldn't move, it was locked, they had locked him out.

There was a gap in the curtains. Mummy hadn't pulled them closed properly. Billy bent down and squinted through them. And he could see Mummy's naked bottom too, and there were her thighs, and there were her boobs, and she was turned away from him, she was looking at George, she only cared about George. And George was naked too, and he was lying upon the bed. Billy stared at George, and George stared back at Billy, and George didn't smile, but he raised his hand in a wave.

And even all this time Billy had still been silent, but now he couldn't help it, he was banging upon the glass. "Let me in!" he cried. "Please, Mummy, let me in!"

It was an age before the door was opened and Billy could tumble into the bedroom. Now Mummy had on a dressing gown, George was wearing a pair of underpants and was putting on a shirt. "What's the matter?" Mummy said. "It isn't just *your* holiday, you know. It isn't all for *you*!" And she slapped him.

The slap didn't hurt. It was one of her gentler slaps, really, and straight away Billy could see Mummy hadn't even meant it. But at that moment Billy made a decision. He'd been going to tell her all about the woman on the balcony, and now he wasn't. He wasn't going to share her after all. She would be all his, his and no one else's – and if that made him feel petty and spiteful, Billy didn't mind, Billy liked how it felt. It made him sting inside and it was such a funny little sting.

Mummy and George were staring at him, and he realised he was dripping wet from the rain. "I'm sorry," he whispered, but he didn't mean it. "I'm sorry, I'm sorry, I'm sorry."

⋆ ⋆ ⋆

Mummy asked him if he wanted anything else to eat. Even ice cream – would he like some more ice cream? Billy said he wasn't hungry, and that was almost true. Mummy gave him a little hug and Billy kept his arms by his sides and refused to hug back. Then he got into his jimjams and brushed his teeth ready for bed. "Would you like to watch TV for half an hour? Any channel you like." So they all cuddled up on the bed and watched the television for a bit, and even though there was nothing on that was fun, that was still quite nice. Mummy in the middle, with Billy cuddling her on one side, and George cuddling the other, nice. Then Billy got into his own little roll-up bed, leaving Mummy and George to theirs. "Night night, sweetie," said Mummy. "We'll do the beach again tomorrow!" "Good night, Billy," said George.

Billy woke up suddenly and thought it must be morning already – the room was so bright! But then he realised that it was nothing but the moonlight streaming through off the balcony. He knew Mummy had closed the curtains but now they were open again. The light was harsh and white, not like daylight with all its warmth and its colour, but Billy preferred this light, he didn't know why, it was just better. *Cleaner*, somehow.

He got up. Mummy and George were still fast asleep. Mummy's arms were clasped tight around George, and George's naked bum was sticking out from beneath the sheets. It wasn't as smooth as the bum of the woman on the balcony. It was the hairiest bum Billy had ever seen.

He looked to the balcony again, and now saw that the door had opened wide for him too. So he went outside.

In the moonlight he thought he could make out the sea in the distance. And the height from the balcony was so much more impressive, he knew without doubt that this time the fall would kill him. He was pleased to see that on her own balcony the woman was still there. Even better, she had woken up too – she was no longer lying on her towel, but standing right at the edge of the barrier looking out into the night air. She was smoking a cigarette. She was still naked.

Billy raised a hand to wave. He decided to be braver still, he would call out to her. He didn't care about being quiet now, Mummy and George weren't doing any bed things this time. "Hello!" But the sound didn't carry, it was strange – his voice was so muffled even he could barely hear it.

But still she seemed to react. She slowly turned her head and looked at him. She only had one eye. He supposed that the seagulls must have come back, perhaps they'd pecked it out. He hoped it hadn't hurt her. She didn't smile. She raised a hand and Billy thought she was going to wave back, but she was just putting her cigarette to her lips. She puffed out smoke through her mouth and down her nostrils and out of that single gaping eye socket, and then she flung the cigarette away.

All the while she didn't take her remaining eye off him. And they looked at each other for a long time.

At length she broke her gaze. She raised her hand to her face again. She stuck out her tongue. She stuck it out a long way, and then she jerked her head back sharply and stuck it out even further. She rubbed the palm of the hand all over it. She was thorough, she tongued all over and between each and every finger. She wasn't *licking* her hand – it wasn't as simple as that. Throughout the operation the tongue seemed quite inert, as if it wasn't a moving part of her body at all, it was the hand that did all the work. The first palm now drenched, the woman raised her other hand and repeated the same procedure. And then, done, she at last lowered her hands to her sides, and Billy could see the drool dripping from them thick like tar. It seemed to glisten in the moonlight.

Only now did she bother to look at Billy again. And she closed her eye, quite deliberately, just for a second, and then opened it again. A playful little wink.

She turned to the wall. She pressed one of her hands against it. Billy heard the squelch, this sound carried, there was nothing muffled about it at all. Above it, she pressed her other hand. Then she heaved herself off the ground, and for a moment she was just hanging there, fixed to the wall with only her sticky hands supporting her.

There was a wet sucking sound as she pulled the lower hand free. She reached higher, pressed it once more against the wall. She climbed up to it. Now she pulled the other hand away, and the wet sucking was louder and turned Billy's stomach, he could see the spit that had supported her was running down the breeze block and pooling thick on the balcony below. She fixed this hand to the wall higher still, and lifted her body up to it. And then with greater ease, and greater speed, she was crawling across the side of the hotel like a spider.

Billy turned his head to the door on his own balcony, and he knew it would be locked tight behind him, and he was right.

When he looked back, the woman had climbed another floor already. Her long blonde hair covered her face so Billy couldn't any longer even see that she was human. There seemed no effort to the climb. It was graceful.

Seagulls tried to stop her, and she pulled one hand free to swipe them away. She caught the ringleader by the neck. She swayed on the wall, supported by only one hand now, the other tight around the seagull's throat. The bird flapped in such a frenzy as it tried to escape, it screamed at her in terror and fury; Billy thought she might fall. But she refused to let go of the wall, and she refused to let go of her prey either – she squeezed hard until the seagull went limp and the entire head came off with a little pop.

She swung her full weight back onto the wall, and resumed her steady, relentless journey towards Billy's balcony.

Billy knew he had to find somewhere to hide. But there was only the small plastic chair – he was only a little boy, but even if he crouched behind it and closed his eyes tight and made himself as tiny as could be, he knew it would do no good.

He dragged the chair against the barrier. He climbed on to it, and then swung both his legs over. Then carefully, so carefully, he lowered himself down the other side of it, his hands grabbing hold of the thin railing. His feet scrambled for something to rest on – he found a little ledge no more than a few centimetres wide, not enough. He pressed his knees tight against the Perspex.

And straightaway he knew he'd made a big mistake. His hands were already smarting in protest, one of his knees buckled. He tried looking down but the ground was too far away for even moonlight to reach, once he fell he'd fall forever.

He wondered whether he could make his own hands sticky enough to support his weight. His tongue felt dry. He couldn't swallow. He decided not to risk it.

The woman still hadn't arrived, and Billy's heart pounded. Maybe she wouldn't come after all? How long should he wait until he came out of hiding? And then he realised he didn't have the strength to pull himself back over the barrier again.

When she dropped on to his balcony, she fluttered in like a bird.

She behaved like a bird too. Her head moved in jerks and twitches as she took in her new surroundings. And for a while Billy thought that maybe he had fooled her, she wouldn't be able to find him. But then her single eye met both of his through the grubby Perspex, and her head stopped twitching and was still.

Billy could now see that her skin was covered with cuts and tears where the seagulls had pecked her and bitten into her and torn away at her flesh. Some of the gashes seemed quite deep. The blood had crusted. Her long blonde hair was blood-crusted too.

She closed her eye at him again, and Billy was less sure it was a wink this time, maybe it was a blink? After all, how could he tell? But it seemed less coy this time, more bemused. And, at last, she raised her hand, and she gave him a wave.

Billy wanted to wave back, but if he did then he would lose his grip and then he'd fall and he wouldn't just break an arm and he wouldn't just break a leg, he'd break into so many tiny pieces. He wanted to wave back, but he knew he mustn't.

He waved back. He fell.

And he understood that he wasn't dead, and he wasn't falling through the air either, and that the woman was gripping him by the wrist. And the grip was strong, but it was smooth and gentle. Then she lifted him high over the barrier and set him down safely on the balcony again, it was the easiest thing in the world. And she let him go.

She stood close and he could see her whole naked body. And no matter how damaged it was, and no matter how dead, it was beautiful.

She opened her arms.

He thought if he put his head into that space between her breasts then he'd drown in there, he'd be sucked down deep in the quicksand and he'd be swallowed up whole and he'd never be heard of again.

He held on to her, and her skin was cold but the contact felt warm, and there was nothing alive inside her chest so it must have been his own heartbeat he could hear.

They held each other for a long time. He thought she would consume him, and then he'd be inside her and he'd be a part of her always and he'd never be free. And maybe that's indeed what happened. And yet at length the hug came to a stop. She slid open the balcony door and took him back to his little roll-up bed. She tucked him under the covers and kissed him, just once, in the middle of his forehead. The kiss burned, and it didn't matter. And then she told him a fairy story, but he would never remember what, and only when he was sleeping soundly did she steal away.

* * *

Mummy shook Billy awake. "Get dressed. We have to go."

Billy did as he was told. Mummy's nostrils were positively quivering, he knew that was when she was at her most dangerous. "Where's George?" he asked.

"I don't know. Out to get some fags. Hurry up."

He was still yawning as she bundled him out of the hotel room. She didn't even bother to close the door. She wheeled her suitcase down to the lift, and stabbed at the button, over and over. "Why won't it come?"

"It's coming, Mummy."

Mummy's face was bleeding; Billy supposed the seagulls must have got to her. They reached the lobby. Mummy looked around nervously, and then she kept her head down and ran, out past reception and on to the street.

"Where are we going?" Billy said.

"Home."

"How are we going to get home? We came here in George's car."

"I don't know!" cried Mummy. "We don't need a car. We'll get a train. We don't need a car. There has to be a train station, come on!" She pulled at his arm, but Billy stopped dead.

"Cars," he said. "I've left my toy cars in the hotel."

"It doesn't matter."

"I want to get my cars."

"I'll buy you new ones."

"But you always say that!" shouted Billy, and Mummy stepped back from him in surprise. "You always say you will get me new cars, and you never do, and I'm left with the same boring old ones!"

Mummy looked around. "Sweetie, people are looking."

"I'll just go back to the room. I'll be quick. I know where they are."

"I can't," Mummy said, "I can't go back up there."

"I'll be quick," Billy said again, and he tried to give his very best grown-up smile. "I will be so quick." *Come on, 'Chelle, don't be a cunt.* And before she could stop him, he raced back into the hotel, ran towards the lift.

The bedroom door was still open. Billy closed it behind him. And took a deep breath. At last, he felt safe.

The toy cars were on the floor, next to the roll-up bed. Billy ignored them. He went out on to the balcony.

The woman was gone. He supposed he knew she would have been. A man with a mop was giving her balcony a clean. He was working hard at some sticky stain on the floor, he was really putting his back into it.

Billy suddenly felt so tired.

From within the room he heard the door open. He turned around.

George stood in the doorway. He didn't speak for a while. He stared at Billy, and Billy stared right back. Billy knew how to do that now. He was good at it.

"Where's your mother?" said George eventually.

"Downstairs."

"What's she doing there?"

Billy shrugged.

"All right," said George. "Come in here. Come in off the balcony."

Billy took a last look at the woman's balcony below him. The man with the mop gave him a wave.

"Off the balcony," said George again. "Come and sit down." George sat on the bed. "Sit here beside me."

Billy did as he was told.

George said, "You're a naughty boy."

Billy didn't know what to say to that.

George grinned. "More than naughty. You're a *dirty* boy, aren't you? I know what you've been up to on that balcony."

Billy started. "What?" he whispered.

"Listening to us. Listening to your mother and me. I know. And trying to get a good look too, I bet. At your own mother! It's disgusting."

"I'm sorry," said Billy.

"It doesn't matter," said George. "I'll tell you a secret. I'm a naughty boy as well. It's just my way. I don't mean anything by it. We have a lot in common, you and I. Your mum and I... we had a disagreement last night. But it doesn't mean anything. All right?"

"All right," said Billy. "Yes."

"I could be a dad to you," said George. "I know we don't discuss your dad. I know he was a wrong 'un. Do you remember your dad?" Billy shook his head. "But I could be a dad for you. I don't know, I'm just jabbering. But I bet I could. We have a lot in common. We could have a lot in common, you and I. Does that sound good?"

"Yes," said Billy.

"So shall we go find Mummy? Shall we have a holiday?"

"Yes," said Billy.

"We can go to the beach, yeah? Have fish and chips?"

"Yes," said Billy.

George now sounded cross. "Don't just keep saying that. For Christ's sake, don't say that."

"I'm sorry," said Billy.

"It's all right."

"I'm sorry, I'm sorry, I'm sorry." He tried to remember what Mummy had done. He reached across to George. He put his hand on George's chin. It felt rough and bristly. George looked at him in surprise. And then Billy kissed him on the mouth.

"What are you doing?" said George. He got off the bed. "What the fuck are you doing?"

Billy didn't say anything.

"You're dirty," said George. "You're *foul.*"

And he went out on to the balcony. He grasped hold of the barrier. Billy watched as George took a series of deep breaths.

Then Billy got up. George turned around just for a moment, but it was too late to stop him – Billy closed the balcony door and locked it fast.

"Hey!" cried George. "What are you doing?"

Billy watched as George pounded on the glass door.

"Open this door! Let me back in! Just you wait until I'm back in!" George thumped the glass again, and then suddenly stopped. He looked around, confused. "What's that?" he asked.

Billy couldn't see, but he could hear it clearly. A strange, wet sucking sound.

George stared out in terror. "No," he said feebly. And then he turned back to the door, began to slam his fists against it, ever more desperate.

Billy closed the curtains. He didn't want to see George anymore. He'd done with George.

As he left the hotel room he heard George scream, but he had no idea if in fear or in pain.

Mummy was waiting for him on the steps outside the hotel. Billy didn't know whether she'd be angry or whether she'd be crying, but he thought he knew how to cope with either. She was crying. "I thought you'd left me," she sobbed. "Don't you ever leave me. You'll be with me always, won't you?"

"Yes," said Billy.

* * *

Billy didn't always think of the dead woman on the balcony, and there were some years he didn't even remember her at all. And then she'd pop into his head again, quite suddenly, and he'd wonder why she'd been hiding away. It wasn't an unwelcome memory. He quite enjoyed teasing at it, picking at the details. Sometimes the woman looked different. The hair wouldn't be so long, or wouldn't be so blonde. He caught a better glimpse of the boobs than he'd originally thought. She wasn't even always beautiful, but he would usually make her beautiful, he preferred that. Sometimes she hadn't lost the eye, but the seagulls had still pecked at it so she'd been blinded and was weeping blood, Billy usually thought it neater to have the eye simply plucked from its socket. But the hug never changed. The hug never changed at all. She held him close, and he got lost within her breasts, and he never found his way back to the surface.

And he'd wonder whether he'd actually seen her die. Whether he'd been watching her at that precise moment when everything had stopped – the breathing, the heart pumping, the whole life thing altogether. Or had he been looking away at the time, had he been playing with his cars or staring out at the view? At the crucial instant when it had mattered, had he simply blinked? For nothing remarkable had happened as she'd passed from one state to the other, from being a living person to being a useless corpse. There hadn't been a glow or an aura, there'd been no beat of a drum or a crack of thunder. There had been nothing to mark her death as anything special and nothing to suggest that her life had been anything special either. So he liked to think he'd missed the moment. He liked to think that he'd squandered that particular privilege, of being the one with her at the very end. That was better. For her sake, it was better.

"She's peaceful today," the nurse told Billy, and he looked at his mother's face and it seemed no more peaceful today than any other day. He thanked the nurse, and she nodded, and left him.

She'd be wrinkling her nose if she could, Billy thought. She'd be wrinkling her nose, and I'd know she wasn't peaceful in the slightest. And then the nurse would have to watch out! But Mummy hadn't wrinkled her nose for ages. It was as if she'd simply forgotten how to express her misery.

He'd brought her some grapes. He didn't know why. She never ate any of them, so he was the one who had to pick at them instead. He didn't like the ones with seeds in, but sometimes they were the best he could get.

George had died that day, and Billy was glad of it. And that was an absolute truth. But it was also true that afterwards George came round to see Mummy several times, and there were more arguments, and Mummy even went out with George again for a little while. But he didn't need to square these opposing truths – George was dead and Billy never had to see him again, not ever, and not talk to him, and not be nice to him, and not stay in the TV room if he were there. And if Mummy *did* make Billy stay in the room with George and talk to George and be nice to George, Billy would just remember that George had been torn apart on a hotel balcony in Bournemouth, he'd had his head ripped off, he'd been sucked up someone's arse. And so he could have no power over him.

Mummy had other men after George, and some of them were kinder and some of them were worse, but they never stayed for long, and Mummy never tried to take Billy on holiday with any of them. That, she said, had been a mistake. And there was one time years later Billy asked after George, but Mummy refused to discuss him, just as she wouldn't discuss Jack, or Curtis, or Dad.

"I've given up on men," Mummy announced to Billy one day when he got home from work. "They're more trouble than they're worth! You can be my man now." "Yes," said Billy, and he wasn't sure what that might entail. But it just meant that they carried on watching TV together on the sofa, she'd cuddle up to him, and she'd sometimes cry. It was just the same as before.

Another nurse came in. "She's peaceful today," the nurse told him. Billy nodded. He didn't say that he'd already heard that from the other nurse, he thought that would be rude. "It's what you hope for," the nurse said, "that they're at peace." Billy stared at his mother intently and hoped that if he ignored the nurse for long enough that she'd eventually just go away, and so she did.

Every afternoon he would come to the hospital reception and he'd be so scared he'd be too late. "I'm here for Michelle Scott," he'd say, "is she still...?" And up till now she'd always been alive, and he'd been taken to the ward. Only then could he relax – he'd sit on the chair beside her bed, and he'd take out the grapes, and he'd keep vigil over her.

This time he'd get it right. He wouldn't get distracted by balcony views or toy cars. He wouldn't blink.

Mummy opened her eyes and seemed to recognise him. She reached out her hand, and he would have liked to have taken it but he didn't. If this were the end, he didn't want to spoil the purity of it.

She sighed, and closed her eyes, and Billy looked hard at her face, but she was still breathing.

He took another grape, put it carefully in his mouth, and chewed it slowly. And he watched for the moment his mother would die.

* * *

Mummy's funeral wasn't expensive but she hadn't had much of an estate and there wasn't a lot of money left over afterwards. Still, Billy didn't quite know what to do with it. The lads at work said he should go on a holiday. Billy knew that the lads made fun of him but they'd been much nicer since Mummy had died, and one of them even helped him book the holiday online and sort out a passport. The night before, Billy packed a suitcase and went to bed and told himself he still needn't go if he decided not to. But in the morning when the taxi came to drive him to the airport he got inside it anyway.

On the flight he studied a phrasebook, and realised with a sinking dismay that he wouldn't be able to learn all the words in time. But it didn't seem to matter, when he landed someone was prepared to listen as he gave directions to the hotel in English, and they drove him there, and charged him well for the privilege.

They all spoke English at the hotel as well. "May I show you to your room, señor?" asked the receptionist, and Billy said, "Yes." They took the lift all the way up to the fourteenth floor. "Here you are, señor. The bed, the bathroom, the minibar, there it is."

"A balcony," said Billy. "No, no balcony. I didn't order a balcony."

"All our rooms have balconies, señor!" Billy gave the receptionist a tip, and then he was left on his own again.

He closed the balcony curtains tight. He lay on the bed, and the mattress was too hard and the pillows were too soft. He turned on the TV, and the programme was English and he had seen it before.

He pulled open the door to the balcony and went outside.

From the balcony there was a view of the sea, right ahead of him. The beach looked sandy. Beneath him there was a swimming pool and a bar. And all around him, all the other balconies were occupied. Couples drinking, children playing. Sunbathing.

Billy peered over the barrier and calculated that if he fell to the side he might just land in the swimming pool and be saved, but if he missed it he'd be very dead indeed.

He looked for the woman, and it took him a while, but he found her eventually.

She wasn't much like how he had remembered her. Her hair was dark and cropped. She was shorter than he'd thought, and her stomach was round and tubby. But she was standing at the barrier and smoking a cigarette, and so he knew it was her.

He stared down, and he raised a hand in a wave. She didn't notice him for the longest time. She just stood there and puffed smoke out towards the Mediterranean, and then at last she tossed her cigarette away. That's when, at last, she saw him.

Billy hoped she recognised him, just as he had recognised her. He knew he must have changed a lot. She gazed up at him, her face curious and unsmiling. And then she raised a hand too. It wasn't a wave. It was a summons. She beckoned him down to join her.

Billy didn't know what to think. This wasn't how the woman was supposed to behave.

He went back into his room. Lay on the bed, and it was still too hard and too soft at the same time. Turned on the TV, and he couldn't get it to work.

He left his room and went to the lift. She was three floors down, four rooms to the right, he'd already counted. He knocked at her door. She was waiting for him.

She took off all her clothes, and that meant she was naked, that was the consequence of that. There was an awful lot of skin, and none of it had been pecked by birds, and Billy supposed that was a good thing, though he had quite liked those peck marks. The boobs were too big and he decided not to look at them.

She spoke to him in Spanish, and he thought that this would have been when the phrasebook could have come in handy. "I don't know what to do," he said, and she smiled, and undid his trousers. So he got naked too, and as he did so he looked around her room, and saw that it had just the same layout as his, TV, minibar, good. She had the curtains drawn, but she hadn't pulled them properly, he could see the balcony clearly through the gap. They lay down on the mattress and it was softer than his one, so that at least was nice. "I don't know what to do," he said again, but she wasn't paying attention to that.

It was all quite nice, until it wasn't. And really, Billy thought, wasn't that true of everything when it came down to it? She kissed him the way he'd seen Mummy do and he tried to respond in kind but he didn't think she was convinced. After a while it seemed wiser just to lay back and try to screen out all of the sensations, and he looked out of the gap in the curtains and imagined what it would be like if his younger self were out there peering in back at him, what would he have made of it all?

She was slowing down, so it was either coming to an end or she'd run out of energy. He pulled away. She smiled and said something in Spanish, and Billy thought it best just to give a nod. She kissed him on the forehead then, and the kiss seemed to burn pleasantly. Then she rolled over and went to sleep.

Billy waited a few minutes, then carefully got off the bed. The woman didn't stir. He looked around for his clothes, but he couldn't see them anywhere. He knew the woman had dropped them on the floor in a heap, but now they were gone.

He thought he should wake her and ask her where she'd put them, but he didn't know the words for it. He touched her gently upon the shoulder anyway. She didn't move. He prodded her harder. Nothing. He looked at her face and one eye was screwed tight shut but the other was half open, and he didn't know how she had managed to do that. She was smiling. "She's peaceful," he said out loud.

He pulled open the curtains, and stepped onto the balcony. And from there he couldn't see the sea, there was a shopping centre, there was a car park. The sun played over his naked body, it felt good.

There was a single plastic chair in the corner. On it there was a towel, and the woman's pack of cigarettes. He took out a cigarette and lit it. He had never smoked before, he didn't know what to expect. It didn't taste of anything. He stood at the Perspex barrier and sucked the smoke in deep, and tried to blow it back out of his mouth and nostrils and eye socket the way he'd seen the woman do. He managed the mouth and the nostrils, but the eye socket was as yet beyond him.

He looked up, and there, a couple of floors above, he saw a little girl on a balcony of her own. If she was alarmed to see a naked man with all his bits flapping about she didn't show it. She stared down at him, and he stared up at her. He raised a hand to her in a wave.

A seagull flew on to the balcony and watched him beadily. He shooed it away, but he knew it would be back. He tossed away his cigarette, and opened up the towel. He didn't bother to look at the girl again, he knew she would be watching. He lay down upon the towel, chest down, arms in front like a swimmer, bum sticking out. And he enjoyed the fading warmth of the sun, and waited.

KITTENS

Keith Rosson

Rich Tuttle had just showered after his shift at the packing plant when his phone started ringing. It was on the edge of the toilet tank, and Tuttle was shaving, one eye squinted against the curl of smoke from his cigarette. Even after his shower he could smell the bleach from the floors, the pink solvent he used to clean the machines. He'd be ninety and still smelling the stuff in his dreams.

The name JOHN DEWEY was on the screen, and Tuttle set his electric razor down, picked up the phone.

"What's up, John?"

"Ah, it's off, man. I'm sorry."

A pause. "What do you mean, it's off?"

"It's off. I'm in the ER."

"You're in the ER? For what?" Tuttle, apparently, tasked with just copying whatever was said to him.

"I broke my collarbone, dude." It was then that Tuttle realised he could hear the squawk of an intercom on the other end of the line, background chatter. "They just took an X-ray, but it's for sure broken."

"Dewey. Man." He looked at himself in the mirror, looked away. "You're screwing us here. Me and Emmett."

"I'm screwing me, too, man. I'm not gonna be able to work for, what? Two months? I think they said two months at least."

"You can't go in and get your cheque or something? Get shit from your locker? Maybe get the addresses then?"

"I can't even lift my arm, Rich. Some fucking newbie picked me up in a fireman's carry and slammed me down."

"At BJJ?"

"Yeah. Doctor's like, 'Oh, it's broken in at least two places, I bet.'"

"Dewey," he said again, but it was pointless.

John Dewey said he was sorry, and then he hung up.

★ ★ ★

Tuttle spent the next hour pounding beers and calling Emmett on his cellphone, trying not to let the panic unspool inside him. The house was stifling hot, the table fans pushing the same hot air around, his eight-year-old daughter Melanie in a pair of Pokémon shorts and a T-shirt that showed the serpentine bumps of her spine, sitting there in front of the TV, laughing huskily every once in a while. Sweat pasted to her forehead. *Money money money*, he thought. *How do people get money? How do I do this? John Dewey with his security gig and his addresses. His little patrol car that he drove around. I am so fucked. I am so abysmally fucked.*

Finally he nuked some chicken nuggets and set them on a plate on the floor next to a faded Big Gulp cup full of water and choked with ice cubes. "You drink that whole thing before you get any pop, you hear me? I'll be home in a couple hours." He told Mel not to answer the door for anyone and not to leave the house, even if her friends came over and wanted to play. Kid was on summer break and Chandra had just left for work as he'd arrived, two broke-ass ships passing in the night; she wouldn't get home until four in the morning. It was a risk, leaving Mel alone, but if this wasn't an emergency, emergency didn't have a name.

He stepped outside into the hottest part of the day, got into his truck. It was 7:00 p.m. and he was angry at the heat, at John Dewey for breaking his collarbone doing dumbass jiu jitsu, at Derrick Davies who he owed sixteen thousand dollars to and who was justifiably insistent that Tuttle pay it back. The only person he was not mad at, pretty much, was Emmett LeRoy, a man he found on his usual stool in front of a beer at the Metropolitan, a dive bar over on Dekum where all the city's rip-off men spent time. He sat down next to Emmett, palmed sweat from his face. Emmett gave him an assessing, mildly curious look.

"What's up, dude?" he said, pushing his hair out of his eyes. Emmett was a small man with a little pooch of beer belly and a greying ponytail that he felt compensated fairly for the fact that he was balding on top. He was ten years Tuttle's senior and tried to act fatherly at times, even though they both were thieves who had met in Snake River Correctional long ago, and Tuttle was the only one of them who supplemented his thievery with hourly, legal work. "Thought I was supposed to meet you at your house at ten."

"It's off," he said. "I tried calling you a million times."

Emmett eyeballed him. Woodenly, he said, "What do you mean, it's off."

"John Dewey broke his collarbone. Where's your phone?"

"Fucking rolling around with dudes on the floor, I bet. Right?"

Tuttle nodded.

"Goddamn it," Emmett said. He wearily signalled the bartender for another. Tuttle asked him again where his phone was.

The bartender came, poured them both beers. Emmett paid. "Forgot it at home. Decided it was too fucking hot to go back and get it."

It was supposed to be a simple thing: John Dewey worked for Saftrol, a security firm that kept eyeballs on a bunch of houses up in the West Hills, the McMansions out in Beaverton. He'd started dating one of the operators in the head office, who gave him, with a little cajoling, a list of the clients' absences that week, as well as the alarm codes to their systems. Good to have in case a security officer had to reset things after a false alarm while folks were on vacation. John Dewey had offered up the addresses and codes to Emmett and Tuttle for a cut. Everything was set, they had a house picked out, a Saftrol client John Dewey said was loaded, and now this.

"What do you want to do?" Tuttle said. Thinking of Derrick Davies, who had loaned him the sixteen thousand for a new truck after his old Ford had finally shit the bed and he couldn't get to work, couldn't get Melanie to school. Derrick, who employed a bevy of mouthbreathers renowned for their willingness to snap fingers, and smack people's elbows and shins with hammers.

"I'm thinking," Emmett said.

"We could still do the house John Dewey picked out," Tuttle offered. "He knows the address."

"Doesn't know the code, though. Was gonna get the code from his lady friend in the office tonight."

"Just smash and grab the place then," said Tuttle. "Fuck it. Look, man, I'm in a bind here—"

"I know a place," Emmett said, nodding. Finally lifting his beer to his lips. "No security system, none of that. Break a window and go."

The relief that flooded through him. "You sure?"

"I am."

"Alright," Tuttle said, leaning forward. "Let's go."

"Tomorrow," Emmett said. "It's a daytime job. They're nine to fivers, these people. We'll go in there with the van tomorrow." He clapped Tuttle on the back. "We're good."

⋆ ⋆ ⋆

He drove home after a few more beers, relatively calmed. It was dusk. There was a way out of this. They had solved the problem. He pulled into his driveway and it was only when he stepped out and shut his door and then heard car doors open and close behind him that that good feeling dissipated like smoke.

"Rich, hold up."

He turned, and there was Derrick Davies, whipcord-thin and wearing an *I Climbed Mount Everest* T-shirt with bleach burns at the hem. The man had half of Portland's dirtbags and tweakers in his pocket and still he dressed like he'd just rolled out of a sleeping bag himself. The grin on his face was wolfish as he scratched at his chin with a yellow fingernail, as he and his man walked Tuttle up against the side of his truck. The guy with Derrick was big, a good head taller than Tuttle, and stupid-looking beyond words. One of those big, joyless dudes with dimples in his knuckles and a face that wouldn't change expression at all as he broke your arm. Immediately, Tuttle needed to piss. His heart suddenly pounding in his throat. Tuttle had a little .22 in his weed box inside the house, and he should have been carrying it with him everywhere.

"Derrick, I'm working on it, I swear."

"Oh, I believe you."

They stood there, the three of them. Tuttle's two-bedroom house with the peeling siding and the late mortgage payments and the last of the daylight making pale fire above the treetops across the street. They just stared at him.

"Something fell through, but I got another th—"

Derrick nodded and the speed of the man beside him was astonishing and terrible. The next thing Tuttle knew, he was on his knees in the driveway, his vision swimming with darkness, Derrick's man shaking out his hand. Tuttle's mouth filled with blood; his tongue probed a new gap in his teeth, right there in the front, a canine, and a distant part of himself was looking at Derrick's feet for the tooth.

"You got a family, right, Rich?"

Tuttle nodded, head buzzing. He could see his own blood pattering onto the cement in front of him.

"I mean, I feel gross for saying it, it's a poor thing to say, but it'd be a shame if something happened to them. Sixteen grand, man, that feels like a thing you can get together. I gave it to you and made very clear the terms. You've put me in a shitty situation here."

"I can," Tuttle said, the words strange in his humming, numbed mouth.

"You can what?"

"I can get you the money."

"By tomorrow," Derrick said, and it wasn't a question, and the two of them got back in their car.

* * *

The next morning Tuttle made eggs and toast for Melanie, who was still eyeballing his new face, the purpled mess of his lips. Tuttle, oddly buoyed, and with a madman's false cheer, had told her that he'd tripped and hit a door. Chandra woke up later that morning and cornered him in the kitchen, her hair corkscrewed with sleep.

"Was it Derrick?"

He nodded, shrugged.

"Christ, Rich. That goddamn truck. You just *had* to have a new truck."

"I'm working it out."

She stood there with her arms folded. "They come to the house?"

"No," he lied. "It was over at the Metro."

Still with this searching look. He looked away, opened the fridge.

"You're a bad liar, Richard."

"I'm taking care of it."

"Derrick Davies comes to this house, with my child here? It's a divorce. I mean it. You hear me?"

He sniffed. "I hear you."

"Sell the truck. Get out from under this."

"I'm not getting sixteen for it, Chan. There's no way."

"You'll get more than you got now," she said, "which is nothing," and went to gather up Melanie to take to her mom's.

★ ★ ★

He got in his truck a half hour later and called in sick to his warehouse gig. Then he went to the McDonald's on Glisan and ordered a hashbrowns and coffee – all he could hold down, the anxiety starting to flex inside him – and ate in the parking lot, leaning against his truck in the sun until Emmett eventually pulled up in the van.

He got in and Emmett tossed him a pair of white coveralls after looking him over. "What happened to you?"

"Derrick came by."

Emmett blinked. He knew about the sixteen grand, the truck. "Jesus wept. Let's get you some folding cash, son." Tuttle started squirming into the coveralls in the passenger seat as they headed out onto the freeway.

"Who we lifting from today?" Tuttle asked, sipping his coffee once he was in his gear, his little white painter's hat.

"Some prick a buddy of mine knows. Dude ripped him off on a contracting gig."

Emmett turned his blinker on, drove carefully. It was one of the things that Tuttle appreciated about him: when they got down to it, there was a reserve of sincerity and seriousness in the man. They were thieves; this was not shit to play around with, to go into high or hungover.

"My buddy," Emmett says, "does a remodel of this guy's kitchen, his bathroom. Giant reno, right? Gets stiffed on it, at least part of it. Tells me the guy has one of the biggest coin and stamp collections he's ever seen. Bunch of rare books too. Occult books and shit. Witchcraft, all that shit. There's gold in them thar hills, Rich, I'm telling you."

"Occult books."

"That's right. And stamps and coins."

"I don't know nothing about stamps, man."

"We'll get it sorted out," Emmett said, but Tuttle was thinking about tonight, about Derrick Davies coming back. Maybe coming inside his house. That dimple-knuckled motherfucker with him, settling his dead gaze on Melanie, on Chandra.

"You think they got cash in there?"

"I think they got all kinds of things in there, bud."

"I'm going for cash, Em." He gestured at his face. "Derrick's not playing."

"I hear you. I got Sam all lined up, ready for us." Their fence.

"You switch the plates on this thing?"

He nodded. "I did, before I come got you." They drove for a bit longer and then Emmett said, "We gotta have the talk."

Tuttle almost smiled. It was why they had managed so many lifts together. Surprises were minimum because they talked things out beforehand. "I got my little .22," he said, and reached into his jacket on the floorboards and put the pistol in the pocket of his coveralls. "I need the money, Emmett. I'm not playing today."

"Sounds good," Emmett said.

★ ★ ★

They parked in the driveway.

If it wasn't a West Hills mansion, one of John Dewey's Saftrol clients, it was a sizeable enough place for Tuttle. Two-car garage, immaculately landscaped lawn flanked by hedges on each side, a pair of big bay windows that looked out onto the street. They stepped out, faces covered by respirators, painter's hats and coveralls. They began unloading equipment out of the back of the van. Paint cans, brushes and trays, a bucket. All of it easily ditched if they had to run. They walked around the side of the house, listening for people, a dog barking inside. There was no car in the driveway, but with a garage that meant nothing.

Big wooden patio out back. A rock garden among a bunch of cactuses, succulents, an eight-foot fence that shut out the neighbour behind them. Tuttle felt a twinge of jealousy at the niceness of the place, the size. Remembered Melanie watching TV the night before, the sweat on her forehead, the house's trapped heat.

A patio, a sliding glass door. Emmett knocked on the glass – if anyone came up, they'd pretend to have the wrong house; the homeowner might call the cops, but the licence plates were lifted and they'd be long gone by the time any cruiser arrived. But no one answered, and Emmett took a glass cutter and drew a section of glass near the handle of the door and punched it in with his elbow. Too loud for Tuttle's liking, and the piece fell inward, shattering on the tile floor inside. More noise. But then Emmett unlocked the door and they crept in.

"Hello?" Emmett called out, his voice muffled from the respirator. Nothing.

They shared a look. "Ten minutes," Tuttle said.

A living room, a dining room, the kitchen off to the left. Emmett took to the cabinets in the dining room; looking for silver. Tuttle, his heart settling now that they were in, was about to tap Emmett's shoulder, tell him he was going to start doing the bedrooms upstairs, when a baby started crying.

Both of them froze.

Tuttle felt ice creep over his scalp, felt his legs go watery. He'd been holding a plastic garbage bag and it drifted to the floor. He pawed at the pocket of his coveralls for the .22, and Emmett, his eyes wide above the respirator, gripped his arm. "The fuck you doing?" he hissed low.

They stood there, unsure. Tuttle had done at least twenty house jobs throughout his life, twenty-five, and never had a baby cry on him. Especially not like this. It was a furious noise, with great expanses of silence between the sobs as the infant hitched in its breath. The sound was coming from upstairs. Tuttle could see in his mind the baby writhing, legs spasming, its face red. How many times had he seen Melanie like that?

Why weren't the parents coming?

Where *were* the parents?

"You want to jet?" This from Emmett, still talking low. The two of them standing there in the living room, Tuttle with his sweat-slicked hand on the .22 in his coveralls.

He imagined it, then – one of the parents dipping out for a minute, going to the grocery store, the post office, some errand, the baby sleeping. Surely it'd be fine for a minute or two, right? Christ, Tuttle had done the same thing with his own child the night before.

But she wasn't a *baby*.

Jesus, it was *screaming* now. High and pinched, a gargling, gravel-edged thread to it.

"What the fuck, man," Tuttle said, angry at himself for being rattled, angry at the baby for crying and fucking everything up, angry at the parents for being absent. He stormed through the living room, Emmett behind him. The stairwell was wide, a floral runner bisecting the stairs, and the landing was tiled and shot through with morning sunlight. A new thought came to him: the baby was dying.

He stalked upstairs and crept forward to the first open door. The .22 was in his hand now. Something was wrong. It was a feeling, but almost tangible for its wrongness. The first door was not the baby's – that was further down, toward the end of the hall – but still, Tuttle's fear was this yawning mouth inside of him, threatening to eat everything up. This was not right.

He peered into the first bedroom and froze. Felt his bladder threaten to loosen. Spit drying up in his mouth.

A bedroom, yes. A vanity, a dresser, more tiled floor, a window showing a wedge of blue sky, the patterned mosaics of the neighbours' roofs. A single large oil painting of a bowl of fruit and a vase done in bold blues and yellows above the bed.

The bed.

"Oh fuck," Emmett said over his shoulder, the words sounding more like an exhalation of breath than anything spoken. Something pulled unwillingly from him.

On the bed – king-sized, silk sheets that matched almost perfectly the colour of the floor tiles – lay two people. A man and a woman? It was hard to tell. Old? Young? The baby's grandparents? Parents?

The baby was still crying.

The corpses – because that's what they were, corpses – seemed to have been… dried out? Their bodies had withered into poses of anguish – ropey muscles tightened so much that their arms had atrophied at a bend, their jaws wrenched open, locked into screams. Tuttle had spent one summer in junior high obsessed with Pompeii, and this reminded him of that. The way people had died so quickly from the superheated volcanic gases they'd had little time to protect themselves against. Dying in mid-event. Running to escape. Trying to burrow themselves beneath a shelf, in a corner. These bodies had that same look of surprise, victims of some singular event that had happened to them in seconds, and also desiccated them. *Husk dolls*, his mind insisted. Grey skin laced over skeletons, over fibrous sinew. The wispy, crackling hair, nipples like blackened pebbles.

The baby just *screaming* and *screaming*.

Emmett, behind him: "The fuck is this, Rich—"

Tuttle pushed away from the door, bounced off Emmett, and pivoted toward the baby's room. His mind with a single pounding cadence to it: *this is wrong this is wrong everything's wrong here—*

Tuttle gently turned the knob, stepped inside.

A crib, a mobile, a window, a dresser tiered with boxes of Pampers on top. The blinds were closed here, but there was light enough for him to see the baby.

See the figure standing over the baby.

Emmett keened behind him, an odd strangled sound, and he briefly put his hand on Tuttle's shoulder, an almost gentle gesture of goodbye. Then the sound of Emmett's feet pounding down the stairs.

The baby, Tuttle saw, was a greyed, shrunken thing. Like the adults across the hall. A shrunken little raisin, devoid of any blood, it seemed, even the eyes wilted, oh, all the living heat and moisture taken from the tiny brittle corpse—

"Hey," Tuttle croaked, and the thing standing above the crib turned and he realised *it* was the one making the noise, *it* was the one making the sounds, this kind of idiot repetition of the last sound the baby had made, the last thing this creature had heard. A mimic.

It may have once been human. The shape, somewhat, of a woman. Emaciated, wearing a gauzy housedress with a tattered hem that may have once been white but was now entirely begrimed in shit and blood. Stringy, filth-clotted hair. Its skeletal fingers were encircled around the baby's grey wrist. It began to turn its face toward him and he thought, *Oh no*. Thought, *Can't have that. Please.* Thought, *It's a fucking vampire, some kind of ghost or vampire and if it looks at me—*

He pissed himself then, a moment of heat sluicing down his leg, and he managed to raise the .22 and fire it; the sound was nothing, inconsequential, and the shot went wide. A small black hole in the wall.

She turned then, let go of the baby, faced him entirely. She lifted her hands and pulled the curtain of dark hair away from her face, and Tuttle shrieked, backpedalled until he hit the doorway. Tried to turn and tripped over his own feet and then she was on him, the sound of the squalling infant coming from those cracked, bloody lips, a sound loud in his ears, his head.

* * *

Sometime later he walked through the house, vomit and blood and sputum clinging to his face, his lips. His respirator was gone, his little hat. He walked downstairs, staggering on the last step and nearly twisting his ankle. There was a sound in his ears now, a whistling sound, which he realised was his own throat trying to seize breath. The patio door was a frill of broken glass, from either Emmett or the thing – *can't think about that now* – escaping after it had done what it had done to him. He unlocked the front door and stepped out into the driveway only to find the van was gone. Of course it was. Emmett had left him.

The midday sun was beating down on him but he felt cold, cold.

* * *

He walked through the residential neighbourhood until he came to a small section of businesses and took off his coveralls. He wiped his face with them and threw them in a garbage can in front of a convenience store. There were bitemarks on the back of his neck and one on his scalp. Both of them had already scabbed up. Though Tuttle was never stupid enough to bring his ID on a job, he had two twenties in his pants pocket for emergencies and went in and bought a bottle of water. The clerk eyeballed his piss-wet jeans, his split lip, the general state of him, but said nothing. Tuttle took the change and sank money into the payphone outside. Whole tremors moved through him. The hard seed of knowledge the thing had imparted to him – *a mother a mother shes hungry and lost and searching* – was a thing he could not avoid but was able to stuff down for the moment.

* * *

Chandra drove him home. It was afternoon by then – she'd had to wait until someone could relieve her at work to come get him – and he'd gone back inside and bought a couple tallboys, managing to sink two of them by the time she pulled into the parking lot. This fact did not endear him to her, not at all, and while she spoke with veiled fury about how they had a kid and how he needed to get his shit straight at some point in his life and what was he even doing out here in the suburbs and was that piss she smelled, all he could think of was what had happened in the baby's room.

How the witch-thing had seized onto Tuttle's neck like a mother with her kittens and thusly marked him. Shared – without speaking somehow – all her grisly life and recriminations. Her appetites.

⋆ ⋆ ⋆

Chandra dropped him off at home, having graduated to not speaking to him save for reminding him that he needed to pick Mel up from daycare at five and she had to get back to work, goddamn it, and he went inside the house – fear finally pushing through the numbness, the place too fucking quiet, too many angles to everything, every room that might hold the witch-thing in the dress – and quickly took a shower, changed his clothes. He had lost his gun in the house and so showered with a knife. He touched the bite on the back of his neck, the pebbled scabs on his scalp softening with the hot water. He tried to weep and it wouldn't come.

⋆ ⋆ ⋆

He walked to the Metro, not trusting himself to drive. It was so hot out. The mother's voice was louder now, but also clearer and less galvanising; he could discern a command of sorts. Tuttle kept seeing the grey baby, the clawed hands of the child's parents.

He stepped inside the Metro and Emmett looked at him and read his face and started running for the back door. The bartender said something as Tuttle passed, slamming through the back door into the sun again, the empty patio.

Emmett stood there in a fighter's stance. His little grey ponytail, his bald spot. His eyes were roving over Tuttle, a look of shock on his face.

"You left me there, fucker."

"You should have run too, Rich. The fuck *happened* to you in there?"

The bartender stepped outside. He had an aluminium bat in one hand and his phone in the other. "Rich, get out," he said. "You're 86'd."

"She's coming for you next," Tuttle said, pointing a finger at Emmett. "You fucking rat. I promise you she is."

Emmett's eyes went big. "Man, please—"

The bartender poked Tuttle's ass with the bat. "Get the fuck out. Now."

★ ★ ★

He walked back home, felt the stirring of the witch-thing louder in his mind. Clearer. He was no longer afraid; there was a kind of order being imposed that he appreciated. It felt almost good, and his problems – Derrick Davies, Chandra and Melanie, his job – were distant and unbothersome. He and the mother were twined now in some way that was not like love – it was more functional and demanding – but Tuttle fingered the hard scabs at the back of his neck and felt, at least, wanted.

He picked up Melanie from daycare, and when Chandra came home from work, he told her she had to take Mel and leave for the night.

"What for?" Chandra said, with this look like she already knew. Like she'd been expecting him to say something like this.

"Derrick," was all he said. He was wearing a button-up shirt with a collar to hide the bitemarks.

mark you as the father i mark you

"I thought you said you were taking care of it."

"I am," he said. "I will."

"He's not coming here."

"He might," Tuttle admitted.

"You motherfucker."

The voice inside him was very loud now, and it was hard to concentrate. He would start yelling soon if Chandra didn't leave, and he thought that he might do more than that once he started. He knew he could invite the mother here, now, and she would steal everything from Chandra, from Melanie, if he let her, but he didn't want that. He still had that much strength at least.

He breathed in, held it.

"Please, Chan."

mark you i mark you

★ ★ ★

– and they did not knock that night, and he didn't lock the door, and they stormed into his house and he was there on the couch, Tuttle was, waiting, and he bolted upright and the sound of the baby screaming was loud in the bedroom down the hall. Derrick and his man looked him up and down; for the first time in all the time Tuttle had known him, Derrick Davies seemed to pause, unsure of his place in the hierarchy of the world. There was something in this house, something he clearly couldn't name or define but that Tuttle recognised as the witch-thing's decimation upon his old life. They had made great advancements toward each other in the interceding hours, he and she; she had marked him and wed him and instructed him on her hunger, this boundless hunger, ancient enough, and he had told her, *Yes, alright. And if you're still hungry after this, I can help you again.*

I know lots of people.

"The fuck is that?" Derrick said at the sound of the crying baby. The look he gave Tuttle as the sound shifted into a low, throaty chuckle.

Tuttle walked slowly past the two men, blocked the front door. Locked it.

"Down the hall," he said. "My room."

Derrick Davies could sense the change, the decimation, and he reached into his waistband and took out a pistol. The other man, the one who had split Tuttle's lips, did a slow circulation around the room.

"Down the hall," Tuttle said again, smiling in a way that pulled at his scabs. "All your answers are there."

BLOOD MOON

C.J. Tudor

It went wrong from the start.

"You said you could read the fucking map."

"I said I could read Google Maps."

"Well, *doh*. We're in the middle of a desert, Chi. There's no internet out here. Fuck me."

Gina thumps the steering wheel. The car swerves on the rough, dusty track. I grip the door handle tighter, but I don't say anything. I hate getting caught in arguments between Gina and Chi. If they can't lob barbs at one other, they'll happily redirect their weapons towards the mug in the middle.

Garrett hasn't learnt this yet. "Hey, let's not argue," he says in his usual laid-back drawl, which I used to find sexy and calming but recently have begun to find kind of irritating. *Like, pick a side, Garrett.*

"No, let's," snaps Gina. "We're lost, we're running out of petrol, and there's no sign of this fucking festival, like literally not even a fucking *sign*. If we don't find it soon, we'll end up snacks for wolves or vultures."

"There aren't any wolves in the desert," Chi says as she attempts to reorganise the paper map. She's small and the map is comically big. She could camp in it, if we ever find the fucking campsite.

"Actually, there are," Gina spits. "They're called *desert* wolves. But who cares? Wolves, coyotes, vultures. I do not want to be a stripped carcass, in a week's—"

"Is that it?" I interrupt.

"No. I am not fucking done yet."

"No. Is that *it*?"

I point ahead to where a battered wooden sign has been nailed to a post stuck in the dusty earth.

Blood Moon Festival ½ mile.

A wobbly arrow points straight down the road.

"At last!" Gina throws her hands up. I grab the door handle again.

"Told you," Chi mutters.

"You are so full of shit."

"Hey, ladies. How about a truce?" Garrett smiles lazily.

I brace. Gina's head whips round. "What the hell did you say, you moron?"

"I said—"

"*Watch out!*" Chi screams.

It happens fast. Gina slams the brakes on. The tyres squeal. The car skids to a halt and we're all jolted forward then back. My head slams against the car seat. Garrett, being Garrett, isn't wearing a seatbelt and his face smashes into the seat in front.

"*Aaaarggh!*" he screams as blood spurts from his nose.

I feel a momentary stab of satisfaction.

"Shit." Gina crouches over the steering wheel, gripping it tightly.

"You almost hit it," Chi gasps.

"Hib whut?" Garrett groans.

"That." Chi points to something skinny, roughly dog-sized, and dusty yellow, which scampers across the road and disappears behind some rocks.

Gina stares after it. Then she glares at Chi.

"I *told* you there were fucking wolves here."

⋆ ⋆ ⋆

Five minutes later, we crest the hill, and the valley spreads out ahead of us. The dying glow of the sun bathes the scene in a blood-orange glow.

The huge effigy commands attention first. A massive straw figure – part man, part beast – it stands at least thirty feet high. Around it, spreading out randomly, are music stages, performance areas, massive sculptures, a fairground, food and drink stalls, then tents, camper vans, trailers. Cars are parked further away, right at the edge of the huge site. You're not allowed to drive into the arena.

The angle of the sun and the distance make it difficult to see how many people are there, but Blood Moon has grown and grown over the years from a few crazy hippies to a few thousand festival goers.

Fairy lights are strung everywhere and flaming torches have been set into stakes around the site. Generators provide some power. But I've heard they're unreliable. Sometimes the only light is the torches, campfires and the moon. And all around, the vastness of the dusty desert. Totally off grid.

"This is awesome," Chi says.

"You said it, sister." Gina grins.

They turn to each other and grasp hands, map argument and near animal collision forgotten. There will be some noisy making-up tonight.

"Aww-urgh," Garrett mumbles. He has an old cloth pressed to his nose. It's stopped bleeding but it's swollen. Irritatingly, Garrett is still hot with a fucked-up nose.

"You're quiet." Chi turns to me.

I shrug. "Just taking it in."

"Yeah, well, take this in." Gina pulls a joint out of her pocket and holds it up.

I smile. "Be rude not to."

* * *

By the time she rolls the car to a halt alongside a battered camper van in the makeshift car park, I'm feeling more mellow. And hungry. I glance at Garrett. And a little horny. Damnit. But that will have to wait. Right now, we have rucksacks, camping gear and beer to lug into the site.

I climb out of the car, feeling my body unknot, and stare around. There must be a few thousand cars and trucks parked up, paintwork coated in fine dust, windscreens reflecting the sun like banks of solar panels. Yet the parking site still feels small against the desert backdrop. Miles and miles of nothing but dry earth and rocks. Temperatures over forty degrees in the day. Nights that can drop to freezing. *No man's land*, I think. Because this isn't a place for people. Not really. It's a place for the creatures that have evolved to adapt to the brutal terrain. *Fierce creatures*. And, despite the acrid heat, a shiver runs through me.

"Hey," Chi says, glancing over her shoulder at me. "Someone turn in your grave?"

One of Chi's endearing qualities – and there are many, from her doll-like face to her anime style dress, though not her map reading, of course

– is her habit of getting common phrases mixed up. *A head and a leg. Growling up the wrong tree. Bark worse than her bike.* It's cute. And only a tiny bit intentional.

I offer a small smile. "No, it's just really hitting home how *out here* we are. This place is wild."

"Sounds like my type of place." Gina grins. "Are we ready, *ladies*?" She directs this barb at Garrett.

He offers a small smile. "Bord redduh."

Gina looks at me and winks. Then she hefts her rucksack onto her back. We all do the same and Garrett grabs the small trailer with the rest of our weekly possessions (booze mainly) piled into it. It occurs to me that it's odd we're the only ones trekking across to the festival site. I mean, we're a day later than most arrivals. The really dedicated festival goers get here two or three days in advance. But I would have expected to see a few other stragglers.

I glance back at the parked cars… and frown. A little further down the haphazard row, I can see a dusty red Corvette. It's a cool car. Retro. The sort of car you might well drive out to a festival in the desert, but you'd still be careful with it. Make sure it was locked tightly before you left.

The driver's door is hanging open. Wide open.

There's something on the ground nearby. It looks like a shoe. A trainer. Converse. High top. Odd.

"Suh, excited?" Garrett falls into step alongside me.

Gina and Chi have taken the lead, holding hands now. Former animosity *definitely* forgotten.

I turn, trainer still in my mind. "Yeah. I guess."

He raises his eyebrows. "You wanted to come."

"I know."

Blood Moon Festival was something I'd heard about for years, and not just in its current influencer-heavy incarnation. My mom came here when she had just turned twenty-one, just like me. Back then it really was a ramshackle gathering of adventurous hippies looking for enlightenment or a higher plane or some such shit.

But Mom told me she had *found her people* out here and she came back year after year. Until she met Dad and had me, and then, as she sometimes said in a slightly sad voice that I tried not to take personally (and failed): "*Things had to change.*" And I guess they did, because I always think of my mom as the archetypal suburban mom. Hard to tally with the hippie chick who drove out to the desert in a VW Beetle to indulge in stuff that was pretty wild (and probably illegal). But I guess we always find it hard to picture our parents as young and carefree.

Sometimes, I find it hard to picture Mom at all. She's only been gone a year and yet she's already fading. She died suddenly, a few days after my twentieth birthday, just over a year ago. Killed in a bizarre and random hunting accident. At least that's what the papers called it.

Mom loved to go hiking in the woods near our house. Often she'd go out early in the morning. *To be at one with nature*, she said. One morning, a stupid man with a gun, whose only intention was to kill nature, somehow mistook her for a startled stag.

He shot her six times. Not once. Not one mistake. Six times – in the stomach, arm and head. The lawyer said we didn't have pockets deep enough to push for a civil manslaughter case. But sometimes I lie awake at night thinking about how the hunter didn't realise after the first shot, or the second. He kept on pumping Mom's body full of lead when it must have already been lifeless on the ground.

The hunter's name was Rodney Gibson. He died too. A few months later. Mauled to death when out on another hunt somewhere in Europe. I suppose that's what they call karma.

Anyway, I guess that's why I'm here. To try to reconnect somehow with Mom.

"Hey. Slowpokes," Gina shouts back over her shoulder. "Pick up the fucking pace. We want to get the tents up before dark."

Both Garrett and I start to walk faster. He's learning. It's wiser not to argue with Gina. Only Chi really gets away with it. Gina is scary: tall, almost six foot, lean and muscular, her body like a sculpted slab of marble. Her eyes are green and her hair is a waist long mass of dark curls. Often, I'm not sure if I really like Gina or I'm just terrified of her. Still, I'd rather have her on my side than not.

We're close enough to the festival site that I can smell the petrol from the huge flaming torches. It reminds me that we still need fuel for the car. Gina seemed confident we'd find some somewhere on site. The bass from a sound system reverberates through the ground and into my stomach. Ahead to my left, I can see a big wheel turning slowly, carriages swaying, and the top of a tall helter-skelter. Other smells waft out. Popcorn, marijuana, burgers and something else, less pleasant. Sweet yet foul at the same time.

"Ahh," Chi says. "The smell of festivals. Food, drugs and shit. Doesn't it make you feel good."

Gina chuckles and even Garrett grins. I attempt a smile, but my facial muscles don't want to co-operate. I can't shake the feeling that something is wrong. Or, as my mom used to say: "*Something feels kind of out of shape, hun'.*"

I always knew what she meant. Like looking at a circle that was slightly off, or a picture that was fuzzy. Something almost imperceptible but that your brain still picked up on. *Out of shape.*

"Isn't there, like, a gate?" Chi pauses and looks around.

We've reached the outer ring of flaming torches. Unlike other festivals there aren't guards or fences here, but I was expecting some kind of security or maybe people to take tickets. Half a dozen small tuk-tuks are parked around the perimeter. They look like they should be manned, but they're all empty.

Further on, past the torches, there are trailers and food stalls. Someone has set up a makeshift stage in the distance, and I can see what looks like a street performance area. Unicycles lie on the ground along with juggling batons.

But there's one thing I can't see.

People.

Which is weird.

Like, this festival is supposed to attract thousands of people.

There are loads of cars parked in the car park.

But I can't see a single soul.

"Is it me, or are things a bit dead?" Gina says, frowning.

"Maybe everyone's in another part of the site?" Chi suggests. "Y'know, maybe there's a band on or something?"

"Must be a fucking quiet band," Gina mutters.

"Or maybe they're all meditating somewhere," Garrett drawls, miming smoking a spliff. He considers. "Or having an orgy."

Chi looks at him. "That's it."

"It is? 'Cos the orgy thing was kind of a joke, man."

Chi turns to the rest of us. "The effigy. The mass meditation area. You remember?"

I do, vaguely. Beneath the effigy is a large domed area where festival goers are encouraged to congregate at certain times for mass meditation '*to move the world*'.

"This must be the time," Chi says happily.

If there's one thing I like about Chi, it's her ability to clutch at the slightest straw of positivity and present it as an absolute certainty. It's also the thing that really aggravates me about her.

"You think?" I ask, trying not to sound sceptical.

"Where else could they be?"

She's stumped me on that one.

"Right. Fine," Gina says, impatiently. "We've answered that question, so let's keep moving."

She strides on and we straggle behind her. There's no real designated camping site at Blood Moon. Obviously, the main arena is for bands, stalls, entertainment and shit, but after that people just camp wherever they want. Some even set up their own stalls and makeshift bars.

The ground throws up dust around our feet. The sun is sinking behind the giant effigy, outlining it in red and gold. I feel sweat trickling down my back. I glance from side to side. Stalls, mostly still with their flaps down, a couple seemingly open but no one behind them. That itching of unease continues. Would vendors desert their wares, even for mass meditation? And then I see something, a flash of movement between two stalls. Something pale, four legs, a tail. An animal.

"Hey. Wait," I say.

"What's up?" Gina looks back.

"I saw something move."

"What? Where? People?"

"No, an animal."

She shrugs. "Maybe it was a rat."

"Bigger."

"A coyote?" Chi suggests.

"Maybe."

"A snake," Garrett adds.

I look at him. "It had *legs*, Garrett."

"Snakes can have legs."

Gina rolls her eyes. "No, they fucking *can't*. By very definition snakes do not have legs."

Garrett muses. "I'm sure I've seen a snake with legs."

"A snake with legs is a lizard," Gina growls. "But you know what else has legs? Us. Legs which should be moving so we can find somewhere to set up our tents so we can start to fucking enjoy ourselves. Comprende, David Attenborough?"

Garrett looks at her and for the briefest moment, his face tenses like he's about to retort. Then it's gone and he shrugs. "Yeah, whatever."

We keep moving past the closed food stalls. I can hear more music, but I think it's just playing on speakers. Not live. Nothing here is alive, I think, except for whatever creature I saw. *Something feels kind of out of shape, hun'.*

"Gina," I say.

"What?"

"Stop."

"Again?"

She turns. In the twilight her eyes gleam fiercely.

"This is wrong," I say. "Look around. There's no one here."

Gina continues to stare at me. Then she sighs. "Yeah. I think you're right."

Chi's face creases. "I thought you agreed with me they were all in the meditation area."

"There would still be *some* people wandering around, Chi."

"Yeah," Garrett says. "One time I went to see the Stones and you'd think everyone would be watching these legends, but there was like a huge queue of people at the hotdog stand – although, to be fair, they were really awesome dogs."

We all stare at him. But I kind of understand what he's saying. Even if there's a big band or a huge meditation area or whatever, there will always be people doing other stuff, milling around, eating, drinking, passed out on the ground. There's none of that here.

"What if everyone is… sick?" Chi suggests. "Like a virus. I heard that happened at a festival once."

"Yeah," Garrett says, sounding unreasonably pleased with the idea. "Maybe they're all infected and turning into zombies."

"Shut up, Garrett," we all say at once.

He stares at us. "Fine." Then he glances sideways. "I'm hungry. I'm gonna check out those stalls."

He ambles off towards a stall that proclaims: *Nevada's BEST organic tofu burgers.*

Low bar, I think.

Gina shakes her head. "Okay, even if something bad has happened here, what can we do? It's getting dark. We have no petrol in the car. Our best bet is still to set up camp, get some rest, drink some fucking beer and figure this shit out in the morning."

"I guess," Chi says. She looks at me. "What do you think, Edie?"

I glance around. The giant torches flicker. To our left, the massive wicker beast towers over the site, thrown into dark silhouette by the sinking sun. Somewhere an animal howls. I shiver.

"You hear that?"

"Hear what?" Gina asks.

"That howl."

"It's a wilderness. There are wild animals."

The howl comes again. Closer.

"It won't come near the festival," Gina says, but she doesn't sound too certain.

"We're probably all just spooked out right now," Chi adds.

"Guys!" Garrett calls.

"Not now, Garrett," I snap.

"Guys, you *really* need to see this."

I turn. "For fuck's sake. What is it? A really great burger and fries? Free beer? Seriously, Garr—"

I stop. Garrett is holding something up in his hand. It's not a burger or fries, or even beer.

It's a severed leg.

⋆ ⋆ ⋆

"Holy fuck," Chi whispers. "What could do this?"

"Animals," Gina says grimly.

"Really?" I look at her. "Can you think of any animal big enough and vicious enough to do this to a human? I mean, they've been… obliterated."

"A pack of animals maybe?"

We look back at the body… or what's left of it. It's hard to tell if it's male or female. Just a bloody, bony, *intestine-y* jumbled mess.

"Do you think that's what happened to the rest of the people here?" Chi says.

"Well, I fucking do *now*," Gina mutters.

"One pack of animals couldn't kill thousands of people," I say. "And even if they did, then why aren't there bodies lying around all over the place? Why aren't there survivors? It still doesn't explain where everyone else is."

Garrett crouches down by the remains and pulls out his phone.

"What the fuck are you doing?" I ask.

"Evidence," he says.

"What?"

"We should record the truth, man. Plus, some sickos will pay good money to see this shit."

"I don't give a fuck. I want to get out of here." I look at the others. "*Now.*"

"Only one problem," Gina says. "We haven't got enough petrol to make it down the road." She looks at us all. "We need to find fuel."

"Or maybe we could steal a car?" Chi says.

Gina looks around at us. "Can anyone here hotwire a car?"

We all shake our heads.

Garrett stands and pockets his phone. "Someone might have left their keys?"

"Yeah." Gina smiles sweetly at him. "Why don't you walk back to the car park and check?"

I watch Garrett's face falter as he considers walking back to the car park on his own, in the dark and searching the rows of abandoned cars.

"You're right," he says. "We should look for fuel."

Gina nods. "Like I said before. It's a festival. There's no electricity. They'll need petrol for generators and shit."

From somewhere, closer than before, comes another howl. We all freeze. And then something answers.

"Shit," Chi whimpers.

Gina's face darkens. "Let's move."

* * *

The sun's last entrails sink beneath the horizon. In its place, I can see the moon, slowly emerging in the dark sky. A swollen, amber globe.

"Flashlights," Gina says. "Everyone got flashlights?"

Our stuff is still dumped in the middle of the path. We start to rummage through.

"Take only what you need," Gina instructs. "Leave anything you don't."

Garrett looks at the crate of booze. "Really?"

"If you think you can run with it, be my guest."

For some reason I'm reminded of the joke – *How do you outrun a lion? You don't have to. You just have to outrun the slowest person.*

With that in mind, I dump half of the stuff from my rucksack onto the ground and shrug it back on, substantially lighter.

"So, what are we looking for?" Garrett asks.

"Generators," Gina says. "Maintenance vans or some shit."

"Some shit. Right."

"The fair," I say. "There must be generators there."

Gina nods. "Good call."

We walk cautiously back down the path and into the fairground. It's brighter here, multicoloured lights flashing from the rides. The music I could hear is coming from here too, but it's distorted, like whatever is playing it is slowly running out of juice.

As well as the big wheel and helter-skelter there's a cycle kart track, some kind of giant spinning ride with swings, dodgems and a waltzer. All look ancient, makeshift and weirdly incongruous here in the middle of nowhere.

"There!" Gina suddenly points, making me jump.

"What?"

"A generator, between the dodgems and the waltzer."

I can see a large, grey box and a truck between the two rides.

"Okay."

We head over, skirting the sedentary dodgems, which are in darkness, like the waltzer. The distorted music is louder here. A deranged, slow-motion version of Abba – 'Dancing Queen'.

Gina darts over to the grey box near the truck. "Okay. Got to be some fuel for this baby somewhere here."

"I'll check the truck," Chi says.

I glance around. I can feel a creeping itch at the back of my neck, an undeniable feeling of being watched. I stare at the waltzer, carriages still and cloaked in darkness.

"I'm just going to check over there," I say.

"'Kay," Gina says, preoccupied with the generator.

Garrett leans against the truck and starts rolling another joint. "I'll be lookout."

Of course. Great. I walk slowly towards the waltzer, pointing my flashlight ahead of me. The beam is weak, and it barely illuminates past my feet. *Should have changed the fucking batteries.* Abba wails about being young and sweet and only seventeen. I can smell something as I get closer to the ride. Foul yet sweet, and unpleasantly familiar. Saliva fills my mouth. I rub at my lips.

I'm close enough now for the flashlight to pick out the shape of the waltzer, the painted carriages, the red seats. So much red. Not just the seats, I realise. All over the walkway, the safety bars, the walls. And mingled amongst the red: limbs, half-eaten heads, the odd foot still in a shoe. A whirling, twirling mash-up of flesh and blood.

I turn and vomit my guts up onto the earth.

I've barely caught my breath when I hear it.

A low, rumbling growl.

I raise my head. From behind one of the waltzer carriages, two silvery discs glint. They're followed by a snout and long yellow teeth.

Fuck. A wolf. But like no wolf I've ever seen before. It emerges and stretches, lengthens, then raises its front two paws, so – *Jesus fucking Christ!* – it's standing semi-upright. Almost as tall as Garrett with fur that's a yellowy white. *Desert wolves.*

It seems like an age, an eternity, that we stare at each other, eyes locked, the smell of blood and death in the air, adrenaline thrumming, breath coming faster. Then I hear a roar. I'm not sure if it's the wolf creature or me.

The wolf launches. It's too late to run. I raise my arms, pointlessly, to protect myself. I can see its open jaws, smell its feral breath. But as it reaches for me, there's another sound. An explosion. *Bang!* The wolf bucks and twists in the air. Two more explosions. *Bang! Bang!* The wolf falls, hitting the ground with a heavy thud. Momentarily, it twitches, blood dribbles from its jaw and then it lies still.

"Whoah. That was epic."

I turn. Garrett stands just behind me, gun in hand.

Alerted by the gunshots, Gina and Chi run over.

"Oh, my Christ-God," Chi wails, hands clutching her face.

Gina stares at the dead creature. "What the fucking *fuck* is that thing?"

Garrett walks over to it. He crouches, touches the fur. "Werewolf," he says casually.

"*What*?"

He stands and slips the gun in his pocket. "What did you think it was – Wile E. Coyote?"

I stare at him. Garrett's different. The dullness, the slouch, the slightly loose drawl. All changed. He's alert, harder, colder.

Gina walks over. "A fucking werewolf. You are shitting me?"

"Nope."

"And you have a gun, Garrett?" Chi says, sounding bewildered.

"Oh yeah. Well, it's still the best weapon for taking them down. Silver bullets only, of course."

"You came prepared," I say. "You knew about this."

He looks at us. "I mean, not *this*. This massacre or whatever the fuck is going on here. But this festival? Yeah, I've heard rumours for years. Most hunters have."

"Hunters?" I shake my head, trying to clear the feeling that I am going fucking insane.

Gina frowns. "How about you explain this to us like we have no fucking clue what you're talking about?"

"Okay." Garrett smiles. "Here's the deal. Werewolves exist. Always have. But they're damn hard to find, let alone track or catch."

"But people try?"

"Right. Hunters, like me. Most of the activity tends to be in northern Europe. Big communities of Lycanthropes there. But they're clever and used to hiding. Plus, they're your common European Lycans. I wanted something special for my first."

"First what?"

"First kill."

"So why here?" I ask.

"According to legend, Blood Moon started as a gathering for a different breed of Lycans. Desert dwellers. Unlike their European or Northern American counterparts, they like the heat, the dry dust of the desert. In human form they're nomads, forming loose communities, some live in caves. But once every year, they come together."

"At Blood Moon Festival."

"Right."

"So, this festival was originally for werewolves?"

"Yeah. Then, over the years it changed. Word spread and it started to pull in normies, humans who claimed it as their own."

"My mom used to be a regular," I say. "It's why I wanted to come here."

Garrett nods. "Yeah. Well, more recently, there have been rumours that Lycans have returned… to feed. People come to Blood Moon and never return home. They just disappear. It's been covered up – written off as kids running away, or wandering off and falling into ravines or even murdered by drug dealers and their bodies buried in the desert but… the hunters know." He taps his nose and for a moment I have an almost irresistible urge to break it again.

"So that's why you're here? For the Lycans?" I can't help feeling a sting of betrayal.

His face falls. "I mean, not *just*. Like, I really like hanging with you too."

"You never told us about any of this werewolf shit," Gina snarls. "You let us walk into a fucking slaughterhouse."

"And would you have believed me?"

The two of them glare at each other. Gina drops her gaze first, cursing under her breath.

"Right." Garrett nods. "Besides, I hoped I might just find one or two. Nothing like this…"

"So what happened here?" I ask. "Why have they killed *everyone*?"

Garrett shrugs. "Maybe they got carried away. Maybe they got sick of hiding. Maybe this is the start of something bigger – an uprising. I don't know."

"Oh. An uprising, Yeah, love the sound of that," Gina drawls.

Chi looks thoughtful. "But don't werewolves only stay werewolves for one night? These people were killed before we got here."

Garrett shakes his head. "That's a common myth. Young Lycans may only change for one night, starting when they turn twenty-one. Mature Lycans stay in form for the entire full moon cycle – around three days." He looks back at the dead wolf creature. "But not this guy." He slings off his rucksack, which still looks pretty heavy. And then I see why. He pulls out a machete.

"Jesus Holy Bull!" Chi exclaims.

Garrett raises the machete and brings it down on the creature's neck. Again and again, hacking through the bone and tendons. Blood spatters his jeans and boots.

I feel a burning in my chest. "You have to do that?"

"Proof of kill."

"You can't just take a photo?"

"Photos can be faked."

He holds up the head. Severed tendons drip dark blood onto the ground. The frozen snarl grimaces at me.

"Yeah, well, that's all very fucking alpha male," Gina says. "But right now you're not showing off your trophy to anyone…" She points back at the generator in disgust. "Diesel. It runs on fucking diesel."

"And?" I say.

"You can't put diesel in a petrol car."

"So, we can't get out of here?"

My voice sounds desperate. I can't help it. The burning in my chest is worse. My whole body is itching. Anxiety, I think, I've had this before. More and more over the last year. I put it down to losing Mom, but maybe it's something more? I take a breath, look up at the sky. The full moon throbs brightly.

"There might be petrol somewhere else," Chi suggests. "I mean, they must use fuel for other things. To light stuff?"

"The effigy," I say. "They burn it, right? They'll need an accelerant."

"Right," says Gina.

Garrett nods. "We should head there."

I frown. He seems a little too enthusiastic, but I don't really have time to dwell on it because distantly – but not distant enough – I hear a chorus of howls.

Garrett pulls open his backpack and stuffs the severed head inside. "I think they can sense one of their own is dead."

"Oh, fucking great." Gina throws her hands up. "I'm so glad we brought you, dude."

"You should be," Garrett smirks. "I'm the one with a gun – and silver bullets."

Gina holds out her hand. "Then you don't need that fucking machete."

★ ★ ★

We move faster, fear driving our feet forward.

This is crazy, I keep telling myself. Lunacy. Insane. A bad, bad dream or maybe a bad trip. But it feels horribly real, so I keep moving, out of the fairground, past the abandoned stalls, towards the centre of the arena and the wicker effigy.

Only when we're near the base do we stop. Up close, it's even more fearsome. Thirty feet of tightly wound wicker that somehow manages to look a lot like coiled tendons. Ready to spring. A massive half man, half animal monster. Which now makes much more sense. *They were telling us all along.*

"Where d'you think they'd keep the petrol?" Chi asks.

"A van or trailer or something?"

We all look around. There's a large trailer a few feet away from the effigy.

"Let's try in there," Gina says.

She walks over and Chi follows. Garrett is staring at the wicker dome beneath the effigy. Around the side, there are entrances covered by loose sheets of hemp fabric.

"What?" I ask.

"I just want to check something out."

"In there?"

"Most Lycans sleep by day and hunt by night. A little like vampires. They want somewhere safe and warm to rest… and they like to stay with their pack."

Now I get why he was so keen to come over here.

"You think they're in *there*?"

"Yep." He starts to walk towards the dome.

I grab his arm. "Are you nuts? There's a pack of sleeping werewolves in there and you want to go and mingle?"

"No, I just want to take a look. This is the biggest discovery in hunter history for decades."

"And that's all you care about?"

"No." He looks at me. "I care about how much money someone will pay me for this head when we get home, so I hope your scary friend finds that fucking petrol."

He strides up to one of the entrances. I glance back over my shoulder and then I follow. Almost immediately, I can smell it. Rotten meat and something musky and dense.

Garrett carefully peels back the covering. I peer over his shoulder.

"Holy fuck."

Inside, there's a large round area scattered with yoga mats and bean bags. Sprawled over them are dozens of wolf creatures, dozing, gently snoring. Piled in the centre, a huge pyramid of dead carcasses and bones, like the remnants of a feast.

"I guess we found the rest of the festival goers," Garrett drawls. "Chi was half-right."

"It's not fu—" I start to say and then jump as a hand lands heavily on my shoulder.

"What gives, fuckheads?"

Gina. Her eyes widen as she takes in the scene. "Whoah. That is one huge pack of dogs."

"Oh my." Chi slides in beside us. "All those poor people."

"Did you get the petrol?" I ask.

Gina holds up a can. "You bet."

"Then let's get out of here."

"Wait," Chi says. "There's more petrol in the trailer. If the lychees—"

"Lycans," I correct.

"If they're in there… we could stop them hurting more people."

She stares at us, her eyes wide.

Garrett grins. "Let's light 'em up."

* * *

We douse the base of the dome liberally with petrol. Gina holds her lighter to the wicker. It takes a moment but then a small flame ignites. She steps back and almost immediately the rest of the wicker catches. Within seconds, flames are swarming up and around the structure.

"Eat fire, bitches!" Gina whispers.

As if in reply, a howl echoes from the dome.

"Shit. They're waking up."

And suddenly, in my mind's eye, I see it. Dozens of the wolf creatures choking on smoke, burning alive. Howling and screaming in pain.

Chi grabs my arm. "Come on, Edie. Hurry."

I turn and run, reminding myself that they are monsters, thousands of people are dead. *But they were hungry, just feeding. We're murdering them.* I glance back. I can see shapes emerging from the smoke and flames.

"Garrett!" I cry.

He turns and fires off a shot. From our right, a guttural growl. Garrett spins and shoots. The creature stumbles and slows but keeps going.

"Shit, shit." Garrett steadies and shoots again, twice. This time the creature goes down. Garrett keeps shooting but the gun is dry clicking.

"Fuck. I'm out of silver bullets."

"Then run faster," Gina shouts.

He doesn't argue. We burst out of the festival site. The moon glints off the rows of cars in the car park. *The car! Where's the fucking car?*

"End of the row. Over there." Chi points.

We reach it, panting. I can't see any more creatures behind us. I bend over, heaving, feeling exhausted and sick. The itching is back, all over my body. My limbs are aching and sweat is pouring off me.

"Okay, let's fuel this baby up," Gina says.

She starts to pour petrol into the tank. Garrett turns away, staring back at the burning effigy and fiddling with his gun. "Clear for now," he says. "But we need to hurry."

"No shit, asshole."

In the distance, I can hear howls, animal cries of terror and agony. My stomach turns. The burning and itching increases.

"You okay?" Chi asks.

I shake my head. "No."

A spasm shoots through my body. I bend double, groaning.

Chi frowns in concern. "Sit down, rest."

I slump to the ground. Chi turns back to Gina. "Edie's not well. We need to go."

"Almost there." She steps back and flips the petrol cap closed. "Done. Let's get out of here."

"Yeah. About that."

Garrett turns. He raises the gun and points it at her.

Gina scowls. "What the fuck are you doing, Garrett?"

"Look. This has all been a bit more than I expected. Originally, I thought we would come here, have some fun, I'd kill a werewolf and no one would be any the wiser."

"Really?" Gina stares at him. "You thought no one would notice a fucking werewolf head in your bag?"

"At a festival like this most people are too drugged or drunk to notice much at all. Even if they did, they probably wouldn't remember, you guys included."

Chi steps forward. "Garrett, we have to tell someone about this. All those poor people are dead."

He shakes his head. "You see, that's what I thought you would say. And here's the thing: if we get the authorities involved, it gets messy and they take this—" He gestures to the head in the bag. "I don't get my big payday. I don't get the respect I'm due."

Gina nods slowly. "Fine. We won't say anything. Now put the gun down."

Garrett flicks off the safety. "Sorry, ladies, but the thing about being a hunter is, we work alone… and we don't leave any witnesses."

Chi's small face crumples. "Garrett, we're your friends."

"No, we're not," Gina says. "And he's bluffing." She reaches for the machete. "He already said, he's all out of bullets."

"Yeah… *silver* bullets." Garrett smiles. "I reloaded, with lead."

He pulls the trigger. Gina jerks, falls back against the car and slides to the ground, leaving a slick bloody trail down the paintwork.

"*Nooo!*" Chi screams.

"Chi, I always liked you—"

She turns to run but only makes it a few paces. *Bang!* Garrett shoots her in the back. She falls to her knees. Garrett walks slowly up to her and points the gun at her head. While his attention is diverted, I edge myself around the other side of the car, body still wracked by spasms, sweat slathering my skin. I hear a final *Bang!* Then the thud of footsteps. Garrett is coming back.

"Edie, honey, I know you're there. You can't hide from me." A pause. "I'm sorry about this. We had some fun, but I'm a hunter first. I hope you understand."

"I do." I look at my hands, thinking of my mom. "I understand everything now."

I hear him walk around the car. His footsteps are so loud, amplified.

"Well, that's sweet."

"You're not going to kill me, Garrett."

"Oh, I think I am."

His dusty boots draw into view. I look up at him. "No, you're not."

His eyes widen, mouth gapes.

I rise to my full height, stretch out my limbs and extend my claws.

"Because you're all out of *silver* bullets."

He shoots anyway, pointlessly. I barely feel the sting. I growl. He screams, tries to turn. But he's so slow and I leap on him, feeling his small, fragile body crumple beneath me. Momentarily, I pin him with my claws, savouring his terror and pain as they dig into his flesh, drawing blood. It's delicious.

"Edie. No. Please. No."

My lips curl back. A smile, but to him it must look like a snarl.

"*Edie!*"

I lower my jaws to his neck… and then I rip his throat out.

★ ★ ★

We watch the effigy burn, flames stretching high into the night sky. A funeral pyre for our fallen brothers and sisters. As one, we raise our heads to the moon and we howl.

Tonight, we mourn.

But soon, we will feed again.

BIOGRAPHIES

The *Oxford Companion to English Literature* calls **Ramsey Campbell** 'Britain's most respected living horror writer', and the *Washington Post* sums up his work as 'one of the monumental accomplishments of modern popular fiction'. In 2015 he was made an Honorary Fellow of Liverpool John Moores University for outstanding services to literature. His latest novels are *Fellstones, The Lonely Lands, The Incubations, An Echo of Children* and *Ancestral.* His Brichester Mythos trilogy consists of *The Searching Dead, Born to the Dark* and *The Way of the Worm.* His most recent collections are *Fearful Implications,* a two-volume retrospective roundup (*Phantasmagorical Stories*) and *The Village Killings and Other Novellas.* From the British Library, *The Show Goes On* is a celebratory collection compiled by Jeremy Dyson. His non-fiction is collected as *Ramsey Campbell, Probably* and *Ramsey Campbell, Certainly. Ramsey's Rambles* collects his video reviews, and *Six Stooges and Counting* is an appreciation of the Three Stooges. *Limericks of the Alarming and Phantasmal* is a history of horror fiction in fifty limericks.

Christa Carmen lives in Rhode Island. She is the Bram Stoker Award-winning and three-time Shirley Jackson Award-nominated author of *The Daughters of Block Island, Beneath the Poet's House,* and *How to Fake a Haunting,* as well as the Indie Horror Book Award-winning *Something Borrowed, Something Blood-Soaked,* the Bram Stoker Award-nominated 'Through the Looking Glass and Straight into Hell' (*Orphans of Bliss: Tales of Addiction Horror*), and co-editor of the Aurealis Award-nominated *We Are Providence* and the Australasian Shadows and Ditmar Award-nominated *Monsters in the Mills.* She has a BA from the University of Pennsylvania, an MA from Boston College, and an MFA from the University of Southern Maine. When she's not writing, she keeps chickens, uses a Ouija board to ghost-hug her dear, departed beagle, and sets out on adventures with her husband, daughter, and bloodhound-golden retriever mix. Most of her work comes from gazing upon the ghosts of the past or else into the dark corners of nature, those places where whorls of bark become owl eyes, and deer step through tunnels of hanging leaves and creeping briars only to disappear.

Eliza Clark is the author of novels *Boy Parts* and *Penance* and short story collection *She's Always Hungry*. *Boy Parts* was adapted for the stage in 2023. She was named one of Granta's Best of Young British Novelists, shortlisted for the Women's Prize Futures 10 award and listed on Forbes' 30 Under 30 Europe. She also writes for film and television.

David Farrow is the author of the *Neverglades* paranormal mystery series, which gained a cult following on Reddit and YouTube and later became an Amazon bestseller. His work has also been published in *Mythaxis*, *Haven Speculative*, and the *NoSleep Podcast*, among others. He holds an MFA in Fiction from Lesley University and teaches with the creative writing non-profit GrubStreet in Boston, Massachusetts. You can find him at davidfarrowwrites.com.

Montanna Rayne Harling (she/her) is a speculative eco-fiction writer from rural California and an alum of the 2024 Clarion Science Fiction and Fantasy Writers' Workshop. She holds an MFA in Prose from University of Massachusetts Amherst. Montanna's writing has been published in *Small Wonders* and *F(r)iction*, and is supported by the Juniper Summer Writing Institute and the DISQUIET International Literary Program. She is working on her debut novel. Find her at montannaharling.com.

Rachel Harrison is the *New York Times* bestselling author of *Kiss Slay Replay*, *Play Nice*, *So Thirsty*, *Black Sheep*, *Such Sharp Teeth*, *Cackle*, and *The Return*. Her short fiction has appeared in numerous anthologies and in her debut story collection *Bad Dolls*. She lives in New Jersey with her husband and their cat/overlord.

Sally Hughes was raised in West Yorkshire and lives in the West Highlands. Her stories have been published by Ghost Orchid Press and *Northwords Now*. She has a PhD in Scottish Literature and has worked in academic and public libraries. Currently she works in the best bookshop in the world and is completing the manuscript of a novel set in Iron-Age Scotland.

Stephen D. Koester is a high school teacher, multi-disciplinary artist, and writer from Warrenton, Missouri. His fiction explores the liminal spaces where the mundane meets the mythic, drawing on folklore, history, and the quiet horror of things glimpsed from the corner of the eye. When not teaching or writing, he paints in oils, composes music, and runs the Substack newsletter *Mono No Aware: The Beauty in Impermanence*, which examines Japanese culture, philosophy, and the stories we tell ourselves about impermanence. 'Monster in the Water' is his first published story. He is currently at work on a historical fantasy novel set in third-century Japan. He lives with his wife Devin, and their four children.

Eric LaRocca (he/they) is a three times Bram Stoker Award finalist, a Shirley Jackson Award nominee, and a two times Splatterpunk Award winner. He was named by *Esquire* as one of the 'Writers Shaping Horror's Next Golden Age' and praised by *Locus* as 'one of the strongest and most unique voices in contemporary horror fiction'. LaRocca's notable works include *Things Have Gotten Worse Since We Last Spoke*, *Everything the Darkness Eats*, *The Trees Grew Because I Bled There*, *At Dark, I Become Loathsome*, the *Burnt Sparrow* trilogy and *Wretch*. He currently resides in Boston, Massachusetts, with his partner.

Josh Malerman is the *New York Times* bestselling author of *Bird Box* and *Incidents Around the House*. His other work includes *Black Mad Wheel*, *Inspection*, *Pearl*, *Daphne*, *Malorie*, *Goblin*, *Unbury Carol* and *Spin a Black Yarn*. He is also one of two singer/songwriters of the Michigan band The High Strung. His documentary *To All The Books* captures the writing of a novel from idea to finish, and is expected to be released in 2026. He lives with his wife, the artist/musician, Allison Laakko.

Mark Morris (Editor) has written and edited over fifty novels, novellas, short story collections and anthologies. His script work includes audio dramas for *Doctor Who*, *Jago & Litefoot* and the *Hammer Chillers* series. Mark's recent work includes the *Obsidian Heart* trilogy, the original *Predator* novel *Stalking Shadows* (co-written with James A. Moore), the official novelisation of the *Doctor Who* sixtieth anniversary special *Wild Blue Yonder*, and the anthologies *New Fears* (winner of the British Fantasy Award for Best Anthology) and *New Fears 2* as editor. He's also written award-winning audio adaptations of the classic 1971 horror movie *Blood on Satan's Claw* and the M.R. James ghost story 'A View from a Hill'. His novels *That Which Stands Outside* and *Bad Things Happen Here* are published by Flame Tree Press.

Originally from Tennessee, **Mo Perkins** is an award-winning screenwriter and a film/TV director who lives and works in Los Angeles. She writes short fiction, mostly horror and sci-fi, for the joy of it. She also teaches screenwriting at Occidental College. When she is not dreaming up creatures from other worlds, she does her best to be a decent mother to one teenager, two cats and a pug.

Laura Purcell is a writer of gothic horror and historical fiction living in Colchester. Her novels – among which are *The Silent Companions, The Corset, Bone China, The Shape of Darkness, The Whispering Muse* and *House of Splinters* – have won various awards including the WH Smith Thumping Good Read Award (2018), Fingerprint Historical Crime Book of the Year (2022) and the Dracula Society's Children of the Night Award (2023). They have also been selected for Radio 2 and Zoe Ball's ITV book clubs. Laura's short stories have been published in a number of bestselling collections. She worked as lead writer on *Roanoke Falls*, a Realm horror podcast executive produced by John Carpenter and Sandy King Carpenter.

Keith Rosson is the author of the novels *Coffin Moon, Fever House, The Devil by Name, Smoke City, Road Seven*, and *The Mercy of the Tide*, as well as the Shirley Jackson Award-winning story collection *Folk Songs for Trauma Surgeons*. His short fiction has appeared in *Southwest Review, Nightmare, Cream City Review, PANK, Redivider, December*, and more. He lives in Portland, Oregon, where he is an ardent admirer of punk cassettes and public libraries.

Michael Rowe was born in Ottawa, and has lived in Beirut, Havana, Geneva and Paris. They are the Shirley Jackson Award-nominated author of three novels, as well as an award-winning essayist and former journalist. Rowe is also the author of two books of essays and a book of interviews, and the editor of four anthologies of original short horror fiction. Rowe is the recipient of the Lambda Literary Award, the Spectrum Award, the New York Publishing Triangle Award, and the New Millennium Writing Award, and was a finalist for the Canadian National Magazine Award and the GLAAD Media Award. In 2022 they were asked to write the introductory essay to *Rolling Stone* magazine photographer Nate Gowdy's *INSURRECTION*, his first-person photojournalistic monograph of the January 6 attack on the US Capitol, which won the 2023 Paris Photography Prize. Michael Rowe lives in Toronto and welcomes readers at michaelrowe.com

Robert Shearman has written six short story collections, which between them have won the World Fantasy Award, the Shirley Jackson Award, the Edge Hill Readers Prize, and five British Fantasy Awards. He began his career in the theatre, and his plays have won the *Sunday Times* Playwriting Award, the World Drama Trust Award, and the Guinness Award for Ingenuity in association with the Royal National Theatre. But he is probably best known for his work on television, bringing back the Daleks for the BAFTA winning first series of the revival of *Doctor Who*, and most recently as script consultant for *Constellation* for Apple TV.

Angela Sylvaine is a Bram Stoker Award-nominated author and self-proclaimed cheerful goth who writes speculative fiction and poetry. Her 90s horror-comedy novels, *Frost Bite* and *Cold Snap*, and her retro 80s YA mall slasher novella, *Chopping Spree*, embody her cheerful side. Her short story collection, *The Dead Spot: Stories of Lost Girls* is fully goth and heartbreaking. Angela's short fiction and poetry have appeared in over sixty anthologies, magazines, and podcasts, including *Southwest Review*, *Apex*, and *PseudoPod*. She lives in the shadow of the Rocky Mountains with her sweetheart and creepy cats. You can find her online at angelasylvaine.com.

Carl Tait is a software engineer, classical pianist, and writer. His work has appeared in *After Dinner Conversation* (Pushcart Prize nominee), *Exquisite Death* (Derringer Award finalist), *Mystery Magazine* (cover story),

NewMyths, *Allegory*, *The Saturday Evening Post*, and *Close to Midnight*, a previous volume of this series. Carl grew up in Atlanta and currently lives in New York City with his wife and twin daughters. For more information, visit carltait.com.

C.J. Tudor's love of writing, especially the dark and macabre, started young. When her peers were reading Judy Blume, she was devouring Stephen King and James Herbert. Over the years she has had a variety of jobs, including trainee reporter, radio scriptwriter, dog walker, voiceover, television presenter and copywriter. She is now the *Sunday Times* bestselling author of *The Chalk Man, The Taking of Annie Thorne, The Other People, The Burning Girls, The Drift* and *The Gathering.* All of her books are in development or optioned for TV. She is also the author of a short story collection, *A Sliver of Darkness.*

Stephen Volk is best known as the creator of BBC TV's notorious Halloween 'mockumentary' *Ghostwatch* and the award-winning paranormal drama series *Afterlife* starring Lesley Sharp and Andrew Lincoln. His many screenplays include *The Awakening* starring Rebecca Hall, Dominic West and Imelda Staunton, the miniseries *Midwinter of the Spirit* starring Anna Maxwell Martin, and Ken Russell's cult classic *Gothic* starring Natasha Richardson as Mary Shelley. For the Bush Theatre he wrote *The Chapel of Unrest*, which featured Jim Broadbent and Reece Shearsmith. He is a BAFTA winner, a two-time British Fantasy Award winner, a Shirley Jackson Award and Bram Stoker Award finalist, and the author of four collections of short stories: *Dark Corners*, *Monsters in the Heart*, *The Parts We Play*, and *Lies of Tenderness*. His acclaimed *Dark Masters Trilogy* consists of three novellas featuring Peter Cushing (*Whitstable*), Alfred Hitchcock (*Leytonstone*) and Dennis Wheatley (*Netherwood*) – with a guest appearance in the latter by Aleister Crowley. His most recent books are *Under a Raven's Wing, The Good Unknown and Other Ghost Stories*, and *The Confirmed Bachelors*. He is also author of *Coffinmaker's Blues*, a collection of nonfiction. stephenvolk.net

After eleven years as a criminal barrister, **Ally Wilkes** decided to become 'professionally spooky'. Her first novel, *All The White Spaces,* was a Bram Stoker Award finalist, and her second novel, *Where The Dead Wait*, was one of *Esquire*'s best horror books of 2023. Her next novel, *Man Eater* – set in the fevered jungles of the Amazon during the late Victorian orchid-hunting craze – will be published in February 2027 by Titan (UK) and Simon & Schuster (US). Her weird and supernatural short stories have appeared in a variety of magazines and anthologies. You can find her at allywilkes.com or on Instagram @av_wilkes.